OXFORD ENGLISH NOVELS

General Editor: JAMES KINSLEY

The Life and Adventures of

SIR LAUNCELOT GREAVES

TOBIAS SMOLLETT

The Life and Adventures of
SIR LAUNCELOT
GREAVES

Edited with an Introduction by
DAVID EVANS

LONDON
OXFORD UNIVERSITY PRESS
NEW YORK   TORONTO
1973

Oxford University Press, Ely House, London W.1

GLASGOW NEW YORK TORONTO MELBOURNE WELLINGTON
CAPE TOWN IBADAN NAIROBI DAR ES SALAAM LUSAKA ADDIS ABABA
DELHI BOMBAY CALCUTTA MADRAS KARACHI LAHORE DACCA
KUALA LUMPUR SINGAPORE HONG KONG TOKYO

ISBN 0 19 255364 X

Introduction, Notes, Bibliography, and Chronology
ⓒ Oxford University Press 1973

*Filmset by BAS Printers Limited, Wallop, Hampshire
and printed in Great Britain
at the University Press, Oxford
by Vivian Ridler
Printer to the University*

CONTENTS

SIR LAUNCELOT GREAVES

ACKNOWLEDGEMENTS

I WOULD like to thank the Canada Council for financial assistance in preparing this edition. To the scholarship of Professor Lewis Knapp everyone who works on Smollett is indebted. The notes have benefited from my discussions with Herbert Rosengarten, a colleague. To Professor Donald S. Taylor I express my appreciation for advice and encouragement. My wife, Barbara Evans, has helped me, with this as with everything, more than anyone.

INTRODUCTION

IN 1760, while contributing to the *Critical Review*, writing weekly instalments for the *Continuation of the Complete History of England* and compiling the *Universal History*, Smollett launched the *British Magazine, or Monthly Repository for Gentlemen and Ladies* in which, from January 1760, to December 1761, appeared *The Life and Adventures of Sir Launcelot Greaves*, his first novel since *Ferdinand Count Fathom* in 1753. The circumstances of the novel's composition are not clear, but it has long been assumed that the journalistic tone of the prison scenes in chapters xx-xxi is evidence that at least some work on the novel was done during or after Smollett's eleven weeks' imprisonment in the King's Bench for libelling Admiral Knowles in the May 1758 issue of the *Critical Review*.[1] Sir Walter Scott claimed that some of the chapters (or parts of chapters, if his time estimate is to be taken literally) were hastily written during Smollett's visit to a friend in Scotland in the summer of 1760; when, as 'post-time drew near, he used to retire for half an hour or an hour, to prepare the necessary quantity of *copy*, as it is technically called in the printing-house, which he never gave himself the trouble to correct or even to read over'.[2] The details of Scott's statement are inaccurate, but that some of the early chapters were composed in Scotland or after the fashion of many of Johnson's periodical essays is both historically possible and believable from the book's pacing, repetitiveness, and occasional inconsistencies[3]—for example, the repeated allusions to the ghost scene in *Hamlet*; the fact that Greaves's mother is described by Clarke as vain and 'ill-tempered', by Mrs. Oakeley as 'my dear lady and benefactress'; the fact that in chapter xvi Greaves knows of Aurelia's London relatives but in chapter xxiv receives Dolly's mention of them as new information.

---

[1] See Chronology, and Knapp (see Bibliography), pp. 230–6.

[2] *Lives of the Novelists* (World's Classics edition, 1906), p. 52.

[3] Cf. Smollett's apology to Alexander Carlyle for the inaccuracies in *Roderick Random* which resulted from haste. (*Letters*, ed. Knapp, p. 8.)

The first critical response to the novel occurred shortly after its serialization began, when an essayist (possibly Goldsmith,[1] one of the most important contributors to the *British Magazine*) wrote an account of a 'wow-wow', or monthly gathering of country people to gossip and read newspapers in the local public house. The account was printed in the *Public Ledger* for 16 February, two weeks after the second chapter of *Launcelot Greaves* had appeared in the *British Magazine* of February 1760:

an Oxford scholar, led there by curiosity, pulled a new magazine out of his pocket, in which he said there were some pieces extremely curious and deserved their attention. He then read the 'Adventures of Sir Launcelot Greaves', to the entire satisfaction of the audience, which being finished, he threw the pamphlet on the table: 'That piece, gentlemen,' says he, 'is written in the very spirit and manner of Cervantes; there is great knowledge of human nature, and evident marks of the master in almost every sentence; and from the plan, the humor, and the execution, I can venture to say that it dropped from the pen of the ingenious Dr. ———.' Everyone was pleased with the performance, and I was particularly gratified in hearing all the sensible part of the company give orders for the British Magazine.[2]

When the novel was published in book form in March 1762, it was noticed, in a single sentence, in the *Monthly Review*. The *Critical Review*, of which Smollett was an editor, reviewed the book favourably, praising Captain Crowe as a successfully drawn sea character and asserting that the principal characters 'resemble without imitating [Don Quixote and Sancho Panza], and remind us of what imparted exquisite enjoyment, without diminishing their own novelty'. The *Library* also carried a short, favourable review.[3] On the whole, though, reception was disappointing; from the beginning, *Launcelot Greaves* has been judged inferior to Smollett's other novels, with the frequent exception of *Ferdinand Count Fathom*.[4] There are no substantive differences between serial and book forms of the novel significant enough to indicate Smollett's interest in revising or improving it (as he had revised

---

[1] For argument against Goldsmith's authorship, see Arthur Friedman, *Collected Works of Oliver Goldsmith* (1966), iii. 156.

[2] Cited in Mayo (see Bibliography), p. 280.

[3] *Monthly Review*, xxvi (1762), 391; *Critical Review*, xiii (1762), 427–9; *Library*, ii (1762), 262.

[4] A history of the book's reputation may be found in Boege (see Bibliography).

Roderick Random and, especially, *Peregrine Pickle*), and there was no other authorized edition during his lifetime.

Launcelot Greaves is firmly grounded in Smollett's personal experiences. Smollett had visited on his journeys to Scotland many of the places along the York to London route travelled by Greaves and his followers.[1] The character of Ferret is modelled on Smollett's long-time opponent in political argument, John Shebbeare, who was a fellow-prisoner in the King's Bench while Smollett was unwillingly absorbing first-hand knowledge for the prison scenes. Because of his admiration for Hogarth, who is alluded to in all the novels except *Ferdinand Count Fathom*, he was probably familiar with Hogarth's *Election* series, based on the Oxfordshire contest of 1754. In particular, both 'The Polling', with its reference to Shebbeare, and 'Chairing the Member', the last two in the series, offer possible visual sources for the conception and details of chapter ix. Although he was never bankrupt himself, Smollett's own tenuous finances probably lie behind his sympathy for Captain Clewlin and other bankrupts exempted from the laws in favour of insolvent debtors. Most importantly, his translation of *Don Quixote* had appeared in 1755 and was about to enjoy a second edition in 1761. Though Carmine Linsalata has demonstrated that Smollett's translation is actually a 'plagiarizing, paraphrasing, rewriting, and inverting' of Jarvis's English translation (1742) and that Smollett probably had little or no Spanish, the significance of his recent preoccupation with Cervantes's story is clear enough in *Launcelot Greaves*.[2] Since *Don Quixote* was one of the books most admired by eighteenth-century writers, Smollett's general interest in it is hardly surprising; though what led him to move from translating the book to writing a novel deriving from it we can only conjecture—either sceptically (that he simply found it easy to re-work Cervantes' mine) or sympathetically—emphasizing his willingness to experiment with the possibilities of novelized satire and to write a book different from those he had written before. *Ferdinand Count Fathom* had been pretty much a failure; he might, however, have been tempted to return to the relatively successful designs of *Roderick Random* and *Peregrine Pickle*.

[1] Kahrl (see Bibliography), pp. 56–60.
[2] Carmine Linsalata, *Smollett's Hoax: Don Quixote in English* (1956), pp. 13, 22.

Quite possibly Smollett was familiar with Fielding's comedy, *Don Quixote in England* (1734), an ephemeral and much more slavish anglicizing of *Don Quixote*, but sharing with *Launcelot Greaves* the satiric intention of showing that most people are at least as mad as the central figure is presumed to be. In any event, there was already a tradition of English works based on the Quixote 'syndrome', ranging from Butler's *Hudibras* (alluded to in the novel) to Charlotte Lennox's *Female Quixote* (1752), and continued in Richard Graves's *Spiritual Quixote* (1772) and such forgotten works as *The Philosophical Quixote* (1782) and *The Amicable Quixote* (1788). Fielding's tribute to Cervantes' influence in the Preface to *Joseph Andrews* is well known, and we can learn something of Smollett's purposes in adapting knight-errantry to an English setting from his own early praise of Cervantes in the Preface to *Roderick Random*:

> ... The world actually began to be infected with the spirit of knight-errantry, when Cervantes, by an inimitable piece of ridicule, reformed the taste of mankind, representing chivalry in the right point of view, and converting romance to purposes far more useful and entertaining, by making it assume the sock, and point out the follies of ordinary life.[1]

Quite clearly, Smollett values *Don Quixote* less for the farcical absurdities of its two central characters than for the comic-satiric exposure of general human folly occasioned by their exploits. In *Launcelot Greaves*, which really has few scenes specifically imitated from *Don Quixote* and which, whatever its merits, is not at all a slavish following of Cervantes, as has been sometimes carelessly claimed,[2] it is the basic metaphor of the hero as both satirist and knight-errant which is Smollett's most important debt to Cervantes.[3] Greaves is rather insipid if looked at as an attempt at realistic characterization, but seen as the vehicle of the book's satire, and the focus of a company of varied caricatures, he becomes much more interesting. In fact, one of the most appealing things about the novel is the group, taken *as* a group, which forms around Sir Launcelot, with its loyalties and shared interests and experiences. Even occasional conflicts and

---

[1] *Roderick Random* (1748), i. vii.

[2] E.g. Martz (see Bibliography), p. 14. Parallels with *Don Quixote* are pointed out in the Explanatory Notes.

[3] Cf. Ronald Paulson (see Bibliography), pp. 199–200.

Ferret's contentiousness are subsumed in the essential good will of the fellow travellers. The exchanges and mutual sympathies among the members of the group recall some of the best scenes in *Don Quixote* in which the curate, the barber, Sancho and Don Quixote debate or travel together, and they anticipate something of the multiple responses to experience rendered in the epistolary form of *Humphry Clinker*. (*The Pickwick Papers* is Dickens's variation and refinement on the possibilities of the travelling cross-section of society.)

The almost inevitable nautical member of Smollett's group is Captain Crowe, who has the winning naïveté of Captain Bowling and outdoes Hawser Trunnion in the relentlessness of his sea-man's terminology. Though overdone, his nautical idiom is often richly metaphorical. He shares Trunnion's superstition and distaste for lawyers as well as his notion that riding horseback is simply another form of navigation. Because they are intended to serve as the voices of common sense, Clarke and Fillet are less interesting, though this does not prevent a certain amount of satire on the undue complexity of the law in Clarke's pretensions to legal expertise. The quickness to respond feelingly to scenes of distress or charity which Smollett attributes to Clarke is only one indication of his attempt in the novel to appeal to the contemporary taste for the sentimental. Crabshaw, like his predecessor Sancho Panza, is a fountain of proverbial expression, most of it aimed at justifying his pragmatic view of things. Unlike Sancho Panza, however, he does not grow in moral stature until his proverbs are taken as genuine wisdom. The reader soon wearies of the countless beatings and afflictions he suffers (*his* master, unlike Sancho's, is exempted from such ignominy), though occasionally he is genuinely funny; for example, when he complains of the price of an astrologer's prophecy that he will be hanged for horse-stealing, because, 'in all likelihood [it] would never be fulfilled'. Among the corrupt public servants the group encounters, the election candidates and the justice of the peace are most sharply delineated, largely through their use and abuse of language. Smollett's attempt at rendering Yorkshire dialect is at best suggestive, but his parody of political speeches in chapter ix is effective in the broad irony with which the candidates are made to expose their selfish motives—to the reader if not to their well-bribed audience. The platform from which they speak is a variation on those wooden devices for elevating one's self above a crowd described in *A Tale of a Tub*. Even more successful, perhaps, is the Gobbles's assault on the English language, which looks forward to the self-revealing diction of Winifred Jenkins and Tabitha Bramble. Dick Distich is only a gesture in the direction of the self-important but second-rate writers satirized in the other novels.

In several respects, the book's most fascinating character is Ferret, the Hobbesian misanthrope. As a caricature of John Shebbeare, he represents Smollett's refusal to give up that satire on specific individuals which he had practised in his early poems *Advice* and *Reproof* and the early novels, and he is scarcely an exaggeration of Shebbeare's real character.[1] Shebbeare had helped Lady Vane to edit, if not write, the *Memoirs of a Lady of Quality* which are included in *Peregrine Pickle*; he appears in the *Memoirs* as the Dr. S——— who attends her. Like Ferret, Shebbeare feigned knowledge of great medical secrets (though no one knew where his medical degree came from) and dabbled in alchemy. Like Ferret, he was known as a political writer who would adjust his opinions to suit his employer. His attacks on the King, the Duke of Newcastle, the Whig ministry, and the legislature were so virulent that, like Ferret, he was hounded by the law and eventually sentenced to three years imprisonment for libel. He also reserved some of his most caustic criticism for what he took to be the Georges' excessive dedication to the interests of Hanover, as Ferret does. Ferret's cynicism, though more specifically political, is reminiscent of the wholesale condemnation of human nature by Cadwallader Crabtree in *Peregrine Pickle*, while his resourcefulness and energy give him something of the attraction of such villains as Volpone, whose machinations, after all, depend on the human capacity for self-deception and greed. In chapter x, even Greaves is forced to admit that in his castigation of government and populace Ferret has 'mixed some melancholy truths'; and many pages of Smollett's *History of England* attest that on a number of important issues, for example, the dishonesty of using the defence of protestantism as a reason for conducting the Seven Years War, he agreed with Shebbeare.[2]

---

[1] My account of Shebbeare derives from James R. Foster, 'Smollett's Pamphleteering Foe Shebbeare', *PMLA*, lvii (1942), 1053–1100.

[2] *The History of England, from the Revolution to the Death of George the Second* (new edition, 5 vols., 1818), iv. 225, 226–8.

In this novel, Smollett's descriptions of the emotions of love are both serious and parodic.[1] Aurelia Darnel, besides being a paragon of virtue and beauty, is intended as the antithesis of the affected wives of the rich yeomen Clarke describes in chapter iii, and in the last chapter the narrator contrasts her wedding attire with the vulgar taste a lesser being would have displayed. As a means of satirizing affectation, however, her contribution is slight. She is no more tolerable than Narcissa, Amelia, or Serafina, the melo-dramatic heroines of the earlier novels.

As in *Roderick Random* and *Peregrine Pickle*, Smollett contrives a central plot which is neither complex nor highly original but which serves the Aristotelian purpose of giving his work a beginning, a middle, and an end. Here, Greaves's knight-errantry, though largely self-conscious, is occasioned by his love-madness, reaches its height when he is most convinced of his rejection by Aurelia and gradually dissolves as the truth of her affection is revealed. However, action directly involving Greaves's pursuit of Aurelia accounts for only about a third of the novel. The remaining two-thirds are essentially social satire and consist of a formally loose but thematically consistent series of episodes in which Greaves and company encounter various corruptions in the public life of both country and town. It is in the best passages of these episodes that Smollett achieves those moments of authenticity and vitality in criticizing eighteenth-century life that suggest Hogarth while bearing the unmistakable stamp of his own view of things.

What holds the novel's satiric episodes together are Greaves and the values he represents. As James Beattie pointed out shortly after the novel was published:

Sir Launcelot Greaves is of Don Quixote's kindred, but a different character. Smollett's design was, not to expose him to ridicule; but rather to recommend him to our pity and admiration. He has therefore given him youth, strength, and beauty, as well as courage, and dignity of mind, has mounted him on a generous steed, and arrayed him in an elegant suit of armour. Yet, that the history might have a comic air, he has been careful to contrast and connect Sir Launcelot with a squire and other associates of very dissimilar tempers and circumstances.[2]

---

[1] Spector (see Bibliography), p. 125.

[2] James Beattie, 'An Essay on Laughter and Ludicrous Composition' (written 1764) in *Essays* (1776), p. 350.

This view does not set with our modern appreciation of *Don Quixote*, and Greaves comes in for more 'ridicule' than the observation allows, but Beattie is right in suggesting that we are intended to admire what Greaves professes, if not always what he does. In fact, *Launcelot Greaves* differs from the earlier novels primarily in having a clear, if exaggerated, set of positive values against which the objects of its satire are measured. If there is a positive criterion against which the vengefulness of Random, the aggressive satire of Peregrine Pickle, and the roguery of Fathom are measured, it is revealed only by implication or (in the case of *Ferdinand Count Fathom*, which can be seen as transitional in this respect)[1] as quite non-ironic and sentimentalized chivalry. By contrast, Greaves is, from the outset, presented as the representative of two sets of ideals, the spirit of chivalry and benevolent squirearchy. In his role as Quixotic knight, representing the values of courage and protection of the weak, he is as archaic as Renaldo in *Ferdinand Count Fathom*. As ideal squire, he represents (as Fielding's Allworthy does) the values of charity and compassion. In this role he is an effective and somewhat realistic embodiment of virtues against which the varieties of injustice he encounters may be gauged. In both roles he personifies the concept of justice, and the vague feudal overtones of the conclusions to *Roderick Random*, *Peregrine Pickle*, and (not so vague) *Ferdinand Count Fathom* suggest that perhaps Greaves's dual roles as knight and ideal squire were not as far apart for Smollett's imagination as they might seem to us.

When Ferret voices what seems to be Smollett's anticipation of the reader's objections to his rehashing of Quixotism, Greaves defines his conception of the role he has adopted:

'What! (said Ferret) you set up for a modern Don Quixote?—The scheme is rather too stale and extravagant. . . .' . . .
'I am neither an affected imitator of Don Quixote [replies Greaves], nor, as I trust in heaven, visited by that spirit of lunacy so admirably displayed in the fictitious character exhibited by the inimitable Cervantes. I have not yet encountered a windmill for a giant; nor mistaken this public house for a magnificent castle. . . . I see and distinguish objects as they are discerned and described by other men. . . . I quarrel with none but the foes

[1] For Renaldo's 'Quixotism', see *Ferdinand Count Fathom*, ed. Grant, Oxford English Novels (1971), p. 346.

of virtue and decorum, against whom I have declared perpetual war, and them I will every where attack as the natural enemies of mankind.'[1]

The description of purpose presented here is a description of the satirist's function. As Ronald Paulson has suggested, Smollett conceives of his hero as satirist-errant, travelling and aggressively searching out injustice and folly.[2] While avoiding the Smollett-or-Fielding controversy, we can say that *Launcelot Greaves* reminds us of Fielding's kind of satire precisely because of the appeal its satire makes to a background of general and ideal values, though the equivalent of the system of values implicitly conveyed by the narrator of *Tom Jones* is, in Smollett's novel, put in the mouth of the central satirist-character. Greaves is a good example of what Sheldon Sacks has called a 'walking concept'; that is, a character who is a spokesman for the values he represents—here the ideals of charity, justice, noblesse oblige.[3]

In set speeches throughout the novel Greaves provides ideal definitions which throw into relief the actual imperfections and abuses the world affords. In chapter iii he reminds his father of the obligations of the truly benevolent landlord. In the election scene, after both candidates have sufficiently revealed their stupidity and self-interest, he outlines the ideal qualifications of a candidate for parliament as well as the considerations that should affect the ideal voter. Similar pictures of the professional ideals to which they should aspire are presented to justice Gobble, the two 'soldiers' (who turn out to be apprentices) and the doctor who collaborates in Greaves's confinement. Whatever unity the novel possesses arises from the consistency with which Greaves can be counted on to invoke (and often to demonstrate) the virtues lacking in those he encounters. This is not to say that Greaves's idealism is always presented with a straight face as a workable alternative to corruption; as in most satire with an internal satiric voice, the satirist-hero comes in for his share of exposure, but Smollett does not allow us to overlook the essential rightness of his hero's ideals. His method in this resembles Fielding's in the treatment of Parson Adams.

---

[1] pp. 12–13.
[2] Paulson (see Bibliography), pp. 189–90, 199–200.
[3] Sheldon Sacks, *Fiction and the Shape of Belief* (1965), p. 100.

Greaves's occasionally excessive zeal is the basis for another of the book's themes, the relationship between the law and satire as means of dealing with human imperfection. When Ferret tries to convince Greaves that he is surely outside the law in riding armed in search of trouble, Greaves replies that his purpose is 'to act as coadjutor to the law, and even to remedy evils which the law cannot reach; to detect fraud and treason, abase insolence, mortify pride, discourage slander, disgrace immodesty, and stigmatize ingratitude'.[1] Even Ferret, in spite of his contempt for the law, regrets that 'impertinence and folly' are not 'felony by the statute', and Swift might have had such a character as Greaves in mind when, in a moment of ethical fervour, he suggested the appointment of 'itinerrary commissioners' to 'inspect everywhere throughout the kingdom, into the conduct . . . of men in office, with respect to their morals and religion'.[2] The contrast between the legal and satiric modes of responding to corruption is well represented in the judgments against Gobble. The lawyers, Clarke and Fenton, are ready with a detailed legal argument and recommendations for proper punishment. Greaves, the bene-volent satirist, on the other hand, attacks the 'malignant heart, devoid of humanity, inflamed with pride, and rankling with revenge', and, positively, asserts the ideal against which Gobble is to be tried.

It has been objected that only Greaves's superior wealth and social standing account for his success in many of his conflicts with vice,[3] but, as in Fielding or Pope, much of the book's satiric point lies precisely in exposing characters who pay to wealth the deference they should pay to virtue. Mrs. Gobble, for example, is made to say that 'Mr. Gobble, thanks be to God, can defy the whole world to prove that he ever said an uncivil word, or did a rude thing to a gentleman, knowing him to be a person of fortune.'[4] Throughout the novel, Greaves's liberal dispensation of charity is, in addition to his descriptions of ideal conduct, the positive half of his role as exposer and righter of wrongs, but one of the

---

[1] p. 14. Cf. *Peregrine Pickle*, ed. Clifford, Oxford English Novels (1964), p. 576.

[2] *A Project for the Advancement of Religion and the Reformation of Morals* (1709), p. 21.

[3] By Milton Goldberg (see Bibliography), p. 117; and Donald Bruce (see Bibliography), pp. 107–8.

[4] p. 96.

subsidiary themes is the definition of 'practical' or effective charity. Clarke says in chapter iii that Greaves as a young man 'made the guineas fly in such a manner, as looked more like madness than generosity'. In the prison scenes, Felton theorizes about human charity and, on the basis of his knowledge of the prisoners, directs Greaves's charity to the most worthy recipients. Greaves learns that a fourth part of what he would have bestowed upon the widow who tries to maintain herself in luxury would make Coleby, the bankrupt tradesman, and his family 'sing for joy'.

Several elements of Smollett's style remind us that *Launcelot Greaves* first appeared in monthly parts. Chapter i, for example, concludes with the self-conscious request for the reader's patience until chapter ii appears. Chapter iii includes an apology for its exceptional length, while throughout there is an effort to make chapters autonomous at the same time that each usually contains a reference to what can be expected to follow. If the early chapters *were* in print before the later ones were written, there are many phrases, such as 'in the sequel' or 'the misanthrope will reappear in due season', to indicate that Smollett had at least a general idea of where things were going. The first year's worth of the novel, even, has a certain self-sufficiency, the conclusion to chapter xii reading more like the end of a book than a chapter. The chapter headings, with their irony at the writer's expense, approach Fielding's narrative *rapport* with the reader more than any of Smollett's other novels do. In this connection, it would be interesting to know if Smollett, like Dickens, had a sense of public response to his work as its serialization progressed, or if he consulted with Walker, his illustrator, as Dickens did with Hablot Browne to ensure compatibility between verbal and visual accounts.[1]

Launcelot Greaves is not a great novel by any means, but there are clear signs that it is more highly regarded today than at any time since its publication, with less attention paid to its vestiges of picaresque and more to its comedy, which is often enjoyable, and its satire, which is often effective.[2] As the representative of certain ideal values, Greaves looks forward to Matthew Bramble, who tests the corruptions of Bath and London against his own Horatian ideals. Smollett's Augustan belief in 'decorum, social

[1] See John Butt and Kathleen Tillotson, *Dickens at Work* (1957).

[2] It is praised in Mayo (see Bibliography), p. 284; and Spector (see Bibliography), p. 126.

order and subordination'[1] is reflected in Greaves's contempt for people who act above their station; the account of the affected yeomen in chapter iii is very much in the vein of Bramble's diatribe against the *nouveau riche* at Bath. So many of the characters set up as orators (Clarke, Ferret, Greaves, Crabshaw, the candidates, the mad-house physician) and so much depends on the specialized languages of law, the sea, politics, or medical diagnosis, that we catch a glimpse of the worlds of Swift and Sterne in which language usurps the power of thought as well as things. The book's 'sociological' value is considerable; we learn a great deal about the texture of eighteenth-century life from it. More important, Smollett's satiric interpretation of that life is memorably robust and distinctive.

[1] Knapp (see Bibliography), p. 305.

NOTE ON THE TEXT

THIS edition is the first to follow the text of the serialized printing, 1760–61; the long 's' has been eliminated and obvious typographical errors have been corrected.

NOTE ON THE ILLUSTRATIONS

THE illustrations originally accompanied the *British Magazine* serialization of *Launcelot Greaves*. It has been said, with considerable authority, that they are the first known magazine illustrations of a work of fiction (Robert Mayo, *The English Novel in the Magazines, 1740–1815* (1962), frontispiece). They are the work of Anthony Walker (1726–65), who was well known for his small book-illustrations executed from his own designs.

SELECT BIBLIOGRAPHY

GENERAL WORKS ON SMOLLET

BIOGRAPHY: Lewis M. Knapp, *Tobias Smollett: Doctor of Men and Manners* (1949); *Letters: The Letters of Tobias Smollett*, ed. Lewis M. Knapp (1970). MODERN STUDIES (in chronological order): Howard S. Buck, *A Study in Smollett, Chiefly 'Peregrine Pickle'* (1925); Howard S. Buck, *Smollett as Poet* (1927); Eugène Joliat, *Smollett et la France* (1935); Louis L. Martz, *The Later Career of Tobias Smollett* (1942); Claude E. Jones, *Smollett Studies* (1942); Alice Parker, 'Tobias Smollett and the Law' (*SP*, xxxix (1942), 545–58); George M. Kahrl, *Tobias Smollett, Traveler-Novelist* (1945); Fred W. Boege, *Smollett's Reputation as a Novelist* (1947); Laurence Brander, *Tobias Smollett* (1951); V. S. Pritchett, 'The Shocking Surgeon', in *The Living Novel* (1954), pp. 18–23; Alan D. McKillop, 'Tobias Smollett', in *The Early Masters of English Fiction* (1956), pp. 147–81; A. R. Humphreys, 'Fielding and Smollett', in *Pelican Guide to English Literature* (1957), iv. 313–31; Milton Orowitz, 'Smollett and the Art of Caricature' (*Spectrum*, ii (1958), 155–67); Albrecht B. Strauss, 'On Smollett's Language', in *English Institute Essays, 1958* (1959), pp. 25–54; Milton A. Goldberg, *Smollett and the Scottish School* (1959); Robert Alter, 'The Picaroon as Fortune's Plaything', in *Rogue's Progress* (1963), pp. 58–79; William B. Piper, 'The Large Diffused Picture of Life in Smollett's Early Novels' (*SP*, lx (1963), 45–56); Donald J. Bruce, *Radical Doctor Smollett* (1964); Robert Giddings, *The Tradition of Smollett* (1967); Ronald Paulson, 'Smollett: The Satirist as Character Type', in *Satire and the Novel in Eighteenth-Century England* (1967), pp. 165–218; Philip Stevick, 'Stylistic Energy in the Early Smollett' (*SP*, lxiv (1967), 712–19); Tuvia Bloch, 'Smollett's Quest For Form' (*MP*, lxv (1967), 103–13); Robert D. Spector, *Tobias Smollett* (1969); Paul-Gabriel Boucé, *Les Romans de Smollett: Etude Critique* (1971); Paul-Gabriel Boucé and George S. Rousseau, eds., *Tobias Smollett: Bicentennial Essays Presented to Lewis M. Knapp* (1971).

EDITIONS OF *LAUNCELOT GREAVES*

First published in monthly instalments in the *British Magazine* from January 1760 to December 1761, with illustrations by A. Walker. First book-form edition 1762, the only authorized edition in Smollett's lifetime. Pirated editions appeared in Dublin (1762) and Cork (1767). In 1774 a 'new' and 'corrected' edition appeared, but there is no evidence that Smollett's intentions were consulted in any way for this edition. For other editions see *CBEL*. *Launcelot Greaves* has, of course, been included in the collected editions of Smollett, including those by Moore (1797), Anderson (1796, 1800, 1820), Saintsbury (1895), Henley (1899–1901), Maynadier (1902), and by the Shakespeare Head (Oxford, 1925–6). With illustrations by T. Stothard (engraving by W. Blake, 1782), R. Corbould (1793), G. Cruikshank (1832). Translated into German (1772, 1791), Danish (1790), and French (1824).

SPECIAL STUDIES OF *LAUNCELOT GREAVES*

There are no critical studies devoted exclusively to *Launcelot Greaves*. However, important material appears in several of the works listed above in the general section or among the editions. Saintsbury has qualified praise for the novel in the Introduction to the *Launcelot Greaves* volume of his *Works* of Smollett. Kahrl gives a few critical comments and information on the geography of the novel in his chapter 'Prose Fiction of the Armchair' (pp. 56–60); Knapp treats the book's composition and reception and gives a brief critical estimate (pp. 228–9, 320–1); McKillop points up similarities to Fielding (pp. 169–70); Goldberg's chapter on *Greaves* is subtitled 'A Study in Social- and Self-Love' (pp. 108–42); much of contemporary understanding of Smollett's satire is indebted to Paulson, who discusses *Greaves* as another of Smollett's attempts to novelize the satirist of formal verse satire (pp. 189–90, 199–200); Spector sees the novel as consistently satiric and makes a good case for a higher assessment (pp. 107–26). Boucé (*Les Romans de Smollett*) discusses the relation of *Greaves* to *Don Quixote* (pp. 144–51) and, in the most penetrating and sympathetic analysis the novel has received, sees the novel as centred on the satiric treatment of madness and reason, while arguing that, like the other novels, it has a thematic unity and subtlety of symbolic pattern hardly compatible with the view of Smollett as an artless writer. Among works not listed in the Bibliography above, three are important: Archer Taylor lists, with references to standard collections, many of the book's proverbs in 'Proverbial Materials in Tobias Smollett, *The Adventures of Sir Launcelot Greaves*' (*Southern Folklore Quarterly* xxi (1957), 85–92; Richard Lettis discusses sources and collates the serial and 1762 editions in 'A Study of Smollett's *Sir Launcelot Greaves*' (unpublished dissertation, Yale University (1957); Robert Mayo, *The English Novel in the Magazines, 1740–1815* (1962), pp. 274–86, has an intelligent evaluation along with interesting observations on the novel's superiority to other serial fiction of its day.

A CHRONOLOGY OF
TOBIAS GEORGE SMOLLETT

XXV

Age

1769 (April)	*The History and Adventures of an Atom*, a political satire, probably by Smollett	48
1771 (June)	*The Expedition of Humphry Clinker*	50
1771 (17 September)	Dies at Il Giardino, a villa near Leghorn. Buried in the English cemetery at Leghorn	50
1773	*Ode to Independence*, published posthumously	
1774	Monument to Smollett erected on the banks of the Leven, near his birthplace, with an inscription by Dr. Johnson	
1776	Translation of Fénelon's *Adventures of Telemachus*, published posthumously	

THE LIFE
AND ADVENTURES OF
SIR LAUNCELOT GREAVES

CHAPTER I

*In which certain personages of this delightful history are
introduced to the reader's acquaintance*

IT was on the great northern road from York to London, about the
beginning of the month October, and the hour of eight in the
evening, that four travellers were by a violent shower of rain driven
for shelter into a little public house on the side of the highway,
distinguished by a sign which was said to exhibit the figure of a
black lion.[1] The kitchen, in which they assembled, was the only
room for entertainment in the house, paved with red bricks,
remarkably clean, furnished with three or four Windsor chairs,
adorned with shining plates of pewter and copper sauce-pans
nicely scoured, that even dazzled the eyes of the beholder; while a
chearful fire of sea-coal[2] blazed in the chimney. Three of the
travellers, who arrived on horseback, having seen their cattle
properly accommodated in the stable, agreed to pass the time, until
the weather should clear up, over a bowl of rumbo,[3] which was
accordingly prepared: but the fourth, refusing to join their
company, took his station at the opposite side of the chimney, and
called for a pint of two-penny,[4] with which he indulged himself
apart. At a little distance, on his left hand, there was another
groupe, consisting of the landlady a decent widow, her two
daughters, the elder of whom seemed to be about the age of
fifteen, and a country lad, who served both as waiter and ostler.

The social triumvirate was composed of Mr. Fillet, a country
practitioner in surgery and midwifery, Capt. Crowe, and his
nephew Mr. Thomas Clarke, an attorney. Fillet was a man of

some education, and a great deal of experience, shrewd, sly, and sensible. Capt. Crowe had commanded a merchant-ship in the Mediterranean-trade for many years, and saved some money by dint of frugality and traffick. He was an excellent seaman, brave, active, friendly in his way, and scrupulously honest; but as little acquainted with the world as a sucking child; whimsical, impatient, and so impetuous that he could not help breaking in upon the conversation, whatever it might be, with repeated interruptions, that seemed to burst from him by involuntary impulse: when he himself attempted to speak, he never finished his period; but made such a number of abrupt transitions, that his discourse seemed to be an unconnected series of unfinished sentences, the meaning of which it was not easy to decypher. His nephew, Tom Clarke, was a young fellow, whose goodness of heart even the exercise of his profession had not been able to corrupt.[1] Before strangers he never owned himself an attorney, without blushing, though he had no reason to blush for his own practice; for he constantly refused to engage in the cause of any client whose character was equivocal, and was never known to act with such industry as when concerned for the widow and the orphan, or any other object that sued *in forma pauperis*.[2] Indeed he was so replete with human kindness, that as often as an affecting story or circumstance was told in his hearing, it overflowed at his eyes. Being of a warm complexion, he was very susceptible of passion, and somewhat libertine in his amours. In other respects, he piqued himself on understanding the practice of the courts, and in private company he took pleasure in *laying down the law*; but he was an indifferent orator, and tediously circumstantial in his explanations: his stature was rather diminutive; but, upon the whole, he had some title to the character of a pretty, dapper, little fellow. The solitary guest had something very forbidding in his aspect, which was contracted by an habitual frown. His eyes were small and red, and so deep set in the sockets, that each appeared like the unextinguished snuff of a farthing-candle, gleaming through the horn of a dark lanthorn.[3] His nostrils were elevated in scorn, as if his sense of smelling had been perpetually offended by some unsavoury odour; and he looked as if he wanted to shrink within himself, from the impertinence of society. He wore a black periwig as straight as the pinions of a raven, and this was covered with an hat flapped, and fastened to his head by a speckled handkerchief tied under his chin. He was wrapped in a great coat of brown frize, under which he seemed to conceal a small bundle. His name was Ferret,[1] and his character distinguished by three peculiarities. He was never seen to smile: he was never heard to speak in praise of any person whatsoever; and he was never known to give a direct answer to any question that was asked: but seemed, on all occasions, to be actuated by the most perverse spirit of contradiction.

Capt. Crowe, having remarked that it was squally weather, asked how far it was to the next market-town; and understanding that the distance was not less than six miles, said he had a good mind to come to an anchor for the night, if so be as he could have a tolerable *berth* in this here harbour. Mr. Fillet, perceiving by his stile that he was a sea-faring gentleman, observed that their land-lady was not used to lodge such company; and expressed some surprize, that he who had no doubt endured so many storms and hardships at sea, should think much of travelling five or six miles a-horseback by moon-light. 'For my part, said he, I ride in all weathers, and at all hours, without minding cold, wet, wind, or darkness. My constitution is so case-hardened, that I believe I could live all the year at Spitzbergen.[2] With respect to this road, I know every foot of it so exactly, that I'll engage to travel forty miles upon it blindfold, without making one false step; and if you have faith enough to put yourselves under my auspices, I will conduct you safe to an elegant inn, where you will meet with the best accommodation.' 'Thank you, brother, (replied the Captain:) we are much beholden to you for your courteous offer; but, how-somever, you must not think I mind foul weather more than my neighbours. I have worked hard aloft and alow[3] in many a taught gale—but this here is the case, d'ye see; we have run down a long day's reckoning: our beasts have had a hard spell; and as for my own hap, brother, I doubt my bottom-planks have lost some of their sheathing,[4] being as how I a'n't used to that kind of scrubbing.'

The Doctor, who had practised on board a man of war in his youth, and was perfectly well acquainted with the Captain's dialect, assured him, that if his bottom was damaged, he would *new-pay*[5] it with an excellent salve, which he always carried about with him, to guard against such accidents on the road: but Tom Clarke, who seemed to have cast the eyes of affection upon the landlady's eldest daughter, Dolly, objected to their proceeding farther without rest and refreshment, as they had already travelled fifty miles since morning; and he was sure his uncle must be fatigued both in mind and body, from vexation as well as from a hard exercise, to which he had not been accustomed. Fillet then desisted, saying, he was sorry to find the Captain had any cause for vexation; but he hoped it was not an incurable evil. This expression was accompanied with a look of curiosity, which Mr. Clarke was glad of an occasion to gratify; for, as we have hinted above, he was a very communicative gentleman, and the affair which now lay upon his stomach interested him nearly. 'I'll assure you, Sir, (said he) this here gentleman, captain Crowe, who is my mother's own brother, has been cruelly used by some of his relations. He bears as good a character as any captain of a ship on the Royal Exchange,[1] and has undergone a variety of hardships at sea. What d'ye think, now, of his bursting all his sinews, and making his eyes start out of his head, in pulling his ship off a rock, whereby he saved to his owners—' Here he was interrupted by the Captain, who exclaimed, 'Belay,[2] Tom, belay:—prithee, don't veer out such a deal of jaw. Clap a stopper upon thy cable,[3] and bring thyself up, my lad.[4]—What a deal of stuff thou hast pumped up concerning bursting, and starting, and pulling ships, Laud have mercy on us!—Look ye here, brother—look ye here—mind these poor crippled joints: two fingers on the starboard, and three on the larboard hand: crooked, d'ye see, like the knees of a bilander.[5]—I'll tell you what, brother, you seem to be a—ship deep laden—rich cargoe—current setting into the bay—hard gale—lee-shore—all hands in the boat—tow round the headland—self pulling for dear blood, against the whole crew.—Snap go the finger-braces[6]—crack went the eye-blocks.[7]—Bounce daylight—flash starlight—down I foundered, dark as hell—whizz went my ears, and my head spun like a whirligig.—That don't signify—I'm a Yorkshire boy, as the saying is—all my life at sea, brother, by reason of an old grandmother and maiden aunt, a couple of old stinking—kept me these forty years out of my grandfather's estate.—Hearing as how they had taken their departure, came ashore, hired horses, and clapped on all my canvas, steering to the northward, to take possession of my—— But it don't signify talking—these two old piratical—had held a palaver with a lawyer—an attorney, Tom, d'ye mind me, an attorney—and by his assistance hove me out of my inheritance:— that is all, brother—hove me out of five hundred pounds a year—

that's all—what signifies—but such windfalls we don't every day pick up along shore.——Fill about,[1] brother——yes, by the Lord! those two smuggling harridans, with the assistance of an attorney— an attorney, Tom—hove me out of five hundred a year.' 'Yes, in- deed, Sir, (added Mr. Clarke) those two malicious old women docked the intail, and left the estate to an alien.'[2]

Here Mr. Ferret thought proper to intermingle in the conver- sation with a '*Pish*, what, do'st talk of docking the intail? Do'st not know that by the Statute Westm. 2, 13 Ed. I.[3] the will and intention of the donor must be fulfilled, and the tenant in *tail* shall not alien after issue had, or before.' 'Give me leave, Sir, (replied Tom) I presume you are a practitioner in the law. Now you know, that in the case of a contingent *remainder*,[4] the intail may be destroyed by levying a fine, and suffering a recovery; or otherwise destroying the particular estate, before the contingency happens. If *feoffees*,[5] who possess an estate only during the life of a son, where divers *remainders* are limited over, make a *feoffment* in fee to him, by the *feoffment* all the future *remainders* are destroyed. Indeed, a person in *remainder* may have a writ of Intrusion,[6] if any do intrude after the death of a tenant for life;[7] and the writ *ex gravi querela*[8] lies to execute a devise in *remainder*, after the death of tenant in tail with- out issue—' 'Spoke like a true disciple of Geber,' cries Ferret. 'No, Sir, (replied Mr. Clarke) counsellor Caper is in the con- veyancing-way[9]—I was clerk to serjeant[10] Croaker.' 'Ay, now you may set up for yourself; (resumed the other) for you can prate as unintelligibly as the best of them.'

'Perhaps (said Tom) I do not make myself understood: if so be as how that is the case, let us change the position; and suppose that this here case is a *tail after a possibility of issue extinct*.[11] If a tenant in *tail*, after possibility, make a *feoffment* of his land, he in reversion may enter for the forfeiture. Then we must make a distinction between *general tail* and *special tail*. It is the word *body* that makes the *intail*:—there must be *body* in the *tail*, devised to heirs male or female, otherwise it is a fee-simple,[12] because it is not limited of what *body*. Thus a corporation cannot be seized in *tail*.[13] For example: here is a young woman—What is your name, my dear?' 'Dolly,' answered the daughter with a curtsy. 'Here's Dolly—I seize Dolly *in tail*—Dolly, I seize you in *tail*.'—'Sha't then,' cried Dolly, pouting. 'I am seized of land in fee—I settle on Dolly in *tail*.'—Dolly, who did not comprehend the nature of the illustration, understood him in a literal sense, and in a whimpering tone exclaimed, 'Sha't then, I tell thee, cursed tuoad!' Tom, however, was so transported with his subject, that he took no notice of poor Dolly's mistake; but proceeded in his harangue upon the different kinds of *tails*, *remainders*, and *seisins*, when he was interrupted by a noise that alarmed the whole company. The rain had been succeeded by a storm of wind, that howled around the house with the most savage impetuosity; and the heavens were overcast in such a manner, that not one star appeared, so that all without was darkness and uproar. This aggravated the horrour of divers loud screams, which even the noise of the blast could not exclude from the astonished ears of our travellers. Capt. Crowe called out, 'Avast, avast:' Tom Clarke sat silent, staring wildly, with his mouth still open: the surgeon himself seemed startled; and Ferret's countenance betrayed evident marks of confusion. The ostler moved nearer the chimney, and the good woman of the house, with her two daughters, crept close to the company.

After some pause, the Captain starting up, 'These (said he) be signals of distress. Some poor souls in danger of foundering.—Let us bear up a-head,[1] and see if we can give them any assistance.' The landlady begged him, for Christis sake, not to think of going out; for it was a spirit that would lead him astray into fens and rivers, and certainly do him a mischief. Crowe seemed to be staggered by this remonstrance, which his nephew reinforced, observing, that it might be a stratagem of rogues to decoy them into the fields, that they might rob them under cloud of night. Thus exhorted, he resumed his seat; and Mr. Ferret began to make very severe strictures upon the folly and fear of those who believed and trembled at the visitation of spirits, ghosts, and goblins. He said, he would engage with twelve pennyworth of phosphorus to frighten a whole parish out of their senses; then he expatiated on the pusillanimity of the nation in general; ridiculed the militia,[2] censured the government; and dropped some hints about a change of hands,[3] which the Captain could not, and the Doctor would not comprehend. Tom Clarke, from the freedom of his discourse, concluded he was a ministerial spy, and communicated his opinion to his uncle in a whisper, while this misanthrope continued to pour forth his invectives with a fluency peculiar to himself. The truth is, Mr. Ferret had been a party-writer,[4] not from principle, but employment, and had felt the rod of power; in order to avoid a second exertion of which, he now found it convenient to sculk about in the country: for he had received intimation of a warrant from the secretary of state, who wanted to be better acquainted with his person. Notwithstanding the ticklish nature of his situation, it was become so habitual to him to think and speak in a certain manner, that even before strangers, whose principles and connexions he could not possibly know, he hardly ever opened his mouth, without uttering some direct or implied sarcasm against the government. He had already proceeded a considerable way in demonstrating, that the nation was bankrupt and beggared, and that those who stood at the helm were steering full into the gulph of inevitable destruction; when his lecture was suddenly suspended by a violent knocking at the door, which threatened the whole house with immediate demolition. Capt. Crowe, believing they should be instantly boarded, unsheathed his hanger, and stood in a posture of defence. Mr. Fillet armed himself with the poker, which happened to be red-hot: the ostler pulled down a rusty firelock, that hung by the roof, over a flitch of bacon. Tom Clarke, perceiving the landlady and her children distracted with terror, conducted them, out of meer compassion, below stairs into the cellar; and as for Mr. Ferret, he prudently withdrew into an adjoining pantry. But as a personage of great importance in this entertaining history was forced to remain some time at the door, before he could gain admittance, so must the reader wait with patience for the next chapter, in which he will see the cause of this disturbance explained much to his comfort and edification.

CHAPTER II

In which the hero of these adventures makes his first appearance on the stage of action

THE outward door of the Black Lion had already sustained two dreadful shocks; but at the third it flew open, and in stalked an apparition, that smote the hearts of our travellers with fear and trepidation. It was the figure of a man armed cap-a-pie,[1] bearing on his shoulder a bundle dropping with water, which afterwards appeared to be the body of a man that seemed to have been drowned, and fished up from the bottom of the neighbouring river.

Sir Launcelot Greaves and his Squire,
Timothy Crabshaw.

Having deposited his burthen carefully on the floor, he addressed himself to the company in these words: 'Be not surprised, good people, at this unusual appearance, which I shall take an opportunity to explain; and forgive the rude and boisterous manner in which I have demanded, and indeed forced admittance. The violence of my intrusion was the effect of necessity. In crossing the river, my squire and his horse were swept away by the stream; and with some difficulty I have been able to drag him ashore, though I am afraid my assistance reached him too late: for, since I brought him to land, he has given no signs of life.' Here he was interrupted by a groan, which issued from the chest of the squire, and terrified the spectators as much as it comforted the master. After some recollection, Mr. Fillet began to undress the body, which was laid in a blanket on the floor, and rolled from side to side by his direction. A considerable quantity of water being discharged from the mouth of this unfortunate squire, he uttered a hideous roar, and, opening his eyes, stared wildly around: then the surgeon undertook for his recovery; and his master went forth with the ostler in quest of the horses, which he had left by the side of the river. His back was no sooner turned than Ferret, who had been peeping from behind the pantry-door, ventured to rejoin the company; pronouncing with a smile, or rather grin of contempt, 'Hey day! what precious mummery is this? What, are we to have the farce of Hamlet's ghost?'[1] 'Adzooks, (cried the Captain) my kinsman Tom has dropped a-stern—hope in God a-has not[2] bulged to, and gone to bottom.' 'Pish, (exclaimed the misanthrope) there's no danger: the young lawyer is only seizing Dolly in tail.'

Certain it is, Dolly squeaked at that instant in the cellar; and Clarke appearing soon after in some confusion, declared she had been frightened by a flash of lightning: but this assertion was not confirmed by the young lady herself, who eyed him with a sullen regard, indicating displeasure, though not indifference; and when questioned by her mother, replied, 'A-doan't maind what a-says, so a-doan't, vor all his goalden jacket, then.'

In the mean time the surgeon had performed the operation of phlebotomy on the squire, who was lifted into a chair, and supported by the landlady for that purpose; but he had not as yet given any sign of having retrieved the use of his senses. And here Mr. Fillet could not help contemplating, with surprize, the strange figure and accoutrements of his patient, who seemed in age to be turned of fifty. His stature was below the middle size: he was thick, squat, and brawny, with a small protuberance on one shoulder, and a prominent belly, which, in consequence of the water he had swallowed, now strutted out beyond its usual dimensions. His forehead was remarkably convex, and so very low, that his black bushy hair descended within an inch of his nose: but this did not conceal the wrinkles of his front, which were manifold. His small glimmering eyes resembled those of the Hampshire porker, that turns up the soil with his projecting snout. His cheeks were shrivelled and puckered at the corners, like the seams of a regimental coat as it comes from the hands of the contractor: his nose bore a strong analogy in shape to a tennis-ball, and in colour to a mulberry; for all the water of the river had not been able to quench the natural fire of that feature. His upper jaw was furnished with two long white sharp-pointed teeth or fangs, such as the reader may have observed in the chaps of a wolf, or full-grown mastiff, and an anatomist would describe as a preternatural elongation of the *dentes canini*. His chin was so long, so peaked and incurvated, as to form in profile with his impending forehead the exact resemblance of a moon in the first quarter. With respect to his equipage, he had a leathern cap upon his head, faced like those worn by the marines, and exhibiting in embroidery the figure of a crescent. His coat was of white cloth, faced with black, and cut in a very antique fashion; and, in lieu of a waistcoat, he wore a buff jerkin.[1] His feet were cased in loose buskins,[2] which, though they rose almost to his knee, could not hide that curvature known by the appellation of bandy legs. A large string of bandaliers garnished a broad belt that graced his shoulders, from whence depended an instrument of war, which was something between a back-sword[3] and a cutlass; and a case of pistols were stuck in his girdle. Such was the figure which the whole company now surveyed with admiration. After some pause, he seemed to recover his recollection. He rolled his eyes around, and, attentively surveying every individual, exclaimed, in a strange tone, 'Bodikins![4] where's Gilbert!' This interrogation did not favour much of sanity, especially when accompanied with a wild stare, which is generally interpreted as a sure sign of a disturbed understanding: nevertheless the surgeon endeavoured to assist his recollection. 'Come, (said he) have a good heart.—How do'st do, friend?' 'Do! (replied the squire) do as well as I can:— that's a lie too: I might have done better. I had no business to be here.' 'You ought to thank God and your master (resumed the surgeon) for the providential escape you have had.' 'Thank my master! (cried the squire) thank the devil! Go and teach your grannum to crack filberds.[1] I know who I'm bound to pray for, and who I ought to curse the longest day I have to live.'

Here the Captain interposing, 'Nay, brother, (said he) you are bound to pray for this here gentleman as your sheet-anchor:[2] for, if so be as he had not cleared your stowage of the water you had taken in at your upper works, and lightened your veins, d'ye see, by taking away some of your blood, adad! you had driven before the gale, and never been brought up in this world again, d'ye see.' 'What, then you would persuade me (replied the patient) that the only way to save my life was to shed my precious blood? Look ye, friend, it shall not be lost blood to me.—I take you all to witness, that there surgeon, or apothecary, or farrier, or dog-doctor, or whatsoever he may be, has robbed me of the balsam[3] of life:—he has not left so much blood in my body as would fatten a starved flea.—O! that there was a lawyer here to serve him with a *siserari*.'[4] Then fixing his eyes upon Ferret, he proceeded: 'An't you a limb of the law, friend?—No, I cry you mercy, you look more like a shew-man or a conjurer.'—Ferret, nettled at this address, answered, 'It would be well for you that I could conjure a little common sense into that numbscull of yours.' 'If I want that commodity, (rejoined the squire) I must go to another market, I trow.— You legerdemain men be more like to conjure the money from our pockets, than sense into our sculls.—Vor my own part, I was once cheated of vorty good shillings by one of your broother cups and balls.'[5] In all probability he would have descended to particulars, had not he been seized with a return of his nausea, which obliged him to call for a bumper of brandy. This remedy being swallowed, the tumult in his stomach subsided. He desired he might be put to-bed without delay, and that half a dozen eggs and a pound of bacon might, in a couple of hours, be dressed for his supper.

He was accordingly led off the scene by the landlady and her daughter; and Mr. Ferret had just time to observe the fellow was a composition, in which he did not know whether knave or fool most predominated, when the master returned from the stable. He had taken off his helmet, and now displayed a very engaging countenance. His age did not seem to exceed thirty: he was tall, and seemingly robust; his face long and oval, his nose aquiline, his mouth furnished with a set of elegant teeth white as the drifted snow; his complexion clear, and his aspect noble. His chesnut hair loosely flowed in short natural curls; and his grey eyes shone with such vivacity, as plainly shewed that his reason was a little discomposed. Such an appearance prepossessed the greater part of the company in his favour: he bowed round with the most polite and affable address; enquired about his squire, and, being informed of the pains Mr. Fillet had taken for his recovery, insisted upon that gentleman's accepting an handsome gratuity: then, in consideration of the cold bath he had undergone, he was prevailed upon to take the post of honour; namely, the great chair fronting the fire, which was reinforced with a billet of wood for his comfort and convenience.

Perceiving his fellow-travellers either over-awed into silence by his presence, or struck dumb with admiration at his equipage, he accosted them in these words, while an agreeable smile dimpled on his cheek.

'The good company wonders, no doubt, to see a man cased in armour, such as hath been for above a whole century disused in this and every other country of Europe; and perhaps they will be still more surprised, when they hear that man profess himself a noviciate of that military order, which hath of old been distinguished in Great Britain, as well as through all Christendom, by the name of Knights Errant. Yes, gentlemen, in that painful and thorny path of toil and danger I have begun my career, a candidate for honest fame; determined, as far as in me lies, to honour and assert the efforts of virtue; to combat vice in all her forms, redress injuries, chastise oppression, protect the helpless and forlorn, relieve the indigent, exert my best endeavours in the cause of innocence and beauty, and dedicate my talents, such as they are, to the service of my country.' 'What! (said Ferret) you set up for a modern Don Quixote?[1]—The scheme is rather too stale and extravagant.—What was an humorous romance, and well-timed satire in Spain, near two hundred years ago,[2] will make but a sorry jest, and appear equally insipid and absurd, when really acted from affectation, at this time a–day, in a country like England.'

The Knight, eying this censor with a look of disdain, replied, in a solemn lofty tone: 'He that from affectation imitates the extravagances recorded of Don Quixote, is an impostor equally wicked and contemptible. He that counterfeits madness, unless he dissembles like the elder Brutus,[1] for some virtuous purpose, not only debases his own soul, but acts as a traytor to heaven, by denying the divinity that is within him.—I am neither an affected imitator of Don Quixote, nor, as I trust in heaven, visited by that spirit of lunacy so admirably displayed in the fictitious character exhibited by the inimitable Cervantes. I have not yet encountered a windmill for a giant;[2] nor mistaken this public house for a magnificent castle:[3] neither do I believe this gentleman to be the constable;[4] nor that worthy practitioner to be master Elizabat,[5] the surgeon recorded in Amadis de Gaul;[6] nor you to be the enchanter Alquife,[7] nor any other sage of history or romance.—I see and distinguish objects as they are discerned and described by other men. I reason without prejudice, can endure contradiction, and, as the company perceives, even bear impertinent censure without passion or resentment. I quarrel with none but the foes of virtue and decorum, against whom I have declared perpetual war, and them I will every where attack as the natural enemies of mankind.' 'But that war (said the cynic) may soon be brought to a conclusion, and your adventures close in Bridewell,[8] provided you meet with some determined constable, who will seize your worship as a vagrant, according to the statute.' 'Heaven and earth! (cried the stranger, starting up and laying his hand to his sword) do I live to hear myself insulted with such an opprobrious epithet, and refrain from trampling into dust the insolent calumniator!'

The tone in which these words were pronounced, and the indignation that flashed from the eyes of the speaker, intimidated every individual of the society, and reduced Ferret to a temporary privation of all his faculties. His eyes retired within their sockets: his complection, which was naturally of a copper hue, now shifted to a leaden colour: his teeth began to chatter; and all his limbs were agitated by a sudden palsy. The Knight observed his condition, and resumed his seat, saying, 'I was to blame: my vengeance must be reserved for very different objects.—Friend, you have nothing to fear—the sudden gust of passion is now blown over. Recollect yourself, and I will reason calmly on the observation you have made.'

This was a very seasonable declaration to Mr. Ferret, who opened his eyes, and wiped his forehead, while the other proceeded in these terms. 'You say I am in danger of being apprehended as a vagrant: I am not so ignorant of the laws of my country, but that I know the description of those who fall within the legal meaning of this odious term. You must give me leave to inform you, friend, that I am neither bearward,[1] fencer, stroller, gipsey, mountebank, nor mendicant; nor do I practice subtle craft to deceive and impose upon the King's lieges; nor can I be held as an idle disorderly person, travelling from place to place, collecting monies by virtue of counterfeited passes, briefs, and other false pretences.—In what respect therefore am I to be deemed a vagrant? Answer boldly, without fear or scruple.' To this interrogation the misanthrope replied, with a faultering accent, 'If not a vagrant, you incur the penalty for riding armed in affray of the peace.' 'But, instead of riding armed in affray of the peace, (resumed the other) I ride in preservation of the peace; and gentlemen are allowed by the law to wear armour for their defence. Some ride with blunderbusses, some with pistols, some with swords, according to their various inclinations. Mine is to wear the armour of my forefathers: perhaps I use them for exercise, in order to accustom myself to fatigue, and strengthen my constitution: perhaps I assume them for a frolick.'

'But if you swagger armed and in disguise,[2] assault me on the highway, or put me in bodily fear, for the sake of the jest, the law will punish you in earnest,' (cried the other.) 'But my intention (answered the Knight) is carefully to avoid all those occasions of offences.' 'Then (said Ferret) you may go unarmed, like other sober people.' 'Not so, (answered the Knight) as I propose to travel all times, and in all places, mine armour may guard me against the attempts of treachery: it may defend me in combat against odds, should I be assaulted by a multitude of plebeians, or have occasion to bring malefactors to justice.' 'What, then (exclaimed the philosopher) you intend to co-operate with the honourable fraternity of thief-takers?' 'I do purpose (said the youth, eying him with a look of ineffable contempt) to act as a coadjutor to the law, and even to remedy evils which the law cannot reach; to detect fraud and treason, abase insolence, mortify pride, discourage slander, disgrace immodesty, and stigmatize ingratitude: but the infamous part of a thief-catcher's character I disclaim. I neither associate with robbers and pickpockets, knowing them to be such, that, in being intrusted with their secrets, I may the more effectually betray them; nor shall I ever pocket the reward granted by the legislature to those by whom robbers are brought to conviction: but I shall always think it my duty to rid my country of that pernicious vermin, which preys upon the bowels of the commonwealth—not but that an incorporated company of licensed thieves might, under proper regulations, be of service to the community.'

Ferret, emboldened by the passive tameness with which the stranger bore his last reflection, began to think he had nothing of Hector but his outside, and gave a loose to all the acrimony of his party rancour. Hearing the Knight mention a company of licensed thieves, 'What else (cried he) is the majority of the nation? What is your standing army[1] at home, that eat up their fellow subjects?[2] What are your mercenaries abroad,[3] whom you hire to fight their own quarrels? What is your militia,[4] that wise measure of this sagacious m——ry,[5] but a larger gang of petty thieves, who steal sheep and poultry through meer idleness; and were they confronted with an enemy, would steal themselves away? What is your . . .[6] but a knot of thieves, who pillage the nation under colour of law, and enrich themselves with the wreck of their country? When you consider the enormous debt of an hundred millions,[7] the intolerable load of taxes and impositions under which we groan, and the manner in which that burthen is yearly accumulating, to support two German electorates,[8] without our receiving any thing in return but the shews of triumph and shadows of conquest: I say, when you reflect on these circumstances, and at the same time behold our cities filled with bankrupts, and our country with beggars; can you be so infatuated as to deny that our m——y[9] is mad, or worse than mad; our wealth exhausted, our people miserable, our credit blasted, and our state on the brink of perdition? This prospect, indeed, will make the fainter impression, if we recollect that we ourselves are a pack of such profligate, corrupted, pusillanimous rascals, as deserve no salvation.'

The stranger, raising his voice to a loud tone, replied, 'Such, indeed, are the insinuations, equally false and insidious, with which the desperate emissaries of a party endeavour to poison the minds of his Majesty's subjects, in defiance of common honesty and common sense. But he must be blind to all perception, and dead to candour, who does not see and own that we are involved in a just and necessary war,[10] which has been maintained on truly British principles,[11] prosecuted with vigour, and crowned with success; that our taxes are easy, in proportion to our wealth; that our conquests are equally glorious and important; that our commerce flourishes, our people are happy, and our enemies reduced to despair.—Is there a man who boasts a British heart, that repines at the success and prosperity of his country? Such there are, O shame to patriotism, and reproach to Great Britain! who act as the emissaries of France both in word and writing; who exaggerate our necessary burthens, magnify our dangers, extol the power of our enemies, deride our victories, extenuate our conquests, condemn the measures of our government, and scatter the seeds of dissatisfaction through the land. Such domestic traitors are doubly the objects of detestation; first, in perverting truth; and, secondly, in propagating falsehoods, to the prejudice of that community of which they have professed themselves members. One of these is well known by the name of Ferret, an old, rancorous, incorrigible instrument of sedition: happy it is for him, that he has never fallen in my way; for, notwithstanding the maxims of forbearance which I have adopted, the indignation which the character of that caitiff inspires, would probably impel me to some act of violence, and I should crush him like an ungrateful viper, that gnawed the bosom which warmed it into life!'

These last words were pronounced with a wildness of look, that even bordered upon frenzy. The misanthrope once more retired to the pantry for shelter, and the rest of the guests were evidently disconcerted.

Mr. Fillet, in order to change the conversation, which was likely to produce serious consequences, expressed uncommon satisfaction at the remarks which the Knight had made, signified his approbation of the honourable office he had undertaken; declared himself happy in having seen such an accomplished cavalier; and observed, that nothing was wanting to render him a compleat knight-errant, but some celebrated beauty, the mistress of his heart, whose idea might animate his breast, and strengthen his arm to the utmost exertion of valour: he added, that love was the soul of chivalry. The stranger started at this discourse. He turned his eyes on the surgeon with a fixed regard: his countenance changed: a torrent of tears gushed down his cheeks: his head sunk upon his bosom: he heaved a profound sigh; and remained in silence with all the external marks of unutterable sorrow. The company were in some measure infected by his despondence; concerning the cause of which, however, they would not venture to inquire.

By this time the landlady, having disposed of the squire, desired to know, with many curtsies, if his honour would not chuse to put off his wet garments; assuring him, that she had a very good feather-bed at his service, upon which many gentlevolks of the virst quality had lain; that the sheets were well aired; and that Dolly should warm them for his worship with a pan of coals. This hospitable offer being repeated, he seemed to wake from a trance of grief; arose from his seat, and, bowing courteously to the company, withdrew.

Captain Crowe, whose faculty of speech had been all this time absorbed in amazement, now broke into the conversation with a volley of interjections: 'Split my snatch-block![1]—Odd's firkin![2]—Splice my old shoes![3]—I have sailed the salt seas, brother, since I was no higher than the Triton's taffril[4]—east, west, north, and south, as the saying is—Blacks, Indians, Moors, Morattos,[5] and Seapoys;[6]—but, smite my timbers! such a man of war——' Here he was interrupted by his nephew Tom Clarke, who had disappeared at the Knight's first entrance, and now produced himself with an eagerness in his look, while the tears started in his eyes.—'Lord bless my soul! (cried he) I know that gentleman, and his servant, as well as I know my own father.—I am his own godson, uncle: he stood for me when he was a boy—yes, indeed, Sir, my father was steward to the estate—I may say I was bred up in the family of Sir Everhard Greaves,[7] who has been dead these two years—this is the only son, Sir Launcelot; the best-natured, worthy, generous gentleman—I care not who knows it: I love him as well as if he was my own flesh and blood—'

At this period Tom, whose heart was of the melting mood, began to sob and weep plenteously, from pure affection. Crowe, who was not very subject to these tendernesses, damned him for a chicken-hearted lubber; repeating, with much peevishness, 'What do'st cry for? what do'st cry for, noddy?' The surgeon, impatient to know the story of Sir Launcelot, which he had heard imperfectly recounted, begged that Mr. Clarke would compose himself, and relate it as circumstantially as his memory could retain the particulars; and Tom, wiping his eyes, promised to give him that satisfaction; which the reader, if he be so minded, may partake in the next chapter.

CHAPTER III

*Which the reader, on perusal, may wish were
chapter the last*

THE Doctor prescribed a *repetatur* of the julep,[1] and mixed the
ingredients *secundum artem*;[2] Tom Clarke hemmed thrice, to clear
his pipes; while the rest of the company, including Dolly and her
mother, who had by this time administred to the knight, composed
themselves into earnest and hushed attention. Then the young
lawyer began his narration to this effect:—'I tell ye what, gemmen,[3]
I don't pretend in this here case to flourish and harangue like a—
having never been called to—but what of that, d'ye see?—perhaps
I may know as much as—Facts are facts, as the saying is.—I shall
tell, repeat, and relate a plain story—matters of fact, d'ye see,
without rhetoric, oratory, ornament, or embellishment; without
repetition, tautology, circumlocution, or going about the bush:
facts which I shall aver, partly on the testimony of my own knowledge, and partly from the information of responsible evidences of
good repute and credit, any circumstance known to the contrary
notwithstanding:—for, as the law saith, if so be as how there is *an
exception* to evidence, that *exception* is in its nature but a denial of
what is taken to be good by the other party, and *exceptio in non
exceptis, firmat regulam*,[4] d'ye see.—But, howsomever, in regard to
this here affair, we need not be so scrupulous as if we were pleading
before a judge *sedente curia*—'[5]

Ferret, whose curiosity was rather more eager than that of any
other person in this audience, being provoked by this preamble,
dashed the pipe he had just filled in pieces against the grate; and
after having pronounced the interjection *pish*, with an acrimony of
aspect altogether peculiar to himself, 'If (said he) impertinence and
folly were felony by the statute, there would be no want of unexceptionable evidence to hang such an eternal babbler.' 'Anan,[6]
babbler! (cried Tom, reddening with passion, and starting up) I'd
have you to know, Sir, that I can bite as well as babble; and that, if
I am so minded, I can run upon the foot after my game without
being in fault,[7] as the saying is; and which is more, I can shake an
old fox by the collar.'

How far this young lawyer might have proceeded to prove

himself staunch on the person of the misanthrope, if he had not been prevented, we shall not determine; but the whole company were alarmed at his looks and expressions. Dolly's rosy cheeks assumed an ash-colour, while she ran between the disputants, crying, 'Naay, naay—vor the love of God doan't then, doan't then!' But captain Crowe exerted a parental authority over his nephew, saying, 'Avast, Tom, avast!—Snug's the word—we'll have no boarding, d'ye see.—Haul forward thy chair again, take thy berth, and proceed with thy story in a direct course, without yawing like a Dutch yanky.'[1]

Tom, thus tutored, recollected himself, resumed his seat, and, after some pause, plunged at once into the current of narration. 'I told you before, gemmen, that the gentleman in armour was the only son of Sir Everhard Greaves, who possessed a free estate of five thousand a year in our county, and was respected by all his neighbours, as much for his personal merit as for his family fortune. With respect to his son Launcelot, whom you have seen, I can remember nothing until he returned from the university, about the age of seventeen, and then I myself was not more than ten years old. The young gemman was at that time in mourning for his mother; though God he knows, Sir Everhard had more cause to rejoice than to be afflicted at her death:—for, among friends, (here he lowered his voice, and looked round the kitchen) she was very whimsical, expensive, and ill-tempered, and, I'm afraid, a little— upon the—flighty order—a little touched or so;—but mum for that—the lady is now dead; and it is my maxim, *de mortuis nil nisi bonum*.[2] The young squire was even then very handsome, and looked remarkably well in his weepers:[3] but he had an aukward air and shambling gait, stooped mortally, and was so shy and silent, that he would not look a stranger in the face, nor open his mouth before company. Whenever he spied a horse or carriage at the gate, he would make his escape into the garden, and from thence into the park; where many's the good time and often he has been found sitting under a tree, with a book in his hand, reading Greek, Latin, and other foreign linguas.

Sir Everhard himself was no great scholar, and my father had forgot his classical learning; and so the rector of the parish was desired to examine young Launcelot. It was a long time before he found an opportunity: the squire always gave him the slip.—At length the parson catched him in bed of a-morning, and, locking the door, to it they went tooth and nail. What passed betwixt them the Lord in heaven knows; but, when the Doctor came forth, he looked wild and haggard as if he had seen a ghost, his face as white as paper, and his lips trembling like an aspen-leaf. "Parson, (said the knight) what is the matter?—how do'st find my son? I hope he won't turn out a ninny, and disgrace his family." The Doctor, wiping the sweat from his forehead, replied, with some hesitation, "he could not tell—he hoped the best—the squire was to be sure a very extraordinary young gentleman——" But the father urging him to give an explicit answer, he frankly declared, that, in his opinion, the son would turn out either a mirrour of wisdom, or a monument óf folly: for his genius and disposition were altogether preternatural. The knight was sorely vexed at this declaration, and signified his displeasure by saying, the doctor, like a true priest, dealt in mysteries and oracles, that would admit of different and indeed contrary interpretations. He afterwards consulted my father, who had served as steward upon the estate for above thirty years, and acquired a considerable share of his favour. "Will. Clarke, (said he, with tears in his eyes) what shall I do with this unfortunate lad? I would to God he had never been born; for I fear he will bring my grey hairs with sorrow to the grave. When I am gone, he will throw away the estate, and bring himself to infamy and ruin by keeping company with rooks and beggars.—O Will! I could forgive extravagance in a young man; but it breaks my heart to see my only son give such repeated proofs of a mean spirit and sordid disposition!"

Here the old gentleman shed a flood of tears, and not without some shadow of reason. By this time Launcelot was grown so reserved to his father, that he seldom saw him, or any of his relations, except when he was in a manner forced to appear at table, and there his bashfulness seemed every day to increase. On the other hand, he had formed some very strange connexions. Every morning he visited the stable, where he not only conversed with the grooms and helpers, but scraped acquaintance with the horses: he fed his favourites with his own hand, stroaked, caressed, and rode them by turns; till at last they grew so familiar, that, even when they were a-field at grass, and saw him at a distance, they would toss their manes, whinny like so many colts at sight of the dam, and, galloping up to the place where he stood, smell him all over.—You must know that I myself, though a child, was his companion in all these excursions. He took a liking to me on account of my being his godson, and gave me more money than I knew what to do with: he had always plenty of cash for the asking, as my father was ordered to supply him liberally, the knight thinking that a command of money might help to raise his thoughts to a proper consideration of his own importance. He never could endure a common beggar, that was not either in a state of infancy or of old age: but, in other respects, he made the guineas fly in such a manner, as looked more like madness than generosity. He had no communication with your rich yeomen; but rather treated them and their families with studied contempt, because forsooth they pretended to assume the dress and manners of the gentry: they kept their footmen, their saddle-horses, and chaises: their wives and daughters appeared in their jewels, their silks, and their sattins, their negligees and trollopees:[1] their clumsy shanks, like so many shins of beef, were cased in silk-hose and embroidered slippers: their raw red fingers, gross as the pipes of a chamber-organ, which had been employed in milching the cows, in twirling the mop or churnstaff, being adorned with diamonds, were taught to thrum the pandola, and even to touch the keys of the harpsichord: nay, in every village they kept a rout,[2] and set up an assembly; and in one place a hog-butcher was master of the ceremonies. I have heard Mr. Greaves ridicule them for their vanity and aukward imitation; and therefore, I believe, he avoided all concerns with them, even when they endeavoured to engage his attention. It was the lower sort of people with whom he chiefly conversed, such as ploughmen, ditchers, and other day-labourers. To every cottager in the parish he was a bounteous benefactor. He was, in the literal sense of the word, a careful overseer of the poor; for he went from house to house, industriously inquiring into the distresses of the people. He repaired their huts, cloathed their backs, filled their bellies, and supplied them with necessaries for exercising their industry and different occupations.

I'll give you one instance now, as a specimen of his character. He and I, strolling one day on the side of a common, saw two boys picking hips and haws[3] from the hedges: one seemed to be about five, and the other a year older: they were both barefoot and ragged; but at the same time fat, fair, and in good condition. "Who do you belong to?" (said Mr. Greaves.) "To Mary Stile, (replied the oldest) the widow that rents one of them housen."[4] "And how

do'st live, my boy? Thou lookest fresh and jolly;" resumed the
squire. "Lived well enough till yesterday," answered the child.
"And pray what happened yesterday, my boy?" continued Mr.
Greaves. "Happened! (said he) why, mammy had a coople of little
Welch keawes, that gi'en milk enough to fill all our bellies;
mammy's, and mine, and Dick's here, and my two little sisters at
hoam: yesterday the squire seized the keawes for rent, God rot'un!
Mammy's gone to bed sick and sulky: my two sisters be crying at
hoam vor vood; and Dick and I be come hither to pick haws and
bullies."[1]—My godfather's face grew red as scarlet: he took one
of the children in either hand, and leading them towards the house,
found Sir Everhard talking with my father before the gate. Instead
of avoiding the old gentleman, as usual, he brushed up to him with
a spirit he had never shewn before, and presenting the two ragged
boys, "Surely, Sir, (said he) you will not countenance that there
ruffian, your steward, in oppressing the widow and the fatherless.
On pretence of distraining[2] for the rent of a cottage, he has robbed
the mother of these and other poor infant-orphans of two cows,
which afforded them their whole sustenance. Shall you be concerned in tearing the hard-earned morsel from the mouth of
indigence? Shall your name, which has been so long mentioned as
a blessing, be now detested as a curse by the poor, the helpless, and
forlorn? The father of these babes was once your game-keeper,
who died of a consumption caught in your service.—You see they
are almost naked—I found them plucking haws and sloes, in order
to appease their hunger.—The wretched mother is starving in a
cold cottage, distracted with the cries of other two infants,
clamorous for food; and while her heart is bursting with anguish
and despair, she invokes heaven to avenge the widow's cause upon
the head of her unrelenting landlord!"

This unexpected address brought tears into the eyes of the good
old gentleman. "Will Clarke, (said he to my father) how durst you
abuse my authority at this rate? You who know I have been always
a protector, not an oppressor of the needy and unfortunate. I charge
you, go immediately and comfort this poor woman with immediate
relief: instead of her own cows, let her have two of the best milch
cows of my dairy: they shall graze in my parks in summer, and be
foddered with my hay in winter.—She shall sit rent-free for life;
and I will take care of these her poor orphans." This was a very
affecting scene. Mr. Launcelot took his father's hand and kissed it,

while the tears ran down his cheeks; and Sir Everhard embraced his son with great tenderness, crying, "My dear boy! God be praised for having given you such a feeling heart." My father himself was moved, thof[1] a practitioner of the law, and consequently used to distresses.—He declared, that he had given no directions to distrain; and that the bailiff must have done it by his own authority.—"If that be the case, (said the young squire) let the inhuman rascal be turned out of our service."

Well, gemmen, all the children were immediately cloathed and fed, and the poor widow had well nigh run distracted with joy. The old knight, being of a humane temper himself, was pleased to see such proofs of his son's generosity: he was not angry at his spending his money, but at squandering away his time among the dregs of the people. For you must know, he not only made matches, portioned[2] poor maidens, and set up young couples that came together without money; but he mingled in every rustic diversion, and bore away the prize in every contest. He excelled every swain of that district in feats of strength and activity: in leaping, running, wrestling, cricket, cudgel-playing, and pitching the bar;[3] and was confessed to be, out of sight, the best dancer at all wakes and holidays: happy was the country-girl who could engage the young squire as her partner! To be sure it was a comely sight for to see as how the buxom country-lasses, fresh and fragrant, and blushing like the rose, in their best apparel dight,[4] their white hose, and clean short dimity petticoats, their gaudy gowns of printed cotton; their top-knots,[5] kissing-strings,[6] and stomachers,[7] bedizened with bunches of ribbons of various colours, green, pink, and yellow; to see them crowned with garlands, and assembled on May-day, to dance before squire Launcelot, as he made his morning's progress through the village. Then all the young peasants made their appearance with cockades,[8] suited to the fancies of their several sweet-hearts, and boughs of flowering hawthorn. The children sported about like flocks of frisking lambs, or the young fry swarming under the sunny bank of some meandering river. The old men and women, in their holiday-garments, stood at their doors to receive their benefactor, and poured forth blessings on him as he passed: the children welcomed him with their shrill shouts; the damsels with songs of praise; and the young men with the pipe and tabor marched before him to the May-pole, which was bedecked with flowers and bloom. There the rural dance began: a plentiful dinner, with oceans of good liquor, was bespoke at the White Hart: the whole village was regaled at the squire's expence; and both the day and the night was spent in mirth and pleasure. Lord help you! he could not rest if he thought there was an aching heart in the whole parish. Every paultry cottage was in a little time converted into a pretty, snug, comfortable habitation, with a wooden porch at the door, glass casements in the windows, and a little garden behind, well stored with greens, roots, and sallads. In a word, the poor's-rate[1] was reduced to a meer trifle, and one would have thought the golden age[2] was revived in Yorkshire. But, as I told you before, the old knight could not bear to see his only son so wholly attached to these lowly pleasures, while he industriously shunned all opportunities of appearing in that superior sphere to which he was designed by nature, and by fortune. He imputed his conduct to meanness of spirit, and advised with my father touching the properest expedient to wean his affections from such low-born pursuits. My father counselled him to send the young gentleman up to London, to be entered as a student in the Temple,[3] and recommended to the superintendance of some person who knew the town, and might engage him insensibly[4] in such amusements, and connexions, as would soon lift his ideas above the humble objects on which they had been hitherto employed. This advice appeared so salutary, that it was followed without the least hesitation. The young squire himself was perfectly well satisfied with the proposal, and in a few days set out for the great city: but there was not a dry eye in the parish at his departure, although he prevailed upon his father to pay in his absence all the pensions he had granted to those who could not live on the fruit of their own industry. In what manner he spent his time at London, it is none of my business to inquire; thof I know pretty well what kind of lives are led by gemmen of your Inns of Court.[5]—I myself once belonged to Serjeant's Inn,[6] and was perhaps as good a wit and a critick as any Templar[7] of them all. Nay, as for that matter, thof I despise vanity, I can aver with a safe conscience, that I had once the honour to belong to the society called *the Town*: we were all of us attorneys clerks, gemmen, and had our meetings at an ale-house in Butcher-row,[8] where we regulated the diversions of the theatre.[9]

But to return from this digression: Sir Everhard Greaves did not seem to be very well pleased with the conduct of his son at London. He got notice of some irregularities and scrapes into which he had fallen; and the squire seldom wrote to his father, except to draw upon him for money, which he did so fast, that in eighteen months the old gemman lost all patience.

At this period squire Darnel chanced to die, leaving an only daughter, a minor, heiress of three thousand a year, under the guardianship of her uncle Anthony, whose brutal character all the world knows. The breath was no sooner out of his brother's body than he resolved, if possible, to succeed him in parliament as representative for the borough of Ashenton.[1] Now you must know, that this borough had been for many years a bone of contention between the families of Greaves and Darnel; and at length the difference was compromised by the interposition of friends, on condition that Sir Everhard and Squire Darnel should alternately represent the place in parliament. They agreed to this compromise for their mutual convenience; but they were never heartily reconciled. Their political principles did not tally; and their wives looked upon each other as rivals in fortune and magnificence: so that there was no intercourse between them, thof they lived in the same neighbourhood. On the contrary, in all disputes, they constantly headed the opposite parties. Sir Everhard understanding that Anthony Darnel had begun to canvass, and was putting every iron in the fire, in violation and contempt of the *pactum familiae*[2] before mentioned, fell into a violent passion, that brought on a severe fit of the gout, by which he was disabled from giving personal attention to his own interest. My father, indeed, employed all his diligence and address, and spared neither money, time, nor constitution, till at length he drank himself into a consumption, which was the death of him. But, after all, there is a great difference between a steward and a principal. Mr. Darnel attended in *propria persona*,[3] flattered and caressed the women, feasted the electors, hired mobs, made processions, and scattered about his money in such a manner, that our friends durst hardly shew their heads in public.

At this very crisis our young squire, to whom father had writ an account of the transaction, arrived unexpectedly at Greavesbury-hall, and had a long private conference with Sir Everhard. The news of his return spread like wild-fire thro' all that part of the country: bonfires were made, and the bells set a-ringing in several towns and steeples; and next morning above seven hundred people were assembled at the gate, with music, flags and streamers, to welcome their young squire, and accompany him to the borough of

Ashenton. He set out on foot with this retinue, and entered one end of the town just as Mr. Darnel's mob had come in at the other. Both arrived about the same time at the market-place; but Mr. Darnel, mounting first into the balcony of the town-house, made a long speech to the people in favour of his own pretensions, not without some invidious reflections glanced at Sir Everhard, his competitor. We did not much mind the acclamations of his party, which we knew had been hired for the purpose: but we were in some pain for Mr. Greaves, who had not been used to speak in public. He took his turn however in the balcony, and, uncovering his head, bowed all round with the most engaging courtesy. He was dressed in a green frock trimmed with gold, and his own dark hair flowed about his ears in natural curls, while his face was overspread with a blush, that improved the glow of youth to a deeper crimson, and I dare say set many a female heart a palpitating. When he made his first appearance, there was just such a humming and clapping of hands as you may have heard when the celebrated Garrick[1] comes upon the stage in King Lear, or King Richard, or any other top character. But how agreeably were we disappointed, when our young gentleman made such an oration as would not have disgraced a Pitt,[2] an Egmont,[3] or a Murray![4] While he spoke, all was hushed in admiration and attention—you could have almost heard a feather drop to the ground. It would have charmed you to hear with what modesty he recounted the services which his father and grandfather had done to the corporation; with what eloquence he expatiated upon the shameful infraction of the treaty subsisting between the two families; and with what keen and spirited strokes of satire he retorted the sarcasms of Darnel. He no sooner concluded his harangue,[5] than there was such a burst of applause as seemed to rend the very sky. Our musick immediately struck up; our people advanced with their ensigns, and, as every man had a good cudgel, broken heads would have ensued, had not Mr. Darnel and his party thought proper to retreat with uncommon dispatch. He never offered to make another public entrance, as he saw the torrent ran so violently against him; but sat down with his loss, and withdrew his opposition, though at bottom extremely mortified and incensed. Sir Everhard was unanimously elected, and appeared to be the happiest man upon earth; for, besides the pleasure arising from his victory over this competitor, he was now fully satisfied that his son, instead of

disgracing, would do honour to his family. It would have moved a
heart of stone, to see with what a tender transport of paternal joy
he received his dear Launcelot, after having heard of his deportment and success at Ashenton; where, by the bye, he gave a ball to
the ladies, and displayed as much elegance and politeness as if he
had been bred at the court of Versailles.

This joyous season was of short duration: in a little time all the
happiness of the family was overcast by a sad incident, which hath
left such an unfortunate impression upon the mind of the young
gentleman, as, I am afraid, will never be effaced. Mr. Darnel's
niece and ward, the great heiress, whose name is Aurelia, was the
most celebrated beauty of the whole country—if I said the whole
kingdom, or indeed all Europe, perhaps I should but barely do her
justice. I don't pretend to be a limner, gemmen; nor does it
become me to delineate such excellence: but surely I may presume
to repeat from the play;

> "O! she is all that painting can express,
> Or youthful poets fancy when they love!"[1]

At that time she might be about seventeen, tall and fair, and so
exquisitely shaped—you may talk of your Venus de Medicis,[2]
your Dianas,[3] your Nymphs, and Galateas;[4] but if Praxiteles,[5]
and Roubillac,[6] and Wilton,[7] were to lay their heads together, in
order to make a complete pattern of beauty, they would hardly
reach her model of perfection.—As for complexion, poets will talk
of blending the lily with the rose, and bring in a parcel of similes of
cowslips, carnations, pinks, and daisies.—There's Dolly, now, has
got a very good complexion:—indeed, she's the very picture of
health and innocence.—You are, indeed, my pretty lass;—but
parva componere magnis.[8]—Miss Darnel is all amazing beauty,
delicacy, and dignity! Then the softness and expression of her fine
blue eyes; her pouting lips of coral hue; her neck, that rises like a
tower of polished alabaster between two mounts of snow.—I tell
you what, gemmen, it don't signify talking: if e'er a one of you was
to meet this young lady alone, in the midst of a heath or common,
or any unfrequented place, he would down on his knees, and think
he kneeled before some supernatural being. I'll tell you more: she
not only resembles an angel in beauty, but a saint in goodness, and
an hermit in humility;—so void of all pride and affectation; so soft,

and sweet, and affable, and humane! Lord! I could tell such instances of her charity!—Sure enough, she and Sir Launcelot were formed by nature for each other: howsoever, the cruel hand of fortune hath intervened, and severed them for ever. Every soul that knew them both, said it was a thousand pities but they should come together, and extinguish in their happy union the mutual animosity of the two families, which had so often embroiled the whole neighbourhood. Nothing was heard but the praises of miss Aurelia Darnel, and Mr. Launcelot Greaves; and no doubt the parties were prepossessed, by this applause, in favour of each other. At length, Mr. Greaves went one Sunday to her parish-church; but, though the greater part of the congregation watched their looks, they could not perceive that she took the least notice of him; or that he seemed to be struck with her appearance. He afterwards had an opportunity of seeing her, more at leisure, at the York-assembly, during the races; but this opportunity was productive of no good effect, because he had that same day quarrelled with her uncle on the turf.—An old grudge, you know, gemmen, is soon inflamed to a fresh rupture. It was thought Mr. Darnel came on purpose to shew his resentment. They differed about a bet upon Miss Cleverlegs, and, in the course of the dispute, Mr. Darnel called him a petulant boy. The young squire, who was hasty as gunpowder, told him he was man enough to chastise him for his insolence; and would do it on the spot, if he thought it would not interrupt the diversion. In all probability they would have come to points immediately, had not the gentlemen interposed; so that nothing further passed, but abundance of foul language on the part of Mr. Anthony, and a repeated defiance to single combat.

Mr. Greaves, making a low bow, retired from the field; and in the evening danced at the assembly with a young lady from the Bishoprick, seemingly in good temper and spirits, without having any words with Mr. Darnel, who was also present. But in the morning he visited that proud neighbour betimes; and they had almost reached a grove of trees on the north-side of the town, when they were suddenly overtaken by half a dozen gentlemen, who had watched their motions. It was in vain for them to dissemble their design, which could not now take effect. They gave up their pistols, and a reconciliation was patched up by the pressing remonstrances of their common friends; but Mr. Darnel's hatred still rankled at bottom, and soon broke out in the sequel. About three months after this transaction, his niece Aurelia, with her mother, having been to visit a lady in the chariot, the horses being young, and not used to the traces, were startled at the braying of a jack-ass on the common, and taking fright, ran away with the carriage like lightning. The coachman was thrown from the box, and the ladies screamed piteously for help. Mr. Greaves chanced to be a-horseback on the other side of an inclosure, when he heard their shrieks; and riding up to the hedge, knew the chariot, and saw their disaster. The horses were then running full speed in such a direction, as to drive headlong over a precipice into a stone-quarry, where they and the chariot, and the ladies, must be dashed in pieces. You may conceive, gemmen, what his thoughts were when he saw such a fine young lady, in the flower of her age, just plunging into eternity; when he saw the lovely Aurelia on the brink of being precipitated among rocks, where her delicate limbs must be mangled and tore asunder; when he perceived that, before he could ride round by the gate, the tragedy would be finished. The fence was so thick and high, flanked with a broad ditch on the outside, that he could not hope to clear it, although he was mounted on *Scipio*, bred out of Miss *Cowslip*, the sire *Muley*, and his *grandsire* the famous Arabian *Mustapha*.—*Scipio* was bred by my father, who would not have taken a hundred guineas for him from any other person but the young squire.—Indeed, I have heard my poor father say—'[1]

By this time Ferret's impatience was become so outrageous, that he exclaimed in a furious tone, 'Damn your father, and his horse, and his colt into the bargain!'

Tom made no reply; but began to strip with great expedition. Captain Crowe was so choaked with passion, that he could utter nothing but disjointed sentences: he rose from his seat, brandished his horse-whip, and seizing his nephew by the collar, cried, 'Odd's heartlikins![2] sirrah, I have a good mind—Devil fire your running tackle,[3] you land-lubber!—can't you steer without all this tacking hither and thither, and the Lord knows whither?—'Noint my block![4] I'd give thee a rope's end[5] for thy supper, if it wasn't——'

Dolly had conceived a sneaking kindness for the young lawyer, and, thinking him in danger of being roughly handled, flew to his relief. She twisted her hand in Crowe's neckcloth without ceremony, crying, 'Sha't then, I tell thee, old coger.—Who kears a vig vor they voolish trantrums?'

While Crowe looked black in the face, and ran the risque of strangulation under the gripe of this amazon, Mr. Clarke having disengaged himself of his hat, wig, coat, and waistcoat, advanced in an elegant attitude of manual offence towards the misanthrope, who snatched up a gridiron from the chimney-corner, and Discord seemed to clap her sooty wings[1] in expectation of battle.—But as the reader may have more than once already cursed the unconscionable length of this chapter, we must postpone to the next opportunity the incidents that succeeded this denunciation of war.

CHAPTER IV

In which it appears that the Knight, when heartily set in for sleeping, was not easily disturbed

IN all probability the kitchen of the Black Lion, from a domestic temple of society, and good-fellowship, would have been converted into a scene or stage of sanguinary dispute, had not Pallas[2] or Discretion interposed in the person of Mr. Fillet, and with the assistance of the hostler disarmed the combatants not only of their arms, but also of their resentment. The impetuosity of Mr. Clarke was a little checked at sight of the gridiron, which Ferret brandished with uncommon dexterity; a circumstance from whence the company were, upon reflection, induced to believe, that before he plunged into the sea of politicks, he had occasionally figured in the character of that facetious droll who accompanies your itinerant physicians, under the familiar appellation of Merry-Andrew, or Jack-Pudding,[3] and on a wooden stage entertains the populace with a solo on the salt-box, or a sonnata on the tongs and gridiron. Be that as it may, the young lawyer seemed to be a little discomposed at the glancing of this extraordinary weapon of offence, which the fair hands of Dolly had scoured, until it shone as bright as the shield of Achilles; or as the emblem of good old English fare, which hangs by a red ribbon round the neck of that thrice-honoured sage's head, in velvet bonnet cased, who presides by rotation at the genial board, distinguished by the title of the *Beef-stake Club*:[4] where the

delicate rumps irresistibly attract the stranger's eye, and, while
they seem to cry 'Come cut me—come cut me,' constrain, by
wondrous sympathy, each mouth to overflow: where the obliging
and humorous Jemmy B———t, the gentle Billy H———d,
replete with human kindness, and the generous Johnny B———d,[1]
respected and beloved by all the world, attend as the priests and
ministers of Mirth, good Cheer, and Jollity, and assist with
culinary art the raw, unpractised, aukward guest.

But, to return from this digressive simile[2]: the hostler no sooner
stept between those menacing antagonists than Tom Clarke very
quietly resumed his cloaths, and Mr. Ferret resigned the gridiron
without further question. The doctor did not find it quite so easy
to release the throat of Capt. Crowe from the masculine grasp of
the virago Dolly, whose fingers could not be disengaged until the
honest seaman was almost at the last gasp. After some pause,
during which he panted for breath, and untied his neckcloth,
'Damn thee, for a brimstone galley (cried he); I was never so
grappled withal since I knew a card[3] from a compass.—Adzooks!
the jade has so taughtened my rigging, d'ye see, that I—Snatch
my bowlings,[4] if I come athwart thy hawser, I'll turn thy keel
upwards—or mayhap set thee a-driving under thy bare poles—I
will—I will, you hell-fire, saucy—I will.'

Dolly made no reply; but seeing Mr. Clarke sit down again with
great composure, took her station likewise at the opposite side of
the apartment. Then Mr. Fillet requested the lawyer to proceed
with his story, which, after three hemms, he accordingly prosecuted in these words.

'I told you, gemmen, that Mr. Greaves was mounted on Scipio,
when he saw miss Darnel and her mother in danger of being hurried
over a precipice. Without reflecting a moment he gave Scipio the
spur, and at one spring he cleared five and twenty feet, over hedge
and ditch, and every obstruction. Then he rode full speed, in order
to turn the coach-horses; and, finding them quite wild and furious,
endeavoured to drive against the counter of the hither horse, which
he missed, and staked poor Scipio on the pole of the coach. The
shock was so great, that the coach-horses made a full stop within
ten yards of the quarry, and Mr. Greaves was thrown forwards
towards the coach-box, which mounting with admirable dexterity,
he seized the reins before the horses could recover of their fright.
At that instant the coachman came running up, and loosed them

from the traces with the utmost dispatch. Mr. Greaves had now time to give his attention to the ladies, who were well nigh distracted with fear. He no sooner opened the chariot-door than Aurelia, with a wildness of look, sprung into his arms; and, clasping him round the neck, fainted away. I leave you to guess, gemmen, what were his feelings at this instant. The mother was not so discomposed but that she could contribute to the recovery of her daughter, whom the young squire still supported in his embrace. At length she retrieved the use of her senses, and perceiving the situation in which she was, the blood revisited her face with a redoubled glow, while she desired him to set her down upon the turf.

'Mrs. Darnel, far from being shy or reserved in her compliments of acknowledgments, kissed Mr. Launcelot without ceremony, the tears of gratitude running down her cheeks: she called him her dear son, her generous deliverer, who, at the hazard of his own life, had saved her and her child from the most dismal fate that could be imagined. Mr. Greaves was so much transported on this occasion, that he could not help disclosing a passion, which he had hitherto industriously concealed. "What I have done (said he) was but a common office of humanity, which I would have performed for any of my fellow-creatures: but, for the preservation of miss Aurelia Darnel, I would at any time sacrifice my life with pleasure." The young lady did not hear this declaration unmoved: her face was again flushed, and her eyes sparkled with pleasure: nor was the youth's confession disagreeable to the good lady her mother, who at one glance perceived all the advantages of such an union between the two families.

'Mr. Greaves proposed to send the coachman to his father's stable for a pair of sober horses, that could be depended upon, to draw the ladies home to their own habitation; but they declined the offer, and chose to walk, as the distance was not great. He then insisted upon his being their conductor; and, each taking him under the arm, supported them to their own gate, where such an apparition filled all the domestics with astonishment. Mrs. Darnel, taking him by the hand, led him into the house, where she welcomed him with another affectionate embrace, and indulged him with an ambrosial kiss of Aurelia, saying, "But for you, we had both been by this time in eternity.—Sure it was heaven that sent you as an angel to our assistance!" She kindly inquired if he had himself sustained any damage in administring that desperate remedy to which they owed their lives. She entertained him with a small collation; and, in the course of the conversation, lamented the animosity which had so long divided two neighbouring families of such influence and character. He was not slow in signifying his approbation of her remarks, and expressing the most eager desire of seeing all those unhappy differences removed: in a word, they parted with mutual satisfaction.

'Just as he advanced from the outward gate, on his return to Greavesbury-hall, he was met by Anthony Darnel on horseback, who, riding up to him with marks of surprize and resentment, saluted him with "Your servant, Sir.—Have you any commands for me?" The other replying with an air of indifference, "None at all," Mr. Darnel asked, what had procured him the honour of a visit. The young gentleman, perceiving by the manner in which he spoke that the old quarrel was not yet extinguished, answered, with equal disdain, that the visit was not intended for him; and that, if he wanted to know the cause of it, he might inform himself by his own servants. "So I shall (cried the uncle of Aurelia); and perhaps let you know my sentiments of the matter—" "Hereafter as it may be," said the youth; who, turning out of the avenue, walked home, and made his father acquainted with the particulars of this adventure.

'The old gentleman chid him for his rashness; but seemed pleased with the success of his attempt, and still more so, when he understood his sentiments of Aurelia, and the deportment of the ladies.

'Next day the son sent over a servant with a compliment, to enquire about their health; and the messenger, being seen by Mr. Darnel, was told that the ladies were indisposed, and did not chuse to be troubled with messages. The mother was really seized with a fever, produced by the agitation of her spirits, which every day became more and more violent, until the physicians despaired of her life. Believing that her end approached, she sent a trusty servant to Mr. Greaves, desiring that she might see him without delay; and he immediately set out with the messenger, who introduced him in the dark. He found the old lady in bed, almost exhausted, and the fair Aurelia, sitting by her, overwhelmed with grief, her lovely hair in the utmost disorder, and her charming eyes inflamed with weeping. The good lady beckoning Mr.

Launcelot to approach, and directing all the attendants to quit the room, except a favourite maid, from whom I learned the story, she took him by the hand, and fixing her eyes upon him with all the fondness of a mother, shed some tears in silence, while the same marks of sorrow trickled down his cheeks. After this affecting pause, "My dear son (said she), Oh! that I could have lived to see you so indeed! you find me hastening to the goal of life—" Here the tender-hearted Aurelia, being unable to contain herself longer, broke out into a violent passion of grief, and wept aloud. The mother, waiting patiently till she had thus given vent to her anguish, calmly intreated her to resign herself submissively to the will of heaven: then turning to Mr. Launcelot, "I had indulged (said she) a fond hope of seeing you allied to my family.—This is no time for me to insist upon the ceremonies and forms of a vain world.—Aurelia looks upon you with the eyes of tender pre-possession." No sooner had she pronounced these words than he threw himself on his knees before the young lady, and, pressing her hand to his lips, breathed the softest expressions which the most delicate love could suggest. "I know (resumed the mother) that your passion is mutually sincere; and I should die satisfied, if I thought your union would not be opposed: but that violent man, my brother-in-law, who is Aurelia's sole guardian, will thwart her wishes with every obstacle that brutal resentment and implacable malice can contrive. Mr. Greaves, I have long admired your virtues, and am confident that I can depend upon your honour.— You shall give me your word, that, when I am gone, you will take no steps in this affair without the concurrence of your own father; and endeavour, by all fair and honourable means, to vanquish the prejudices and obtain the consent of her uncle: the rest we must leave to the dispensations of Providence."

'The squire promised, in the most solemn and fervent manner, to obey all her injunctions, as the last dictates of a parent whom he should never cease to honour. Then she favoured them both with a great deal of salutary advice, touching their conduct before and after marriage; and presented him with a ring, as a memorial of her affection: at the same time he pulled another off his finger, and made a tender of it as a pledge of his love to Aurelia, whom her mother permitted to receive this token. Finally, he took a last farewel of the good matron, and returned to his father with the particulars of this interview.

'In two days Mrs. Darnel departed this life, and Aurelia was removed to the house of a relation, where her grief had like to have proved fatal to her constitution.

'In the mean time, the mother was no sooner committed to the earth than Mr. Greaves, mindful of her exhortations, began to take measures for a reconciliation with the guardian. He engaged several gentlemen to interpose their good offices; but they always met with the most mortifying repulse: and at last Anthony Darnel declared, that his hatred to the house of Greaves was hereditary, habitual, and unconquerable. He swore he would spend his heart's blood to perpetuate the quarrel; and that, sooner than his niece should match with young Launcelot, he would sacrifice her with his own hand. The young gentleman, finding his prejudice so rancorous and invincible, left off making further advances; and, since he found it impossible to obtain his consent, resolved to cultivate the good graces of Aurelia, and wed her in despite of her implacable guardian. He found means to establish a literary correspondence with her, as soon as her grief was a little abated; and even to effect an interview, after her return to her own house: but he soon had reason to repent of this indulgence. The uncle entertained spies upon the young lady, who gave him an account of this meeting; in consequence of which she was suddenly hurried to some distant part of the country, which we never could discover.

'It was then we began to think Mr. Launcelot a little disordered in his brain, his grief was so wild, and his passion so impetuous. He refused all sustenance, neglected his person, renounced his amusements, rode out in the rain, sometimes bare headed, strolled about the fields all night, and became so peevish, that none of the domestics, durst speak to him, without the hazard of broken bones. Having played these pranks for about three weeks, to the unspeakable chagrin of his father, and the astonishment of all that knew him, he suddenly grew calm, and his good-humour returned. But this, as your sea-faring people say, was a deceitful calm, that soon ushered in a dreadful storm.

'He had long sought an opportunity to tamper with some of Mr. Darnel's servants, who could inform him of the place where Aurelia was confined; but there was not one about the family who could give him that satisfaction: for the persons who accompanied her, remained as a watch upon her motions, and none of the other domestics were privy to the transaction. All attempts proving fruitless, he could no longer restrain his impatience; but throwing himself in the way of the uncle, upbraided him in such harsh terms, that a formal challenge ensued. They agreed to decide their difference without witnesses; and one morning, before sun-rise, met on that very common where Mr. Greaves had saved the life of Aurelia. The first pistol was fired on each side without taking effect; but Mr. Darnel's second wounded the young squire in the flank: nevertheless, having a pistol in reserve, he desired his antagonist to ask his life. The other, instead of submitting, drew his sword; and Mr. Greaves, firing his piece in the air, followed his example. The contest then became very hot, tho' of short continuance. Darnel being disarmed at the first onset, our young squire gave him back the sword, which he was base enough to use a second time against his conqueror. Such an instance of repeated ingratitude and brutal ferocity diverted Mr. Greaves of his temper and forbearance. He attacked Mr. Anthony with great fury, and at the first longe ran him up to the hilt, at the same time seizing with his left hand the shell of his enemy's sword, which he broke in disdain. Mr. Darnel having fallen, the other immediately mounted his horse, which he had tied to a tree before the engagement; and riding full speed to Ashenton, sent a surgeon to Anthony's assistance. He afterwards ingenuously confessed all these particulars to his father, who was overwhelmed with consternation, for the wounds of Darnel were judged mortal; and as no person had seen the particulars of the duel, Mr. Launcelot might have been convicted of murder.

'On these considerations, before a warrant could be served upon him, the old knight, by dint of the most eager intreaties, accompanied with marks of horrour and despair, prevailed upon his son to withdraw himself from the kingdom, until such time as the storm should be overblown. Had his heart been unengaged, he would have chose to travel; but at this period, when his whole soul was engrossed and so violently agitated by his passion for Aurelia, nothing but the fear of seeing the old gentleman run distracted, would have induced him to desist from the pursuit of that young lady, far less quit the kingdom where she resided. Well then, gemmen, he repaired to Harwich, where he embarked for Holland, from whence he proceeded to Brussels, where he procured a passport from the French king, by virtue of which he travelled to Marseilles, and there took a tartan[1] for Genoa. The first letter sir Everhard received from him was dated at Florence. Mean while the surgeon's prognostic was not altogether verified. Mr. Darnel did not die immediately of his wounds; but he lingered a long time, as it were in the arms of death, and even partly recovered: yet, in all probability he will never be wholly restored to the enjoyment of health; and is obliged every summer to attend the hot well at Bristol. As his wounds began to heal, his hatred to Mr. Greaves seemed to revive with augmented violence; and he is now, if possible, more than ever determined against all reconciliation. Mr. Launcelot, after having endeavoured to amuse his imagination with a succession of curious objects, in a tour of Italy, took up his residence at a town called Pisa, and there fell into a deep melancholy, from which nothing could rouse him but the news of his father's death.

'The old gentleman (God rest his soul) never held up his head after the departure of his darling Launcelot; and the dangerous condition of Darnel kept up his apprehension: this was reinforced by the obstinate silence of the youth, and certain accounts of his disordered mind, which he had received from some of those persons who take pleasure in communicating disagreeable tidings. A complication of all these grievances, co-operating with a severe fit of the gout and gravel, produced a fever, which in a few days brought sir Everhard to his long home; after he had settled his affairs with heaven and earth, and made his peace with God and man. I'll assure you, gemmen, he made a most edifying and christian end: he died regretted by all his neighbours except Anthony, and might be said to be embalmed by the tears of the poor, to whom he was always a bounteous benefactor.

'When the son, now sir Launcelot, came home, he appeared so meagre, wan, and hollow-ey'd, that the servants hardly knew their young master. His first care was to take possession of his fortune, and settle accounts with the steward who had succeeded my father. These affairs being discussed, he spared no pains to get intelligence concerning miss Darnel; and soon learned more of that young lady than he desired to know; for it was become the common talk of the county, that a match was agreed upon between her and young squire Sycamore, a gentleman of a very great fortune. These tidings were probably confirmed under her own hand, in a letter which she wrote to Sir Launcelot. The contents were never exactly known but to the parties themselves: nevertheless, the effects were too visible; for, from that blessed moment, he spoke not one word to any living creature for the space of three days: but was seen sometimes to shed a flood of tears, and sometimes to burst out into a fit of laughing. At last he broke silence, and seemed to wake from his disorder. He became more fond than ever of the exercise of riding, and began to amuse himself again with acts of benevolence. One instance of his generosity and justice deserves to be recorded in brass or marble: you must know, gemmen, the rector of the parish was lately dead, and Sir Everhard had promised the presentation to another clergyman. In the mean time, Sir Launcelot, chancing one sunday to ride through a lane, perceived a horse saddled and bridled feeding on the side of a fence; and casting his eyes around, beheld on the other side of the hedge an object lying extended on the ground, which he took to be the body of a murdered traveller. He forthwith alighted; and, leaping into the field, descried a man at full length wrapped in a great coat, and writhing in agony. Approaching nearer, he found it was a clergyman, in his gown and cassock. When he inquired into the case, and offered his assistance, the stranger rose up, thanked him for his courtesy, and declared that he was now very well. The knight, who thought there was something mysterious in this incident, expressed a desire to know the cause of his rolling on the grass in that manner; and the clergyman, who knew his person, made no scruple in gratifying his curiosity. "You must know, sir, said he, I serve the curacy of your own parish, for which the late incumbent payed me twenty pounds a year; but this sum being scarce sufficient to maintain my wife and children, who are five in number, I agreed to read prayers in the afternoon at another church about four miles from hence; and for this additional duty I receive ten pounds more: as I keep a horse, it was formerly an agreeable exercise rather than a toil, but of late years I have been afflicted with a rupture, for which I consulted the most eminent operators in the kingdom; but I have no cause to rejoice in the effects of their advice, tho' one of them assured me I was completely cured. The malady is now more troublesome than ever, and often comes upon me so violently while I am on horseback, that I am forced to alight, and lie down upon the ground, until the cause of the disorder can for the time be reduced."

'Sir Launcelot not only condoled with him upon his misfortune, but desired him to throw up the second cure; and he would pay him ten pounds a year out of his own pocket. "Your generosity confounds me, good sir: (cried the clergyman) and yet I ought not to be surprised at any instance of benevolence in Sir Launcelot Greaves, but I will check the fullness of my heart. I shall only observe, that your good intention towards me can hardly take effect. The gentleman, who is to succeed the late incumbent, has given me notice to quit the premises, as he hath provided a friend of his own for the curacy." "What! (cried the knight) does he mean to take your bread from you, without assigning any other reason?" "Surely, sir, replied the ecclesiastic, I know of no other reason. I hope my morals are irreproachable, and that I have done my duty with a conscientious regard: I may venture an appeal to the parishioners among whom I have lived these seventeen years. After all, it is natural for every man to favour his own friends in preference to strangers. As for me, I propose to try my fortune in the great city; and I doubt not but providence will provide for me and my little ones." To this declaration Sir Launcelot made no reply; but riding home set on foot a strict enquiry into the character of this man, whose name was Jenkins. He found that he was a reputed scholar, equally remarkable for his modesty and good life; that he visited the sick, assisted the needy, compromised disputes among his neighbours, and spent his time in such a manner as would have done honour to any christian divine. Thus informed, the knight sent for the gentleman to whom the living had been promised; and accosted him to this effect: "Mr. Tootle, I have a favour to ask of you. The person who serves the cure of this parish, is a man of good character, beloved by the people, and has a large family. I shall be obliged to you if you will continue him in the curacy." The other told him he was sorry he could not comply with his request, being that he had already promised the curacy to a friend of his own." "No matter: (replied Sir Launcelot) since I have not interest with you, I will endeavour to provide for Mr. Jenkins in some other way."

'That same afternoon he walked over to the curate's house, and told him that he had spoken in his behalf to Dr. Tootle, but the curacy was pre-engaged. The good man having made a thousand acknowledgments for the trouble his honour had taken; "I have not interest sufficient to make you curate, (said the knight) but I can give you the living itself, and that you shall have." So saying, he retired; leaving Mr. Jenkins incapable of uttering one syllable, so powerfully was he struck with this unexpected turn of fortune. The presentation was immediately made out; and in a few days Mr. Jenkins was put in possession of his benefice, to the inexpressible joy of the congregation. Hitherto every thing went right, and every unprejudiced person commended the knight's conduct: but, in a little time, his generosity seemed to overleap the bounds of discretion; and even in some cases might be thought tending to a breach of the king's peace. For example, he compelled, *vi et armis*,[1] a rich farmer's son to marry the daughter of a cottager, whom the young fellow had debauched. Indeed it seems there was a promise of marriage in the case, though it could not be legally ascertained. The wench took on dismally; and her parents had recourse to Sir Launcelot, who, sending for the delinquent, expostulated with him severely on the injury he had done the young woman, and exhorted him to save her life and reputation by performing his promise; in which case he (Sir Launcelot) would give her three hundred pounds to her portion. Whether the farmer thought there was something interested in this uncommon offer, or was a little elevated by the consciousness of his father's wealth; he rejected the proposal with rustic disdain, and said, if so be as how the wench would swear the child to him, he would settle it with the parish:[2] but declared, that no squire in the land should oblige him to buckle with such a cracked pitcher.[3] This resolution, however, he could not maintain: for, in less than two hours, the rector of the parish had direction to publish the banns, and the ceremony was performed in due course.

'Now, though we know not precisely the nature of the arguments that were used with the farmer, we may conclude they were of the minatory species; for the young fellow could not, for some time, look any person in the face. The knight acted as the general redresser of grievances. If a woman complained to him of being ill treated by her husband, he first inquired into the foundation of the complaint; and if he found it just, catechised the defendant. If this warning had no effect, and the man proceeded to fresh acts of violence; then this judge took the execution of the law in his own hand, and horsewhipped the party. Thus he involved himself in several law-suits, that drained him of pretty large sums of money. He seemed particularly incensed at the least appearance of oppression; and supported divers poor tenants against the extortion of the land-lords. Nay, he has been known to travel two hundred miles as a volunteer, to offer his assistance in the cause of a person, who he heard was by chicanery and oppression wronged of a considerable estate. He accordingly took her under his protection, relieved her distresses, and was at a vast expence in bringing the suit to a determination; which being unfavourable to his client, he resolved to bring an appeal into the house of lords, and certainly would have executed his purpose, if the gentlewoman had not died in the interim.'

At this period Ferret interrupted the narrator, by observing that the said Greaves was a common nuisance, and ought to be prosecuted on the statute of barretry. 'No, sir (resumed Mr. Clarke) he cannot be convicted of barretry, unless he is always at variance with some person or other, a mover of suits and quarrels, who disturbs the peace under colour of law. Therefore he is in the indictment stiled, *Communis malefactor, calumniator and seminator litium.*'[1] 'Prithee, truce with thy definitions, (cried Ferret) and make an end of thy long-winded story. Thou hast no title to be so tedious, until thou comest to have a coif in the court of common pleas.'[2] Tom smiled contemptuous, and had just opened his mouth to proceed, when the company were disturbed by a hideous repetition of groans, that seemed to issue from the chamber in which the body of the squire was deposited. The land-lady snatched the candle, and ran into the room, followed by the doctor and the rest; and this accident naturally suspended the narration. In like manner we shall conclude the chapter, that the reader may have time to breathe and digest what he has already heard.

CHAPTER V

In which this recapitulation draws to a close

WHEN the landlady entered the room from whence the groaning proceeded, she found the squire lying on his back, under the dominion of the night-mare, which rode him so hard, that he not only groaned and snorted, but the sweat ran down his face in streams. The perturbation of his brain, occasioned by this pressure and the fright he had lately undergone, gave rise to a very terrible dream, in which he fancied himself apprehended for a robbery.

The horror of the gallows was strong upon him, when he was suddenly awaked by a violent shock from the doctor; and the company broke in upon his view, still perverted by fear, and bedimmed by slumber. His dream was now realized by a full persuasion that he was surrounded by the constable and his gang. The first object that presented itself to his disordered view was the figure of Ferret, who might very well have passed for the finisher of the law: against him therefore the first effort of his despair was directed. He started upon the floor; and, seizing a certain utensil,[1] that shall be nameless, launched it at the misanthrope with such violence, that had not he cautiously slipped his head aside, it is supposed that actual fire would have been produced from the collision of two such hard and solid substances. All future mischief was prevented by the strength and agility of captain Crowe, who, springing upon the assailant, pinioned his arms to his sides, crying, 'O damn ye, if you are for running a-head, I'll soon bring you to your bearings.' The squire thus restrained, soon recollected himself, and gazing upon every individual in the apartment, 'Wounds![2] (said he) I've had an ugly dream. I thought, for all the world, they were carrying me to Newgate;[3] and that there was Jack Ketch[4] coom to vetch me before my taim.' Ferret, who was the person he had thus distinguished, eying him with a look of the most emphatic malevolence, told him, it was very natural for a knave to dream of Newgate; and that he hoped to see the day when this dream would be found a true prophecy, and the commonwealth purged of all such rogues and vagabonds: but it could not be expected that the vulgar would be honest and conscientious, while the great were distinguished by profligacy and corruption. The squire was disposed to make a practical reply to this insinuation, when Mr. Ferret prudently withdrew himself from the scene of altercation. The good woman of the house persuaded his antagonist to take out his nap, assuring him that the eggs and bacon, with a mug of excellent ale, should be forthcoming in due season. The affair being thus fortunately adjusted, the guests returned to the kitchen, and Mr. Clarke resumed his story to this effect. 'You'll please to take notice, gemmen, that besides the instances I have alleged of Sir Launcelot's extravagant benevolence, I could recount a great many others of the same nature, and particularly the laudable vengeance he took of a country lawyer.—I'm sorry that any such miscreant should belong to the profession. He was clerk of the assize,[1] gemmen, in a certain town, not a great way distant, and having a blank pardon left by the judges for some criminals, whose cases were attended with favourable circumstances, he would not insert the name of one who could not procure a guinea for the fee; and the poor fellow, who had only stole an hour-glass out of a shoemaker's window, was actually executed after a long respite; during which he had been permitted to go abroad, and earn his subsistence by his daily labour.

'Sir Launcelot, being informed of this barbarous act of avarice, and having some ground that bordered on the lawyer's estate, not only rendered him contemptible and infamous, by exposing him as often as they met on the grand jury, but also, being vested with the property of the great tythes,[2] proved such a troublesome neighbour, sometimes by making waste among his hay and corn, sometimes by instituting suits against him for petty trespasses, that he was fairly obliged to quit his habitation, and remove into another part of the kindom. All these avocations could not divert Sir Launcelot from the execution of a wild scheme, which has carried his extravagance to such a pitch, that I am afraid if a statute —you understand me, gemmen, were sued, the jury would—I don't choose to explain myself further on this circumstance. Be that as it may, the servants at Greavesbury-hall were not a little confounded, when their master took down from the family armoury a compleat suit of armour, which had belonged to his great grandfather, Sir Marmaduke Greaves, a great warrior, who lost his life in the service of his king. This armour being scoured, repaired, and altered so as to fit Sir Launcelot, a certain knight, whom I don't choose to name, because I believe he cannot be proved *compos mentis*, came down seemingly on a visit with two attendants; and, on the eve of the festival of St. George,[3] the armour being carried into the chapel, Sir Launcelot (Lord have mercy upon us!) remained all night in that dismal place alone and without light, though it was confidently reported, all over the country, that the place was haunted by the spirit of his great great uncle, who, being lunatic, had cut his throat from ear to ear, and was found dead on the communion table.'

It was observed, that while Mr. Clarke rehearsed this circumstance, his eyes began to stare, and his teeth to chatter; while Dolly, whose looks were fixed invariably on this narrator, growing pale, and hitching her joint stool nearer the chimney, exclaimed in a frighten'd tone, 'Moother, moother, in the neame of God, look to 'un! how a quakes! as I'm a precious faowl, a looks as if a saw soomething,' Tom forced a smile, and thus proceeded:

'While Sir Launcelot tarried within the chapel, with the doors all locked, the other knight stalked round and round it on the outside, with his sword drawn, to the terror of divers persons who were present at the ceremony. As soon as day broke he opened one of the doors, and, going in to Sir Launcelot, read a book for some time, which we did suppose to be the constitutions of knighterrantry: then we heard a loud flap which ecchoed through the whole chapel, and the stranger pronounce with an audible and solemn voice, "In the name of God, St. Michael, and St. George, I dub thee knight—be faithful, bold, and fortunate." You cannot imagine, gemmen, what an effect this strange ceremony had upon the people who were assembled. They gazed at one another in silent horror; and, when Sir Launcelot came forth completely armed, took to their heels in a body, and fled with the utmost precipitation. I myself was overturned in the crowd; and this was the case with that very individual person who now serves him as a squire. He was so frightened that he could not rise, but lay roaring in such a manner, that the knight came up, and gave him a thwack with his launce across the shoulders, which roused him with a vengeance. For my own part, I freely own I was not altogether unmoved at seeing such a figure come stalking out of a church in the grey of the morning; for it recalled to my remembrance the idea of the ghost in Hamlet,[1] which I had seen acted in Drurylane,[2] when I made my first trip to London; and I had not yet got rid of the impression.

'Sir Launcelot, attended by the other knight, proceeded to the stable; from whence, with his own hands, he drew forth one of his best horses, a fine mettlesome sorrel, who had got blood in him, ornamented with rich trappings. In a trice the two knights, and the other two strangers, who now appeared to be trumpeters, were mounted. Sir Launcelot's armour was lacquered black; and on his shield was represented the moon in her first quarter, with the motto *impleat orbem*.[3] The trumpets having sounded a charge, the stranger pronounced with a loud voice, "God preserve this gallant knight in all his honourable atchievements; and may he long continue to press the sides of his now adopted steed, which I denominate Bronzomarte, hoping that he will rival in swiftness and spirit Bayardo, Brigliadoro,[1] or any other steed of past or present chivalry!" After another flourish of the trumpets, all four clapped spurs to their horses, Sir Launcelot couching his lance, and galloped to and fro, as if they had been mad, to the terror and astonishment of all the spectators. What should have induced our knight to choose this here man for his squire, it is not easy to determine; for, of all the servants about the house, he was the least likely either to please his master, or engage in such an undertaking. His name is Timothy Crabshaw, and he acted in the capacity of whipper-in[2] to Sir Everhard. He afterwards married the daughter of a poor cottager, by whom he has several children, and was employed about the house as a ploughman and carter. To be sure the fellow has a dry sort of humour about him: but he was universally hated among the servants for his abusive tongue and perverse disposition, which often brought him into trouble; for though the fellow is as strong as an elephant, he has no more courage naturally than a chicken—I say naturally, because, since his being a member of knight-errantry, he has done some things that appear altogether incredible and præternatural.

'Timothy kept such a bawling, after he had received the blow from Sir Launcelot, that every body on the field thought some of his bones were broken; and his wife, with five bantlings, came snivelling to the knight, who ordered her to send the husband directly to his house. Tim accordingly went thither, groaning piteously all the way, creeping along with his body bent like a Greenland canoe.[3] As soon as he entered the court, the outward door was shut; and Sir Launcelot coming down stairs with a horse-whip in his hand, asked what was the matter with him that he complained so dismally. To this question he replied, that it was as common as duck-weed in his country, for a man to complain when his bones were broke. "What should have broke your bones?" said the knight. "I cannot guess (answered the other) unless it was that delicate switch that your honour in your mad pranks handled so dextrously upon my carcase." Sir Launcelot then told him there was nothing so good for a bruise as a sweat, and he had the remedy in his hand. Timothy eying the horsewhip askance, observed that there was another still more speedy; to wit, a moderate pill of lead, with a sufficient dose of gunpowder. "No, rascal, (cried the knight) that must be reserved for your betters.

So saying, he employed the instrument so effectually, that Crabshaw soon forgot his fractured ribs, and capered about with great agility. When he had been disciplined in this manner to some purpose, the knight told him he might retire; but ordered him to return next morning, when he should have a repetition of the medicine, provided he did not find himself capable of walking in an erect posture. The gate was no sooner thrown open, than Timothy ran home with all the speed of a greyhound, and corrected his wife, by whose advice he had pretended to be so grievously damaged in his person. No body dreamed that he would next day present himself at Gravesbury-hall; nevertheless, he was there very early in the morning, and even closetted a whole hour with Sir Launcelot. He came out making wry faces, and several times slapped himself on the forehead, crying, "Bodikins! thof he be creazy, I an't, that I an't!" When he was asked what was the matter, he said he believed the devil had got into him, and he should never be his own man again. That same day the knight carried him to Ashenton, where he bespoke those accoutrements which he now wears; and while these were making, it was thought the poor fellow would have run distracted. He did nothing but growl, and curse, and swear to himself, run backwards and forwards between his own hutt and Greavesbury-hall, and quarrel with the horses in the stable. At length his wife and family were removed into a snug farm-house that happened to be empty, and care taken that they should be comfortably maintained.

'These precautions being taken, the knight, one morning, at day-break, mounted Bronzomarte, and Crabshaw as his squire ascended the back of a clumsy cart horse, called Gilbert. This again was looked upon as an instance of insanity in the said Crabshaw; for of all the horses in the stable, Gilbert was the most stubborn and vicious, and had often like to have done a mischief to Timothy, while he drove the cart and plough. When he was out of humour he would kick and plunge as if the devil was in him. He once thrust Crabshaw into the middle of a quickset-hedge, where he was terribly torn; another time he canted him over his head into a quagmire, where he stuck with his heels up, and must have perished if people had not been passing that way; a third time he seized him in the stable with his teeth by the rim of the belly, and swung him off the ground, to the great danger of his life; and I'll be hanged if it was not owing to Gilbert that Crabshaw was now thrown into the river. Thus mounted and accoutred, the knight and his squire set out on their first excursion. They turned off from the common highway, and travelled all that day without meeting any thing worth recounting: but, in the morning of the second day, they were favoured with an adventure. The hunt was upon a common, through which they travelled, and the hounds were in full cry after a fox, when Crabshaw, prompted by his own mischievous disposition, and neglecting the order of his master, who called aloud to him to desist, rode up to the hounds, and crossed them at full gallop. The huntsman, who was not far off, running towards the squire, bestowed upon his head such a memento with his pole, as made the landschape dance before his eyes; and in a twinkling he was surrounded by all the fox-hunters, who plied their whips about his ears with infinite agility. Sir Launcelot advancing at an easy pace, instead of assisting the disastrous squire, exhorted his adversaries to punish him severely for his insolence, and they were not slow in obeying this injunction. Crabshaw, finding himself in this disagreeable situation, and that there was no succour to be expected from his master, on whose prowess he had depended, grew desperate; and, clubbing his whip, laid about him with great fury, wheeling about Gilbert, who was not idle; for he, having received some of the favours intended for his rider, both bit with his teeth, and kicked with his heels; and at last made his way through the ring that encircled him, though not before he had broke the huntsman's leg, lamed one of the best horses on the field, and killed half a score of the hounds. Crabshaw, seeing himself clear of the fray, did not tarry to take leave of his master, but made the most of his way to Greavesbury-hall, where he appeared with hardly any vestige of the human countenance, so much had he been defaced in this adventure. He did not fail to raise a great clamour against Sir Launcelot, whom he cursed as a coward in plain terms, swearing he would never serve him another day: but whether he altered his mind on cooler reflection, or was lectured by his wife, who well understood her own interest, he rose with the cock, and went again in quest of Sir Launcelot, whom he found on the eve of a very hazardous enterprize. In the midst of a lane the knight happened to meet with a party of about forty recruits, commanded by a serjeant, a corporal, and a drummer, which last had his drum slung at his back; but seeing such a strange figure mounted on a high-spirited horse, he was seized with an inclination to divert his company. With this view he braced his drum, and, hanging it in its proper position, began to beat a point of war, advancing under the very nose of Bronzomarte; while the corporal exclaimed, "Damn my eyes, who have we got here? old king Stephen, from the horse armoury,[1] in the tower; or the fellow that rides armed at my lord mayor's shew."[2] The knight's steed seemed at least as well pleased with the sound of the drum as were the recruits that followed it; and signified his satisfaction in some curvettings and caprioles, which did not at all discompose the rider, who, addressing himself to the serjeant, "Friend, said he, you ought to teach your drummer better manners. I would chastise the fellow on the spot for his insolence, were it not out of the respect I bear to his majesty's service." "Respect mine a———! (cried this ferocious commander) what, d'ye think to frighten us with your pewter pisspot on your scull, and your lacquer'd potlid on your arm? get out of the way and be dammed, or I'll raise with my halbert such a clutter upon your target, that you'll remember it the longest day you have to live." At that instant, Crabshaw arriving upon Gilbert, "So, rascal, said Sir Launcelot, you are returned. Go and beat in that scoundrel's drum-head."

'The squire, who saw no weapons of offence about the drummer but a sword, which he hoped the owner durst not draw; and being resolved to exert himself in making atonement for his desertion, advanced to execute his master's orders: but Gilbert, who liked not the noise, refused to proceed in the ordinary way. Then the squire turning his tail to the drummer, he advanced in a retrograde motion, and with one kick of his heels, not only broke the drum into a thousand pieces, but laid the drummer in the mire, with such a blow upon his hip-bone that he halted all the days of his life. The recruits, perceiving the discomfiture of their leader, armed themselves with stones; the serjeant raised his halbert in a posture of defence, and immediately a severe action ensued. By this time, Crabshaw had drawn his sword, and begun to lay about him like a devil incarnate; but, in a little time, he was saluted by a volley of stones, one of which knocked out two of his grinders, and brought him to the earth, where he had like to have found no quarter; for the whole company crowded about him, with their cudgels brandished; and perhaps he owed his preservation to their pressing so hard that they hindered one another from using their weapons. Sir Launcelot, seeing with indignation the unworthy treatment his

squire had received, and scorning to stain his launce with the blood
of plebeians, instead of couching it in the rest, seized it by the middle,
and fetching one blow at the serjeant, broke in twain the halbert
which he had raised as a quarter-staff for his defence. The second
stroke encountered his pate, which being the hardest part about
him, sustained the shock without damage; but the third, lighting
on his ribs, he honoured the giver with immediate prostration. The
general being thus overthrown, Sir Launcelot advanced to the
relief of Crabshaw, and handled his weapon so effectually, that the
whole body of the enemy were disabled or routed, before one
cudgel had touched the carcase of the fallen squire. As for the
corporal, instead of standing by his commanding officer, he had
overleaped the hedge, and run to the constable of an adjoining
village for assistance. Accordingly, before Crabshaw could be
properly remounted, the peace-officer arrived with his posse; and
by the corporal was charged with Sir Launcelot and his squire, as
two highwaymen. The constable, astonished at the martial figure
of the knight, and intimidated at sight of the havock he had made,
contented himself with standing at a distance, displaying the badge
of his office, and reminding the knight that he represented his
majesty's person. Sir Launcelot, seeing the poor man in great
agitation, assured him that his design was to enforce, not violate
the laws of his country; and that he and his squire would attend
him to the next justice of the peace; but in the mean time, he, in his
turn, charged the peace-officer with the serjeant and the drummer,
who had begun the fray. The justice had been a pettifogger, and
was a sycophant to a nobleman in the neighbourhood, who had a
post at court. He therefore thought he should oblige his patron,
by shewing his respect for *the military*; and treated our knight with
the most boorish insolence; but refused to admit him into his house,
until he had surrendered all his weapons of offence to the constable.
Sir Launcelot and his squire being found the aggressors, the
justice insisted upon making out their mittimus,[1] if they did not
find bail immediately; and could hardly be prevailed upon to
agree that they should remain at the house of the constable, who,
being a publican, undertook to keep them in safe custody, until the
knight could write to his steward. Mean while he was bound over
to the peace; and the serjeant with his drummer were told they had
a good action against him for assault and battery, either by information or indictment.[2] They were not, however, so fond of the law as

the justice seemed to be. Their sentiments had taken a turn in favour of Sir Launcelot, during the course of his examination, by which it appeared that he was really a gentleman of fashion and fortune; and they resolved to compromise the affair without the intervention of his worship. Accordingly, the serjeant repaired to the constable's house, where the knight was lodged; and humbled himself before his honour, protesting with many oaths, that if he had known his quality he would have beaten the drummer's brains about his ears, for presuming to give his honour or his horse the least disturbance; thof the fellow, he believed, was sufficiently punished in being a cripple for life. Sir Launcelot admitted of his apologies; and taking compassion on the fellow who had suffered so severely for his folly, resolved to provide for his maintenance. Upon the representation of the parties to the justice, the warrant was next day discharged; and the knight returned to his own house, attended by the serjeant and the drummer mounted on horseback, the recruits being left to the corporal's charge.

'The halberdeer found the good effects of Sir Launcelot's liberality; and his companion being rendered unfit for his majesty's service by the heels of Gilbert, is now entertained at Greavesbury-hall, where he will probably remain for life. As for Crabshaw, his master gave him to understand, that if he did not think him pretty well chastised for his presumption and flight by the discipline he had undergone in the last two adventures, he would turn him out of his service with disgrace. Timothy said he believed it would be the greatest favour he could do him to turn him out of a service in which he knew he should be rib-roasted every day, and murdered at last. In this situation were things at Greavesbury-hall about a month ago, when I crossed the country to Ferry-bridge,[1] where I met my uncle: probably, this is the first incident of their second excursion; for the distance between this here house and Sir Launcelot's estate, does not exceed fourscore or ninety miles.'

CHAPTER VI

In which the reader will perceive that in some cases madness is catching

MR. CLARKE having made an end of his narrative, the surgeon thanked him for the entertainment he had received; and Mr. Ferret shrugged up his shoulders in silent disapprobation. As for captain Crowe, who used at such pauses to pour in a broadside of dismembered remarks, linked together like chain-shot, he spoke not a syllable for some time; but, lighting a fresh pipe at the candle, began to roll such voluminous clouds of smoke as in an instant filled the whole apartment, and rendered himself invisible to the whole company. Though he thus shrouded himself from their view, he did not long remain concealed from their hearing. They first heard a strange dissonant cackle, which the doctor knew to be a sea-laugh, and this was followed by an eager exclamation of 'rare pastime, strike my yards and top-masts!—I've a good mind—why shouldn't—many a losing. voyage I've—smite my taffrel but I wool—' By this time, he had relaxed so much in his fumigation, that the tip of his nose and one eye reappeared; and as he had drawn his wig forwards so as to cover his whole forehead, the figure that now saluted their eyes was much more ferocious and terrible than the fire-breathing chimæra of the antients. Notwithstanding this dreadful appearance there was no indignation in his heart; but, on the contrary, an agreeable curiosity which he was determined to gratify. Addressing himself to Mr. Fillet, 'Prithee, doctor (said he) can'st tell, whether a man without being rated a lord or a baron, or a what d'ye call um, d'ye see, may'nt take to the highway in the way of a frolick, d'ye see?—adad! for my own part, brother, I'm resolved as how to cruise a bit in the way of an arrant—if so be as I can't at once be commander, mayhap I may be bore upon the books as a petty officer or the like d'ye see.'

'Now, the Lord forbid! (cried Clarke with tears in his eyes) I'd rather see you dead than brought to such a dilemma.' 'Mayhap thou would'st (answered the uncle); for then, my lad, there would be some picking—aha! do'st thou tip me the traveller,[1] my boy—' Tom assured him he scorned any such mercenary views. 'I am only concerned (said he) that you should take any step that might tend

to the disgrace of yourself or your family; and I say again I had
rather die than live to see you reckoned any otherwise than
compos—' 'Die and be damned! you shambling, half-timber'd
son of a —— (cried the choleric Crowe) do'st talk to me of keeping
reckoning and compass!—I could keep a reckoning, and box my
compass,[1] long enough before thy keelstone was laid—Sam Crowe
is not come here to ask thy counsel how to steer his course—'
'Lord, sir, (resumed the nephew) consider what people will say—
all the world will think you mad—' 'Set thy heart at ease, Tom,
(cried the seaman) I'll have a trip to and again in this here channel.
Mad! what then? I think for my part one half of the nation is mad—
and the other not very sound—I don't see why I ha'n't as good a
right to be mad as another man—but, doctor, as I was saying I'd be
bound to you, if you would direct me where I can buy that same
tackle that an arrant must wear. As for the matter of the long pole
headed with iron, I'd never desire a better than a good boat-hook;
and I could make a special good target of that there tin sconce that
holds the candle—mayhap any blacksmith will hammer me a
scull-cap, d'ye see, out of an old brass kettle: and I can call my
horse by the name of my ship, which was *Mufti*.'

The surgeon was one of those wags who can laugh inwardly
without exhibiting the least outward mark of mirth or satisfaction.
He at once perceived the amusement which might be drawn from
this strange disposition of the sailor, together with the most likely
means which could be used to divert him from such an extravagant
pursuit. He therefore tipped Clarke the wink[2] with one side of his
face, while the other was very gravely turned to the captain, whom
he addressed to this effect: 'It is not far from hence to Sheffield,
where you might be fitted compleatly in half-a-day—then you must
wake your armour in church or chapel, and be dubbed. As for this
last ceremony, it may be performed by any person whatsoever.
Don Quixote was dubbed by his landlord;[3] and there are many
instances on record, of errants obliging and compelling the next
person they met to cross their shoulders, and dub them knights. I
myself would undertake to be your godfather; and I have interest
enough to procure the keys of the parish church that stands hard
by; besides, this is the eve of St. Martin,[4] who was himself a knight-
errant, and therefore a proper patron to a noviciate. I wish we could
borrow Sir Launcelot's armour for the occasion.'

Crowe, being struck with this hint, started up, and laying his fingers on his lips to enjoin silence, walked off softly on his tiptoes, to listen at the door of our knight's apartment, and judge whether or not he was asleep. Mr. Fillet took this opportunity to tell his nephew, that it would be in vain for him to combat this humour with reason and argument: but the most effectual way of diverting him from the plan of knight-errantry would be to frighten him heartily while he should be keeping his vigil in the church. Towards the accomplishment of which purpose he craved the assistance of the misanthrope as well as the nephew. Clarke seemed to relish the scheme; and observed that his uncle, though endued with courage enough to face any human danger, had at bottom a strong fund of superstition, which he seemed to have acquired, or at least improved, in the course of a sea life. Ferret, who perhaps would not have gone ten paces out of his road to save Crowe from the gallows, nevertheless, engaged as an auxiliary, meerly in hope of seeing a fellow-creature miserable; and even undertook to be the principal agent in this adventure. For this office, indeed, he was better qualified than they could have imagined: in the bundle which he kept under his great coat, there was, together with divers nostrums, a small vial of liquid phosphorus, sufficient, as he had already observed, to frighten a whole neighbourhood out of their senses. In order to concert the previous measures, without being overheard, these confederates retired with a candle and lanthorn into the stable; and their backs were scarce turned, when captain Crowe came in loaded with pieces of the knight's armour, which he had conveyed from the apartment of Sir Launcelot, whom he had left fast asleep.

Understanding that the rest of the company were gone out for a moment, he could not resist the inclination he felt of communicating his intention to the landlady, who, with her daughter, had been too much engaged in preparing Crabshaw's supper, to know the purport of their conversation. The good woman, being informed of the captain's design to remain alone all night in the church, began to oppose it with all her rhetorick. She said it was setting his maker at defiance, and a wilful running into temptation. She assured him all the country knew that the church was haunted by spirits and hobgoblins: that lights had been seen in every corner of it; and a tall woman in white had one night appeared upon the top of the tower: that dreadful shrieks were often heard to come from the south aile, where a murdered man had been buried: that she herself had seen the cross on the top of the steeple all a-fire; and one evening as she passed a horseback close by the stile at the entrance into the church-yard, the horse stood still sweating and trembling, and had not power to proceed until she had repeated the Lord's Prayer.

These remarks made a strong impression on the imagination of Crowe, who asked in some confusion, if she had got that same prayer in print. She made no answer; but reaching the prayer-book from a shelf, and turning up the leaf, put it into his hand: then the captain, having adjusted his spectacles, began to read or rather spell aloud with equal eagerness and solemnity. He had refreshed his memory so well as to remember the whole; when the doctor, returning with his companions, gave him to understand that he had procured the key of the chancel, where he might watch his armour as well as in the body of the church; and that he was ready to conduct him to the spot. Crowe was not now quite so forward as he had appeared before to atchieve this adventure. He begun to start objections with respect to the borrowed armour: he wanted to stipulate the comforts of a can of flip, and a candle's end, during his vigil; and hinted something of the damage he might sustain from your malicious imps of darkness.

The doctor told him the constitutions of chivalry absolutely required that he should be left in the dark alone and fasting, to spend the night in pious meditations; but that if he had any fears which disturbed his conscience, he had much better desist, and give up all thoughts of knight-errantry, which could not consist with the least shadow of apprehension. The captain, stung by this remark, replied not a word; but gathering up the armour into a bundle, threw it on his back, and set out for the place of probation, preceded by Clarke with the lanthorn. When they arrived at the church, Fillet, who had procured the key from the sexton who was his patient, opened the door, and conducted our novice into the middle of the chancel, where the armour was deposited. Then bidding Crowe draw his hanger, committed him to the protection of heaven, assuring him he would come back, and find him either dead or alive by day break, and perform the remaining part of the ceremony. So saying, he and the other associates shook him by the hand and took their leave, after the surgeon had tilted up the lanthorn in order to take a view of his visage, which was pale and haggard.

Before the door was locked upon him, he called aloud, 'Hilloa! doctor, hip—another word, d'ye see—.' They forthwith returned, to know what he wanted, and found him already in a sweat. 'Heark ye, brother (said he wiping his face) I do suppose as how one may pass away the time in whistling black joke,[1] or singing black-ey'd Susan,[2] or some such sorrowful ditty.' 'By no means, (cried the doctor) such pastimes are neither suitable to the place, nor the occasion, which is altogether a religious exercise. If you have got any psalms by heart, you may sing a stave or two, or repeat the doxology.' 'Would I had Tom Laverick here, (replied our noviciate) he would sing you anthems like a sea-mew[3]—a had been a clerk ashore—many's the time and often I've given him a rope's end for singing psalms in the larboard watch—would I had hired the son of a bitch to have taught me a cast of his office—but it can't be holp, brother—if we can't go large, we must haul upon a wind,[4] as the saying is—if we can't sing, we must pray.' The company again left him to his devotion, and returned to the public house in order to execute the essential part of their project.

CHAPTER VII

In which the knight resumes his importance

DOCTOR FILLET having borrowed a couple of sheets from the landlady, dressed the misanthrope and Tom Clarke in ghostly apparel, which was reinforced by a few drops of liquid phosphorus, from Ferret's phial, rubbed on the foreheads of the two adventurers. Thus equipped they returned to the church with their conductor, who entered with them softly at an aile which was opposite to a place where the novice kept watch. They stole unperceived through the body of the church; and though it was so dark that they could not distinguish the captain with the eye, they heard the sound of his steps, as he walked backwards and forwards on the pavement with uncommon expedition, and an ejaculation now and then escape in a murmur from his lips.

The triumvirate having taken their station, with a large pew in their front, the two ghosts uncovered their heads, which, by help of the phosphorus, exhibited a pale and lambent flame extremely dismal and ghastly to the view; then Ferret, in a squeaking tone exclaimed, 'Samuel Crowe! Samuel Crowe!' The captain hearing himself accosted in this manner, at such a time, and in such a place, replied, 'Hilloah'; and turning his eyes towards the quarter whence the voice seemed to proceed, beheld the terrible apparition. This no sooner saluted his view, than his hair bristled up, his knees began to knock, and his teeth to chatter, while he cried aloud, 'In the name of God, where are you bound, ho?' To this hail, the misanthrope answered, 'We are the spirits of thy grandmother Jane and thy aunt Bridget.'

At mention of these names, Crowe's terrors began to give way to his resentment, and he pronounced in a quick tone of surprize, mixed with indignation, 'What d'ye want? what d'ye want? what d'ye want, ho?' The spirit replied, 'We are sent to warn thee of thy fate.' 'From whence, ho?' cried the captain, whose choler had by this time well nigh triumphed over his fear. 'From heaven,' said the voice. 'Ye lie, ye b——s of hell! (did our novice exclaim) ye are damned for heaving me out of my right, five fathom and a half by the lead,[1] in burning brimstone. Don't I see the blue flames come out of your hawse-holes[2]—mayhap you may be the devil himself for aught I know—but, I trust in the Lord, d'ye see—I never disrated[3] a kinsman, d'ye see; so don't come along side of me—put about on t'other tack, d'ye see—you need not clap hard aweather,[4] for you'll soon get to hell again with a flowing sail.'

So saying, he had recourse to his Pater-noster; but perceiving the apparitions approach, he thundered out, 'Avast—avast—sheer off, ye babes of hell, or I'll be foul of your forelights.' He accordingly sprung forwards with his hanger, and very probably would have set the spirits on their way to the other world, had not he fallen over a pew in the dark, and intangled himself so much among the benches, that he could not immediately recover his footing. The triumvirate took this opportunity to retire; and such was the precipitation of Ferret in his retreat, that he encountered a post, by which his right eye sustained considerable damage: a circumstance which induced him to inveigh bitterly against his own folly, as well as the impertinence of his companions who had inveigled him into such a troublesome adventure. Neither he nor Clarke could be prevailed upon to revisit the novice. The doctor himself thought his disease was desperate; and, mounting his horse, returned to his own habitation.

Ferret finding all the beds of the public house were occupied, composed himself to sleep in a windsor-chair at the chimney-corner; and Mr. Clarke, whose disposition was extremely amorous, resolved to renew his practices on the heart of Dolly. He had reconnoitred the apartments in which the bodies of the knight and his squire were deposited, and discovered close by the top of the staircase a sort of a closet or hovel just large enough to contain a truckle-bed, which, from some other particulars, he supposed to be the bedchamber of his beloved Dolly, who had by this time retired to her repose. Full of this idea, and instigated by the dæmon of desire, Mr. Thomas crept softly up stairs; and lifting the latch of the closet-door, his heart began to palpitate with joyous expectation: but before he could breathe the gentle effusions of his love, the supposed damsel started up, and, seizing him by the collar with an Herculean gripe, uttered in the voice of Crabshaw, 'It wa'n't for nothing that I dreamed of Newgate, sirrah; but I'd have thee to know, an arrant squire is not to be robbed by such a peddling[1] thief as thee—here I'll howld thee vast, an the devil were in thy doublet—help! murder! vire! help!'

It was impossible for Mr. Clarke to disengage himself, and equally impracticable to speak in his own vindication; so that here he stood trembling and half throttled, until the whole house being alarmed, the landlady and her ostler ran up stairs with a candle. When the light rendered objects visible, an equal astonishment prevailed on all sides: Crabshaw was confounded at sight of Mr. Clarke, whose person he well knew; and releasing him instantly from his grasp, 'Bodikins! (cried he) I believe as how this hawse is haunted—who thought to meet with Measter Laayer Clarke at midnight and so far from hoam.' The landlady could not comprehend the meaning of this rencounter; nor could Tom conceive how Crabshaw had transported himself hither from the room below, in which he saw him quietly reposed. Yet nothing was more easy than to explain this mystery: the apartment below was the chamber which the hostess and her daughter reserved for their own convenience; and this particular having been intimated to the squire while he was at supper, he had resigned the bed quietly, and been conducted hither in the absence of the company: Tom recollecting himself as well as he could, professed himself of Crabshaw's opinion, that the house was haunted, declaring that he could not well account for his being there in the dark; and leaving those that were assembled to discuss this knotty point, retired down stairs in hope of meeting with his charmer, whom accordingly he found in the kitchen just risen, and wrapped in a loose dishabillé.

The noise of Crabshaw's cries had awakened and aroused his master, who, rising suddenly in the dark, snatched up his sword that lay by his bedside, and hastened to the scene of tumult, where all their mouths were opened at once to explain the cause of the disturbance, and make an apology for breaking his honour's rest. He said nothing; but taking the candle in his hand, beckoned to his squire to follow him into his apartment, resolving to arm and take horse immediately. Crabshaw understood his meaning; and while he shuffled on his cloaths, yawning hideously all the while, wished the lawyer at the devil for having visited him so unseasonably; and even cursed himself for the noise he had made, in consequence of which he foresaw he should now be obliged to forfeit his night's rest, and travel in the dark exposed to the inclemencies of the weather. 'Pox rot thee, Tom Clarke, for a wicked laayer! (said he to himself) hadst thou been hanged at Bartlemey-tide,[1] I should this night have slept in peace, that I should—an I would there was a blister on this plaguy tongue of mine for making such a hollow-balloo; that I do—five gallons of cold water has my poor belly been drenched with since night fell; so as my reins[2] and my liver are all one as if they were turned into ice, and my whole harslet[3] shakes and shivers like a vial of quicksilver. I have been dragged, half drowned like a rotten ewe, from the bottom of a river; and who knows but I may be next dragged quite dead from the bottom of a coal-pit—if so be as I am, I shall go to hell to be sure, for being consarned like in my own moorder; that I will: so I will: for a plague on it, I had no business with the vagaries of this crazy-peated measter of mine, a pox on him, say I.'

He had just finished this soliloquy as he entered the apartment of his master, who desired to know what was become of his armour. Timothy understanding that it had been left in the room when the knight undressed, began to scratch his head in great perplexity; and at last declared it as his opinion that it must have been carried off by witchcraft. Then he related his adventure with Tom Clarke, who he said was conveyed to his bedside he knew not how; and concluded, with affirming they were no better than Papishes,[4] who did not believe in witchcraft. Sir Launcelot could not help smiling at his simplicity; but assuming a peremptory air, he commanded him to fetch the armour without delay, that he might afterwards saddle the horses, in order to prosecute their journey. Timothy retired in great tribulation to the kitchen, where finding the misanthrope, whom the noise had also disturbed, and still impressed with the notion of his being a conjurer, he offered him a shilling if he would cast a figure,[1] and let him know what was become of his master's armour.

Ferret, in hope of producing more mischief, informed him without hesitation, that one of the company conveyed it into the chancel of the church, where he would now find it deposited; at the same time presenting him with the key, which Mr. Fillet had left in his custody. The squire, who was none of those who set hobgoblins at defiance, being afraid to enter the church alone at these hours, bargained with the ostler to accompany and light him with a lanthorn. Thus attended he advanced to the place, where the armour lay in a heap, and loaded it upon the back of his attendant without molestation, the lance being shouldered over the whole. In this equipage they were just going to retire, when the ostler hearing a noise at some distance, wheeled about with such velocity, that one end of the spear saluting Crabshaw's pate, the poor squire measured his length on the ground; and crushing the lanthorn in his fall, the light was extinguished. The other terrified at these effects of his own sudden motion, threw down his burthen, and would have betaken himself to flight had not Crabshaw laid fast hold on his leg, that he himself might not be deserted. The sound of the pieces clattering on the pavement, roused captain Crowe from a trance or slumber in which he had lain since the apparition vanished; and he hollowed, or rather bellowed, with vast vociferation. Timothy and his friend were so intimidated by this terrific strain, that they thought no more of the armour, but ran home arm in arm, and appeared in the kitchen with all the marks of horror and consternation.

When Sir Launcelot came forth wrapped in his cloak, and demanded his arms, Crabshaw declared that the devil had them in possession; and this assertion was confirmed by the ostler, who pretended to know the devil by his roar. Ferret sat in his corner, maintaining the most mortifying silence, and enjoying the impatience of the knight, who in vain requested an explanation of this mystery. At length his eyes began to lighten, when seizing Crabshaw in one hand and the ostler in the other, he swore by heaven he would dash their souls out, and raze the house to the foundation, if they did not instantly disclose the particulars of this transaction. The good woman fell on her knees, protesting in the name of the Lord that she was innocent as the child unborn, thof she had lent the captain a Prayer Book to learn the Lord's Prayer, a lanthorn and candle to light him to the church, and a couple of clean sheets for the use of the other gentlemen. The knight was more and more puzzled by this declaration; when Mr. Clarke, coming into the kitchen, presented himself with a low obeisance to his old patron.

Sir Launcelot's anger was immediately converted into surprize. He set at liberty the squire and the ostler; and stretching out his hand to the lawyer, 'My good friend Clarke, (said he) how came you hither? Can you solve this knotty point which hath involved us all in such confusion?'

Tom forthwith began a very circumstantial recapitulation of what had happened to his uncle; in what manner he had been disappointed of the estate; how he had accidentally seen his honour, been enamoured of his character, and become ambitious of following his example. Then he related the particulars of the plan which had been laid down to divert him from his design, and concluded with assuring the knight, that the captain was a very honest man, though he seemed to be a little disordered in his intellects. 'I believe it, (replied Sir Launcelot): madness and honesty are not incompatible—indeed I feel it by experience.'

Tom proceeded to ask pardon in his uncle's name, for his having made so free with the knight's armour; and begged his honour, for the love of God, would use his authority with Crowe that he might quit all thoughts of knight-errantry, for which he was by no means qualified; for being totally ignorant of the laws of the land, he would be continually committing trespasses, and bring himself into trouble. He said in case he should prove refractory, he might be apprehended by virtue of a friendly warrant, for having feloniously carried off the knight's accoutrements. 'Taking away another man's moveables, (said he) and personal goods against the will of the owner, is *furtum*[1] and felony according to the statute: different indeed from robbery, which implies putting in fear on the king's highway, *in alta via regia violenter, & felonice captum & asportatum in magnum terrorem, &c.*[2] for if the robbery be laid in the indictment as done *in quadam via pedestri*, in a foot-path, the offender will not be ousted of his clergy.[3] It must be *in alta via regia*; and your honour will please to take notice, that robberies committed on the river Thames, are adjudged as done *in alta via regia*; for the king's high-stream is all the same as the king's highway.'

Sir Launcelot could not help smiling at Tom's learned investigation. He congratulated him on the progress he had made in the study of the law. He expressed his concern at the strange turn the captain had taken; and promised to use his influence in persuading him to desist from the preposterous design he had formed. The lawyer thus assured, repaired immediately to the church, accompanied by the squire, and held a parley with his uncle, who, when he understood that the knight in person desired a conference, surrendered up the arms quietly, and returned to the publick-house. Sir Launcelot received the honest seaman with his usual complacency, and perceiving great discomposure in his looks, said, he was sorry to hear he had passed such a disagreable night to so little purpose. Crowe having recruited his spirits with a bumper of brandy, thanked him for his concern, and observed that he had passed many a hard night in his time; but such another as this, he would not be bound to weather for the command of the whole British navy. 'I have seen Davy Jones in the shape of a blue flame, d'ye see, hopping to and fro, on the spritsail yard arm; and I've seen your Jacks o'the Lanthorn, and Wills o'the Wisp, and many such spirits both by sea and land: but, to-night I've been boarded by all the devils and damn'd souls in hell, squeaking and squalling, and glimmering and glaring. Bounce, went the door—crack, went the pew—crash, came the tackle—white-sheeted ghosts dancing in one corner by the glow-worm's light—black devils hobbling in another—Lord, have mercy upon us! and I was hailed, Tom, I was, by my grand-mother Jane, and my aunt Bridget, d'ye see—a couple of damn'd—but they're roasting; that's one comfort, my lad.'

When he had thus disburthened his conscience, Sir Launcelot introduced the subject of the new occupation at which he aspired. 'I understand, said he, that you are desirous of treading the paths of errantry, which I assure you, are thorny and troublesome. Nevertheless, as your purpose is to exercise your humanity and benevolence, so your ambition is commendable. But towards the practice of chivalry, there is something more required than the virtues of courage and generosity. A knight-errant ought to understand the sciences,[1] to be master of ethics or morality, to be well versed in theology, a compleat casuist, and minutely acquainted with the laws of his country. He should not only be patient of cold, hunger, and fatigue, righteous, just, and valiant; but also, chaste, religious, temperate, polite, and conversible; and have all his passions under the rein, except love, whose empire he should submissively acknowledge. He said, this was the very essence of chivalry, and no man had ever made such a profession of arms, without having first placed his affection upon some beauteous object, for whose honour, and at whose command he would chearfully encounter the most dreadful perils:

He took notice that nothing could be more irregular than the manner in which Crowe had attempted to keep his vigil: for he had never served his noviciate—he had not prepared himself with abstinence and prayer—he had not provided a qualified godfather for the ceremony of dubbing—he had no armour of his own to wake; but, on the very threshold of chivalry, which is the perfection of justice, had unjustly purloined the arms of another knight: that this was a meer mockery of a religious institution, and therefore, unpleasing in the sight of heaven; witness, the demons and hob-goblins that were permitted to disturb and torment him in his trial.

Crowe having listened to these remarks, with earnest attention, replied, after some hesitation: 'I am bound to you, brother, for your kind and christian counsel—I doubt as how I've steered by a wrong chart, d'ye see—as for the matter of the sciences, to be sure, I know plain sailing[1] and mercator;[2] and am an indifferent good seamen, thof I say it that should not say it: but as to all the rest, no better than the viol block[3] or the geer capstan.[4] Religion I ha'n't much over-hauled; and we tars laugh at your polite conversation, thof, mayhap, we can chaunt a few ballads to keep the hands awake in the night watch; then for chastity, brother, I doubt that's not to be expected in a sailor just come a-shore, after a long voyage—sure all those poor hearts won't be damned for steering in the wake of nature. As for a sweet-heart, Bet Mizen of St. Catherine's[5] would fit me to a hair—she and I are old messmates; and—what signifies talking, brother, she knows already the trim of my vessel, d'ye see.' He concluded with saying, 'He thought he wa'n't too old to learn; and if Sir Launcelot would take him in tow, as his tender, he would stand by him all weathers, and it should not cost his consort a farthing's expence.'

The knight said, he did not think himself of consequence enough to have such a pupil; but should always be ready to give him his best advice, as a specimen of which he exorted him to weigh all the circumstances, and deliberate calmly and leisurely, before he actually engaged in such a boisterous profession, assuring him that if, at the end of three months, his resolution should continue, he would take upon himself the office of his instructor. In the mean time, he gratified the hostess for his lodging, put on his armour, took leave of the company, and mounting *Bronzomarte*, proceeded southerly, being attended by his squire Crabshaw, grumbling on the back of Gilbert.

CHAPTER VIII

*Which is within a hair's breadth of proving
highly interesting*

LEAVING captain Crowe and his nephew for the present, though they and even the misanthrope will reappear in due season, we are now obliged to attend the progress of the knight, who proceeded in a southerly direction, insensible of the storm that blew, as well as of the darkness, which was horrible. For some time Crabshaw ejaculated curses in silence; till at length his anger gave way to his fear, which waxed so strong upon him, that he could no longer resist the desire of alleviating it, by entering into a conversation with his master. By way of introduction, he gave Gilbert the spur, directing him towards the flank of Bronzomarte, which he encountered with such a shock that the knight was almost dismounted. When sir Launcelot, with some warmth, asked the reason of this attack, the squire replied in these words: 'The devil, (God bless us) mun be playing his pranks with Gilbert too, as sure as I'm a living soul!— I'se wage a teaster,[1] the foul fiend has left the seaman, and got into Gilbert, that he has—when a has passed through an ass and a horse, I'se marvel what beast a will get into next.' 'Probably into a mule, (said the knight;) in that case you will be in some danger— but I can, at any time, dispossess[2] you with a horsewhip.'—'Aye, aye, (answered Timothy) your honour has a mortal good hand at giving a flap with a fox's tail, as the saying is—'tis a wonderment you did not try your hand on that there wiseacre that stole your honour's harness, and wants to be an arrant with a murrain[3] to 'un—Lord help his fool's head! it becomes him as a sow doth a cart-saddle.' 'There is no guilt in infirmity (said the knight;) I punish the vicious only.' 'I would your honour would punish Gilbert then, (cried the squire) for 'tis the most vicious tuoad that ever I laid a leg over—but as to that same sea-faring man, what may his distemper be?' 'Madness;' (answered sir Launcelot.) 'Bodikins, (exclaimed the squire) I doubt as how other volks are leame of the same leg—but a'n't vor such small gentry as he to be mad: they mun leave that to their betters.' 'You seem to hint at me, Crabshaw: do you really think I am mad?' 'I may say as how I have looked your honour in the mouth; and a sorry dog should I be, if I did not know your humours as well as I know e'er a beast in the steable at Greaves-bury-hall.' 'Since you are so well acquainted with my madness, (said the knight) what opinion have you of yourself, who serve and follow a lunatic?' 'I hope I han't served your honour for nothing, but I shall inherit some of your cast vagaries—when your honour is pleased to be mad, I should be very sorry to be found right in my senses. Timothy Crabshaw will never eat the bread of unthankful-ness—It shall never be said of him that he was wiser than his master: as for the matter of following a madman, we may say your honour's face is made of a fiddle; every one that looks on you loves you.' This compliment the knight returned by saying, 'If my face is a fiddle, Crabshaw, your tongue is a fiddle-stick that plays upon it—yet your music is very disagreeable—you don't keep time.' 'Nor you neither, measter, (cried Timothy) or we shouldn't be here wandering about under cloud of night, like sheep-stealers, or evil spirits with troubled consciences.'

Here the discourse was interrupted by a sudden disaster, in consequence of which the squire uttered an inarticulate roar that startled the knight himself, who was very little subject to the sensa-tion of fear: but his surprize was changed into vexation when he perceived Gilbert without a rider passing by, and kicking his heels with great agility. He forthwith turned his steed, and, riding back a few paces, found Crabshaw rising from the ground. When he asked what was become of his horse, he answered in a whimpering tone, 'Horse! would I could once see him fairly carrion for the hounds—for my part I believe as how 'tis no horse but a devil incarnate; and yet I've been worse mounted, that I have—I'd like to have rid a horse that was foaled of an acorn.'[1]

This accident happened in a hollow way, overshadowed with trees, one of which the storm had blown down, so that it lay over the road, and one of its boughs projecting horizontally, encountered the squire as he trotted along in the dark. Chancing to hitch under his long chin, he could not disengage himself; but hung suspended like a flitch of bacon, while Gilbert, pushing forward left him dangling, and, by his aukward gambols, seemed to be pleased with the joke. This capricious animal was not retaken without the personal endeavours of the knight: for Crabshaw absolutely refusing to budge a foot from his honour's side, he was obliged to alight, and fasten Bronzomarte to a tree: then they set out together, and with some difficulty found Gilbert with his neck stretched over a five-barred gate, snuffing up the morning-air. The squire, however, was not remounted, without having first undergone a severe reprehension from his master, who upbraided him with his cowardice, threatened to chastise him on the spot, and declared that he would divorce his dastardly soul from his body, should he ever be incommoded or affronted with another instance of his base-born apprehension. Though there was some risque in carrying on the altercation at this juncture, Timothy having bound up his jaws, could not withstand the inclination he had to confute his master. He therefore, in a muttering accent, protested that if the knight would give him leave, he should prove that his honour had tied a knot with his tongue which he could not untie with all his teeth. 'How, caitiff, (cried sir Launcelot) presume to contend with me in argument!' 'Your mouth is scarce shut, (said the other) since you declared that a man was not to be punished for madness, because it was a distemper: now I will maintain that cowardice is a distemper as well as madness; for nobody would be afraid if he could help it.' 'There is more logic in that remark (resumed the knight) than I expected from your clod-pate, Crabshaw: but I must explain the difference between cowardice and madness. Cowardice, tho' sometimes the effect of natural imbecility, is generally a prejudice of education, or bad habit contracted from misinformation, or misapprehension, and may certainly be cured by experience, and the exercise of reason: but this remedy cannot be applied in madness, which is a privation or disorder of reason itself.' 'So is cowardice, as I'm a living soul, (exclaimed the squire) don't you say a man is frightened out of his senses? for my peart, measter, I can neither see nor hear, much less argufy when I'm in such a quandary: wherefore, I believe, odds bodikins! that cowardice and madness are both distempers, and differ no more than the hot and cold fits of an ague. When it teakes your honour, you're all heat and fire and fury, Lord bless us! but when it catches poor Tim, he's cold and dead-hearted, he sheakes and shivers like an aspen-leaf, that he does.' 'In that case, (answered the knight) I shall not punish you for the distemper which you cannot help, but for engaging in a service exposed to perils, when you knew your own infirmity: in the same manner as a man deserves punishment, who enlists himself for a soldier, while he labours under any secret disease.' 'At that rate (said the squire) my bread is like to be rarely buttered o'both sides, I faith. But, I hope, as by the blessing of God, I have run mad, so I shall in good time grow valiant, under your honour's precept and example.'

By this time a very disagreeable night was succeeded by a fair, bright morning, and a market-town appeared at the distance of three or four miles, when Crabshaw, having no longer the fear of hobgoblins before his eyes, and being moreover cheared by the sight of a place where he hoped to meet with comfortable entertainment, began to talk big, to expatiate on the folly of being afraid, and finally set all danger at defiance; when all of a sudden he was presented with an opportunity of putting in practice those new adopted maxims. In an opening between two lanes, they perceived a gentleman's coach stopped by two highwaymen on horse-back, one of whom advanced to reconnoitre and keep the coast clear, while the other exacted contribution from the travellers in the coach. He who acted as centinel, no sooner saw our adventurer appearing from the lane, than he rode up with a pistol in his hand, and ordered him to halt on pain of immediate death.

To this peremptory mandate the knight made no other reply than charging him with such impetuosity that he was unhorsed in a twinkling, and lay sprawling on the ground, seemingly sore bruised with his fall. Sir Launcelot commanding Timothy to alight and secure the prisoner, couched his launce, and rode full speed at the other highwayman, who was not a little disturbed at sight of such an apparition. Nevertheless, he fired his pistol without effect; and, clapping spurs to his horse, fled away at full gallop. The knight pursued him with all the speed that Bronzomarte could exert; but the robber being mounted on a swift hunter, kept him at a distance; and, after a chace of several miles, escaped thro' a wood so entangled with coppice, that Sir Launcelot thought proper to desist. He then, for the first time, recollected the situation in which he had left the other thief, and remembering to have heard a female shriek, as he passed by the coach-window, resolved to return with all expedition, that he might make a proffer of his service to the lady, according to the obligation of knight-errantry. But he had lost his way; and after an hour's ride, during which he traversed many a field, and circled divers hedges, he found himself in the market-town aforementioned. Here the first object that presented itself to his eyes, was Crabshaw, on foot, surrounded by a mob, tearing his hair, stamping with his feet, and roaring out in manifest distraction, 'Shew me the mayor, (for the love of God) shew me the mayor!—O Gilbert, Gilbert! a murrain take thee, Gilbert! sure thou wast foaled for my destruction!'

From these exclamations, and the antic dress of the squire, the people, not without reason, concluded that the poor soul had lost his wits; and the beadle was just going to secure him, when the knight interposed, and at once attracted the whole attention of the populace. Timothy, seeing his master, fell down on his knees, crying, 'The thief has run away with Gilbert—you may pound me into a peaste, as the saying is: but now I'se as mad as your worship; and an't afeard of the devil and all his works.' Sir Launcelot desiring the beadle would forbear, was instantly obeyed by that officer, who had no inclination to put the authority of his place in competition with the power of such a figure armed at all points, mounted on a fiery steed, and ready for the combat. He ordered Crabshaw to attend him to the next inn, where he alighted; then taking him into a separate apartment, demanded an explanation of the unconnected words he had uttered. The squire was in such agitation, that with infinite difficulty, and by dint of a thousand different questions, his master learned the adventure to this effect: Crabshaw, according to Sir Launcelot's command, had alighted from his horse, and drawn his cutlass, in hope of intimidating the discomfited robber into a tame surrender, though he did not at all relish the nature of the service: but the thief was neither so much hurt, nor so tame as Timothy had imagined. He started on his feet with his pistol still in his hand; and presenting it to the squire, swore with dreadful imprecations, that he would blow his brains out in an instant. Crabshaw, unwilling to hazard the trial of this experiment, turned his back, and fled with great precipitation; while the robber, whose horse had run away, mounted Gilbert, and rode off across the country. It was at this period, that two footmen belonging to the coach, who had stayed behind to take their morning's whet, at the inn where they had lodged, came up to the assistance of the ladies, armed with blunderbusses; and the carriage proceeded, leaving Timothy alone in distraction and despair. He knew not which way to turn, and was afraid of remaining on the spot, lest the robbers should come back and revenge themselves upon him for the disappointment they had undergone. In this distress, the first thought that occurred, was to make the best of his way to the town, and demand the assistance of the civil magistrate towards the retrieval of what he had lost: a design which he executed in such a manner, as justly entailed upon him the imputation of lunacy.

While Timothy stood fronting the window, and answering the interrogations of his master, he suddenly exclaimed, 'Bodikins! there's Gilbert!' and sprung into the street with incredible agility. There finding his strayed companion brought back by one of the footmen who attended the coach, he imprinted a kiss on his forehead; and hanging about his neck, with the tears in his eyes, hailed his return with the following salutation:[1] 'Art thou come back, my darling? ah Gilbert, Gilbert! a pize upon thee! thou hadst like to have been a dear Gilbert to me! how couldst thou break the heart of thy old friend, who has known thee from a colt? seven years next grass have I fed thee and bred thee; provided thee with sweet hay, delicate corn, and fresh litter, that thou mought lie warm, dry, and comfortable. Ha'n't I curry-combed thy carcase 'till it was as sleek as a sloe, and cherished thee as the apple of mine eye? for all that thou hast played me an hundred dog's-tricks; biting, and kicking, and plunging, as if the devil was in thy body; and now thou couldst run away with a thief, and leave me to be flea'd alive by master: what canst thou say for thyself, thou cruel, hard-hearted, unchristian tuoad!' To this tender expostulation, which afforded much entertainment to the boys, Gilbert answered not one word; but seemed altogether insensible to the caresses of Timothy, who forthwith led him into the stable. On the whole, he seems to have been an unsocial animal:[2] for it does not appear that he ever contracted any degree of intimacy, even with Bronzomarte, during the whole course of their acquaintance and fellowship. On the contrary, he has been more than once known to signify his aversion by throwing out behind, and other eruptive marks of contempt for that elegant charger, who excelled him as much in personal merit, as his rider Timothy was outshone by his all-accomplished master. While the squire accommodated Gilbert in the stable, the knight sent for the footman who had brought him back; and, having presented him with a liberal acknowledgment, desired to know in what manner the horse had been retrieved.

The stranger satisfied him in this particular, by giving him to understand, that the highwayman, perceiving himself pursued across the country, plied Gilbert so severely with whip and spur, that the animal resented the usage, and being besides, perhaps, a little struck with remorse for having left his old friend Crabshaw, suddenly halted, and stood stock still, notwithstanding all the stripes and tortures he underwent; or if he moved at all, it was in a retrograde direction. The thief, seeing all his endeavours ineffectual, and himself in danger of being overtaken, wisely quitted his acquisition, and fled into the bosom of a neighbouring wood.

Then the knight inquired about the situation of the lady in the coach, and offered himself as her guard and conductor: but was told that she was already safely lodged in the house of a gentleman at some distance from the road. He likewise learned that she was a person disordered in her senses, under the care and tuition of a widow lady her relation; and that in a day or two they should pursue their journey northward to the place of her habitation. After the footman had been some time dismissed, the knight recollected that he had forgot to ask the name of the person to whom he belonged; and began to be uneasy at this omission, which indeed was more interesting than he could imagine: for an explanation of this nature would, in all likelihood, have led to a discovery, that the lady in the coach was no other than Miss Aurelia Darnel, who seeing him unexpectedly in such an equipage and attitude, as he passed the coach, (for his helmet was off) had screamed with surprize and terror, and fainted away. Nevertheless, when she recovered from her swoon, she concealed the real cause of her agitation, and none of her attendants were acquainted with the person of Sir Launcelot.

The circumstances of the disorder, under which she was said to labour, shall be revealed in due course. In the mean time, our adventurer, though unaccountably affected, never dreamed of such an occurrence; but being very much fatigued, resolved to indemnify himself for the loss of last night's repose; and this happened to be one of the few things in which Crabshaw felt an ambition to follow his master's example.

Sir L. Greaves and his Squire T. Crabshaw
at a Country Election.

CHAPTER IX

Which may serve to shew, that true patriotism is of no party

THE knight had not enjoyed his repose above two hours, when he was disturbed by such a variety of noises, as might have discomposed a brain of the firmest texture. The rumbling of carriages, and the rattling of horses feet on the pavement, was intermingled with loud shouts, and the noise of fiddle, french-horn, and bagpipe. A loud peal was heard ringing in the church-tower, at some distance, while the inn resounded with clamour, confusion, and uproar.

Sir Launcelot being thus alarmed, started from his bed, and running to the window, beheld a cavalcade of persons well mounted, and distinguished by blue cockades. They were generally attired like jockies, with gold-laced hats and buckskin breeches, and one of them bore a standard of blue silk, inscribed in white letters, LIBERTY AND THE LANDED INTEREST. He who rode at their head was a jolly figure, of a florid complexion and round belly, seemingly turned of fifty, and, in all appearance, of a choleric disposition. As they approached the market-place they waved their hats, huzza'd, and cried aloud, NO FOREIGN CONNECTIONS,—OLD-ENGLAND FOR EVER.[1] This acclamation, however, was not so loud or universal, but that our adventurer could distinctly hear a counter-cry from the populace, of NO SLAVERY,—NO POPISH PRETENDER.[2] An insinuation so ill relished by the cavaliers, that they began to ply their horse-whips among the multitude, and were, in their turn, saluted with a discharge or volley of stones, dirt, and dead cats; in consequence of which some teeth were demolished, and many surtouts defiled.

Our adventurer's attention was soon called off from this scene, to contemplate another procession of people on foot, adorned with bunches of orange ribbons,[3] attended by a regular band of musick, playing *God save great George our king*, and headed by a thin, swarthy personage, of a sallow aspect and large goggling eyes, arched over with two thick semicircles of hair, or rather bristles, jet black, and frowzy. His apparel was very gorgeous, though his address was aukward; he was accompanied by the mayor, recorder, and heads of the corporation, in their formalities. His ensigns were known by the inscription, LIBERTY OF CON-SCIENCE AND THE PROTESTANT SUCCESSION; and the people saluted him as he passed with repeated cheers, that seemed to prognosticate success. He had particularly ingratiated himself with the good women, who lined the street, and sent forth many ejaculatory petitions in his favour.

Sir Launcelot immediately comprehended the meaning of this solemnity: he perceived it was the prelude to the election of a member to represent the county in parliament, and he was seized with an eager desire to know the names and characters of the competitors. In order to gratify this desire, he made repeated application to the bell-rope that depended from the ceiling of his apartment; but this produced nothing, except the repetition of the words 'Coming, Sir,' which ecchoed from three or four different corners of the house. The waiters were so distracted by a variety of calls, that they stood motionless, in the state of the schoolman's ass[1] between two bundles of hay, incapable of determining where they should first offer their attendance.

Our knight's patience was almost exhausted, when Crabshaw entered the room, in a very strange equipage: one half of his face appeared close shaved, and the other covered with lather, while the blood trickled in two rivulets from his nose, upon a barber's cloth that was tucked under his chin; he looked grim with indignation, and, under his left arm carried his cutlass, un-sheathed. Where he had acquired so much of the profession of knight-errantry we shall not pretend to determine; but, certain it is, he fell on his knees before sir Launcelot, crying, with an accent of rage and distraction, 'In the name of St. George for England, I beg a boon, sir knight, and thy compliance I demand, before the peacock and the ladies.'[2]

Sir Launcelot, astonished at this address, replied in a lofty strain, 'Valiant squire, thy boon is granted, provided it doth not con-travene the laws of the land, and the constitutions of chivalry.' 'Then I crave leave (answered Crabshaw) to challenge and defy to mortal combat, that caitif barber who hath left me in this piteous condition; and I vow by the peacock, that I will not shave my beard, until I have shaved his head from his shoulders: so may I thrive in the occupation of an arrant squire.'

Before his master had time to enquire into particulars, they were joined by a decent man in boots, who was likewise a traveller, and had seen the rise and progress of Timothy's disaster. He gave the knight to understand, that Crabshaw had sent for a barber, and already undergone one half of the operation, when the operator received the long expected message from both the gentlemen, who stood candidates at the election. The double summons was no sooner intimated to him, than he threw down his bason and retired with precipitation, leaving the squire in the suds. Timothy, incensed at this desertion, followed him with equal celerity into the street, where he collared the shaver, and insisted upon being entirely trimmed, on pain of the bastinado. The other finding himself thus arrested, and having no time to spare for altercation, lifted up his fist, and discharged it upon the snout of Crabshaw with such force, that the unfortunate aggressor was fain to bite the ground, while the victor hastened away, in hope of touching the double wages of corruption.

The knight being informed of these circumstances, told Timothy with a smile, that he should have liberty to defy the barber; but in the mean time, he ordered him to saddle Bronzomarte, and prepare for immediate service. While the squire was thus employed, his master engaged in conversation with the stranger, who happened to be a London dealer travelling for orders, and was well acquainted with the particulars which our adventurer wanted to know. It was from this communicative tradesman he learned, that the competitors were sir Valentine Quickset[1] and Mr. Isaac Vanderpelft;[2] the first a meer fox-hunter, who depended for success in this election upon his interest among the high-flying[3] gentry; the other a stock-jobber[4] and contractor, of foreign extract, not without a mixture of Hebrew blood, immensely rich, who was countenanced by his grace of ——, and supposed to have distributed large sums in securing a majority of votes among the yeomanry of the county, possessed of small freeholds, and copy-holders,[5] a great number of which last resided in this burrough. He said these were generally dissenters[6] and weavers; and that the mayor, who was himself a manufacturer, had received a very considerable order for exportation, in consequence of which, it was believed, he would support Mr. Vanderpelft with all his influence and credit.

Sir Launcelot, rouzed at this intelligence, called for his armour, which being buckled on in a hurry, he mounted his steed, attended by Crabshaw on Gilbert, and rode immediately into the midst of the multitude by which the hustings were surrounded, just as sir Valentine Quickset began to harangue the people from an occasional theatre, formed of a plank supported by the upper board of the publick stocks, and an inferior rib of a wooden cage pitched also for the accommodation of petty delinquents.

Though the singular appearance of sir Launcelot at first attracted the eyes of all the spectators, yet they did not fail to yield attention to the speech of his brother knight, sir Valentine, which ran in the following strain: 'Gentlemen vreehoulders of this here county, I shan't pretend to meake a vine vlourishing speech, — I'm a plain spoken man, as you all know. I hope I shall always speak my maind without vear or vavour, as the zaying is. 'Tis the way of the Quicksets—we are no upstarts, nor vorreigners, nor have we any Jewish blood in our veins;—we have lived in this here neighbour-hood time out of maind, as you all know; and possess an estate of vive thousand clear, which we spend at whoam, among you, in old English hospitality—all my vorevathers have been parliament-men, and I can prove that ne'r a one o'um gave a zingle vote for the court since the revolution. Vor my own peart, I value not the ministry three skips of a louse, as the zaying is,—I ne'er knew but one minister that was an honest man; and vor all the rest I care not if they were hanged as high as Haman,[1] with a pox to 'un—I am, thank God, a vree-born, true-hearted Englishman, and a loyal, thof unworthy, son of the church—vor all they have done vor H——r,[2] I'd vain know what they have done vor the church, with a vengeance—vor my oun peart, I hate all vorreigners, and vorreign measures, whereby this poor nation is broken-backed with a dismal load of debt, and taxes rise so high that the poor cannot get bread. Gentlemen vreehoulders of this county, I value no minister a vig's end, d'ye see; if you will vavour me with your votes and interest, whereby I may be returned, I'll engage one half of my estate that I never cry yea to vour shillings in the pound;[3] but will cross the ministry in every thing, as in duty bound, and as becomes an honest vreehoulder in the ould interest—but, if you sell your votes and your country for hire, you will be detested in this here world, and damned in the next to all eternity: so I leave every man to his own conscience.'

This eloquent oration was received by his own friends with loud peals of applause; which, however, did not discourage his competitor, who, confident of his own strength, ascended the rostrum, or, in other words, an old cask, set upright for the purpose. Having bowed all round to the audience, with a smile of gentle condescension, he told them, how ambitious he was of the honour to represent this county in parliament; and how happy he found himself in the encouragement of his friends, who had so unanimously agreed to support his pretensions. He said, over and above the qualification he possessed among them, he had fourscore thousand pounds in his pocket, which he had acquired by commerce, the support of the nation, under the present happy establishment, in defence of which he was ready to spend the last farthing. He owned himself a faithful subject to his majesty king George, sincerely attached to the protestant succession, in detestation and defiance of a popish, an abjured, and outlawed pretender; and declared that he would exhaust his substance and his blood, if necessary, in maintaining the principles of the glorious revolution. 'This (cried he) is the solid basis and foundation upon which I stand.'

These last words had scarce proceeded from his mouth, when the head of the barrel or puncheon on which he stood, being frail and infirm, gave way; so that down he went with a crash, and in a twinkling disappeared from the eyes of the astonished beholders. The fox-hunters perceiving his disaster, exclaimed, in the phrase and accent of the chace, 'Stole away! stole away!' and, with hideous vociferation, joined in the sylvan chorus which the hunters hollow when the hounds are at fault.

The disaster of Mr. Vanderpelft was soon repaired by the assiduity of his friends, who disengaged him from the barrel in a trice, hoisted him on the shoulders of four strong weavers, and resenting the unmannerly exultation of their antagonists, began to form themselves in order of battle. An obstinate fray would have undoubtedly ensued, had not their mutual indignation given way to their curiosity, at the motion of our knight, who had advanced into the middle between the two fronts, and waving his hand, as a signal for them to give attention, addressed himself to them with graceful demeanor, in these words: 'Countrymen, friends, and fellow-citizens, you are this day assembled to determine a point of the utmost consequence to yourselves and your posterity; a point that ought to be determined by far other weapons than brutal force and factious clamour. You, the freemen of England, are the basis of that excellent constitution, which hath long flourished the object of envy and admiration. To you belongs the inestimable privilege of choosing a delegate properly qualified to represent you in the high court of parliament. This is your birth-right, inherited from your ancestors, obtained by their courage, and sealed with their blood. It is not only your birthright, which you should maintain in defiance of all danger, but also a sacred trust, to be executed with the most scrupulous care and fidelity. The person whom you trust ought not only to be endued with the most inflexible integrity, but should likewise possess a fund of knowledge that may enable him to act as a part of the legislature. He must be well acquainted with the history, the constitution, and the laws of his country: he must understand the forms of business, the extent of the royal prerogative, the privilege of parliament, the detail of government, the nature and regulation of the finances, the different branches of commerce, the politicks that prevail, and the connections that subsist among the different powers of Europe: for, on all these subjects, the deliberations of a house of commons occasionally turn: but, these great purposes will never be answered by electing an illiterate savage, scarce qualified, in point of understanding, to act as a country justice of the peace, a man who has scarce ever travelled beyond the excursion of a fox-chace, whose conversation never rambles farther than his stable, his kennel, and his barn-yard; who rejects decorum as degeneracy, mistakes rusticity for independence, ascertains his courage by leaping over gates and ditches, and sounds his triumph on feats of drinking; who holds his estate by a factious tenure, professes himself the blind slave of a party, without knowing the principles that gave it birth, or the motives by which it is actuated, and thinks that all patriotism consists in railing indiscriminately at ministers, and obstinately opposing every measure of the administration. Such a man, with no evil intentions of his own, might be used as a dangerous tool in the hands of desperate faction, by scattering the seeds of disaffection, embarrassing the wheels of government, and reducing the whole kingdom to anarchy.'

Here the knight was interrupted, by the shouts and acclamations of the Vanderpelftites, who cried aloud, 'Hear him! hear him! long life to the iron-cased orator.' This clamour subsiding, he prosecuted his harangue to the following effect:

'Such a man as I have described may be dangerous from

ignorance, but is neither so mischievous nor so detestable as the wretch who knowingly betrays his trust, and sues to be the hireling and prostitute of a weak and worthless minister; a sordid knave, without honour or principle, who belongs to no family whose example can reproach him with degeneracy; who has no country to command his respect, no friends to engage his affection, no religion to regulate his morals, no conscience to restrain his iniquity, and who worships no God but mammon. An insinuating miscreant, who undertakes for the dirtiest work of the vilest administration; who practises national usury, receiving by whole-sale the rewards of venality, and distributing the wages of corruption by retail.'

In this place our adventurer's speech was drowned in the acclamations of the fox-hunters, who now triumphed in their turn, and hoicksed[1] the speaker, exclaiming, 'Well opened Jowler— to 'un, to 'un, to 'un again, Sweetlips! hey, Merry, Whitefoot!' After a short interruption, he thus resumed his discourse:

'When such a caitif presents himself to you, like the devil, with a temptation in his hand, avoid him as if he were in fact the devil—it is not the offering of disinterested love; for, what should induce him, who has no affections, to love you, to whose persons he is an utter stranger? alas! it is not a benevolence, but a bribe. He wants to buy you at one market, that he may sell you at another. Without doubt his intention is to make an advantage of his purchase; and this aim he cannot accomplish, but by sacrificing, in some sort, your interest, your independency, to the wicked designs of a minister, as he can expect no gratification for the faithful dis-charge of his duty. But, even if he should not find an opportunity of selling you to advantage, the crime, the shame, the infamy, will still be the same in you, who, baser than the most abandoned prostitutes, have sold yourselves and your posterity for hire—for a paltry price, to be refunded with interest by some minister, who will indemnify himself out of your own pockets: for, after all, you are bought and sold with your own money—the miserable pittance you may now receive, is no more than a pitcher full of water thrown in to moisten the sucker of that pump which will drain you to the bottom. Let me therefore advise and exhort you, my countrymen, to avoid the opposite extremes of the ignorant clown and the designing courtier, and choose a man of honesty, intelli-gence, and moderation, who will—'

The doctrine of moderation was a very unpopular subject in such an assembly; and, accordingly, they rejected it as one man. They began to think the stranger wanted to set up for himself,[1] a supposition that could not fail to incense both sides equally, as they were both zealously engaged in their respective causes. The Whigs and the Tories joined against this intruder, who being neither, was treated like a monster, or chimæra in politics. They hissed, they hooted, and they hollowed; they annoyed him with missiles of dirt, sticks, and stones; they cursed, they threatened and reviled, till at length his patience was exhausted.

'Ungrateful, and abandoned miscreants! (he cried) I spoke to you as men and christians, as free-born Britons and fellow-citizens: but I perceive you are a pack of venal, infamous scoundrels, and I will treat you accordingly.' So saying he brandished his lance, and riding into the thickest of the concourse, laid about him with such dexterity and effect, that the multitude was immediately dispersed, and he retired without further molestation.

The same good fortune did not attend squire Crabshaw in his retreat. The ludicrous singularity of his features, and the half-mown crop of hair that bristled from one side of his countenance, invited some wags to make merry at his expence: one of them clapped a furzebush under the tail of Gilbert, who, feeling himself thus stimulated *a posteriori*, kicked and plunged and capered in such a manner, that Timothy could hardly keep the saddle. In this commotion he lost his cap and his periwig, while the rabble pelted him in such a manner, that, before he could join his master, he looked like a pillar, or rather a pillory, of mud.

CHAPTER X

Which sheweth that he who plays at bowls, will sometimes meet with rubbers [2]

Sir Launcelot, boiling with indignation at the venality and faction of the electors, whom he had harrangued to so little purpose, retired with the most deliberate disdain towards one of the gates of the town, on the outside of which his curiosity was attracted by a concourse of people, in the midst of whom stood Mr. Ferret, mounted upon a stool, with a kind of satchel hanging round his neck, and a vial displayed in his right hand, while he held forth to the audience in a very vehement strain of elocution.

Crabshaw thought himself happily delivered, when he reached the suburbs, and proceeded without halting; but his master mingled with the crowd, and heard the orator express himself to this effect: 'Very likely, you may undervalue me and my medicine, because I don't appear upon a stage of rotten boards, in a shabby velvet coat and tye-periwig,[1] with a foolish fellow in motley, to make you laugh by making wry faces: but I scorn to use these dirty arts for engaging your attention. These paultry tricks, *ad captandum vulgus*,[2] can have no effect but on ideots, and if you are ideots, I don't desire you should be my customers. Take notice, I don't address you in the stile of a mountebank, or a high German doctor;[3] and yet the kingdom is full of mountebanks, empirics, and quacks. We have quacks in religion, quacks in physic, quacks in law, quacks in politics; quacks in patriotism; quacks in government; high German quacks that have blistered, sweated, bled, and purged the nation into an atrophy. But this is not all: they have not only evacuated her into a consumption, but they have intoxicated her brain, until she is become delirious: she can no longer pursue her own interest; or, indeed, rightly distinguish it: like the people of Nineveh,[4] she can hardly tell her right hand from her left; but, as a changeling, is dazzled and delighted by an *ignis fatuus*, a Will o' the wisp, an exhalation from the vilest materials in nature, that leads her astray through Westphalian[5] bogs and deserts, and will one day break her neck over some barren rock, or leave her sticking in some H——n[6] pit or quagmire. For my part, if you have a mind to betray your country, I have no objection. In selling yourselves and your fellow-citizens, you only dispose of a pack of rascals who deserve to be sold—If you sell one another, why should not I sell this here Elixir of Long Life, which if properly used, will protract your days till you shall have seen your country ruined? I shall not pretend to disturb your understandings, which are none of the strongest, with a hotch-potch of unintelligible terms, such as Aristotle's four principles[7] of generation, unformed matter, privation, efficient and final causes. Aristotle was a pedantic blockhead, and still more knave than fool. The same censure we may safely put on that wise-acre Dioscorides, with his faculties[8] of simples, his seminal, specific, and principal virtues; and that crazy commentator Galen, with his four elements,[9] elementary qualities, his eight complexions, his harmonies, and discords. Nor shall I expatiate on the alkahest of that mad scoundrel Paracelsus,[1] with which he pretended to reduce flints into salt; nor the *archœus* or *spiritus rector* of that visionary Van Helmont,[2] his simple, elementary water, his *gas*, ferments, and transmutations; nor shall I enlarge upon the salt, sulphur, and oil, the *acidum vagum*,[3] the mercury of metals, and the volatilized vitriol of other modern chymists, a pack of ignorant, conceited, knavish rascals, that puzzle your weak heads with such jargon, just as a Germanized m—r[4] throws dust in your eyes, by lugging in and ringing the changes on the balance of power, the protestant religion, and your allies on the continent; acting like the juggler who picks your pockets, while he dazzles your eyes and amuses your fancy with twirling his fingers, and reciting the gibberish of *hocus pocus*; for, in fact, the balance of power is a meer chimera; as for the protestant religion, no body gives himself any trouble about it; and allies on the continent we have none; or at least, none that would raise an hundred men to save us from perdition, unless we paid an extravagant price for their assistance. But, to return to this here Elixir of Long Life, I might embellish it with a great many high-sounding epithets; but I disdain to follow the example of every illiterate vagabond, that from idleness turns quack, and advertises his nostrum in the public papers. I am neither a felonious dry-salter[5] returned from exile, an hospital stump-turner,[6] a decayed stay-maker, a bankrupt printer, or insolvent debtor, released by act of parliament.[7] I did not pretend to administer medicines, without the least tincture of letters, or suborn wretches to perjure themselves in false affidavits of cures that were never performed; nor employ a set of led-captains[8] to harrangue in my praise, at all public places. I was bred regularly to the profession of chymistry, and have tried all the processes of alchemy, and I may venture to say, that this here Elixir is, in fact, the *chrusion pepuromenon ek puros*,[9] the visible, glorious, spiritual body, from whence all other beings derive their existence, as proceeding from their father the sun, and their mother the moon; from the sun, as from a living and spiritual gold, which is meer fire; consequently, the common and universal first created mover, from whence all moveable things have their distinct and particular motions; and also from the moon, as from the wife of the sun, and the common mother of all sublunary things: and for as much as man is, and must be the comprehensive end of all creatures, and the microcosm, he is counselled in the Revelations,[1] to buy gold that is thoroughly fired, or rather pure fire, that he may become rich and like the sun; as on the contrary, he becomes poor, when he abuses the arsenical poison; so that his silver, by the fire, must be calcined to a *caput mortuum*,[2] which happens, when he will hold and retain the menstruum[3] out of which he partly exists, for his own property, and doth not daily offer up the same in the fire of the sun, that the woman may be cloathed with the sun, and become a sun, and thereby rule over the moon; that is to say, that he may get the moon under his feet.—Now this here Elixir, sold for no more than six-pence a vial, contains the essence of the alkahest, the archæus, the catholicon,[4] the menstruum, the sun, moon, and to sum up all in one word, is the true, genuine, un-adulterated, unchangeable, immaculate and specific *chrusion pepuromenon ek puros.*'

The audience were variously affected by this learned oration: some of those who favoured the pretensions of the whig candidate, were of opinion that he ought to be punished for his presumption in reflecting so scurrilously on ministers and measures. Of this sentiment was our adventurer, though he could not help admiring the courage of the orator, and owning within himself, that he had mixed some melancholy truths with his scurrility. Mr. Ferret would not have stood so long in his rostrum unmolested, had not he cunningly chosen his station immediately without the jurisdiction of the town, whose magistrates therefore could not take cognizance of his conduct; but, application was made to the constable of the other parish, while our nostrum-monger pro-ceeded in his speech, the conclusion of which produced such an effect upon his hearers, that his whole cargo was immediately exhausted. He had just stepped down from his stool, when the constable, with his staff, arrived, and took him under his guidance. Mr. Ferret, on this occasion, attempted to interest the people in his behalf, by exhorting them to vindicate the liberty of the subject, against such an act of oppression; but finding them deaf to the tropes and figures of his elocution, he addressed himself to our knight, reminding him of his duty to protect the helpless and the injured, and earnestly soliciting his interposition.

Sir Launcelot, without making the least reply to his intreaties, resolved to see the end of this adventure; and being joined by his squire, followed the prisoner at a distance, measuring back the ground he had travelled the day before, until he reached another small borough, where Ferret was housed in the common prison. While he sat a-horse-back, deliberating on the next step he should take, he was accosted by the voice of Tom Clarke, who called in a whimpering tone, through a window grated with iron, 'For the love of God! Sir Launcelot, do, dear Sir, be so good as to take the trouble to alight and come up stairs—I have something to communicate of consequence to the community in general, and you in particular—Pray, do, dear Sir Knight. I beg a boon in the name of St. Michael and St. George for England.'

Our adventurer, not a little surprized at this address, dismounted without hesitation, and being admitted to the common jail, there found not only his old friend Tom, but also the uncle, sitting on a bench with an woolen night-cap on his head, and a pair of spectacles on his nose, reading very earnestly in a book, which he afterwards understood was intituled, 'The Life and Adventures of Valentine and Orson.'[1] The captain, no sooner saw his great pattern enter, than he rose and received him with the salutation of 'What cheer, brother?' and before the knight could answer, added these words: 'You see how the land lies—here have Tom and I been fast a-shore these four and twenty hours; and this berth we have got by attempting to tow your galley, brother, from the enemy's harbour.—Adds bobs! if we had this here fellow whoreson for a consort, with all our tackle in order, brother, we'd soon shew 'em the topsail, slip our cable, and down with their barricadoes.[2] But, howsomever, it don't signify talking,—patience is a good stream-anchor,[3] and will hold, as the saying is,—but, damn my—as for the matter of my boltsprit.[4]—Hearkye, hearkye, brother, damn'd hard to engage with three at a time, one upon my bow, one upon my quarter, and one right a-head, rubbing, and drubbing, lying athwart hawse,[5] raking fore and aft, battering and grappling, and lashing and clashing—adds heart, brother; crash went the bolt-sprit—down came the round-top[6]—up with the dead lights[7]—I saw nothing but the stars at noon, lost the helm of my seven senses, and down I broached upon my broadside—.'[8]

As Mr. Clarke rightly conceived that his uncle would need an interpreter, he began to explain these hints by giving a circumstantial detail of his own and the captain's disaster. He told Sir Launcelot, that notwithstanding all his persuasion and remon-

strances, captain Crowe insisted upon appearing in the character
of a knight errant; and with that view had set out from the
public-house on the morning that succeeded his vigil in the church:
that upon the high-way they had met with a coach, containing two
ladies, one of whom seemed to be under great agitation; for, as
they passed she struggled with the other, thrust out her head at the
window, and said something which he could not distinctly hear;
that captain Crowe was struck with admiration of her unequalled
beauty; and he, (Tom) no sooner informed him who she was, than
he resolved to set her at liberty, on the supposition that she was
under restraint and in distress: that he accordingly unsheathed his
cutlass, and riding back after the coach, commanded the driver
to bring to, on pain of death: that one of the servants believing the
captain to be an highwayman, presented a blunderbuss, and in all
probability would have shot him on the spot, had not he (the
nephew) rode up and assured them the gentleman was *non compos*:
that notwithstanding his intimation, all the three attacked him with
the butt ends of their horse-whips, while the coach drove on, and
although he laid about him with great fury, at last brought him to
the ground by a stroke on the temple: that Mr. Clarke himself
then interposed in defence of his kinsman, and was also severely
beaten: that two of the servants, upon application to a justice of
the peace, residing near the field of battle, had granted a warrant
against the captain and his nephew, and without examination,
committed them as idle vagrants, after having seized their horses
and their money, on pretence of their being suspected for
highwaymen. 'But, as there was no just cause of suspicion, (added
he) I am of opinion, the justice is guilty of a trespass, and may be
sued for *falsum imprisonamentum*, and considerable damages
obtained; for, you will please to observe, Sir, no justice has a right
to commit any person 'till after due examination; besides, we were
not committed for an assault and battery, *auditâ querela*,[1] nor as
wandering lunatics by the statute, who, to be sure, may be
apprehended by a justice's warrant, and locked up and chained,
if necessary, or be sent to their last legal settlement:[2] but, we were
committed as vagrants, and suspected highwaymen. Now we do not
fall under the description of vagrants; nor did any circumstance
appear to support the suspicion of robbery; for to constitute
robbery, there must be something taken; but, here nothing was
taken but blows, and they were upon compulsion: even an

attempt to rob, without any taking, is not felony, but a misdemeanour. To be sure there is a taking in deed, and a taking in
law: but still the robber must be in possession of a thing stolen;
and we attempted to steal nothing, but to steal ourselves away—
My uncle indeed, would have released the young lady *vi et armis,*[1]
had his strength been equal to his inclination; and in so doing, I
would have willingly lent my assistance, both from a desire to serve
such a beautiful young creature, and also in regard to your honour,
for I thought I heard her call upon your name.'——

'Ha! how! what! whose name? say, speak—heaven and earth!'
(cried the Knight, with marks of the most violent emotion.)
Clarke terrified at his looks, replied, 'I beg your pardon a
thousand times; I did not say positively she did speak those words:
but, I apprehended she did speak them. Words, which may be
taken or interpreted by law in a general, or common sense, ought
not to receive a strained, or unusual construction; and am-
biguous words'.——'Speak, or be dumb for ever! (exclaimed Sir
Launcelot in a terrific tone, laying, his hand on his sword) what
young lady, ha! What name did she call upon?' Clarke falling on
his knees, answered, not without stammering, 'Miss Aurelia
Darnel; to the best of my recollection, she called upon Sir
Launcelot Greaves.' 'Sacred powers! (cried our adventurer) which
way did the carriage proceed?'

When Tom told him that the coach quitted the post-road, and
struck away to the right, at full speed, Sir Launcelot was seized
with a pensive fit; his head sunk upon his breast, and he mused in
silence for several minutes, with the most melancholy expression
on his countenance: then recollecting himself, he assumed a more
composed and chearful air, and asked several questions, with
respect to the arms on the coach, and the liveries worn by the
servants. It was in the course of this interrogation, that he discovered he had actually conversed with one of the foot-men, who
had brought back Crabshaw's horse: a circumstance that filled him
with anxiety and chagrin, as he had omitted to inquire the name of
his master, and the place to which the coach was travelling;
though, in all probability, had he made these inquiries, he would
have received very little satisfaction, there being reason to think
the servants were enjoined secrecy. The knight, in order to medi-
tate on this unexpected adventure, sat down by his old friend, and
entered into a reverie, which lasted about a quarter of an hour, and

might have continued longer, had it not been interrupted by the voice of Crabshaw, who bawled aloud, 'Look to it, my masters—as you brew you must drink—this shall be a dear day's work to some of you, for my part I say nothing—the braying ass eats little grass—one barber shaves not so close, but another finds a few stubble—you wanted to catch a capon, and you've stole a cat. He that takes up his lodgings in a stable, must be contented to lie upon litter.—'[1]

The knight, desirous of knowing the cause that prompted Timothy to apothegmatize in this manner, looked through the grate, and perceived the squire fairly set in the stocks, surrounded by a mob of people. When he called to him, and asked the reason of this disgraceful restraint, Crabshaw replied, 'There's no cake, but there's another of the same make—who never climbed never fell—after clouds comes clear weather. 'Tis all long of[2] your honour I've met with this preferment; no deservings of my own, but the interest of my master. Sir Knight, if you will slay the justice, hang the constable, release your squire, and burn the town, your name will be famous in story: but, if you are content, I am thankful. Two hours are soon spent in such good company; in the mean time look to'un jailor, there's a frog in the stocks.'[3]

Sir Launcelot, incensed at this affront offered to his servant, advanced to the prison-door, but found it fast locked, and when he called to the turnkey, he was given to understand that he himself was prisoner. Enraged at this intimation, he demanded at whose suit; and was answered through the wicket, 'At the suit of the king, in whose name I will hold you fast, with God's assistance.'

The knight's looks now began to lighten, he rolled his eyes around, and snatching up an oaken bench, which three ordinary men could scarce have lifted from the ground, he, in all likelihood, would have shattered the door in pieces, had not he been restrained by the interposition of Mr. Clarke, who intreated him to have a little patience, assuring him he would suggest a plan that would avenge him amply on the justice, without any breach of the peace. 'I say, the justice (added Tom) because it must be his doing.—He is a little petulant sort of a fellow, ignorant of the law, guilty of numberless irregularities; and if properly managed, may for this here act of arbitrary power, be not only cast[4] in a swinging sum, but even turned out of the commission with disgrace.—'

This was a very seasonable hint, in consequence of which, the bench was softly replaced, and captain Crowe deposited the poker, with which he had armed himself to second the efforts of Sir Launcelot. They now, for the first time, perceived that Ferret had disappeared; and, upon inquiry, found that he was in fact the occasion of the knight's detention and the squire's disgrace.

CHAPTER XI

Description of a modern Magistrate

BEFORE the knight would take any resolution for extricating himself from his present embarrassment, he desired to be better acquainted with the character and circumstances of the justice by whom he had been confined, and likewise to understand the meaning of his own detention. To be informed in this last particular, he renewed his dialogue with the turnkey, who told him, through the grate, that Ferret no sooner perceived him in the jail, without his offensive arms, which he had left below, than he desired to be carried before the justice, where he had given information against the knight, as a violator of the public peace, who strolled about the country with unlawful arms, rendering the highways unsafe, encroaching upon the freedom of elections, putting his majesty's liege subjects in fear of their lives, and, in all probability, harbouring more dangerous designs under an affected cloak of lunacy. Ferret, upon this information, had been released, and entertained as an evidence for the king; and Crabshaw was put in the stocks, as an idle stroller.

Sir Launcelot, being satisfied in these particulars, addressed himself to his fellow-prisoners, and begged they would communicate what they knew respecting the worthy magistrate, who had been so premature in the execution of his office. This request was no sooner signified than a crew of naked wretches crowded around him, and, like a congregation of rooks, opened their throats all at once, in accusation of justice Gobble. The knight was moved at this scene, which he could not help comparing, in his own mind, to what would appear upon a much more awful occasion, when the cries of the widow and the orphan, the injured and oppressed, would be uttered at the tribunal of an unerring Judge against the villainous and insolent authors of their calamity.

When he had, with some difficulty, quieted their clamours, and confined his interrogation to one person of a tolerably decent appearance, he learned that justice Gobble, whose father was a taylor, had for some time served as a journeyman hosier in London, where he had picked up some law-terms, by conversing with hackney-writers[1] and attorneys' clerks of the lowest order; that, upon the death of his master, he had insinuated himself into the good graces of the widow, who took him for her husband, so that he became a person of some consideration, and saved money apace; that his pride, increasing with his substance, was re-inforced by the vanity of his wife, who persuaded him to retire from business, that they might live genteelly in the country; that his father dying, and leaving a couple of houses in this town, Mr. Gobble had come down with his lady to take possession, and liked the place so well as to make a more considerable purchase in the neighbourhood; that a certain peer being indebted to him a large sum in the way of his business, and either unwilling or unable to pay the money, had compounded the debt, by inserting his name in the commission; since which period his own insolence, and his wife's ostentation, had exceeded all bounds: that, in the exertion of his authority, he had committed a thousand acts of cruelty and injustice against the poorer sort of people, who were unable to call him to a proper account: that his wife domineered with a more ridiculous, though less pernicious usurpation, among the females of the place: that, in a word, she was the subject of continual mirth, and he the object of universal detestation. Our adventurer, though extremely well disposed to believe what was said to the prejudice of Gobble, would not give intire credit to this description, without first inquiring into the particulars of his conduct. He therefore asked the speaker, what was the cause of his particular complaint. 'For my own part, Sir, (said he) I lived in repute, and kept a shop in this here town, well furnished with a great variety of articles. All the people in the place were my customers; but what I and many others chiefly depended upon, was the extraordinary sale at two annual customary fairs, to which all the country people in the neighbourhood resorted to lay out their money. I had employed all my stock, and even engaged my credit to procure a large assortment of goods for the Lammas-market:[2] but having given my vote, in the election of a vestry-clerk, contrary to the interest of justice Gobble, he resolved to work my ruin. He suppressed the annual fairs, by which a great many people, especially publicans, earned the best part of their subsistence. The country people resorted to another town. I was over-stocked with a load of perishable commodities; and found myself deprived of the best part of my home customers by the ill-nature and revenge of the justice, who employed all his influence among the common people, making use of threats and promises, to make them desert my shop, and give their custom to another person, whom he settled in the same business under my nose. Being thus disabled from making punctual payments, my commodities spoiling, and my wife breaking her heart, I grew negligent and careless, took to drinking, and my affairs went to wreck. Being one day in liquor, and provoked by the fleers and taunts of the man who had set up against me, I struck him at his own door; upon which I was carried before the justice, who treated me with such insolence, that I became desperate, and not only abused him in the execution of his office, but also made an attempt to lay violent hands upon his person. You know, Sir, when a man is both drunk and desperate, he cannot be supposed to have any command of himself. I was sent hither to jail. My creditors immediately seized my effects; and, as they were not sufficient to discharge my debts, a statute of bankruptcy was taken out against me: so that here I must lie, until they think proper to sign my certificate,[1] or the parliament shall please to pass an act for the relief of insolvent debtors.'

The next person who presented himself in the croud of accusers was a meagre figure, with a green apron, who told the knight that he had kept a public house in town for a dozen years, and enjoyed a good trade, which was in a great measure owing to a skittle-ground, in which the best people of the place diverted themselves occasionally: that justice Gobble, being disobliged at his refusing to part with a gelding which he had bred for his own use, first of all shut up the skittle-ground; but finding the publican still kept his house open, he took care that he should be deprived of his licence, on pretence that the number of ale-houses was too great, and that this man had been bred to another employment. The poor publican, being thus deprived of his bread, was obliged to try the stay-making business, to which he had served an apprenticeship: but being very ill-qualified for this profession, he soon fell to decay, and contracted debts, in consequence of which he was now in prison, where he had no other support but what arose from the labour of his wife, who had gone to service.

The next prisoner who preferred his complaint against the un-righteous judge was a poacher, at whose practices justice Gobble had for some years connived, so as even to screen him from punishment, in consideration of being supplied with game gratis, till at length he was disappointed by accident. His lady had invited guests to an entertainment, and bespoke a hare, which the poacher undertook to furnish. He laid his snares accordingly over night; but they were discovered, and taken away by the game-keeper of the gentleman to whom the ground belonged. All the excuses the poacher could make, proved ineffectual in appeasing the resentment of the justice and his wife, at being thus disconcerted. Measures were taken to detect the delinquent in the exercise of his illicit occupation: he was committed to safe custody; and his wife with five bantlings, was passed to her husband's settlement in a different part of the country.

A stout squat fellow, rattling with chains, had just taken up the ball of accusation, when Sir Launcelot was startled with the appearance of a woman, whose looks and equipage indicated the most piteous distress. She seemed to be turned of the middle age, was of a lofty carriage, tall, thin, weather-beaten, and wretchedly attired: her eyes were inflamed with weeping, and her looks displayed that wildness and peculiarity which denote distraction. Advancing to Sir Launcelot, she fell upon her knees, and clasping her hands together, uttered the following rhapsody in the most vehement tone of affliction:

'Thrice potent, generous, and august emperor, here let my knees cleave to the earth, until thou shalt do me justice on that inhuman caitiff Gobble. Let him disgorge my substance which he hath devoured: let him restore to my widowed arms my child, my boy, the delight of my eyes, the prop of my life, the staff of my sustenance, whom he hath torn from my embrace, stolen, betrayed, sent into captivity, and murdered!—Behold these bleeding wounds upon his lovely breast! see how they mangle his lifeless coarse! Horrour! give me my child, barbarians! his head shall lie upon his Suky's bosom—she will embalm him with her tears.—Ha! plunge him in the deep! shall my boy then float in a watry tomb!—Justice, most mighty emperor! justice upon the villain who hath ruined us all!—May heaven's dreadful vengeance overtake him! may the keen storm of adversity strip him of all his leaves and fruit! may peace forsake his mind, and rest be banished from his pillow, so that all his days shall be filled with reproach and sorrow; and all his nights be haunted with horrour and remorse! may he be stung by jealousy without cause, and maddened by revenge without the means of execution! may all his offspring be blighted and consumed, like the mildewed ears of corn, except one that shall grow up to curse his old age, and bring his hoary head with sorrow to the grave, as he himself has proved a curse to me and mine!'

The rest of the prisoners, perceiving the knight extremely shocked at her misery and horrid imprecation, removed her by force from his presence, and conveyed her to another room; while our adventurer underwent a violent agitation, and could not for some minutes compose himself so well as to inquire into the nature of this wretched creature's calamity. The shop-keeper, of whom he demanded this satisfaction, gave him to understand that she was born a gentlewoman, and had been well educated: that she married a curate, who did not long survive his nuptials; and afterwards became the wife of one Oakely, a farmer, in opulent circumstances: that, after twenty years cohabitation with her husband, he sustained such losses by the distemper among the cattle, as he could not repair; and that this reverse of fortune was supposed to have hastened his death: that the widow, being a woman of spirit, determined to keep up and manage the farm, with the assistance of an only son, a very promising youth, who was already contracted in marriage with the daughter of another wealthy farmer. Thus the mother had a fair prospect of retrieving the affairs of her family, when all her hopes were dashed and destroyed by a ridiculous pique which Mrs. Gobble conceived against the young farmer's sweet-heart, Mrs. Susan Sedgemoor. This young woman chancing to be at a country assembly, where the grave-digger of the parish acted as master of the ceremonies, was called out to dance before miss Gobble, who happened to be there present also with her mother. The circumstance was construed into an unpardonable affront by the justice's lady, who abused the director, in the most opprobrious terms, for his insolence and ill-manners; and, retiring in a storm of passion, vowed revenge against the saucy minx who had presumed to vie in gentility with miss Gobble. The justice entered into her resentment. The grave-digger lost his place; and Suky's lover, young Oakely, was pressed for a soldier. Before his mother could take any steps for his discharge, he was hurried away to the East Indies, by the industry and contrivance of the justice.

Poor Suky wept and pined until she fell into a consumption. The forlorn widow, being thus deprived of her son, was overwhelmed with grief to such a degree, that she could no longer manage her concerns. Every thing went backward: she ran in arrears with her landlord, and the prospect of bankruptcy aggravated her affliction, while it added to her incapacity. In the midst of these disastrous circumstances, news arrived that her son Greaves had lost his life in a sea-engagement with the enemy; and these tidings almost instantly deprived her of her reason. Then the landlord seized for his rent; and she was arrested at the suit of justice Gobble, who had bought up one of her debts, in order to distress her, and now pretended that her madness was feigned.

When the name of Greaves was mentioned our adventurer started, and changed colour; and, now the story was ended, asked, with marks of eager emotion, if the name of the woman's first husband was not Wilford. When the prisoner answered in the affirmative, he rose up, and striking his breast, 'Good heaven! (cried he) the very woman who watched over my infancy, and even nourished me with her milk!—She was my mother's humble friend.—Alas! poor Dorothy! how would your old mistress grieve to see her favourite in this miserable condition!' While he pronounced these words, to the astonishment of the hearers, a tear stole softly down each cheek. Then he desired to know if the poor lunatic had any intervals of reason; and was given to understand, that she was always quiet, and generally supposed to have the use of her senses, except when she was disturbed by some extraordinary noise, or when any person touched upon her misfortune, or mentioned the name of her oppressor, in all which cases she started out into extravagance and frenzy. They likewise imputed great part of her disorder to the want of quiet, proper food, and necessaries, with which she was but poorly supplied by the cold hand of chance charity. Our adventurer was exceedingly affected by the distress of this woman, whom he resolved to relieve; and in proportion as his commiseration was excited, his resentment rose against the miscreant, who seemed to have insinuated himself into the commission of the peace on purpose to harrass and oppress his fellow-creatures. Thus animated, he entered into consultation with Mr. Thomas Clarke concerning the steps he should take, first for their deliverance, and then for prosecuting and punishing the justice. In result of this conference, the knight called aloud for the jaylor, and demanded to see a copy of his commitment, that he might know the cause of his imprisonment, and offer bail; or, in case that should be refused, move for a writ of Habeas Corpus. The jaylor told him the copy of the writ should be forthcoming; but after he had waited some time, and repeated the demand before witnesses, it was not yet produced. Mr. Clarke then, in a solemn tone, gave the jaylor to understand, that an officer, refusing to deliver a true copy of the commitment warrant, was liable to the forfeiture of one hundred pounds for the first offence; and for the second to a forfeiture of twice that sum, besides being disabled from executing his office.

Indeed, it was no easy matter to comply with Sir Launcelot's demand; for no warrant had been granted, nor was it now in the power of the justice to remedy this defect, as Mr. Ferret had taken himself away privately, without having communicated the name and designation of the prisoner. A circumstance the more mortifying to the jaylor, as he perceived the extraordinary respect which Mr. Clarke and the captain payed to the knight, and was now fully convinced that he would be dealt with according to law. Disordered with these reflections, he imparted them to the justice, who had in vain caused search to be made for Ferret, and was now extremely well inclined to set the knight and his friends at liberty, though he did not at all suspect the quality and importance of our adventurer. He could not, however, resist the temptation of displaying the authority of his office; and therefore ordered the prisoners to be brought before his tribunal, that, in the capacity of a magistrate, he might give them a severe reproof, and proper caution, with regard to their future behaviour.

They were accordingly led thro' the street in procession, guarded by the constable and his gang, followed by Crabshaw, who had by this time been released from the stocks, and surrounded by a croud of people, attracted by curiosity. When they arrived at the justice's house, they were detained for some time in the passage: then a voice was heard, commanding the constable to bring in the prisoners, and they were introduced to the hall of audience, where Mr. Gobble sat in judgment, with a crimson velvet night cap on his head; and on his right hand appeared his lady, puffed up with the pride and insolence of her husband's office, fat, frowzy, and not over-clean, well stricken in years, without the least vestige of an agreeable feature, having a rubicond nose, ferret eyes, and imperious aspect.

The justice himself was a little, affected, pert prig, who endeavoured to solemnize his countenance by assuming an air of consequence, in which pride, impudence, and folly were strangely blended. He aspired at nothing so much as the character of an able spokesman; and took all opportunities of holding forth at vestry and quarter-sessions,[1] as well as in the administration of his office in private. He would not, therefore, let slip this occasion of exciting the admiration of his hearers, and, in an authoritative tone, thus addressed our adventurer:

'The laws of this land has provided—I says, as how provision is made by the laws of this here land, in reverence to delinquems and manefactors, whereby the king's peace is upholden by we magistrates, who represents his majesty's person, better than in e'er a contagious nation under the sun: but, howsoemever, that there king's peace, and this here magistrate's authority, cannot be adequably and identically upheld, if so be as how criminals escapes unpunished. Now, friend, you must be confidentious in your own mind, as you are a notorious criminal, who have trespassed again the laws on divers occasions and importunities; if I had a mind to exercise the rigour of the law, according to the authority wherewith I am wested, you and your companions in iniquity would be sewerely punished by the statue: but we magistrates has a power to litigate the sewerity of justice, and so I am contented that you shoulds be mercifully dealt withal, and even dismissed.'

To this harangue the knight replied, with solemn and deliberate accent, 'If I understand your meaning aright, I am accused of being a notorious criminal; but nevertheless you are contented to let me escape with impunity. If I am a notorious criminal, it is the duty of you, as a magistrate, to bring me to condign punishment; and if you allow a criminal to escape unpunished, you are not only unworthy of a place in the commission, but become accessory to his guilt, and, to all intents and purposes, *socius criminis*.[2] With respect to your proffered mercy, I shall decline the favour; nor do I deserve any indulgence at your hands: for, depend upon it, I shall shew no mercy to you, in the steps I intend to take for bringing you to justice. I understand that you have been long hackneyed in the ways of oppression, and I have seen some living monuments of your inhumanity—of that hereafter. I myself have been detained in prison, without cause assigned. I have been treated with indignity, and insulted by jaylors and constables, led thro' the streets like a felon, as a spectacle to the multitude, obliged to dance attendance in your passage, and afterwards branded with the name of a notorious criminal.—I now demand to see the information in consequence of which I was detained in prison, the copy of the warrant of commitment or detainer, and the face of the person by whom I was accused. I insist upon a compliance with these demands, as the privileges of a British subject; and if it is refused, I shall seek redress before a higher tribunal.'

The justice seemed to be not a little disturbed at this peremptory declaration; which, however, had no other effect upon his wife, but that of enraging her choler and inflaming her countenance. 'Sirrah! sirrah! (cried she) do you dares to insult a worshipful magistrate on the bench?—Can you deny that you are a vagram, and a dilatory sort of a person? Han't the man with the satchel made an affidavy of it?—If I was my husband, I'd lay you fast by the heels for your resumption, and ferk you with a primineery[1] into the bargain, unless you could give a better account of yourself—I would.'

Gobble, encouraged by this fillip, resumed his petulance, and proceeded in this manner:—'Heark ye, friend, I might, as Mrs. Gobble very justly observes, trounce you for your audacious behaviour; but I scorn to take such advantages: howsomever, I shall make you give an account of yourself and your companions; for I believes as how you are all in a gang, and all in a story, and perhaps you may be found one day all in a cord.—What are you, friend? What is your station and degree?' 'I am a gentleman,' replied the knight. 'Ay, that is English for a sorry fellow, (said the justice.) Every idle vagabond, who has neither home nor habitation, trade nor profession, designs himself a gentleman. But I must know how you live?' 'Upon my means,' 'What are your means?' 'My estate.' 'Whence doth it arise?' 'From inheritance.' 'Your estate lies in brass, and that you have inherited from nature: but do you inherit lands and tenements?' 'Yes.' 'But they are neither here nor there, I doubt.—Come, come, friend, I shall bring you about presently.' Here the examination was interrupted by the arrival of Mr. Fillet the surgeon, who chancing to pass, and seeing a croud about the door, went in to satisfy his curiosity.

CHAPTER XII

Which shews there are more ways to kill a dog than hanging

MR. FILLET no sooner appeared in the judgment-chamber of justice Gobble than captain Crowe, seizing him by the hand, exclaimed, 'Body o'me! Doctor, thou'rt come up in the nick of time to lend us a hand in putting about.—We're a little in the stays here —but howsomever we've got a good pilot, who knows the coast, and can weather the point, as the saying is. As for the enemy's vessel, she has had a shot or two already a-thwart her fore-foot:[1] the next, I do suppose, will strike the hull, and then you'll see her taken all a-back.' The doctor, who perfectly understood his dialect, assured him he might depend upon his assistance; and advancing to the knight, accosted him in these words: 'Sir Launcelot Greaves, your most humble servant.—When I saw a croud at the door, I little thought of finding you within, treated with such indignity.— Yet, I can't help being pleased with an opportunity of proving the esteem and veneration I have for your person and character:—you will do me a particular pleasure in commanding my best services.'

Our adventurer thanked him for this instance of his friendship, which he told him he would use without hesitation; and desired he would procure immediate bail for him and his two friends, who had been imprisoned, contrary to law, without any cause assigned. During this short dialogue, the justice, who had heard of Sir Launcelot's family and fortune, though an utter stranger to his person, was seized with such pangs of terror and compunction, as a groveling mind may be supposed to have felt in such circumstances; and they seemed to produce the same unsavoury effects that are so humorously delineated by the inimitable Hogarth in the print of Felix on his tribunal, done in the Dutch stile.[2] Nevertheless, seeing Fillet retire to execute the knight's commands, he recollected himself so far as to tell the prisoners there was no occasion to give themselves any further trouble; for he would release them without bail or mainprize.[3] Then discarding all the insolence from his features, and assuming an aspect of the most humble adulation, he begged the knight ten thousand pardons for the freedoms he had taken, which were intirely owing to his ignorance of Sir Launcelot's quality. 'Yes, I'll assure you, Sir (said the wife), my husband would have bit off his tongue, rather than say black is the white of your eye, if so be he had known your capacity.—Thank God, we have been used to deal with gentle-folks, and many's the good pound we have lost by them; but what of that? Sure we know how to behave to our betters. Mr. Gobble, thanks be to God, can defy the whole world to prove that he ever said an uncivil word, or did a rude thing to a gentleman, knowing him to be a person of fortune. Indeed, as to your poor gentry and riff-raff, your tag, rag, and bobtail, or such vulgar scoundrelly people, he has always behaved like a magistrate, and treated them with the rigger of authority.' 'In other words (said the knight), he has tyrannized over the poor, and connived at the vices of the rich: your husband is little obliged to you for this confession, woman.' 'Woman! (cried Mrs. Gobble, impurpled with wrath, and fixing her hands on her sides by way of defiance) I scorn your words—Marry come up, woman! quotha: no more a woman than your worship.' Then bursting into tears, 'Husband (continued she), if you had the soul of a louse, you would not suffer me to be abused at this rate: you would not sit still on the bench, and hear your spouse called such contemptible epitaphs.—Who cares for his title and his knightship? You and I, husband, knew a taylor that was made a knight: but, thank God, I have noblemen to stand by me, with their privilegs and beroguetifs.'

At this instant Mr. Fillet returned with his friend, a practitioner in the law, who freely offered to join in bailing our adventurer, and the other two prisoners, for any sum that should be required. The justice, perceiving the affair began to grow more and more serious, declared that he would discharge the warrants, and dismiss the prisoners. Here Mr. Clarke interposing, observed, that against the knight no warrant had been granted, nor any information sworn to; consequently, as the justice had not complied with the form of pro-ceeding directed by statute, the imprisonment was *coram non judice*,[1] and void. 'Right, Sir (said the other lawyer), if a justice commits a felon for trial, without binding over the prosecutor to the assizes, he shall be fined.'—'And again (cried Clarke), if a justice issues a warrant for commitment, where there is no accusa-tion, action will lie against the justice.' 'Moreover (replied the stranger), if a justice of peace is guilty of any misdemeanour in his office, information lies against him in *Banco Regis*,[2] where he shall be punished by fine and imprisonment.' 'And besides (resumed the accurate Tom), the same court will grant an information against a justice of peace, on motion, for sending even a servant to the house of correction, or common jail, without sufficient cause.' 'True! (exclaimed the other limb of the law) and, for contempt of law, attachment may be had against justices of peace in *Banco Regis*. A justice of peace was fined a thousand marks for corrupt practices.' With these words advancing to Mr. Clarke, he shook him by the hand, with the appellation of Brother, saying, 'I doubt the justice has got into a cursed hovel.' Mr. Gobble himself seemed to be of the same opinion. He changed colour several times during the remarks which the lawyers had made; and now, declaring that the gentlemen were at liberty, begged, in the most humble phrase, that the company would eat a bit of mutton with him, and after dinner the affair might be amicably compromised. To this proposal our adventurer replied, in a grave and resolute tone, 'If your acting in the commission as a justice of the peace concerned my own particular only, perhaps I should wave any further inquiry, and resent your insolence no other way but by silent contempt. If I thought the errors of your administration proceeded from a good intention, defeated by want of understanding, I should pity your ignorance, and, in compassion, advise you to desist from acting a part for which you are so ill qualified: but the preposterous conduct of such a man deeply affects the interest of the community, especially that part of it which, from its helpless situation, is the more intitled to our protection and assistance. I am moreover convinced, that your misconduct is not so much the consequence of an uninformed head, as the poisonous issue of a malignant heart, devoid of humanity, inflamed with pride, and rankling with revenge. The common prison of this little town is filled with the miserable objects of your cruelty and oppression. Instead of protecting the helpless, restraining the hands of violence, preserving the public tranquillity, and acting as a father to the poor, according to the intent and meaning of that institution of which you are an unworthy member, you have distressed the widow and the orphan, given a loose to all the insolence of office, embroiled your neighbours by fomenting suits and animosities, and played the tyrant among the indigent and forlorn. You have abused the authority with which you were invested, intailed a reproach upon your office, and, instead of being revered as a blessing, you are detested as a curse among your fellow-creatures. This, indeed, is generally the case of low fellows, who are thrust into the magistracy without sentiment, education, or capacity. Among other instances of your iniquity, there is now in prison an unhappy woman, infinitely your superior in the advantages of birth, sense, and education, whom you have, even without provocation, persecuted to ruin and distraction, after having illegally and inhumanly kidnapped her only child, and exposed him to violent death in a foreign land. Ah caitiff! if you were to forego all the comforts of life, distribute your means among the poor, and do the severest penance that ever priestcraft prescribed for the rest of your days, you could not attone for the ruin of that hapless family; a family through whose sides you cruelly and perfidiously stabbed the heart of an innocent young woman, to gratify the pride and diabolical malice of that wretched low-bred woman, who now sits at your right hand as the associate of your power and presumption. Oh! if such a despicable reptile shall annoy mankind with impunity, if such a contemptible miscreant shall have it in his power to do such deeds of inhumanity and oppression, what avails the law? Where is our admired constitution, the freedom, the security of the subject, the boasted humanity of the British nation? Sacred Heaven! if there was no human institution to take cognizance of such atrocious crimes, I would listen to the dictates of eternal Justice, and, arming myself with the right of nature, exterminate such villains from the face of the earth!'

These last words he pronounced in such a strain, while his eyes lightened with indignation, that Gobble and his wife underwent the most violent agitation; the constable's teeth chattered in his head, the jailer trembled, and the whole audience was overwhelmed with consternation.

After a short pause, Sir Launcelot proceeded in a milder strain: 'Thank Heaven, the laws of this country have exempted me from the disagreeable task of such an execution. To them we shall have immediate recourse, in three separate actions against you for false imprisonment; and any other person who has been injured by your arbitrary and wicked proceedings, in me shall find a warm protector, until you shall be expunged from the commission with disgrace, and have made such retaliation as your circumstances will allow for the wrongs you have done the community.'

In order to compleat the mortification and terror of the justice, the lawyer, whose name was Fenton, declared, that, to his certain knowledge, these actions would be reinforced with divers prosecutions for corrupt practices, which had lain dormant until some person of courage and influence should take the lead against justice Gobble, who was the more dreaded as he acted under the patronage of lord Sharpington. By this time fear had deprived the justice and his help-mate of the faculty of speech. They were indeed almost petrified with dismay, and made no effort to speak, when Mr. Fillet, in the rear of the knight, as he retired with his company, took his leave of them in these words:

'And now, Mr. Justice, to dinner with what appetite you may.' Our adventurer, though warmly invited to Mr. Fenton's house, repaired to a public inn, where he thought he should be more at his ease, fully determined to punish and depose Gobble from his magistracy, to effect a general jail-delivery of all the debtors whom he had found in confinement; and, in particular, to rescue poor Mrs. Oakley from the miserable circumstances in which she was involved.

In the mean time, he insisted upon entertaining his friends at dinner, during which many sallies of sea-wit and good-humour passed between captain Crowe and doctor Fillet, which last had just returned from a neighbouring village, whither he was summoned to fish a man's yard-arm, which had snapt in the slings.[1] Their enjoyment, however, was suddenly interrupted by a loud scream from the kitchen, whither Sir Launcelot immediately sprung, with equal eagerness and agility. There he saw the landlady, who was a woman in years, embracing a man dressed in a sailor's jacket, while she exclaimed, 'It is thy own flesh and blood, so sure as I'm a living soul.—Ah! poor Greaves, poor Greaves, many a poor heart has grieved for thee!' To this salutation the youth replied, 'I'm sorry for that, mistress.—How does poor mother? how does Sukey Sedgemore?'

The good woman of the house could not help shedding tears at these interrogations; while Sir Launcelot, interposing, said, not without emotion, 'I perceive you are the son of Mrs. Oakely.— Your mother is in a bad state of health; but in me you will find a real parent.' Perceiving that the young man eyed him with astonishment, he gave him to understand, that his name was Launcelot Greaves.

Oakely no sooner heard these words pronounced, than he fell upon his knees, and seizing the knight's hand, kissed it eagerly, crying, 'God for ever bless your honour: I am your name-son, sure enough—but what of that? I can earn my bread, without being beholden to any man.'

When the knight raised him up, he turned to the woman of the house, saying, 'I want to see mother. I'm afraid as how times are hard with her; and I have saved some money for her use.' This instance of filial duty brought tears into the eyes of our adventurer, who assured him his mother should be carefully attended, and want for nothing: but that it would be very improper to see her at present, as the surprize might shock her too much, considering that she believed him dead. 'Ey, indeed, (cried the landlady) we were all of the same opinion, being as the report went that poor Greaves Oakely was killed in battle.' 'Lord, mistress, (said Oakely) there wa'n't a word of truth in it, I'll assure you.—What, d'ye think I'd tell a lie about the matter? Hurt I was, to be sure; but that don't signify: we gave 'em as good as they brought, and so parted.— Well, if so be I can't see mother, I'll go and have some chat with Sukey.—What d'ye look so glum for? she an't married, is she?' 'No, no, (replied the woman) not married; but almost heart-broken. Since thou wast gone, she has done nothing but sighed, and wept, and pined herself into a decay. I'm afraid thou ha'st come home too late to save her life.'

Oakely's heart was not proof against this information. Bursting into tears, he exclaimed, 'O my dear, sweet, gentle Sukey! Have I then lived to be the death of her whom I loved more than the whole world!' He would have gone instantly to her father's house; but was restrained by the knight and his company, who had now joined him in the kitchen. The young man was seated at table, and gave them to understand, that the ship to which he belonged having arrived in England, he was indulged with a month's leave to see his relations; and that he had received about fifty pounds in wages and prize-money.[1] After dinner, just as they began to deliberate upon the measures to be taken against Gobble, that gentleman arrived at the inn, and humbly craved admittance. Fillet, struck with a sudden idea, retired into another apartment with the young farmer; while the justice, being admitted to the company, declared that he came to propose terms of accommodation. He accordingly offered to ask pardon of Sir Launcelot in the public papers, and pay fifty pounds to the poor of the parish, as an attonement for his mis-behaviour, provided the knight and his friends would grant him a general release. Our adventurer told him, he would willingly wave all personal concessions; but, as the case concerned the community, he insisted upon his leaving off acting in the commission, and making satisfaction to the parties he had injured and oppressed. This declaration introduced a discussion, in the course of which the justice's petulance began to revive; when Fillet, entering the room, told them he had a reconciling measure to propose, if Mr. Gobble would for a few minutes withdraw. He rose up immediately, and was shewn into the room which Fillet had prepared for his reception. While he sat musing on this untoward adventure, so big with disgrace and disappointment, young Oakely, according to the instructions he had received, appeared all at once before him, pointing to a ghastly wound, which the doctor had painted on his forehead. The apparition no sooner presented itself to the eyes of Gobble, than, taking it for granted it was the spirit of the young farmer whose death he had occasioned, he roared aloud, 'Lord have mercy upon us!' and fell insensible on the floor. There being found by the company, to whom Fillet had communicated his contrivance, he was conveyed to bed, where he lay some time before he recovered the perfect use of his senses. Then he earnestly desired to see the knight, and assured him he was ready to comply with his terms, inasmuch as he believed he had not long to live. Advantage was immediately taken of this salutary disposition. He bound himself not to act as a justice of the peace, in any part of Great Britain, under the penalty of five thousand pounds. He burned Mrs. Oakely's note; payed the debts of the shopkeeper; undertook to compound those of the publican, and to settle him again in business; and, finally, discharged them all from prison, paying the dues[1] out of his own pocket. These steps being taken with peculiar eagerness, he was removed to his own house, where he assured his wife he had seen a vision that prognosticated his death; and had immediate recourse to the curate of the parish for spiritual consolation.

The most interesting part of the talk that now remained, was to make the widow Oakely acquainted with her good fortune, in such a manner as might least disturb her spirits, already but too much discomposed. For this purpose they chose the landlady, who, after having received proper directions how to regulate her conduct, visited her in prison that same evening. Finding her quite calm, and her reflection perfectly restored, she began with exhorting her to put her trust in Providence, which would never forsake the cause of the injured widow and fatherless: she promised to assist and befriend her on all occasions, as far as her abilities would reach: she gradually turned the conversation upon the family of the Greaves; and by degrees informed her, that Sir Launcelot, having learned her situation, was determined to extricate her from all her troubles. Perceiving her astonished, and deeply affected at this intimation, she artfully shifted the discourse, recommended resignation to the Divine Will, and observed that this circumstance seemed to be an earnest of further happiness. 'O! I'm incapable of receiving more! (cried the disconsolate widow, with streaming eyes)—Yet I ought not to be surprised at any blessing that flows from that quarter.—The family of Greaves were always virtuous, humane, and benevolent.—This young gentleman's mother was my dear lady and benefactress:—he himself was suckled at these breasts.—O! he was the sweetest, comliest, best conditioned babe! —I loved not my own Greaves with greater affection—but he, alas! is now no more!' 'Have patience, good neighbour, (said the land-lady of the White Hart) that is more than you have any right to affirm.—All that you know of the matter is by common report, and common report is commonly false: besides, I can tell you I have seen a list of the men that were killed in admiral P——'s[1] ship, when he fought the French in the East Indies, and your son was not in the number.' To this intimation she replied, after a consider-able pause, 'Don't, my good neighbour, don't feed me with false hope.—My poor Greaves too certainly perished in a foreign land— yet he is happy:—had he lived to see me in this condition, grief would soon have put a period to his days.' 'I tell you then, (cried the visitant) he is not dead. I have seen a letter that mentions his being well since the battle. You shall come along with me—you are no longer a prisoner; but shall live at my house comfortably, till your affairs are settled to your wish.'

The poor widow followed her in silent astonishment, and was immediately accommodated with necessaries.

Next morning her hostess proceeded with her in the same cautious manner, until she was assured that her son had returned. Being duly prepared, she was blessed with a sight of poor Greaves, and fainted away in his arms.

We shall not dwell upon this tender scene, because it is but of a secondary concern in the history of our knight-errant: let it suffice

to say, their mutual happiness was unspeakable. She was afterwards visited by Sir Launcelot, whom she no sooner beheld, than,
springing forwards with all the eagerness of maternal affection, she
clasped him to her breast, crying, 'My dear child! my Launcelot!
my pride! my darling! my kind benefactor! This is not the first
time I have hugged you in these arms! O! you are the very image of
Sir Everhard in his youth; but you have got the eyes, the complexion, the sweetness, and complacency of my dear and ever-
honoured lady.' This was not the strain of hireling praise; but the
genuine tribute of esteem and admiration. As such, it could not but
be agreeable to our hero, who undertook to procure Oakely's discharge, and settle him in a comfortable farm on his own estate.

In the mean time, Greaves went with a heavy heart to the house
of farmer Sedgemoor, where he found Sukey, who had been prepared for his reception, in a transport of joy, though very weak,
and greatly emaciated. Nevertheless, the return of her sweetheart
had such an happy effect on her constitution, that in a few weeks
her health was perfectly restored.

This adventure of our knight was crowned with every happy
circumstance that could give pleasure to a generous mind. The
prisoners were released, and reinstated in their former occupations.
The justice performed his articles from fear; and afterwards turned
over a new leaf from remorse. Young Oakely was married to Sukey,
with whom he received a considerable portion. The new-married
couple found a farm ready stocked for them on the knight's estate;
and the mother enjoyed a happy retreat in the character of the
housekeeper at Greavesbury-hall.

CHAPTER XIII

In which our Knight is tantalized with a transient glimpse of felicity

THE success of our adventurer, which we have particularized in
the last chapter, could not fail of inhancing his character, not only
among those who knew him, but also among the people of the town
to whom he was an utter stranger. The populace surrounded the
house, and testified their approbation in loud huzzas. Captain
Crowe was more than ever inspired with veneration for his ad-

mired patron, and more than ever determined to pursue his foot-steps in the road of chivalry. Fillet, and his friend the lawyer, could not help conceiving an affection, and even a profound esteem, for the exalted virtue, the person, and the accomplishments of the knight, dashed as they were with a mixture of extravagance and insanity. Even Sir Launcelot himself was elevated to an extra-ordinary degree of self-complacency on the fortunate issue of his adventure, and became more and more persuaded that a knight-errant's profession might be exercised, even in England, to the advantage of the community. The only person of the company who seemed unanimated with the general satisfaction was Mr. Thomas Clarke. He had, not without good reason, laid it down as a maxim, that knight-errantry and madness were synonimous terms; and that madness, though exhibited in the most advantageous and agreeable light, could not change its nature, but must continue a perversion of sense to the end of the chapter. He perceived the additional impression which the brain of his uncle had sustained, from the happy manner in which the benevolence of Sir Launcelot had so lately operated; and began to fear it would be, in a little time, quite necessary to have recourse to a commission of lunacy, which might not only disgrace the family of the Crowes, but also tend to invalidate the settlement which the captain had already made in favour of our young lawyer.

Perplexed with these cogitations, Mr. Clarke appealed to our adventurer's own reflection. He expatiated upon the bad conse-quences that would attend his uncle's perseverance in the execution of a scheme so foreign to his faculties; and intreated him, for the love of God, to divert him from his purpose, either by arguments or authority; as, of all mankind, the knight alone had gained such an ascendency over his spirit, that he would listen to his exhorta-tions with respect and submission. Our adventurer was not so mad, but that he saw and owned the rationality of these remarks. He readily undertook to employ all his influence with Crowe to dis-suade him from his extravagant design; and seized the first oppor-tunity of being alone with the captain, to signify his sentiments on this subject. 'Captain Crowe (said he), you are then determined to proceed in the course of knight-errantry?' 'I am, (replied the seaman) with God's help, d'ye see, and the assistance of wind and weather—' 'What, do'st thou talk of wind and weather! (cried the knight, in an elevated tone of affected transport:) without the help of Heaven, indeed, we are all vanity, imbecility, weakness, and wretchedness; but if thou art resolved to embrace the life of an errant, let me not hear thee so much as whisper a doubt, a wish, an hope, or sentiment, with respect to any other obstacle, which wind or weather, fire or water, sword or famine, danger or disappointment, may throw in the way of thy career.—When the duty of thy profession calls, thou must singly rush upon innumerable hosts of armed men: thou must storm the breach in the mouth of batteries loaded with death and destruction, while, every step thou movest, thou art exposed to the horrible explosion of subterranean mines, which, being sprung, will whirl thee aloft in air, a mangled corse, to feed the fowls of heaven. Thou must leap into the abyss of dismal caves and caverns, replete with poisonous toads and hissing serpents. Thou must plunge into seas of burning sulphur: thou must launch upon the ocean in a crazy bark,[1] when the foaming billows roll mountain high, when the lightning flashes, the thunder roars, and the howling tempest blows, as if it would commix the jarring elements of air and water, earth and fire, and reduce all nature to the original anarchy of chaos. Thus involved, thou must turn thy prow full against the fury of the storm, and stem the boisterous surge to thy destined port, though at the distance of a thousand leagues—thou must—'

'Avast, avast, brother, (exclaimed the impatient Crowe) you've got into the high latitudes, d'ye see:—if so be as you spank[2] it away at that rate, adad, I can't continue in tow—we must cast off the rope, or 'ware timbers.[3]—As for your 'osts and breeches, and hurling aloft, d'ye see, your caves and caverns, whistling tuoads and serpents, burning brimstone and foaming billows, we must take our hap;[4] I value 'em not a rotten ratline:[5]—but, as for sailing in the wind's eye, brother, you must give me leave—no offence, I hope—I pretend to be a thoroughbred seaman, d'ye see—and I'll be damned if you, or e'er an arrant that broke biscuit, ever sailed in a three-mast vessel within five points of the wind, allowing for variation and lee-way.—No, no, brother, none of your tricks upon travellers[6]—I a'n't now to learn my compass.' 'Tricks! (cried the knight, starting up, and laying his hand on the pummel of his sword) what! suspect my honour!'

Crowe, supposing him to be really incensed, interrupted him with great earnestness, saying, 'Nay, don't—what a-pize![7]—addsbunt-lines![8]—I did n't go to give you the lie, brother, smite my limbs: I only said as how to sail in the wind's eye was impossible—' 'And I say unto thee, (resumed the knight) nothing is impossible to a true knight-errant, inspired and animated by love.' 'And I say unto thee, (hollowed Crowe) if so be as how love pretends to turn his hawse-holes to the wind, he's no seaman, d'ye see, but a snotty-nose lubberly boy, that knows not a cat from a capstan—a-don't.' 'He that does not believe that love is an infallible pilot, must not embark upon the voyage of chivalry; for, next to the protection of Heaven, it is from love that the knight derives all his prowess and glory. The bare name of his mistress invigorates his arm: the remembrance of her beauty infuses in his breast the most heroic sentiments of courage, while the idea of her chastity hedges him round like a charm, and renders him invulnerable to the sword of his antagonist. A knight without a mistress is a meer non-entity, or at least a monster in nature, a pilot without compass, a ship without rudder, and must be driven to and fro upon the waves of discomfiture and disgrace.' 'An that be all, (replied the sailor) I told you before as how I've got a sweetheart, as true a hearted girl as ever swung in canvas.—What tho'f she may have started a hoop in rolling[1]—that signifies nothing—I'll warrant her tight as a nut-shell.'[2] 'She must, in your opinion, be a paragon either of beauty or virtue. Now, as you have given up the last, you must uphold her charms unequalled, and her person without a parallel.' 'I do, I do uphold she will sail upon a parallel,[3] as well as e'er a frigate that was rigged to the northward of fifty.'[4] 'At that rate she must rival the attractions of her whom I adore; but that, I say, is impossible: the perfections of my Aurelia are altogether supernatural; and as two suns cannot shine together in the same sphere with equal splendour, so I affirm, and will prove with my body, that your mistress, in comparison with mine, is as a glow-worm to the meridian sun, a rush-light to the full moon, or a stale mackarel's eye to a pearl of orient.' 'Hearkye, brother, you might give good words, however: an we once fall a-jawing, d'ye see, I can heave out as much bilge-water as another; and since you besmear my sweetheart Besselia, I can as well bedaub your mistress Aurelia, whom I value no more than old junk, pork-slush, or stinking stockfish.' 'Enough, enough—such blasphemy shall not pass unchastised. In consideration of our having fed from the same table, and maintained together a friendly tho' short intercourse, I will not demand the combat before you are duly prepared. Proceed to the first great town where you can be furnished with horse and harnessing, with arms offensive and defensive: provide a trusty squire, assume a motto and device—declare yourself a son of chivalry; and proclaim the excellence of her who rules your heart. I shall fetch a compass; and wheresoever we may chance to meet, let us engage with equal arms in mortal combat, that shall decide and determine this dispute.'

So saying, our adventurer stalked with great solemnity into another apartment; while Crowe, being sufficiently irritated, snapped his fingers in token of defiance. Honest Crowe thought himself scurvily used by a man whom he had cultivated with such humility of veneration; and, after an incoherent ejaculation of sea-oaths, went in quest of his nephew, in order to make him acquainted with this unlucky transaction.

In the mean time Sir Launcelot, having ordered supper, retired into his own chamber, and gave a loose to the most tender emotions of his heart. He recollected all the fond ideas which had been excited in the course of his correspondence with the charming Aurelia. He remembered, with horror, the cruel letter he had received from that young lady, containing a formal renunciation of his attachment, so unsuitable to the whole tenour of her character and conduct. He resolved the late adventure of the coach, and the declaration of Mr. Clarke, with equal eagerness and astonishment; and was seized with the most ardent desire of unravelling a mystery so interesting to the predominant passion of his heart.—All these mingled considerations produced a kind of ferment in the œconomy of his mind, which subsided into a profound reverie, compounded of hope and perplexity.

From this trance he was waked by the arrival of his squire, who entered the room with the blood trickling over his nose, and stood before him without speaking. When the knight asked whose livery was that he wore, he replied, ''Tis your honour's own livery:—I received it on your account, and hope as you will quit the score.' Then he proceeded to inform his master, that two officers of the army having come into the kitchen, insisted upon having for their supper the victuals which Sir Launcelot had bespoke; and that he, the squire, objecting to the proposal, one of them had seized the poker, and basted him with his own blood; that when he told them he belonged to a knight-errant, and threatened them with the vengeance of his master, they cursed and abused him, calling him

Sancho Panza, and such dogs names; and bade him tell his master Don Quicksot, that, if he made any noise, they would confine him to his cage,[1] and lie with his mistress Dulcinea.[2] 'To be sure, Sir, (said he) they thought you as great a nicompoop as your squire—trim tram, like master, like man;—but I hope as how you will give them a Rowland for their Oliver.'[3]

'Miscreant! (cried the knight) you have provoked the gentlemen with your impertinence, and they have chastised you as you deserve. I tell thee, Crabshaw, they have saved me the trouble of punishing thee with my own hands; and well it is for thee, sinner as thou art, that they themselves have performed the office: for, had they complained to me of thy insolence and rusticity, by Heaven! I would have made thee an example to all the impudent squires upon the face of the earth. Hence then, avaunt, caitif.—Let his majesty's officers, who are perhaps fatigued with hard duty in the service of their country, comfort themselves with the supper which was intended for me, and leave me undisturbed to my own meditations.'

Timothy did not require a repetition of this command, which he forthwith obeyed, growling within himself, that thenceforward he should let every cuckold wear his own horns; but he could not help entertaining some doubts with respect to the courage of his master, who, he supposed, was one of those Hectors who have their fighting days, but are not at all times equally prepared for the combat.

The knight, having taken a slight repast, retired to his repose; and had for some time enjoyed a very agreeable slumber, when he was startled by a knocking at his chamber-door. 'I beg your honour's pardon, (said the landlady) but there are two uncivil persons in the kitchen, who have well nigh turned my whole house topsy-turvy. Not contented with laying violent hands on your honour's supper, they want to be rude to two young ladies who are just arrived, and have called for a post-chaise to go on. They are afraid to open their chamber-door to get out—and the young lawyer is like to be murdered for taking the ladies part.'

Sir Launcelot, though he refused to take notice of the insult which had been offered to himself, no sooner heard of the distress of the ladies than he started up, huddled on his cloaths, and, girding his sword to his loins, advanced with a deliberate pace to the kitchen, where he perceived Thomas Clarke warmly engaged in altercation with a couple of young men dressed in regimentals, who, with a peculiar air of arrogance and ferocity, treated him with great insolence and contempt. Tom was endeavouring to persuade them, that, in the constitution of England, the military was always subservient to the civil power; and that their behaviour to a couple of helpless young women was not only unbecoming gentlemen, but expressly contrary to the law, inasmuch as they might be sued for an assault on an action of damages.

To this remonstrance the two heroes in red replied by a volley of dreadful oaths, intermingled with threats, which put the lawyer in some pain for his ears. While one thus endeavoured to intimidate honest Tom Clarke, the other thundered at the door of the apartment to which the ladies had retired, demanding admittance, but received no other answer than a loud shriek. Our adventurer advancing to this uncivil champion, accosted him thus in a grave and solemn tone: 'Assuredly I could not have believed, except upon the evidence of my own senses, that persons who have the appearance of gentlemen, and bear his majesty's honourable commission in the army, could behave so wide of the decorum due to society, of a proper respect to the laws, of that humanity which we owe to our fellow-creatures, and that delicate regard for the fair-sex, which ought to prevail in the breast of every gentleman, and which in particular dignifies the character of a soldier. To whom shall that weaker, tho' more amiable part of the creation, fly for protection, if they are insulted and outraged by those whose more immediate duty it is to afford them security and defence from injury and violence? What right have you, or any man upon earth, to excite riot in a public inn, which may be deemed a temple sacred to hospitality, to disturb the quiet of your fellow-guests, some of them perhaps exhausted by fatigue, some of them invaded by distemper, to interrupt the king's lieges in their course of journeying upon their lawful occasions? Above all, what motive but wanton barbarity could prompt you to violate the apartment, and terrify the tender hearts of two helpless young ladies travelling no doubt upon some cruel emergency, which compels them unattended to encounter in the night the dangers of the highway.'

'Hark ye, Don Bethlem,[1] (said the captain, strutting up and cocking his hat in the face of our adventurer) you may be as mad as e'er a straw-crowned monarch in Moorfields, for aught I care; but damme! don't you be saucy, otherwise I shall dub your worship with a good stick across your shoulders.' 'How! petulant boy (cried the knight) since you are so ignorant of urbanity, I will give you a lesson that you shall not easily forget.' So saying, he unsheathed his sword, and called upon the soldier to draw in his defence.

The reader may have seen the physiognomy of a stockholder at Jonathan's when the rebels were at Derby,[1] or the features of a bard when accosted by a bailiff, or the countenance of an alderman when his banker stops payment; if he has seen either of these phænomena, he may conceive the appearance that was now exhibited by the visage of the ferocious captain, when the naked sword of Sir Launcelot glanced before his eyes: far from attempting to produce his own, which was of unconscionable length, he stood motionless as a statue, staring with the most ghastly look of terror and astonishment. His companion, who partook of his panic, seeing matters brought to a very serious crisis, interposed with a crest-fallen countenance, assuring Sir Launcelot they had no intention to quarrel, and what they had done was intirely for the sake of the frolick.

'By such frolicks (cried the knight) you become nuisances to society, bring yourselves into contempt, and disgrace the corps to which you belong. I now perceive the truth of the observation, that cruelty always resides with cowardice. My contempt is changed into compassion; and as you are probably of good families, I must insist upon this young man's drawing his sword, and acquitting himself in such a manner as may screen him from the most infamous censure which an officer can undergo.' 'Lack a day, Sir (said the other) we are no officers, but 'prentices to two London haberdashers, travellers for orders. Captain is a good travelling name, and we have dressed ourselves like officers to procure more respect upon the road.'

The knight said he was very glad, for the honour of the service, to find they were impostors; tho' they deserved to be chastised for arrogating to themselves an honourable character, which they had not spirit to sustain.

These words were scarce pronounced, when Mr. Clarke approaching one of the bravadoes, who had threatened to crop his ears, bestowed such a benediction on his jaw, as he could not receive without immediate humiliation; while Timothy Crabshaw, smarting from his broken head and his want of supper, saluted the other with a Yorkshire hug, that layed him across the body of his companion. In a word, the two pseudo-officers were very roughly handled for their presumption in pretending to act characters for which they were so ill qualified.

While Clarke and Crabshaw were thus laudably employed, the two young ladies passed through the kitchen so suddenly, that the knight had only a transient glimpse of their backs, and they disappeared before he could possibly make a tender of his services. The truth is, they dreaded nothing so much as their being discovered, and took the first opportunity of gliding into the chaise, which had been for some time waiting in the passage.

Mr. Clarke was much more disconcerted than our adventurer, by their sudden escape. He ran with great eagerness to the door, and, perceiving they were flown, returned to Sir Launcelot, saying, 'Lord bless my soul, Sir, didn't you see who it was?' 'Hah! how! (exclaimed the knight, reddening with alarm) who was it?' 'One of them (replied the lawyer) was Dolly, our old landlady's daughter at the Black Lyon.—I knew her when first she lighted, notwithstanding her being neatly dressed in a green joseph,[1] which, I'll assure you, Sir, becomes her remarkably well.—I'd never desire to see a prettier creature. As for the other, she's a very genteel woman; but whether old or young, ugly or handsome, I can't pretend to say; for she was masqued.—I had just time to salute Dolly, and ask a few questions;—but all she could tell me was, that the masqued lady's name was miss Meadows; and that she, Dolly, was hired as her waiting-woman.'

When the name of Meadows was mentioned, Sir Launcelot, whose spirits had been in violent commotion, became suddenly calm and serene, and he began to communicate to Clarke the dialogue which had passed between him and capt. Crowe, when the hostess, addressing herself to our errant, 'Well, (said she) I have had the honour to accommodate many ladies of the first fashion at the White Hart, both young and old, proud and lowly, ordinary and handsome; but such a miracle as miss Meadows I never yet did see. Lord, let me never thrive but I think she is of something more than a human creature.—O, had your honour but set eyes on her, you would have said it was a vision from Heaven, a cherubim of beauty:—for my part, I can hardly think it was any thing but a dream:—then so meek, so mild, so good-natured and generous! I say, blessed is the young woman who tends upon such a heavenly creature:—and poor dear young lady! she seems to be under grief and affliction; for the tears stole down her lovely cheeks, and looked for all the world like orient pearl.'

Sir Launcelot listened attentively to the description, which reminded him of his dear Aurelia, and, sighing bitterly, withdrew to his own apartment.

CHAPTER XIV

Which shews,
That a man cannot always sip,
When the cup is at his lip

THOSE who have felt the doubts, the jealousies, the resentments, the humiliations, the hopes, the despair, the impatience, and, in a word, the infinite disquiets of love, will be able to conceive the sea of agitation on which our adventurer was tossed all night long, without repose or intermission. Sometimes he resolved to employ all his industry and address in discovering the place in which Aurelia was sequestered, that he might rescue her from the supposed restraint to which she had been subjected. But, when his heart beat high with the anticipation of this exploit, he was suddenly invaded, and all his ardour checked, by the remembrance of that fatal letter, written and signed by her own hand, which had divorced him from all hope, and first unsettled his understanding. The emotions waked by this remembrance were so strong, that he leaped from the bed, and, the fire being still burning in the chimney, lighted a candle, that he might once more banquet his spleen by reading the original billet, which, together with the ring he had received from miss Darnel's mother, he kept in a small box, carefully deposited within his portmanteau. This being instantly unlocked, he unfolded the paper, and recited the contents in these words:

'Sir, Obliged as I am by the passion you profess, and the eagerness with which you endeavour to give me the most convincing proof of your regard, I feel some reluctance in making you acquainted with a circumstance, which, in all probability, you will not learn without some disquiet. But the affair is become so interesting, I am compelled to tell you, that however agreeable your proposals may have been to those whom I thought it my duty to please by every reasonable concession, and howsoever you may have been flattered by the seeming complacency with which I have heard your addresses, I now find it absolutely necessary to speak in a decisive strain, to assure you, that, without sacrificing my own peace, I cannot admit a continuation of your correspondence; and that your regard for me will be best shewn by your desisting from a pursuit, which is altogether inconsistent with the happiness of

AURELIA DARNEL.'

Having pronounced aloud the words that composed this dismission, he hastily replaced the cruel scroll; and, being too well acquainted with the hand to harbour the least doubt of its being genuine, threw himself into his bed in a transport of despair, mingled with resentment; during the predominancy of which, he determined to proceed in the career of adventure, and endeavour to forget the unkindness of his mistress, amidst the avocations of knight-errantry. Such was the resolution that governed his thoughts, when he rose in the morning, ordered Crabshaw to saddle Bronzomarte, and demanded a bill of his expence. Before these orders could be executed, the good woman of the house, entering his apartment, told him, with marks of concern, that the poor young lady, miss Meadows, had dropped her pocket-book in the next chamber, where it was found by the hostess, who now presented it unopened.

Our knight, having called in Mrs. Oakely and her son as witnesses, unfolded the book, without reading one syllable of the contents, and found in it five bank-notes, amounting to two hundred and thirty pounds. Perceiving, at once, that the loss of this treasure might be attended with the most embarrassing consequences to the owner, and reflecting that this was a case which demanded the immediate interposition and assistance of chivalry, he declared, that he himself would convey it safely into the hands of miss Meadows; and desired to know the road she had pursued, that he might set out in quest of her, without a moment's delay. It was not without some difficulty that this information was obtained from the post-boy, who had been enjoined secrecy by the lady, and even gratified with a handsome reward for his promised discretion. The same method was used to make him disgorge his trust: he undertook to conduct Sir Launcelot, who hired a post-chaise for dispatch, and immediately departed, after having directed his squire to follow his tract[1] with the horses.

Yet, whatever haste he made, it is absolutely necessary for the reader's satisfaction, that we should outstrip the chaise, and visit the ladies before his arrival. We shall therefore, without circumlocution, premise, that miss Meadows was no other than that paragon of beauty and goodness, the all-accomplished miss Aurelia Darnel. She had, with that meekness of resignation peculiar to herself, for some years, submitted to every species of oppression which her uncle's tyranny of disposition could plan, and his unlimited power of guardianship execute, till, at length, it rose to such a pitch of despotism as she could not endure. He had projected a match between his niece and one Philip Sycamore, Esq; a young man who possessed a pretty considerable estate in the North Country; who liked Aurelia's person, but was enamoured of her fortune, and had offered to purchase Anthony's interest and alliance with certain concessions, which could not but be agreeable to a man of loose principles, who would have found it a difficult task to settle the accounts of his wardship.

According to the present estimate of matrimonial felicity, Sycamore might have found admittance as a future son-in-law in any private family of the kingdom. He was by birth a gentleman, tall, straight, and muscular, with a fair, sleek, unmeaning face, that promised more simplicity than ill-nature. His education had not been neglected, and he inherited an estate of five thousand a year. Miss Darnel, however, had penetration enough to discover and despise him as a strange composition of rapacity and profusion, absurdity and good-sense, bashfulness and impudence, self-conceit and diffidence, aukwardness and ostentation, insolence and good-nature, rashness and timidity. He was continually surrounded and preyed upon by certain vermin called led-captains and buffoons, who shewed him in leading-strings like a sucking giant,[2] rifled his pockets without ceremony, ridiculed him to his face, traduced his character, and exposed him in a thousand ludicrous attitudes for the diversion of the public; while, all the time, he knew their knavery, saw their drift, detested their morals, and despised their understanding. He was so infatuated by indolence of thought, and communication with folly, that he would have rather suffered himself to be led into a ditch with company, than be at the pains of going over a bridge alone; and involved himself in a thousand difficulties, the natural consequences of an error in the first concoction, which, though he plainly saw it, he had not resolution enough to avoid.

Such was the character of squire Sycamore, who professed himself the rival of Sir Launcelot Greaves in the good graces of miss Aurelia Darnel. He had in this pursuit persevered with more constancy and fortitude, than he ever exerted in any other instance. Being generally needy, from extravagance, he was stimulated by his wants, and animated by his vanity, which was artfully instigated by his followers, who hoped to share the spoils of his success. These motives were reinforced by the incessant and eager exhortations of Anthony Darnel, who, seeing his ward in the last year of her minority, thought there was no time to be lost in securing his own indemnification, and snatching his niece for ever from the hopes of Sir Launcelot, whom he now hated with redoubled animosity. Finding Aurelia deaf to all his remonstrances, proof against ill-usage, and resolutely averse to the proposed union with Sycamore, he endeavoured to detach her thoughts from Sir Launcelot, by forging tales to the prejudice of his constancy and moral character; and, finally, by recapitulating the proofs and instances of his distraction, which he particularized with the most malicious exaggerations.

In spite of all his arts, he found it impracticable to surmount her objections to the purposed alliance, and therefore changed his battery. Instead of transferring her to the arms of his friend, he resolved to detain her in his own power by a legal claim, which would invest him with the uncontrouled management of her affairs. This was a charge of lunacy, in consequence of which he hoped to obtain a commission, to secure a jury to his wish, and be appointed sole committee of her person, as well as steward on her estate, of which he would then be heir apparent. As the first steps towards the execution of this honest scheme, he had subjected Aurelia to the superintendency and direction of an old duenna, who had been formerly the procuress of his pleasures; and hired a new set of servants, who were given to understand, at their first admission, that the young lady was disordered in her brain.

An impression of this nature is easily preserved among servants, when the master of the family thinks his interest is concerned in supporting the imposture. The melancholy produced from her confinement, and the vivacity of her resentment under ill-usage, were, by the address of Anthony, and the prepossession of his domesticks, perverted into the effects of insanity; and the same interpretation was strained upon her most indifferent words and actions. The tydings of miss Darnel's disorder were carefully cir- culted in whispers, and soon reached the ears of Mr. Sycamore, who was not at all pleased with the information. From his know- ledge of Anthony's disposition, he suspected the truth of the report; and unwilling to see such a prize ravished, as it were, from his grasp, he, with the advice and assistance of his myrmidons, re- solved to set the captive at liberty, in full hope of turning the adventure to his own advantage; for he argued in this manner: 'If she is in fact *compos mentis*, her gratitude will operate in my behalf, and even prudence will advise her to embrace the proffered asylum from the villany of her uncle. If she is really disordered, it will be no great difficulty to deceive her into a marriage, and then I become her trustee of course.'

The plan was well conceived; but Sycamore had not discretion enough to keep his own counsel. From weakness and vanity, he blabbed the design, which in a little time was communicated to Anthony Darnel, and he took his precautions accordingly. Being infirm in his own person, and consequently unfit for opposing the violence of some desperadoes, whom he knew to be the satellites of Sycamore, he prepared a private retreat for his ward at the house of an old gentleman, the companion of his youth, whom he had imposed upon with the fiction of her being disordered in her under- standing, and amused with a story of a dangerous design upon her person. Thus cautioned and instructed, the gentleman had gone with his own coach and servants to receive Aurelia and her governante at a third house, to which she had been privately removed from her uncle's habitation; and in this journey it was, that she had been so accidentally protected from the violence of the robbers by the interposition and prowess of our adventurer.

As he did not wear his helmet in that exploit, she recognized his features as he passed the coach, and, struck with the apparition, shrieked aloud. She had been assured by her guardian, that his design was to convey her to her own house; but perceiving, in the sequel, that the carriage struck off upon a different road, and finding herself in the hands of strangers, she began to dread a much more disagreeable fate, and conceive doubts and ideas that filled her tender heart with horror and affliction. When she expostulated with the duenna, she was treated like a changeling, admonished to be quiet, and reminded that she was under the direction of those who would manage her with a tender regard to her own welfare, and the honour of her family. When she addressed herself to the old gentleman, who was not much subject to the emotions of humanity, and besides firmly persuaded that she was deprived of her reason, he made no answer; but laid his finger on his mouth, by way of enjoining silence.

This mysterious behaviour aggravated the fears of the poor hapless young lady; and her terrors waxed so strong, that when she saw Tom Clarke, whose face she knew, she called aloud for assistance, and even pronounced the name of his patron Sir Launcelot Greaves, which she imagined might stimulate him the more to attempt something for her deliverance.

The reader has already been informed in what manner the endeavours of Tom and his uncle miscarried. Miss Darnel's new keeper having, in the course of his journey, halted for refreshment at the Black Lyon, of which being landlord, he believed the good woman and her family were intirely devoted to his will and pleasure, Aurelia found an opportunity of speaking in private to Dolly, who had a very prepossessing appearance. She conveyed a purse of money into the hands of this young woman, telling her, while the tears trickled down her cheeks, that she was a young lady of fortune, in danger, as she apprehended, of assassination. This hint, which she communicated in a whisper, while the governante stood at the other end of the room, was sufficient to interest the compassionate Dolly in her behalf. As soon as the coach departed, she made her mother acquainted with the transaction; and as they naturally concluded that the young lady expected their assistance, they resolved to approve themselves worthy of her confidence.

Dolly having inlisted in their design a trusty countryman, one of her own professed admirers, they set out together for the house of the gentleman in which the fair prisoner was confined, and waited for her in secret at the end of a pleasant park, in which they naturally concluded she might be indulged with the privilege of taking the air. The event justified their conception: on the very first day of their watch they saw her approach, accompanied by her duenna. Dolly and her attendant immediately tied their horses to a stake, and retired into a thicket, which Aurelia did not fail to enter. Dolly forthwith appeared, and, taking her by the hand, led her to the horses, one of which she mounted in the utmost hurry and trepidation, while the countryman bound the duenna with a cord, prepared for the purpose, gagged her mouth, and tied her to a tree, where he left her to her own meditations. Then he mounted before Dolly, and thro' unfrequented paths conducted his charge to an inn on the post-road, where a chaise was ready for their reception.

As he refused to proceed farther, lest his absence from his own home should create suspicion, Aurelia rewarded him liberally; but would not part with her faithful Dolly, who, indeed, had no inclination to be discharged: such an affection and attachment had she already acquired for the amiable fugitive, though she knew neither her story, nor her true name. Aurelia thought proper to conceal both, and assumed the fictitious appellation of Meadows, until she should be better acquainted with the disposition and discretion of her new attendant. The first resolution she could take in the present flutter of her spirits, was to make the best of her way to London, where she thought she might find an asylum in the house of a female relation, married to an eminent physician, known by the name of Kawdle. In the execution of this hasty resolve, she travelled at a violent rate, from stage to stage, in a carriage drawn by four horses, without halting for necessary refreshment or repose, until she judged herself out of danger of being overtaken. As she appeared overwhelmed with grief and consternation, the good-natured Dolly endeavoured to alleviate her distress with diverting discourse; and, among other less interesting stories, entertained her with the adventures of Sir Launcelot and captain Crowe, which she had seen and heard recited while they remained at the Black Lyon: nor did she fail to introduce Mr. Thomas Clarke, in her narrative, with such a favourable representation of his person and character, as plainly discovered that her own heart had received a rude shock from the irresistible force of his qualifications.

The history of Sir Launcelot Greaves was a theme which effectually fixed the attention of Aurelia, distracted as her ideas must have been by the circumstances of her present situation. The particulars of his conduct, since the correspondence between her and him had ceased, she heard with equal concern and astonishment; for, how far soever she deemed herself detached from all possibility of future connexion with that young gentleman, she was not made of such indifferent stuff, as to learn without emotion the calamitous disorder of an accomplished youth, whose extraordinary virtues she could not but revere.

As they had deviated from the post-road, taken precautions to conceal their route, and made such progress, that they were now within one day's journey of London, the careful and affectionate Dolly seeing her dear lady quite exhausted with fatigue, used all her natural rhetorick, which was very powerful, mingled with tears that flowed from the heart, in persuading Aurelia to enjoy some repose; and so far she succeeded in the attempt, that for one night the toil of travelling was intermitted. This recess from incredible fatigue, was a pause that afforded our adventurer time to overtake them before they reached the metropolis, that vast labyrinth, in which Aurelia might have been for ever lost to his inquiry.

It was in the afternoon of the day which succeeded his departure from the White Hart, that Sir Launcelot arrived at the inn, where miss Aurelia Darnel had bespoke a dish of tea, and a post-chaise for the next stage. He had, by inquiry, traced her a considerable way, without ever dreaming who the person really was whom he thus pursued, and now he desired to speak with her attendant. Dolly was not a little surprised to see Sir Launcelot Greaves, of whose character she had conceived a very sublime idea, from the narrative of Mr. Thomas Clarke; but she was still more surprised when he gave her to understand, that he had charged himself with the pocket-book, containing the bank-notes, which miss Meadows had dropped in the house where they had been threatened with insult. Miss Darnel had not yet discovered her disaster, when her attendant, running into the apartment, presented the prize, which she had received from our adventurer, with his compliments to miss Meadows, implying a request to be admitted into her presence, that he might make a personal tender of his best services.

It is not to be supposed that the amiable Aurelia heard unmoved such a message from a person, whom her maid discovered to be the very identical Sir Launcelot Greaves, whose story she had so lately related: but as the ensuing scene requires fresh attention in the reader, we shall defer it till another opportunity, when his spirits shall be recruited from the fatigue of this chapter.

CHAPTER XV

Exhibiting an interview, which, it is to be hoped, will interest the curiosity of the reader

THE mind of the delicate Aurelia was strangely agitated by the intelligence which she received, with her pocket-book, from Dolly. Confounded as she was by the nature of her situation, she at once perceived that she could not, with any regard to the dictates of gratitude, refuse complying with the request of Sir Launcelot; but, in the first hurry of her emotion, she directed Dolly to beg, in her name, that she might be excused for wearing a masque at the interview which he desired, as she had particular reasons, which concerned her peace, for retaining that disguise. Our adventurer submitted to this preliminary with a good grace, as he had nothing in view but the injunctions of his order, and the duties of humanity; and he was admitted without further preamble. When he entered the room, he could not help being struck with the presence of Aurelia. Her stature was improved since he had seen her; her shape was exquisitely formed; and she received him with an air of dignity, which impressed him with a very sublime idea of her person and character. She was no less affected at sight of our adventurer, who, though cased in armour, appeared with his head uncovered; and the exercise of travelling had thrown such a glow of health and vivacity on his features, which were naturally elegant and expressive, that we will venture to say, there was not in all England a couple that excelled this amiable pair in personal beauty and accomplishments. Aurelia shone with all the fabled graces of nymph or goddess; and to Sir Launcelot might be applied what the divine poet Ariosto says of the prince Zerbino:

> *Natura il fece e poi ruppe la stampa.*[1]
> 'When Nature stamp'd him, she the dye destroy'd.'

Our adventurer, having made his obeisance to this supposed miss Meadows, told her, with an air of pleasantry, that altho' he thought himself highly honoured in being admitted to her presence, and allowed to pay his respects to her, as superior beings are adored, unseen; yet his pleasure would receive a very considerable addition, if she would be pleased to withdraw that invidious veil, that he might have a glimpse of the divinity which it concealed. Aurelia immediately took off her masque, saying, with a faultering accent, 'I cannot be so ungrateful as to deny such a small favour to a gentleman who has laid me under the most important obligations.'

The unexpected apparition of Miss Aurelia Darnel, beaming with all the emanations of ripened beauty, blushing with all the graces of the most lovely confusion, could not but produce a violent effect upon the mind of Sir Launcelot Greaves. He was, indeed, overwhelmed with a mingled transport of astonishment, admiration, affliction, and awe. The colour vanished from his cheeks, and he stood gazing upon her, in silence, with the most emphatic expression of countenance. Aurelia was infected by his disorder: she began to tremble, and the roses fluctuated on her face.—'I cannot forget (said she) that I owe my life to the courage and humanity of Sir Launcelot Greaves, and that he at the same time rescued from the most dreadful death a dear and venerable parent.' 'Would to heaven she still survived! (cried our adventurer with great emotion.) She was the friend of my youth, the kind patroness of my felicity! my guardian angel forsook me when she expired! her last injunctions are deep engraven on my heart!'

While he pronounced these words she lifted her handkerchief to her fair eyes, and, after some pause, proceeded in a tremulous tone, 'I hope, Sir—I hope you have—I should be sorry—pardon me, Sir, I cannot reflect upon such an interesting subject unmoved—' Here she fetched a deep sigh, that was accompanied with a flood of tears; while the knight continued to bend his eyes upon her with the utmost eagerness of attention. Having recollected herself a little, she endeavoured to shift the conversation: 'You have been abroad since I had the pleasure to see you—I hope you were agreeably amused in your travels.' 'No, madam, (said our hero, drooping his head) I have been unfortunate.' When she, with the most enchanting sweetness of benevolence, expressed her concern to hear he had been unhappy, and her hope that his misfortunes were not past remedy; he lifted up his eyes, and fixing them upon her again with a look of tender dejection, 'Cut off (said he) from the possession of what my soul held most dear, I wished for death, and was visited by distraction.—I have been abandoned by my reason—my youth is for ever blasted—'

The tender heart of Aurelia could bear no more—her knees began to totter: the lustre vanished from her eyes, and she fainted in the arms of her attendant. Sir Launcelot, aroused by this circumstance, assisted Dolly in seating her mistress on a couch, where she soon recovered, and saw the knight on his knees before her. 'I am still happy (said he) in being able to move your compassion, though I have been held unworthy of your esteem.' 'Do me justice, (she replied:) my best esteem has been always inseparably connected with the character of Sir Launcelot Greaves—' 'Is it possible? (cried our hero) then surely I have no reason to complain. If I have moved your compassion, and possess your esteem, I am but one degree short of supreme happiness—that, however, is a gigantic step.—O miss Darnel! when I remember that dear, that melancholy moment—' So saying, he gently touched her hand, in order to press it to his lips, and perceived on her finger the very individual ring which he had presented in her mother's presence, as an interchanged testimony of plighted faith. Starting at the well-known object, the sight of which conjured up a strange confusion of ideas, 'This (said he) was once the pledge of something still more cordial than esteem.' Aurelia, blushing at this remark, while her eyes lightened with unusual vivacity, replied, in a severer tone, 'Sir, you best know how it lost its original signification.' 'By heaven! I do not, madam, (exclaimed our adventurer.) With me it was ever held a sacred idea throned within my heart, cherished with such fervency of regard, with such reverence of affection, as the devout anchorite more unreasonably pays to those sainted reliques that constitute the object of his adoration—' 'And, like those reliques, (answered miss Darnel) I have been insensible of my votary's devotion.—A saint I must have been, or something more, to know the sentiments of your heart by inspiration.' 'Did I forbear (said he) to express, to repeat, to enforce the dictates of the purest passion that ever warmed the human breast, until I was denied access, and formally discarded by that cruel dismission—' 'I must beg your pardon, Sir, (cried Aurelia, interrupting him hastily) I know not what you mean.' 'That fatal sentence, (said he) if not pronounced by your own lips, at least written by your own fair hand, which drove me out an exile for ever from the paradise of your affection.' 'I would not (she replied) do Sir Launcelot Greaves the injury to suppose him capable of imposition: but you talk of things to which I am an utter stranger.—I have a right, Sir, to demand of your honour, that you will not impute to me your breaking off a connection, which—I would—rather wish—had never—' 'Heaven and earth! what do I hear? (cried our impatient knight) have I not the baleful letter to produce? What else but miss Darnel's explicit and express declaration could have destroyed the sweetest hope that ever cheared my soul; could have obliged me to resign all claim to that felicity for which alone I wished to live; could have filled my bosom with unutterable sorrow and despair; could have even divested me of reason, and driven me from the society of men, a poor, forlorn, wandering lunatic, such as you see me now prostrate at your feet; all the blossoms of my youth withered, all the honours of my family decayed?'

Aurelia looking wistfully at her lover, 'Sir, (said she) you overwhelm me with amazement and anxiety! you are imposed upon, if you have received any such letter: you are deceived, if you thought Aurelia Darnel could be so insensible, ungrateful, and—inconstant.'

This last word she pronounced with some hesitation, and a downcast look, while her face underwent a total suffusion, and the knight's heart began to palpitate with all the violence of emotion. He eagerly imprinted a kiss upon her hand, exclaiming, in interrupted phrase, 'Can it be possible?—Heaven grant—Sure this is no illusion.—O, madam!—shall I call you my Aurelia? My heart is bursting with a thousand fond thoughts and presages. You shall see that dire paper which hath been the source of all my woes—it is the constant companion of my travels.—Last night I nourished my chagrin with the perusal of its horrid contents.'

Aurelia expressed great impatience to view the cruel forgery; for such she assured him it must be: but he could not gratify her desire till the arrival of his servant with the portmanteau. In the mean time, tea was called. The lovers were seated: he looked and languished; she flushed and faultered: all was doubt and delirium, fondness and flutter. Their mutual disorder communicated itself to the kind-hearted sympathizing Dolly, who had been witness to the interview, and deeply affected with the disclosure of the scene. Unspeakable was her surprize when she found her mistress miss Meadows was no other than the celebrated Aurelia Darnel, whose eulogium she had heard so eloquently pronounced by her sweetheart Mr. Thomas Clarke; a discovery which still more endeared her lady to her affection. She had wept plentifully at the progress of their mutual explanation; and was now so disconcerted, that she scarce knew the meaning of the orders she had received. She set the

kettle on the table, and placed the tea-board on the fire. Her confusion, by attracting the notice of her mistress, helped to relieve
her from her own embarrassing situation. She, with her own
delicate hands, rectified the mistake of Dolly; who still continued
to sob, and said, 'Yaw may think, my leady Darnel, as haw I 'aive
yeaten hool-cheese;[1] but it y'an't soa.—I'se think, vor maai peart,
as how I'aive bean bewitched.' Sir Launcelot could not help
smiling at the simplicity of Dolly, whose goodness of heart, and
attachment, Aurelia did not fail to extol, as soon as her back was
turned. It was in consequence of this commendation, that, the next
time she entered the room, our adventurer, for the first time, considered her face, and seemed to be struck with her features. He
asked her some questions, which she could not answer to his satisfaction, applauded her regard for her lady, and assured her of his
friendship and protection. He now begged to know the cause that
obliged his Aurelia to travel at such a rate, and in such an equipage;
and she informed him of those particulars which we have already
communicated to the reader.

Sir Launcelot glowed with resentment, when he understood how
his dear Aurelia had been oppressed by her perfidious and cruel
guardian. He bit his nether lip, rolled his eyes around, started from
his seat, and striding across the room, 'I remember (said he) the
dying words of her who is now a saint in heaven—"That violent
man, my brother-in-law, who is Aurelia's sole guardian, will
thwart her wishes with every obstacle that brutal resentment and
implacable malice can contrive."—What followed, it would ill
become me to repeat: but she concluded with these words—"The
rest we must leave to the dispensations of Providence."—Was it
not Providence that sent me hither, to guard and protect the
injured Aurelia?' Then turning to miss Darnel, whose eyes
streamed with tears, he added, 'Yes, divine creature! heaven, careful of your safety, and in compassion to my sufferings, hath guided
me hither, in this mysterious manner, that I might defend you from
violence, and enjoy this transition from madness to deliberation,
from despair to felicity.' So saying, he approached this amiable
mourner, this fragrant flower of beauty, glittering with the dew-
drops of the morning; this sweetest, gentlest, loveliest ornament of
human nature: he gazed upon her with looks of love ineffable: he
sat down by her; he pressed her soft hand in his; he began to fear
that all he saw was the flattering vision of a distempered brain. He

looked, and sighed; and turning up his eyes to heaven, breathed, in broken murmurs, the chaste raptures of his soul. The tenderness of this communication was too painful to be long endured. Aurelia industriously interposed other subjects of discourse, that his attention might not be dangerously overcharged, and the afternoon passed insensibly away.

Though he had determined, in his own mind, never more to quit this idol of his soul, they had not yet concerted any plan of conduct, when their happiness was all at once interrupted by a repetition of cries, denoting horror; and a servant, coming in, said he believed some rogues were murdering a traveller on the highway. The supposition of such distress operated like gun-powder on the disposition of our adventurer, who, without considering the situation of Aurelia, and indeed without seeing, or being capable to think on her, or any other subject, for the time being, ran directly to the stable, and mounting the first horse which he found saddled, issued out in the twilight, having no other weapon but his sword. He rode full speed to the spot whence the cries seemed to proceed; but they sounded more remote as he advanced. Nevertheless he followed them to a considerable distance from the road, over fields, ditches, and hedges; and at last came so near, that he could plainly distinguish the voice of his own squire, Timothy Crabshaw, bellowing for mercy, with hideous vociferation. Stimulated by this recognition, he redoubled his career in the dark, till at length his horse plunged into a hole, the nature of which he could not comprehend; but he found it impracticable to disengage him. It was with some difficulty that he himself clambered over a ruined wall, and regained the open ground. Here he groped about, in the utmost impatience of anxiety, ignorant of the place, mad with vexation for the fate of his unfortunate squire, and between whiles invaded with a pang of concern for Aurelia, left among strangers, unguarded, and alarmed. In the midst of this emotion, he bethought himself of hollowing aloud, that, in case he should be in the neighbourhood of any inhabited place, he might be heard and assisted. He accordingly practised this expedient, which was not altogether without effect; for he was immediately answered by an old friend, no other than his own steed Bronzomarte, who, hearing his master's voice neighed strenuously at a small distance. The knight, being well acquainted with the sound, heard with astonishment; and, advancing in the right direction, found his noble charger fastened to a tree. He forthwith untied and mounted him; then, laying the reins upon his neck, allowed him to chuse his own path, in which he began to travel with equal steadiness and expedition. They had not proceeded far when the knight's ears were again saluted by the cries of Crabshaw; which Bronzomarte no sooner heard than he pricked up his ears, neighed, and quickened his pace, as if he had been sensible of the squire's distress, and hastened to his relief. Sir Launcelot, notwithstanding his own disquiet, could not help observing and admiring this generous sensibility of his horse: he began to think himself some hero of romance mounted upon a winged steed,[1] inspired with reason, directed by some humane inchanter, who pitied virtue in distress. All circumstances considered, it is no wonder that the commotion in the mind of our adventurer produced some such delirium. All night he continued the chace; the voice, which was repeated at intervals, still retreating before him, till the morning began to appear in the East, when, by divers piteous groans, he was directed to the corner of a wood, where he beheld his miserable squire stretched upon the grass, and Gilbert feeding by him altogether unconcerned, the helmet and the launce suspended at the saddle-bow, and the portmanteau safely fixed upon the crupper.

The knight, riding up to Crabshaw, with equal surprize and concern, asked what had brought him there; and Timothy, after some pause, during which he surveyed his master with a rueful aspect, answered, 'The devil.' 'One would imagine, indeed, you had some such conveyance, (said Sir Launcelot.) I have followed your cries since last evening I know not how, nor whither, and never could come up with you till this moment. But, say, what damage have you sustained, that you lie in that wretched posture, and groan so dismally?' 'I can't guess, (replied the squire) if it bean't that mai hoole carcase is drilled into oilet hools,[2] and my flesh pinched into a jelly.'—'How! wherefore? (cried the knight)—who were the miscreants that treated you in such a barbarous manner? Do you know the ruffians?' 'I know nothing at all, (answered the peevish squire) but that I was tormented by vive hoondred and vifty thousand legions of devils, and there's an end oan't.' 'Well, you must have a little patience, Crabshaw—there's a salve for every sore.'—'Yaw mought as well tell ma, for every zow there's a zirreverence.'[3] 'For a man in your condition, methinks you talk very much at your ease.—Try if you can get up and mount Gilbert, that you may be conveyed to some place where you can have proper assistance.—So—well done—chearly—'

Timothy actually made an effort to rise; but fell down again, and uttered a dismal yell. Then his master exhorted him to take advantage of a park-wall, by which he lay, and raise himself gradually upon it. Crabshaw, eying him askance, said, by way of reproach, for his not alighting and assisting him in person, 'Thatch your house with t——d, and you'll have more teachers than reachers.'[1]—Having pronounced this inelegant adage, he made shift to stand upon his legs; and now, the knight lending a hand, was mounted upon Gilbert, though not without a world of oh's! and ah's! and other ejaculations of pain and impatience. As they jogged on together, our adventurer endeavoured to learn the particulars of the disaster which had befallen the squire; but all the information he could obtain, amounted to a very imperfect sketch of the adventure. By dint of a thousand interrogations he understood, that Crabshaw had been, in the preceding evening, encountered by three persons on horseback with Venetian masques[2] on their faces, which he mistook for their natural features, and was terrified accordingly: that they not only presented pistols to his breast, and led his horse out of the highway; but pricked him with goads, and pinched him, from time to time, till he screamed with the torture: that he was led through unfrequented places across the country, sometimes at an easy trot, sometimes at full gallop, and tormented all night by those hideous dæmons, who vanished at day break, and left him lying on the spot where he was found by his master. This was a mystery which our hero could by no means unriddle: it was the more unaccountable, as the squire had not been robbed of his money, horses, and baggage. He was even disposed to believe, that Crabshaw's brain was disordered, and the whole account he had given, no more than a chimera. This opinion, however, he could no longer retain, when he arrived at an inn on the post-road, and found, upon examination, that Timothy's lower extremities were covered with blood, and all the rest of his body speckled with livid marks of contusion. But he was still more chagrined when the landlord informed him, that he was thirty miles distant from the place where he had left Aurelia, and that his way lay through crossroads, which were almost impassable at that season of the year. Alarmed at this intelligence, he gave directions that his squire should be immediately conveyed to bed in a comfortable chamber, as he complained more and more; and indeed was seized with a fever, occasioned by the fatigue, the pain, and terror he had undergone. A neighbouring apothecary being called, and giving it as his opinion that he could not for some days be in a condition to travel, his master deposited a sum of money in his hands, desiring he might be properly attended, till he should hear further. Then mounting Bronzomarte, he set out with a guide for the place he had left, not without a thousand fears and perplexities, arising from the reflection of having left the jewel of his heart with such precipitation.

CHAPTER XVI

Which, it is to be hoped, the reader will find an agreeable medley of mirth and madness, sense and absurdity

I T was not without reason that our adventurer afflicted himself: his fears were but too prophetic. When he alighted at the inn, which he had left so abruptly the preceding evening, he ran directly to the apartment where he had been so happy in Aurelia's company; but her he saw not—all was solitary. Turning to the woman of the house, who had followed him into the room, 'Where is the lady?' cried he, in a tone of impatience. Mine hostess, screwing up her features into a very demure aspect, said she saw so many ladies, she could not pretend to know who he meant. 'I tell thee, woman, (exclaimed the knight, in a louder accent) thou never sawest such another—I mean that miracle of beauty—' 'Very like, (replied the dame, as she retired to the room-door.) Husband, here's one as axes concerning a miracle of beauty; hi, hi, hi. Can you give him any information about this miracle of beauty?—Ola! hi, hi, hi.' Instead of answering this question, the inn-keeper advancing, and surveying Sir Launcelot, 'Friend, (said he) you are the person that carried off my horse out of the stable.' 'Tell not me of a horse—where is the young lady?' 'Now I will tell you of the horse; and I'll make you find him too, before you and I part.' 'Wretched animal! how dar'st thou dally with my impatience?—Speak, or despair.—What is become of miss Meadows? Say, did she leave this place of her own accord, or was she—hah!—speak—answer, or, by the Powers above—' 'I'll answer you flat—she you call miss Meadows is in very good hands—so you may make yourself easy on that score—'

'Sacred Heaven! explain your meaning, miscreant, or I'll make you a dreadful example to all the insolent publicans of the realm.' So saying, he seized him with one hand, and dashing him on the floor, set one foot on his belly, and kept him trembling in that prostrate attitude. The hostler and waiter flying to the assistance of their master, our adventurer unsheathed his sword, declaring he would dismiss their souls from their bodies, and exterminate the whole family from the face of the earth, if they would not immediately give him the satisfaction he required.

The hostess, being by this time terrified almost out of her senses, fell on her knees before him, begging he would spare their lives, and promising to declare the whole truth. He would not, however, remove his foot from the body of her husband, until she told him, that, in less than half an hour after he had sallied out upon the supposed robbers, two chaises arrived, each drawn by four horses; that two men, armed with pistols, alighting from one of them, laid violent hands upon the young lady; and, notwithstanding her struggling and shrieking, forced her into the other carriage, in which was an infirm gentleman, who called himself her guardian: that the maid was left to the care of a third servant, to follow with a third chaise, which was got ready with all possible dispatch, while the other two proceeded at full speed on the road to London. It was by this communicative lacquey the people of the house were informed, that the old gentleman his master was squire Darnel, the young lady his niece and ward, and our adventurer a needy sharper, who wanted to make prey of her fortune. The knight, fired even almost to frenzy by this intimation, spurned the carcase of his host; and, his eye gleaming terror, rushed into the yard, in order to mount Bronzomarte, and pursue the ravisher, when he was diverted from his purpose by a new incident.

One of the postilions, who had driven the chaise in which Dolly was conveyed, happened to arrive at that instant; when, seeing our hero, he ran up to him cap in hand, and, presenting a letter, accosted him in these words: 'Please your noble honour, if your honour be Sir Launcelot Greaves of the West Riding, here's a letter from a gentlewoman, that I promised to deliver into your honour's own hands.'

The knight, snatching the letter with the utmost avidity, broke it up, and found the contents couched in these terms:

'Honoured Sir,

'The man az gi'en me leave to lat yaw knaw my dear leady is going to Loondon with her unkle squaire Darnel.—Be not con-zarned, honoured sir, vor I'se teake it on mai laife, to let yaw knaw wheare we be zettled, if zo be I can vind wheare you loadge in Loondon.—The man zays yaw may put it in the pooblic prints.—I houp the bareheir will be honest enuff to deliver this scrowl; and that your honour will pardon

Your umbil servant to command

DOROTHY COWSLIP.

'P. S. Please my kaind sarvice to laayer Clarke. Squire Darnel's man is very civil vor sartain; but I'ave no thoughts on him I'll assure yaw.—Marry hap, worse ware may have a better chap, as the zaying goes.'[1]

Nothing could be more seasonable than the delivery of this billet; which he had no sooner perused, than his reflection returned, and he entered into a serious deliberation with his own heart. He considered that Aurelia was by this time far beyond a possibility of being overtaken; and that by a precipitate pursuit he should only expose his own infirmities. He confided in the attachment of his mistress, and in the fidelity of her maid, who would find oppor-tunities of communicating her sentiments, by the means of this lacquey, of whom he perceived by the letter she had already made a conquest. He therefore resolved to bridle his impatience, to pro-ceed leisurely to London, and, instead of taking any rash step which might induce Anthony Darnel to remove his niece from that city, remain in seeming quiet until she should be settled, and her guardian returned to the country. Aurelia had mentioned to him the name of doctor Kawdle, and from him he expected, in due time, to receive the most interesting information.

These reflections had an instantaneous effect upon our hero, whose rage immediately subsided, and whose visage gradually resumed its natural cast of courtesy and good humour. He forth-with gratified the postilion with such a remuneration, as sent him dancing into the kitchen, where he did not fail to extol the generosity and immense fortune of Sir Launcelot Greaves.

Our adventurer's next step was to see Bronzomarte properly accommodated; then he ordered a refreshment for himself, and retired into an apartment, where mine host with his wife and all the servants waited on him, to beseech his honour to forgive their impertinence, which was owing to their ignorance of his honour's quality, and the false information they had received from the gentleman's servant. He had too much magnanimity to retain the least resentment against such inconsiderable objects. He not only pardoned them without hesitation; but assured the landlord he would be accountable for the horse, which, however, was that same evening brought home by a countryman, who had found him pounded as it were within the walls of a ruined cottage. As the knight had been greatly fatigued, without enjoying any rest for eight and forty hours, he resolved to indulge himself with one night's repose, and then return to the place where he had left his squire indisposed: for by this time even his concern for Timothy had recurred.

On a candid scrutiny of his own heart, he found himself much less unhappy than he had been before his interview with Aurelia; for, instead of being as formerly tormented with the pangs of despairing love, which had actually unsettled his understanding, he was now happily convinced that he had inspired the tender breast of Aurelia with mutual affection; and though she was invidiously snatched from his embrace, in the midst of such endearments as had wound up his soul to extasy and transport, he did not doubt of being able to rescue her from the power of an inhuman kinsman, whose guardianship would soon of course expire; and in the mean time, he rested with the most perfect dependence on her constancy and virtue.

As he next day crossed the country, ruminating on the disaster that had befallen his squire, and could now compare circumstances coolly, he easily comprehended the whole scheme of that adventure, which was no other than an artifice of Anthony Darnel and his emissaries, to draw him from the inn where he proposed to execute his design upon the innocent Aurelia. He took it for granted, that the uncle, having been made acquainted with his niece's elopement, had followed her track by the help of such information as he received from one stage to another; and that, receiving more particulars at the White Hart touching Sir Launcelot, he had formed the scheme in which Crabshaw was an involuntary instrument towards the seduction of his master.

Amusing himself with these and other cogitations, our hero in the afternoon reached the place of his destination; and entering the inn where Timothy had been left at sick quarters, chanced to meet the apothecary retiring precipitately in a very unsavoury pickle from the chamber of his patient. When he inquired about the health of his squire, this retainer to medicine, wiping himself all the while with a napkin, answered in manifest confusion, That he apprehended him to be in a very dangerous way, from an inflammation of the *pia mater*,[1] which had produced a most furious delirium. Then he proceeded to explain, in technical terms, the method of cure he had followed; and concluded with telling him the poor squire's brain was so outrageously disordered, that he had rejected all administration, and just thrown an urinal in his face.

The knight's humanity being alarmed at this intelligence, he resolved that Crabshaw should have the benefit of further advice, and asked if there was not a physician in the place. The apothecary, after some interjections of hesitation, owned there was a doctor in the village, an odd sort of a humourist; but he believed he had not much to do in the way of his profession, and was not much used to the forms of prescription. He was counted a scholar, to be sure; but as to his medical capacity,—he would not take upon him to say—'No matter, (cried Sir Launcelot) he may strike out some lucky thought for the benefit of the patient; and I desire you will call him instantly.'—

While the apothecary was absent on this service, our adventurer took it in his head to question the landlord about the character of this physician, which had been so unfavourably represented, and received the following information:

'For my peart, measter, I knows nothing amiss of the doctor—he's a quiet sort of an inoffensive man; uses my house sometimes, and pays for what he has, like the rest of my customers. They says he deals very little in physic stuff, but cures his patients with fasting and water-gruel, whereby he can't expect the pothecary to be his friend.[2] You knows, master, one must live, and let live, as the saying is. I must say, he, for the value of three guineas, set up my wife's constitution in such a manner, that I have saved within these two years, I believe, forty pounds in pothecary's bills. But what of that? Every man must eat, thof at another's expence; and I should be in a deadly hole myself, if all my customers should take it in their heads to drink nothing but water-gruel, because it is good for the constitution. Thank God, I have as good a constitution as e'er a man in England; but for all that, I and my whole family bleed and purge and take a diet-drink twice a-year, by way of serving the pothecary, who is a very honest man, and a very good neighbour.'

Their conversation was interrupted by the return of the apothe-cary with the doctor, who had very little of the faculty in his appearance. He was dressed remarkably plain; seemed to be turned of fifty; had a careless air, and a sarcastical turn in his countenance. Before he entered the sick man's chamber, he asked some questions concerning the disease; and when the apothecary, pointing to his own head, said, 'It lies all here;' the doctor, turning to Sir Launcelot, replied, 'If that be all, there's nothing in it.'

Upon a more particular enquiry about the symptoms, he was told that the blood was seemingly viscous, and salt upon the tongue; the urine remarkably acrosaline;[1] and the fæces atrabilious[2] and fœtid. When the doctor said he would engage to find the same phænomena in every healthy man of the three kingdoms; the apothecary added, that the patient was manifestly comatous, and moreover afflicted with griping pains and borborygmata.[3]—'A f——t for your borborygmata, (cried the physician.) What has been done?' To this question he replied, that venæsection[4] had been three times performed: that a vesicatory had been applied *inter scapulas*:[5] that the patient had taken occasionally of a cathartic apozem,[6] and, between whiles, alexipharmic[7] boluses[8] and neutral[9] draughts.—'Neutral, indeed, (said the doctor;) so neutral, that I'll be crucified if ever they declare either for the patient or the disease.' So saying, he brushed into Crabshaw's chamber, followed by our adventurer, who was almost suffocated at his first entrance. The day was close, the window-shutters were fastened; a huge fire blazed in the chimney; thick harateen curtains were close drawn round the bed, where the wretched squire lay extended under an enormous load of blankets. The nurse, who had all the exteriors of a bawd given to drink, sat stewing in this apartment, like a damned soul in some infernal bagnio: but rising, when the company entered, made her curtsies with great decorum. 'Well, (said the doctor) how does your patient, nurse?' 'Blessed be God for it, I hope in a fair way:—to be sure his apozem has had a blessed effect— five and twenty stools since three o'clock in the morning.—But then a'would not suffer the blisters to be put upon his thighs.— Good lack! a'has been mortally obstropolous, and out of his senses all this blessed day.'—'You lie, (cried the squire) I a'n't out of my seven senses, thof I'm half mad with vexation.'

The doctor having withdrawn the curtain, the hapless squire appeared very pale and ghastly; and having surveyed his master with a rueful aspect, addressed him in these words: 'Sir knight, I beg a boon: be pleased to tie a stone about the neck of the apothecary, and a halter about the neck of the nurse, and throw the one into the next river, and the other over the next tree, and in so doing you will do a charitable deed to your fellow-creatures; for he and she do the devil's work in partnership, and have sent many a score of their betters home to him before their time.' 'Oh, he begins to talk sensibly.' 'Have a good heart, (said the physician.) What is your disorder?' 'Physick.' 'What do you chiefly complain of?' 'The doctor.' 'Does your head ake?' 'Yea, with impertinence.' 'Have you a pain in your back?' 'Yes, where the blister lies.' 'Are you sick at stomach?' 'Yes, with hunger.' 'Do you feel any shiverings?' 'Always at sight of the apothecary.' 'Do you perceive any load in your bowels?' 'I would the apothecary's conscience was as clear.' 'Are you thirsty?' 'Not thirsty enough to drink barley-water.' 'Be pleased to look into his fauces, (said the apothecary:) he has got a rough tongue, and a very foul mouth, I'll assure you.' 'I have known that the case with some limbs of the faculty, where they stood more in need of correction than of physick.—Well, my honest friend, since you have already undergone the proper purgations in due form, and say you have no other disease than the doctor, we will set you on your legs again, without further question. Here, nurse, open that window, and throw these vials into the street. Now lower the curtain, without shutting the casement, that the man may not be stifled in his own steam. In the next place, take off two thirds of these coals, and one third of these blankets.— How do'st feel now, my heart?' 'I should feel heart-whole, if so be as yow would throw the noorse a'ter the bottles, and the pothecary a'ter the noorse, and oorder me a pound of chops for my dinner; for I be so hoongry, I could eat a horse behind the saddle.'

The apothecary, seeing what passed, retired of his own accord, holding up his hands in sign of astonishment. The nurse was dismissed in the same breath. Crabshaw rose, dressed himself without assistance, and made a hearty meal on the first eatable that presented itself to his view. The knight passed the evening with the physician, who from his first appearance, concluded he was mad; but, in the course of the conversation, found means to resign that opinion, without adopting any other in lieu of it, and parted with him under all the impatience of curiosity. The knight, on his part, was very well entertained with the witty sarcasms and erudition of the doctor, who appeared to be a sort of cynic philosopher, tinctured with misanthropy, and at open war with the whole body of apothecaries, whom, however, it was by no means his interest to disoblige.

Next, day, Crabshaw being to all appearance perfectly recovered, our adventurer reckoned with the apothecary, payed the landlord, and set out on his return for the London-road, resolving to lay aside his armour at some distance from the metropolis: for, ever since his interview with Aurelia, his fondness for chivalry had been gradually abating. As the torrent of his despair had disordered the current of his sober reflection, so now, as that despair subsided, his thoughts began to flow deliberately in their antient channel. All day long he regaled his imagination with plans of connubial happiness, formed on the possession of the incomparable Aurelia; determined to wait with patience, until the law should supersede the authority of her guardian, rather than adopt any violent expedient which might hazard the interest of his passion.

He had for some time travelled in the turnpike road, when his reverie was suddenly interrupted by a confused noise; and when he lifted up his eyes, he beheld at a little distance a rabble of men and women, variously armed with flails, pitchforks, poles, and muskets, acting offensively against a strange figure on horseback, who, with a kind of lance, laid about him with incredible fury. Our adventurer was not so totally abandoned by the spirit of chivalry, as to see without emotion a single knight in danger of being overpowered by such a multitude of adversaries. Without staying to put on his helmet, he ordered Crabshaw to follow him in the charge against those plebeians: then couching his lance, and giving Bronzomarte the spur, he began his career with such impetuosity as overturned all that happened to be in his way; and intimidated the rabble to such a degree, that they retired before him like a flock of sheep, the greater part of them believing he was the devil *in propria persona*. He came in the very nick of time to save the life of the other errant, against whom three loaded musquets were actually levelled, at the very instant that our adventurer began his charge. The unknown knight was so sensible of the seasonable interposition, that riding up to our hero, 'Brother, (said he) this is the second time you have holp me off, when I was bump ashore.—Bess Mizen, I must say, is no more than a leaky bumboat,[1] in comparison of the glorious galley you want to man.

I desire that henceforth we may cruise in the same latitudes, brother; and I'll be damned if I don't stand by you as long as I have a stick standing, or can carry a rag of canvas.'

By this address our knight recognized the novice captain Crowe, who had found means to accommodate himself with a very strange suit of armour. By way of helmet, he wore one of the caps used by the light horse, with straps buckled under his chin, and contrived in such a manner as to conceal his whole visage, except the eyes. Instead of cuirass, mail, greaves, and the other pieces of complete armour, he was cased in a postilion's leathern jerkin, covered with thin plates of tinned iron: his buckler was a potlid, his lance a hop-pole[1] shod with iron, and a basket-hilt broad sword, like that of Hudibras,[2] depended by a broad buff belt, that girded his middle. His feet were defended by jack-boots, and his hands by the gloves of a trooper. Sir Launcelot would not lose time in examining particulars, as he perceived that some mischief had been done, and that the enemy had rallied at a distance: he therefore commanded Crowe to follow him, and rode off with great expedition; but he did not perceive that his squire was taken prisoner; nor did the captain recollect that his nephew, Tom Clarke, had been disabled and secured in the beginning of the fray. The truth is, the poor captain had been so belaboured about the pate, that it was a wonder he remembered his own name.

CHAPTER XVII

Containing adventures of chivalry, equally new and surprising

THE knight Sir Launcelot, and the novice Crowe, retreated with equal order and expedition to the distance of half a league from the field of battle, where the former, halting, proposed to make a lodgment in a very decent house of entertainment, distinguished by the sign of St. George of Cappadocia encountering the dragon, an atchievement in which temporal and spiritual chivalry were happily reconciled.[3] Two such figures alighting at the inn-gate, did not pass through the yard unnoticed and unadmired by the guests and attendants; some of whom fairly took to their heels, on the supposition that these outlandish creatures were the avant couriers, or heralds of a French invasion. The fears and doubts, however, of those who ventured to stay were soon dispelled, when our hero accosted them in the English tongue, and with the most courteous demeanour desired to be shewn into an apartment. Had captain Crowe been the spokesman, perhaps their suspicions would not have so quickly subsided; for he was, in reality, a very extraordinary novice, not only in chivalry, but also in his external appearance, and particularly in those dialects of the English language which are used by the terrestrial animals of this kingdom. He desired the hostler to take his horse in tow, and bring him to his moorings in a safe riding. He ordered the waiter, who shewed them into a parlour, to bear-a-hand, ship his oars, mind his helm, and bring along-side a short allowance of brandy or grog, that he might cant a slug into his bread-room; for there was such a heaving and pitching, that he believed he should shift his ballast. The fellow understood no part of this address but the word *brandy*, at mention of which he disappeared. Then Crowe, throwing himself into an elbow-chair, 'Stop my hawse-holes, (cried he) I can't think what's the matter, brother; but, a-gad, my head sings and simmers like a pot of chowder.—My eye-sight yaws to and again, d'ye see:— then there's such a walloping and whushing in my hold—smite my—Lord have mercy upon us.—Here, you swab, ne'er mind a glass—hand me the noggin—.'

The latter part of this address was directed to the waiter, who had returned with a quartern of brandy, which Crowe, snatching eagerly, started into his bread-room at one cant. Indeed there was no time to be lost, inasmuch as he seemed to be on the verge of fainting away when he swallowed this cordial, by which he was instantaneously revived. He then desired the servant to unbuckle the straps of his helmet; but this was a task which the drawer could not perform, even though assisted with the good offices of Sir Launcelot: for the head and jaws were so much swelled with the discipline they had undergone, that the straps and buckles lay buried, as it were, in pits formed by the tumefaction of the adjacent parts. Fortunately for the novice, a neighbouring surgeon passed by the door on horseback; a circumstance which the waiter, who saw him from the window, no sooner disclosed, than the knight had recourse to his assistance. This practitioner having viewed the whole figure, and more particularly the head of Crowe, in silent wonder, proceeded to feel his pulse; and then declared, that as the inflammation was very great, and going on with violence to its akme, it would be necessary to begin with copious phlebotomy, and then to empty the intestinal canal. So saying, he began to strip the arm of the captain, who perceiving his aim, 'Avast, brother, (cried he) you go the wrong way to work—you may as well rummage the afterhold, when the damage is in the forecastle.—I shall right again, when my jaws are unhooped.'

With these words he drew a clasp-knife from his pocket, and, advancing to a glass, applied it so vigorously to the leather straps of his headpiece, that the Gordian-knot was cut, without any other damage to his face than a moderate scarification, which, added to the tumefaction of features, naturally strong, and a whole week's growth of a very bushy beard, produced, on the whole, a most hideous caricatura. After all, there was a necessity for the administration of the surgeon, who found divers contusions on different parts of the skull, which even the tin-cap had not been able to protect from the weapons of the rusticks.

These being shaved, and dressed *secundum artem*, and the operator dismissed with a proper acknowledgement, our knight detached one of the post-boys to the field of action for intelligence, concerning Mr. Clarke and squire Timothy; and, in the interim, desired to know the particulars of Crowe's adventures since he parted from him at the White Hart. A connected relation, in plain English, was what he had little reason to expect from the novice, who, nevertheless, exerted his faculties to the uttermost for his satisfaction: he gave him to understand, that in steering his course to Birmingham, where he thought of fitting himself with tackle, he had fallen in, by accident, at a public house, with an itinerant tinker, in the very act of mending a kettle: that, seeing him do his business like an able workman, he had applied to him for advice; and the tinker, after having considered the subject, had undertaken to make him such a suit of armour as neither sword nor lance should penetrate: that they adjourned to the next town, where the leather coat, the plates of tinned iron, the lance, and the broad sword, were purchased, together with a copper sauce-pan, which the artist was now at work upon, in converting it to a shield: but, in the mean time, the captain, being impatient to begin his career of chivalry, had accommodated himself with a pot-lid, and taken to the highway, notwithstanding all the intreaties, tears, and remonstrances of his nephew Tom Clarke, who could not however be prevailed upon to leave him in the dangerous voyage he had undertaken: that this being but the second day of his journal,[1] he descried five or six men on horseback, bearing up full in his teeth; upon which he threw his sails a-back, and prepared for action: that he hailed them at a considerable distance, and bad them bring-to:[2] that, when they came along-side, notwithstanding his hail, he ordered them to clew up[3] their corses, and furl their topsails, otherwise he would be foul of their quarters: that, hearing this salute, they luffed all at once, till their cloth shook in the wind: then he hollowed in a loud voice, that his sweetheart Besselia Mizzen wore the broad pendant[4] of beauty, to which they must strike their topsails, on pain of being sent to the bottom: that, after having eyed him for some time with astonishment, they clapped on all their sails, some of them running under his stern, and others athwart his forefoot, and got clear off: that, not satisfied with running a-head, they all of a sudden tacked about, and one of them boarding him on the lee-quarter, gave him such a drubbing about his upper works, that the lights danced in his lanthorns: that he returned the salute with his hop-pole so effectually, that his aggressor broached-to[5] in the twinkling of an hand-spike;[6] and then he was engaged with all the rest of the enemy, except one who sheered off, and soon returned with a mosqueto fleet[7] of small craft, who had done him considerable damage, and, in all probability, would have made prize of him, hadn't he been brought off by the knight's gallantry. He said, that in the beginning of the conflict Tom Clarke rode up to the foremost of the enemy, as he did suppose, in order to prevent hostilities; but before he got up to him, near enough to hold discourse, he was pooped with a sea[8] that almost sent him to the bottom, and then towed off he knew not whither.

Crowe had scarce finished his narration, which consisted of broken hints, and unconnected explosions of sea-terms, when a gentleman of the neighbourhood, who acted in the commission of the peace, arrived at the gate, attended by a constable, who had in custody the bodies of Thomas Clarke and Timothy Crabshaw, surrounded by five men on horseback, and an innumerable posse of men, women, and children, on foot. The captain, who always kept a good lookout, no sooner descried this cavalcade and procession than he gave notice to Sir Launcelot, and advised that they should crowd away[9] with all the cloth they could carry. Our adventurer was of another opinion, and determined at any rate to procure the enlargement of the prisoners. The justice, ordering his attendants to stay without the gate, sent his compliments to Sir Launcelot Greaves, and desired to speak with him for a few minutes. He was immediately admitted, and could not help starting at sight of Crowe, who, by this time, had no remains of the human physiognomy, so much was the swelling increased and the skin discoloured. The gentleman, whose name was Mr. Elmy, having made a polite apology for the liberty he had taken, proceeded to unfold his business. He said, information had been lodged with him, as a justice of the peace, against two armed men on horseback, who had stopped five farmers on the king's highway, put them in fear and danger of their lives, and even assaulted, maimed, and wounded divers persons, contrary to the king's peace, and in violation of the statute: that, by the description, he supposed the knight and his companion to be the persons against whom the complaint had been lodged; and understanding his quality from Mr. Clarke, whom he had known in London, he was come to wait on him, and, if possible, effect an accommodation.

Our adventurer, having thanked him for the polite and obliging manner in which he proceeded, frankly told him the whole story, as it had been just related by the captain; and Mr. Elmy had no reason to doubt the truth of the narrative, as it confirmed every circumstance which Clarke had before reported. Indeed, Tom had been very communicative to this gentleman, and made him acquainted with the whole history of Sir Launcelot Greaves, as well as with the whimsical resolution of his uncle, captain Crowe. Mr. Elmy now told the knight, that the persons whom the captain had stopped were farmers, returning from a neighbouring market, a set of people naturally boorish, and at that time elevated with ale to an uncommon pitch of insolence: that one of them, in particular, called Prickle, was the most quarrelsome fellow in the whole country; and so litigious, that he had maintained above thirty law-suits, in eight and twenty of which he had been condemned in costs. He said the others might be easily influenced in the way of admonition; but there was no way of dealing with Prickle, except by the form and authority of the law: he therefore proposed to hear evidence in a judicial capacity, and, his clerk being in attendance, the court was immediately opened in the knight's apartment.

By this time Mr. Clarke had made such good use of his time in explaining the law to his audience, and displaying the great wealth and unbounded liberality of Sir Launcelot Greaves, that he had actually brought over to his sentiments the constable and the commonalty, tag, rag, and bob-tail, and even staggered the majority of the farmers, who, at first, had breathed nothing but defiance and revenge. Farmer Stake, being first called to the bar, and sworn, touching the identity of Sir Launcelot Greaves and captain Crowe, declared, that the said Crowe had stopped him on the king's highway, and put him in bodily fear: that he afterwards saw the said Crowe with a pole or weapon, value three pence, breaking the king's peace, by committing assault and battery against the heads and shoulders of his majesty's liege subjects, Geoffrey Prickle, Hodge Dolt, Richard Bumpkin, Mary Fang, Catherine Rubble, and Margery Litter; and that he saw Sir Launcelot Greaves, baronet, aiding, assisting, and comforting the said Crowe, contrary to the king's peace, and against the form of the statute.

Being asked if the defendant, when he stopped them, demanded their money, or threatened violence, he answered, he could not say, inasmuch as the defendant spoke in an unknown language. Being interrogated if the defendant did not allow them to pass without using any violence, and if they did not pass unmolested, the deponent replied in the affirmative: being required to tell for what reason they returned, and if the defendant Crowe was not assaulted before he began to use his weapon, the deponent made no answer. The depositions of farmer Bumpkin and Muggins, as well as of Madge Litter and Mary Fang, were taken much to the same purpose; and his worship earnestly exhorted them to an accommodation, observing, that they themselves were in fact the aggressors, and that captain Crowe had done no more than exerted himself in his own defence.

They were all pretty well disposed to follow his advice, except farmer Prickle, who, entering the court with a bloody handkerchief about his head, declared, that the law should determine it at next 'size;[1] and in the mean time insisted, that the defendants should find immediate bail, or go to prison, or be set in the stocks. He affirmed, that they had been guilty of an *affray*, in appearing with armour and weapons not usually worn, to the terror of others, which is in itself a breach of the peace: but that they had, moreover, with force of arms, that is to say, with swords, staves, and other warlike instruments, by turns, made an assault and *affray*, to the terror and disturbance of him and divers subjects of our lord the king then and there being, and to the evil and pernicious example of the liege people of the said lord the king, and against the peace of our said lord the king, his crown, and dignity.

This peasant had purchased a few law-terms at a considerable expence, and he thought he had a right to turn his knowledge to the annoyance of all his neighbours. Mr. Elmy, finding him obstinately deaf to all proposals of accommodation, held the defendants to very moderate bail, the landlord and the curate of the parish freely offering themselves as sureties. Mr. Clarke, with Timothy Crabshaw, against whom nothing appeared, were now set at liberty; when the former, advancing to his worship, gave information against Geoffrey Prickle, and declared upon oath, that he had seen him assault captain Crowe, without any provocation; and when he, the deponent, interposed to prevent further mischief, the said Prickle had likewise assaulted and wounded him the deponent, and detained him for some time in false imprisonment, without warrant or authority.

In consequence of this information, which was corroborated by divers evidences, selected from the mob at the gate, the tables were turned upon farmer Prickle, who was given to understand, that he must either find bail, or be forthwith imprisoned. This *honest* boor, who was in opulent circumstances, had made such popular use of the benefits he possessed, that there was not an housekeeper in the parish who would not have rejoiced to see him hanged. His dealings and connections however were such, that none of the other four would have refused to bail him, had not Clarke given them to understand, that, if they did, he would make them all principals and parties, and have two separate actions against each. Prickle happened to be at variance with the inn-keeper, and the curate durst not disoblige the vicar, who at that very time was suing the farmer for the small tythes.[1] He offered to deposit a sum equal to the recognizance of the knight's bail; but this was rejected as an expedient contrary to the practice of the courts. He sent for the attorney of the village, to whom he had been a good customer; but the lawyer was hunting evidence in another county. The exciseman presented himself as a surety; but he not being an housekeeper, was not accepted. Divers cottagers, who depended on farmer Prickle, were successively refused, because they could not prove that they had payed scot and lot,[1] and parish taxes.

The farmer, finding himself thus forlorn, and in imminent danger of visiting the inside of a prison, was seized with a paroxysm of rage; during which he inveighed against the bench, reviled the two adventurers errant, declared that he believed, and would lay a wager of twenty guineas, that he had more money in his pocket than e'er a man in the company; and in the space of a quarter of an hour swore forty oaths, which the justice did not fail to number. 'Before we proceed to other matters, (said Mr. Elmy) I order you to pay forty shillings for the oaths you have swore; otherwise I will cause you to be set in the stocks, without further ceremony.'

Prickle, throwing down a couple of guineas, with two execrations more to make up the sum, declared, that he could afford to pay for swearing as well as e'er a justice in the county; and repeated his challenge of the wager, which our adventurer now accepted, protesting, at the same time, that it was not a step taken from any motive of pride, but intirely with a view to punish an insolent plebeian, who could not otherwise be chastised without a breach of the peace. Twenty guineas being deposited on each side in the hands of Mr. Elmy, Prickle, with equal confidence and dispatch, produced a canvas bag, containing two hundred and seventy pounds, which, being spread upon the table, made a very formidable shew, that dazzled the eyes of the beholders, and induced many of them to believe he had ensured his conquest.

Our adventurer, asking if he had any thing further to offer, and being answered in the negative, drew forth, with great deliberation, a pocket-book, in which there was a considerable parcel of bank-notes, from which he selected three of one hundred pounds each, and exhibited them upon the table, to the astonishment of all present. Prickle, mad with his overthrow and loss, said it might be necessary to make him prove the notes were honestly come by; and Sir Launcelot started up, in order to take vengeance upon him for this insult; but was withheld by the arms and remonstrances of Mr. Elmy, who assured him that Prickle desired nothing so much as another broken head, to lay the foundation of a new prosecution.

The knight, calmed by this interposition, turned to the audience, saying, with the most affable deportment, 'Good people, do not imagine that I intend to pocket the spoils of such a contemptible rascal. I shall beg the favour of this worthy gentleman to take up these twenty guineas, and distribute them as he shall think proper, among the poor of the parish: but, by this benefaction, I do not hold myself acquitted for the share I had in the bruises some of you have received in this unlucky fray; and therefore I give the other twenty guineas to be divided among the sufferers, to each according to the damage he or she shall appear to have sustained; and I shall consider it as an additional obligation, if Mr. Elmy will likewise superintend this retribution.'

At the close of this address, the whole yard and gate-way rung with acclamation: while honest Crowe, whose generosity was not inferior even to that of the accomplished Greaves, pulled out his purse, and declared that as he had begun the engagement, he would at least go share and share alike in new caulking their seams and repairing their timbers. The knight, rather than enter into a dispute with his novice, told him he considered the twenty guineas as given by them both in conjunction, and that they would confer together on that subject hereafter.

This point being adjusted, Mr. Elmy assumed all the solemnity of the magistrate, and addressed himself to Prickle in these words: 'Farmer Prickle, I am both sorry and ashamed to see a man of your years and circumstances so little respected, that you cannot find sufficient bail for forty pounds; a sure testimony that you have neither cultivated the friendship, nor deserved the goodwill of your neighbours. I have heard of your quarrels and your riots, your insolence, and litigious disposition; and often wished for an opportunity of giving you a proper taste of the law's correction. That opportunity now offers—You have in the hearing of all these people poured forth a torrent of abuse against me, both in the character of a gentleman and of a magistrate: your abusing me personally, perhaps I should have overlooked with the contempt it deserves; but I should ill vindicate the dignity of my office as magistrate, by suffering you to insult the bench with impunity. I shall therefore imprison you for contempt; and you shall remain in jail, until you can find bail on the other prosecutions.'

Prickle, the first transports of his anger having subsided, began to be pricked with the thorns of compunction. He was indeed exceedingly mortified at the prospect of being sent to jail so disgracefully. His countenance fell, and, after a hard internal struggle while the clerk was employed in writing the mittimus, he said he hoped his worship would not send him to prison. He begged pardon of him and our adventurers for having abused them in his passion, and observed, that as he had received a broken head, and payed two and twenty guineas for his folly, he could not be said to have escaped altogether without punishment, even if the plaintiff should agree to exchange releases.

Sir Launcelot, seeing this stubborn rustic effectually humbled, became an advocate in his favour with Mr. Elmy and Tom Clarke, who forgave him at his request, and a mutual release being executed, the farmer was permitted to depart. The populace were regaled at our adventurer's expence; and the men, women, and children, who had been wounded or bruised in the battle, to the number of ten or dozen, were desired to wait upon Mr. Elmy in the morning to receive the knight's bounty. The justice was prevailed upon to spend the evening with Sir Launcelot and his two companions, for whom supper was bespoke; but the first thing the cook prepared was a poultice for Crowe's head, which was now enlarged to a monstrous exhibition. Our knight, who was all kindness and complacency, shook Mr. Clarke by the hand, expressing his satisfaction at meeting with his old friends again, and told him softly that he had compliments for him from Mrs. Dolly Cowslip, who now lived with his Aurelia.

Clarke was confounded at this intelligence, and after some hesitation, 'Lord bless my soul! (cried he) I'll be shot then if the pretended miss Meadows wa'n't the same as miss Darnel!' he then declared himself extremely glad that poor Dolly had got into such an agreeable situation, passed many warm encomiums on her goodness of heart and virtuous inclinations, and concluded with appealing to the knight whether she did not look very pretty in her green Joseph. In the mean time, he procured a plaister for his own head, and helped to apply the poultice to that of his uncle, who was sent to bed betimes with a moderate dose of sack-whey[1] to promote perspiration. The other three passed the evening to their mutual satisfaction; and the justice in particular grew enamoured of the knight's character, dashed as it was with extravagance.

Let us now leave them to the enjoyment of a sober and rational conversation; and give some account of other guests who arrived late in the evening, and here fixed their night-quarters—But as we have already trespassed on the reader's patience, we shall give him a short respite until the next chapter makes its appearance.

CHAPTER XVIII

In which the Rays of Chivalry shine with renovated Lustre

OUR hero little dreamed that he had a formidable rival in the person of the knight who arrived about eleven at the sign of the St. George, and, by the noise he made, gave intimation of his importance. This was no other than squire Sycamore, who, having received advice that Miss Aurelia Darnel had eloped from the place of her retreat, immediately took the field, in quest of that lovely fugitive; hoping, that should he have the good fortune to find her in her present distress, his good offices would not be rejected. He had followed the chace so close, that, immediately after our adventurer's departure, he alighted at the inn from whence Aurelia had been conveyed; and there he learned the particulars which we have related above. Mr. Sycamore had a great deal of the childish romantic in his disposition, and, in the course of his amours, is said to have always taken more pleasure in the pursuit than in the final possession. He had heard of Sir Launcelot's extravagance, by which he was in some measure infected; and he dropped an insinuation, that he could eclipse his rival even in his own lunatic sphere. This hint was not lost upon his companion, counsellor, and buffoon, the facetious Davy Dawdle, who had some humour and a great deal of mischief in his composition. He looked upon his patron as a fool, and his patron knew him to be both knave and fool: yet the two characters suited each other so well, that they could hardly exist asunder. Davy was an artful sycophant, but he did not flatter in the usual way; on the contrary, he behaved *en cavalier*, and treated Sycamore, on whose bounty he subsisted, with the most sarcastic familiarity. Nevertheless, he seasoned his freedom with certain qualifying ingredients that subdued the bitterness of it, and was now become so necessary to the squire, that he had no idea of enjoyment with which Dawdle was not some how or other connected. There had been a warm dispute betwixt them about the scheme of contesting the prize with Sir Launcelot in the lists of chivalry. Sycamore had insinuated, that if he had a mind to play the fool, he could wear armour, wield a launce, and manage a charger, as well as Sir

Launcelot Greaves. Dawdle snatching the hint, 'I had some time ago, (said he) contrived a scheme for you, which I was afraid you had not address enough to execute—It would be no difficult matter, in imitation of the batchelor Sampson Carrasco, to go in quest of Greaves as a knight errant, defy him as a rival, and establish a compact, by which the vanquished should obey the injunctions of the victor'[1]—'That is my very idea.' (cried Sycamore) 'Your idea (replied the other) had you ever an idea of your own conception.'—Thus the dispute began, and was maintained with great vehemence; until other arguments failing, the squire offered to lay a wager of twenty guineas. To this proposal Dawdle answered by the interjection *Pish*! which inflamed Sycamore to a repetition of the defiance.'—'You are in the right (said Dawdle) to use such an argument, as you know is by me unanswerable. A wager of twenty guineas will at any time overthrow and confute all the logick of the most able syllogist, who has not got a shilling in his pocket.'

Sycamore looked very grave at this declaration, and, after a short pause, said, 'I wonder, Dawdle, what you do with all your money!' 'I am surprised you should give yourself that trouble—I never ask what you do with yours.'—'You have no occasion to ask: you know pretty well how it goes.' 'What! do you upbraid me with your favours?—'tis mighty well, Sycamore.'—'Nay Dawdle, I did not intend to affront.'—'Z——s![2] affront! what d'ye mean?'—'I'll assure you Davy, you don't know me, if you think I could be so ungenerous as to—a—to—' 'I always thought, whatever faults or foibles you might have, Sycamore, that you was not deficient in generosity,—tho' to be sure it is often very absurdly displayed.' 'Ay, that's one of my greatest foibles: I can't refuse even a scoundrel, when I think he's in want.—Here Dawdle, take that note.'—'Not I, sir,—what d'ye mean?—what right have I to take your notes.' 'Nay but Dawdle—come.'—'By no means, —it looks like the abuse of good nature,—all the world knows you're good natured to a fault.'—'Come dear Davy, you shall— you must oblige me.'—Thus urged, Dawdle accepted the bank note with great reluctance, and restored the idea to the right owner.

A suit of armour being brought from the garret or armoury of his ancestors, he gave orders for having the pieces scoured and furbished up; and his heart dilated with joy, when he reflected upon the superb figure he should make when cased in complete steel, and armed at all points for the combat.

When he was fitted with the other parts, Dawdle insisted on buckling on his helmet, which weighed fifteen pounds, and the head-piece being adjusted, made such a clatter about his ears with a cudgel, that his eyes had almost started from their sockets. His voice was lost within the vizor, and his friend affected not to understand his meaning when he made signs with his gauntlets, and endeavoured to close with him that he might wrest the cudgel from his hand. At length he desisted, saying, 'I'll warrant the helmet sound, by its ringing;' and taking it off, found the squire in a cold sweat. He would have atchieved his first exploit on the spot, had his strength permitted him to assault Dawdle; but, what with want of air, and the discipline he had undergone, he had well nigh swooned away; and before he retrieved the use of his members, he was appeased by the apologies of his companion, who protested he meant nothing more than to try if the helmet was free of cracks, and whether or not it would prove a good protection for the head it covered. His excuses were accepted: the armour was packed up, and next morning Mr. Sycamore set out from his own house, accompanied by Dawdle, who undertook to perform the part of his squire at the approaching combat. He was also attended by a servant on horseback, who had charge of the armour, and another who blowed the trumpet. They no sooner understood that our hero was housed at the George, than the trumpeter sounded a charge, which alarmed Sir Launcelot and his company, and disturbed honest captain Crowe in the middle of his first sleep. Their next step was to pen a challenge, which, when the stranger departed, was by the trumpeter delivered with great ceremony into the hands of Sir Launcelot, who read it in these words. 'To the Knight of the Crescent, greeting. Whereas I am informed you have the presumption to lay claim to the heart of the peerless Aurelia Darnel, I give you notice that I can admit no rivalship in the affection of that paragon of beauty; and I expect that you will either resign your pretensions, or make it appear in single combat, according to the law of arms, and the institutions of chivalry, that you are worthy to dispute her favour with him of the Griffin. POLYDORE.'

Our adventurer was not a little surprised at this address, which, however, he pocketed in silence; and began to reflect, not without mortification, that he was treated as a lunatic by some person who wanted to amuse himself with the infirmities of his fellow creatures. Mr. Thomas Clarke, who saw the ceremony with which the letter was delivered, and the emotions with which it was read, hied him to the kitchen for intelligence, and there learned that the stranger was squire Sycamore. He forthwith comprehended the nature of the billet, and, in the apprehension that bloodshed would ensue, resolved to alarm his uncle, that he might assist in keeping the peace. He accordingly entered the apartment of the captain, who had been waked by the trumpet, and now peevishly asked the meaning of that damned piping, as if all hands were called upon deck. Clarke having imparted what he knew of the transaction, together with his own conjectures, the captain said, he did not suppose as how they would engage by candle-light; and that for his own part he should turn out in the larboard watch, long enough before any signals could be hove out for forming the line. With this assurance the lawyer retired to his nest, where he did not fail to dream of Mrs. Dolly Cowslip; while Sir Launcelot passed the night awake, in ruminating on the strange challenge he had received. He had got notice that the sender was Mr. Sycamore, and hesitated with himself whether he should not punish him for his impertinence: but when he reflected on the nature of the dispute, and the serious consequences it might produce, he resolved to decline the combat, as a trial of right and merit, founded upon absurdity. Even in his maddest hours, he never adopted those maxims of knight-errantry which related to challenges. He always perceived the folly and wickedness of defying a man to mortal fight, because he did not like the colour of his beard, or the complexion of his mistress; or of deciding by homicide, whether he or his rival deserved the preference, when it was the lady's prerogative to determine which should be the happy lover. It was his opinion that chivalry was an useful institution while confined to its original purposes of protecting the innocent, assisting the friendless, and bringing the guilty to condign punishment: but he could not conceive how these laws should be answered by violating every suggestion of reason, and every precept of humanity. Captain Crowe did not examine the matter so philosophically. He took it for granted that in the morning the two knights would come to action, and slept sound on that supposition. But he rose before it was day, resolved to be some how concerned in the fray; and understanding that the stranger had a companion, set him down immediately for his own antagonist. So impatient was he to establish this secondary contest, that by day-break he entered the chamber of Dawdle, to which he was directed by the waiter, and roused him with a hilloah, that might have been heard at the distance of half a league. Dawdle, startled by this terrific sound, sprung out of bed, and stood upright on the floor, before he opened his eyes upon the object by which he had been so dreadfully alarmed. But when he beheld the head of Crowe, so swelled and swathed, so livid, hideous, and griesly, with a broad sword by his side, and a case of pistols in his girdle, he believed it was the apparition of some murthered man; his hair bristled up, his teeth chattered, and his knees knocked; he would have prayed, but his tongue denied its office. Crowe seeing his perturbation, 'May-hap friend, said he, you take me for a buccaneer: but I am no such person.—My name it is captain Crowe.—I come not for your silver nor your gold; your rigging nor your stowage, but hearing as how your friend intends to bring my friend Sir Launcelot Greaves to action, d'ye see; I desire in the way of friendship, that, while they are engaged, you and I as their seconds may lie board and board for a few glasses,[1] to divert one another, d'ye see.' Dawdle hearing this request, began to retrieve his faculties, and throwing himself into the attitude of Hamlet, when the ghost appears, exclaimed in theatrical accent, 'Angels and ministers of grace defend us!—Art thou a spirit of grace, or goblin damn'd?'[2]——As he seemed to bend his eye on vacancy, the captain began to think that he really saw something preternatural, and stared wildly around. Then addressing himself to the terrified Dawdle, 'Damn'd (said he) for what should I be damn'd? if you are afeard of goblins brother, put your trust in the Lord, and he'll prove a sheet-anchor to you.' The other having by this time recollected himself perfectly, continued, not withstanding, to spout tragedy, and in the words of Macbeth pronounced,

> 'What man dare, I dare:
> Approach thou like the rugged Russian bear,
> The armed rhinoceros, or Hyrcanian tyger;
> Take any shape but that, and my firm nerves
> Shall never tremble. . . .'[3]

"Ware names Jack, (cried the impatient mariner) if so be as how you'll bear a hand and rig yourself, and take a short trip with me into the offing, we'll overhaul this here affair in the turning of a capstan.'

At this juncture they were joined by Mr. Sycamore in his night-gown and slippers. Disturbed by Crowe's first salute he had sprung up; and now expressed no small astonishment at first sight of the novice's countenance. After having gazed alternately at him and Dawdle, 'Who have we got here, said he, raw head and bloody bones?'[1] when his friend, slipping on his cloaths, gave him to understand that this was a friend of Sir Launcelot Greaves, and explained the purport of his errand, he treated him with more civility. He assured him that he should have the pleasure to break a spear with Mr. Dawdle; and signified his surprise that Sir Launcelot had made no answer to his letter. It being by this time clear day-light, and Crowe extremely interested in this affair, he broke without ceremony into the knight's chamber, and told him abruptly that the enemy had brought to, and waited for his coming up, in order to begin the action. 'I've hailed his consort, said he, a shambling chattering fellow: he took me first for an hobgoblin, then called me names, a tyger, a wrynose o'ross, and a Persian bear: but egad, if I come athwart him, I'll make him look like the bear and ragged staff[2] before we part.—I wool.—'

This intimation was not received with that alacrity which the captain expected to find in our adventurer, who told him in a peremptory tone, that he had no design to come to action, and desired to be left to his repose. Crowe forthwith retired, crest-fallen; and muttered something which was never distinctly heard.

About eight in the morning Mr. Dawdle brought him a formal message from the knight of the Griffin, desiring he would appoint the lists, and give security of the field. To which request he made answer in a very composed and solemn accent, 'If the person who sent you, thinks I have injured him, let him without disguise, or any such ridiculous ceremony, explain the nature of the wrong; and then I shall give such satisfaction as may suit my conscience and my character. If he hath bestowed his affection upon any par-ticular object, and looks upon me as a favoured rival, I shall not wrong the lady so much as to take any step that may prejudice her choice, especially a step that contradicts my own reason as much as it would outrage the laws of my country. If he who calls himself knight of the Griffin, is really desirous of treading in the paths of true chivalry, he will not want opportunities of signalizing his valour in the cause of virtue.—Should he, notwithstanding this declaration, offer violence to me in the course of my occasions, he will always find me in a posture of defence: or, should he persist in repeating his importunities, I shall without ceremony chastise the messenger.' His declining the combat was interpreted into fear by Mr. Sycamore, who now became more insolent and ferocious, on the supposition of our knight's timidity. Sir Launcelot, mean while, went to breakfast with his friends; and having put on his armour, ordered the horses to be brought forth. Then he payed the bill, and walking deliberately to the gate, in presence of squire Sycamore and his attendants, vaulted at one spring into the saddle of Bronzomarte, whose neighing and curvetting proclaimed the joy he felt in being mounted by his accomplished master.

Though the knight of the Griffin did not think proper to insult his rival personally, his friend Dawdle did not fail to crack some jokes on the figure and horsemanship of Crowe; who again declared he should be glad to fall in with him upon the voyage: nor did Mr. Clarke's black patch and rueful countenance pass un-noticed and unridiculed. As for Timothy Crabshaw, he beheld his brother squire with the contempt of a veteran: and Gilbert payed him his compliments with his heels at parting: but when our adventurer and his retinue were clear of the inn, Mr. Sycamore ordered his trumpeter to sound a retreat, by way of triumph over his antagonist. Perhaps he would have contented himself with this kind of victory had not Dawdle further inflamed his envy and ambition by launching out in praise of Sir Launcelot. He observed that his countenance was open and manly; his joints strong knit, and his form unexceptionable; that he trod like Hercules, and vaulted into the saddle like a winged Mercury: nay he even hinted it was lucky for Sycamore that the knight of the Crescent happened to be so pacifically disposed. His patron sickened at these praises, and took fire at the last observation. He affected to under-value personal beauty, though the opinion of the world had been favourable to himself in that particular: he said he was at least two inches taller than Greaves; and as to shape and air, he would make no comparisons; but with respect to riding, he was sure he had a better seat than Sir Launcelot, and would wager five hundred to fifty guineas, that he would unhorse him at the first encounter. 'There is no occasion for laying wagers, replied Mr. Dawdle, the doubt may be determined in half an hour—Sir Launcelot is not a man to avoid you at full gallop.' Sycamore, after some hesitation, declared he would follow and provoke him to battle, on condition that Dawdle would engage Crowe; and this condition was accepted: for though Davy had no stomach to the tryal, he could not readily find an excuse for declining it: besides, he had discovered the captain to be a very bad horseman, and resolved to eke out his own scanty valour with a border of ingenuity. The servants were immediately ordered to unpack the armour, and in a little time, Mr. Sycamore made a very formidable appearance. But the scene that followed is too important to be huddled in at the end of a chapter, and therefore we shall reserve it for a more conspicuous place in these memoirs.

CHAPTER XIX

Discomfiture of the Knight of the Griffin

MR. SYCAMORE, alias the knight of the Griffin, so denominated from a gryphon painted on his shield, being armed at all points, and his friend Dawdle provided with a certain implement, which he flattered himself, would ensure a victory over the novice Crowe; they set out from the George, with their attendants, in all the elevation of hope, and pranced along the highway that led towards London, that being the road which our adventurer pursued. As they were extremely well mounted, and proceeded at a round pace, they, in less than two hours, came up with Sir Launcelot and his company; and Sycamore sent another formal defiance to the knight, by his trumpeter, Dawdle having, for good reasons, declined that office.

Our adventurer hearing himself thus addressed, and seeing his rival, who had passed him, posted to obstruct his progress, armed capapie, with his lance in the rest; determined to give the satisfaction that was required, and desired that the regulations of the combat might be established. The knight of the Griffin proposed, that the vanquished party should resign all pretensions to Miss Aurelia Darnel, in favour of the victor; that while the principals were engaged, his friend Dawdle should run a tilt with captain Crowe; that squire Crabshaw, and Mr. Sycamore's servant, should keep themselves in readiness to assist their respective masters occasionally, according to the law of arms; and that Mr. Clarke should observe the motions of the trumpeter, whose province was to sound the charge to battle.[1]

Our knight agreed to these regulations, notwithstanding the earnest and pathetic remonstrances of the young lawyer, who, with tears in his eyes, conjured all the combatants, in their turns, to refrain from an action that might be attended with bloodshed and murder; and was contrary to the laws both of God and man. In vain he endeavoured to move them by tears and intreaties, by threatening them with prosecutions in this world, and pains and penalties in the next: they persisted in their resolution, and his uncle would have begun hostilities on his carcase, had not he been prevented by Sir Launcelot, who exhorted Clarke to retire from the field, that he might not be involved in the consequences of the combat. He relished this advice so well, that he had actually moved off to some distance; but his apprehension and concern for his friends co-operating with an insatiable curiosity, detained him in sight of the engagement.

The two knights having fairly divided the ground, and the same precautions being taken by the seconds, on another part of the field, Sycamore began to be invaded with some scruples, which were probably engendered by the martial appearance, and well known character of his antagonist. The confidence which he had derived from the reluctance of Sir Launcelot, now vanished, because it plainly appeared, that the knight's backwardness was not owing to personal timidity; and he foresaw that the prosecution of this joke might be attended with very serious consequences to his own life and reputation. He, therefore, desired a parley, in which he observed his affection for Miss Darnel was of such a delicate nature, that should the discomfiture of his rival contribute to make her unhappy, his victory must render him the most miserable wretch upon earth. He proposed, therefore, that her sentiments and choice should be ascertained before they proceeded to extremity.

Sir Launcelot declared that he was much more afraid of combating Aurelia's inclination, than of opposing the knight of the Griffin in arms; and that if he had the least reason to think Mr. Sycamore, or any other person, was distinguished by her preference, he would instantly give up his suit as desperate. At the same time, he observed that Sycamore had proceeded too far to retract; that he had insulted a gentleman, and not only challenged, but even pursued him, and blocked up his passage in the public highway; outrages which he (Sir Launcelot) would not suffer to pass unpunished. Accordingly, he insisted on the combat, on pain of treating Mr. Sycamore as a craven, and a recreant. This declaration was reinforced by Dawdle, who told him that should he now decline the engagement, all the world would look upon him as an infamous poltroon.

These two observations gave a necessary fillip to the courage of the challenger. The parties took their stations: the trumpet sounded to charge, and the combatants began their career with great impetuosity. Whether the gleam of Sir Launcelot's arms affrighted Mr. Sycamore's steed, or some other object had an unlucky effect on his eyesight; certain it is he started, at about midway, and gave his rider such a violent shake as discomposed his attitude, and disabled him from using his lance to the best advantage. Had our hero continued his career, with his launce couched, in all probability Sycamore's armour would have proved but a bad defence to his carcase: but Sir Launcelot perceiving his rival's spear unrested, had just time to throw up the point of his own, when the two horses closed with such a shock, that Sycamore, already wavering in the saddle, was overthrown, and his armour crashed around him as he fell.

The victor, seeing him lie without motion, alighted immediately and began to unbuckle his helmet, in which office he was assisted by the trumpeter. When the head-piece was removed, the hapless knight of the Griffin appeared in the pale livery of death, tho' he was only in a swoon, from which he soon recovered by the effect of the fresh air, and the aspersion of cold water, brought from a small pool in the neighbourhood. When he recognized his conqueror doing the offices of humanity about his person, he closed his eyes from vexation, told Sir Launcelot that his was the fortune of the day, tho' he himself owed his mischance to the fault of his own horse; and observed that this ridiculous affair would not have happened, but for the mischievous instigation of that scoundrel Dawdle, on whose ribs he threatened to revenge his mishap.

Perhaps captain Crowe might have saved him this trouble, had that wag honourably adhered to the institutions of chivalry, in his conflict with our novice: but on this occasion, his ingenuity was more commendable than his courage. He had provided at the inn a blown bladder, in which several smooth pebbles[1] were inclosed; and this he slily fixed to the head of his pole, when the captain obeyed the signal to battle. Instead of bearing the brunt of the encounter, he turned out of the straight line, so as to avoid the launce of his antagonist, and rattled his bladder with such effect, that Crowe's horse pricking up his ears, took to his heels, and fled across some ploughed land with such precipitation, that the rider was obliged to quit his spear, and lay fast hold on the mane, that he might not be thrown out of the saddle. Dawdle, who was much better mounted, seeing his condition, rode up to the unfortunate novice, and belaboured his shoulders without fear of retaliation. Mr. Clarke, seeing his kinsman so roughly handled, forgot his fears, and flew to his assistance; but, before he came up, the aggressor had retired, and now perceiving that fortune had declared against his friend and patron, very honourably abandoned him in his distress, and went off at full speed for London.

Nor was Timothy Crabshaw without his share in the noble atchievements of this propitious day. He had by this time imbibed such a tincture of errantry, that he firmly believed himself and his master equally invincible; and this belief operating upon a perverse disposition, rendered him as quarrelsome in his sphere, as his master was mild and forbearing. As he sat on horseback, in the place assigned to him and Sycamore's lacquey, he managed Gilbert in such a manner, as to invade with his heels, the posteriors of the other's horse; and this insult produced some altercation, which ended in mutual assault. The footman handled the butt-end of his horse-whip with great dexterity about the head of Crabshaw, who declared afterwards, that it sung and simmered like a kettle of cod-fish: but the squire, who understood the nature of long lashes, as having been a carter from his infancy, found means to twine his thong about the neck of his antagonist, and pull him off his horse half strangled, at the very instant his master was thrown by Sir Launcelot Greaves.

Having thus obtained the victory, he did not much regard the punctilios of chivalry; but taking it for granted he had a right to make the most of his advantage, resolved to carry off the *spolia optima*.[2] Alighting with great agility, 'Brother, (cried he) I think as haw yawrs bean't a butcher's horse, a doan't carry calves[3] well—I'se make yaw knaw your churning days, I wool—what yaw look as if yaw was crow-trodden,[1] you do—now, you shall pay the score you have been running on my peate, you shall, brother.'

So saying, he rifled his pockets, stripped him of his hat and coat, and took possession of his master's portmanteau. But he did not long enjoy his plunder: for the lacquey complaining to Sir Launcelot, of his having been despoiled, the knight commanded his squire to refund, not without menaces of subjecting him to the severest chastisement, for his injustice and rapacity. Timothy represented, with great vehemence, that he had won the spoils in fair battle, at the expence of his head and shoulders, which he immediately uncovered, to prove his allegation: but his remonstrance having no effect upon his master, 'Wounds! (cried he) an I mun gee thee back the pig, I'se gee thee back the poke also; I'm a drubbing still in thy debt.'

With these words, he made most furious attack upon the plaintiff, with his horse-whip, and before the knight could interpose, repayed the lacquey with interest. As an appurtenance to Sycamore and Dawdle, he ran the risque of another assault from the novice Crowe, who was so transported with rage, at the disagreeable trick which had been played upon him, by his fugitive antagonist, that he could not for some time pronounce an articulate sound, but a few broken interjections, the meaning of which could not be ascertained. Snatching up his pole, he ran towards the place where Mr. Sycamore sat on the grass, supported by the trumpeter, and would have finished what our adventurer had left undone, if the knight of the Crescent, with admirable dexterity, had not warded off the blow which he aimed at the knight of the Griffin, and signified his displeasure in a resolute tone: then he collared the lacquey, who was just disengaged from the chastising hand of Crabshaw, and swinging his launce with his other hand, encountered the squire's ribs by accident.

Timothy was not slow in returning the salutation, with the weapon which he still wielded: Mr. Clarke, running up to the assistance of his uncle, was opposed by the lacquey, who seemed extremely desirous of seeing the enemy revenge his quarrel, by falling foul of one another. Clarke, thus impeded, commenced hostilities against the footman, while Crowe grappled with Crabshaw; a battle-royal insued, and was maintained with great vigour, and some bloodshed on all sides, until the authority of Sir Launcelot, reinforced by some weighty remonstrances, applied to the squire, put an end to the conflict. Crabshaw immediately desisted, and ran roaring to communicate his grievances to Gilbert, who seemed to sympathize very little with his distress. The lacquey took to his heels; Mr. Clarke wiped his bloody nose, declaring he had a good mind to put the aggressor in the Crown-office;[1] and captain Crowe continued to ejaculate unconnected oaths, which, however, seemed to imply that he was almost sick of his new profession. 'D—n my eyes, if you call this—start my timbers, brother—look ye, d'ye see—a lousy, lubberly, cowardly son of a—among the breakers, d'ye see—lost my steerage way—split my binnacle; haul away—O! damn all arrantry—give me a tight vessel, d'ye see, brother—mayhap you may'nt—snatch my—sea room[2] and a spanking gale—odds heart, I'll hold a whole year's —smite my limbs: it don't signify talking.—'

Our hero consoled the novice for his disaster, by observing, that if he had got some blows, he had lost no honour. At the same time, he observed that it was very difficult, if not impossible, for a man to succeed in the paths of chivalry, who had passed the better part of his days in other occupations; and hinted that as the cause which had engaged him in this way of life no longer existed, he was determined to relinquish a profession, which, in a peculiar manner, exposed him to the most disagreeable incidents. Crowe chewed the cud upon this insinuation, while the other personages of the Drama were employed in catching the horses, which had given their riders the slip. As for Mr. Sycamore, he was so bruised by his fall, that it was necessary to procure a litter for conveying him to the next town, and the servant was dispatched for this convenience; Sir Launcelot staying with him until it arrived.

When he was safely deposited in the carriage, our hero took leave of him in these terms. 'I shall not insist upon your submitting to the terms, you yourself proposed before this rencounter. I give you free leave to use all your advantages, in an honourable way, for promoting your suit with the young lady, of whom you profess yourself enamoured. Should you have recourse to sinister practices, you will find Sir Launcelot Greaves ready to demand an account of your conduct, not in the character of a lunatic knight-errant, but as a plain English gentleman, jealous of his honour, and resolute in his purpose.'

To this address, Mr. Sycamore made no reply, but with a sullen aspect ordered the carriage to proceed; and it moved accordingly to the right, our hero's road to London, lying in the other direction. Sir Launcelot had already exchanged his armour for a riding-coat, hat, and boots; and Crowe parting with his skull-cap and leathern jerkin, regained in some respects the appearance of a human creature. Thus metamorphosed, they pursued their way in an easy pace, Mr. Clarke endeavouring to amuse them with a learned dissertation on the law, tending to demonstrate that Mr. Sycamore was, by his behaviour of that day, liable to three different actions, besides a commission of lunacy; and that Dawdle might be prosecuted for having practised subtle craft, to the annoyance of his uncle, over and above an action for assault and battery; because, for why? The said Crow having run away, as might be easily proved, before any blows were given, the said Dawdle by pursuing him even out of the high road, putting him in fear, and committing battery on his body, became, to all intents and purposes, the aggressor; and an indictment would lie in *Banco Regis.*[1]

The Captain's pride was so shocked at these observations, that he exclaimed with equal rage and impatience, 'You lie, you dog, in *Bilkum Regis*[2]—you lie, I say, you lubber, I did not run away; nor was I in fear, d'ye see. It was my son of a bitch of a horse that would not obey the helm, d'ye see, whereby I coudn't use my metal, d'ye see—As for the matter of fear, you and fear may kiss my——So don't go and heave your stink-pots[3] at my character, d'ye see, or agad I'll trim thee fore and aft with a—I wool.' Tom protested he meant nothing but a little speculation, and Crowe was appeased.

In the evening they reached the town of Bugden,[4] without any farther adventure, and passed the night in great tranquility. Next morning, even after the horses were ordered to be saddled, Mr. Clarke, without ceremony, entered the apartment of Sir Launcelot, leading in a female, who proved to be the identical Mrs. Dolly Cowslip. This young woman advancing to the knight, cried, 'O, Sir Launcelot! my dear leady, my dear leady'—but was hindered from proceeding by a flood of tears, which the tender-hearted lawyer mingled with a plentiful shower of sympathy.

Our adventurer starting at this exclamation, 'O heavens! (cried he) where is my Aurelia? speak, where did you leave that jewel of my soul? answer me in a moment—I am all terror and impatience!' Dolly having recollected herself, told him that Mr. Darnel had lodged his niece in the new buildings by May-fair;[5]

that on the second night after their arrival, a very warm expostulation had passed between Aurelia and her uncle, who next morning dismissed Dolly, without permitting her to take leave of her mistress, and that same day moved to another part of the town, as she afterwards learned of the landlady, though she could not inform her whither they were gone. That when she was turned away, John Clump, one of the footmen, who pretended to have a kindness for her, had faithfully promised to call upon her and let her know what passed in the family; but as he did not keep his word, and she was an utter stranger in London, without friends or settlement, she had resolved to return to her mother, and travelled so far on foot since yesterday morning.

Our knight, who had expected the most dismal tidings from her lamentable preamble, was pleased to find his presaging fears disappointed; tho' he was far from being satisfied, with the dismission of Dolly, from whose attachment to his interest, joined to her influence over Mr. Clump, he had hoped to reap such intelligence as would guide him to the haven of his desires. After a minute's reflection, he saw it would be expedient to carry back Mrs. Cowslip, and lodge her at the place where Mr. Clump had promised to visit her with intelligence; for, in all probability, it was not for want of inclination that he had not kept his promise.

Dolly did not express any aversion to the scheme of returning to London, where she hoped once more to rejoin her dear lady, to whom by this time, she was attached by the strongest ties of affection; and her inclination, in this respect, was assisted by the consideration of having the company of the young lawyer, who, it plainly appeared, had made strange havock in her heart, tho' it must be owned, for the honour of this blooming damsel, that her thoughts had never once deviated from the paths of innocence and virtue. The more Sir Launcelot surveyed this agreeable maiden, the more he felt himself disposed to take care of her fortune; and from this day he began to ruminate on a scheme which was afterwards consummated in her favour—In the mean time, he laid injunctions on Mr. Clarke to conduct his addresses to Mrs. Cowslip, according to the rules of honour and decorum, as he valued his countenance and friendship. His next step was to procure a saddle-horse for Dolly, who preferred this to any other sort of carriage; and thereby gratified the wish of her admirer, who longed to see her on horseback in her green joseph.

The armour, including the accoutrements of the novice and the squire, were left in the care of the inn-keeper, and Timothy Crabshaw was so metamorphosed by a plain livery-frock, that even Gilbert with difficulty recognized his person. As for the novice Crowe, his head had almost resumed its natural dimensions; but then his whole face was so covered with a livid suffusion; his nose appeared so flat, and his lips so tumified, that he might very well have passed for a Caffre[1] or Æthiopian. Every circumstance being now adjusted, they departed from Bugden in a regular cavalcade, dined at Hatfield,[2] and in the evening arrived at the Bull and Gate inn in Holborn,[3] where they established their quarters for the night.

CHAPTER XX

In which our Hero descends into the Mansions of the Damned

THE first step which Sir Launcelot took in the morning that succeeded his arrival in London, was to settle Mrs. Dolly Cowslip in lodgings at the house where John Clump had promised to visit her; as he did not doubt, that tho' the visit was delayed, it would some time or other be performed; and in that case, he might obtain some intelligence of Aurelia. Mr. Thomas Clarke was permitted to take up his habitation in the same house, on his earnestly desiring he might be intrusted with the office of conveying information and instruction between Dolly and our adventurer. The knight himself resolved to live retired until he should receive some tidings relating to miss Darnel, that would influence his conduct; but he proposed to frequent places of public resort incognito, that he might have some chance of meeting by accident with the mistress of his heart. Taking it for granted that the oddities of Crowe would help to amuse him in his hours of solitude and disappointment, he invited that original to be his guest at a small house which he determined to hire ready furnished in the neighbourhood of Golden-square.[4] The captain thanked him for his courtesy, and frankly embraced his offer; tho' he did not much approve of the knight's choice, in point of situation. He said he would recommend him to a special good upper-deck hard by St. Catherine's in Wapping,[5] where he would be delighted with the prospect of the street forwards, well frequented by passengers, carts, drays, and other carriages; and having backwards, an agreeable view of alderman Parsons' great brewhouse,[1] with two hundred hogs feeding almost under the window. As a further inducement, he mentioned the vicinity of the Tower guns, which would regale his hearing on days of salutation: nor did he forget the sweet sound of mooring and unmooring ships in the river, and the pleasing objects on the other side of the Thames, displayed in the oozy docks and cabbage-gardens of Rotherhithe.[2] Sir Launcelot was not insensible to the beauties of this landschape; but, his pursuit lying another way, he contented himself with a less enchanting situation, and Crowe accompanied him out of pure friendship. At night Mr. Clarke arrived at our hero's house with tidings that were by no means agreeable. He told him that Clump had left a letter for Dolly, informing her that his master 'squire Darnel was to set out early in the morning for Yorkshire; but he could give no account of her lady, who had, the day before, been convey'd, he knew not whither, in a hackney-coach, attended by her uncle and an ill-looking fellow who had much the appearance of a bailiff or turnkey; so that he feared she was in trouble.

Sir Launcelot was deeply affected by this intimation. His apprehension was even roused by a suspicion that a man of Darnel's violent temper, and unprincipled heart, might have practised upon the life of his lovely niece: but, upon recollection, he could not supose that he had recourse to such infamous expedients, knowing, as he did, that an account of her would be demanded at his hands, and that it would be easily proved he had conveyed her from the lodging in which she resided. His first fears now gave way to another suggestion, that Anthony, in order to intimidate her into a compliance with his proposals, had trumped up a spurious claim against her, and by virtue of a writ confined her in some prison or spunging-house.[3] Possessed with this idea, he desired Mr. Clarke to search the sheriff's office in the morning, that he might know whether any such writ had been granted; and he himself resolved to make a tour of the great prisons belonging to the metropolis, to enquire if perchance she might not be confined under a borrowed name. Finally, he determined, if possible, to apprise her of his place of abode by a paragraph in all the daily papers, signifying that Sir Launcelot Greaves had arrived at his house by Golden-square.

All these resolutions were punctually executed. No such writ had been taken out in the sheriff's office; and therefore, our hero set out on his jail expedition, accompanied by Mr. Clarke, who had contracted some acquaintance with the commanding officers in these garrisons, in the course of his clerkship, and practice as an attorney. The first day they spent in prosecuting their inquiry through the Gate-house, Fleet, and Marshalsea; the next they allotted to the King's-bench,[1] where they understood there was a great variety of prisoners. There they proposed to make a minute scrutiny, by the help of Mr. Norton the deputy-marshal, who was Mr. Clarke's intimate friend, and had nothing at all of the jailor either in his appearance or in his disposition, which was remarkably humane and benevolent towards all his fellow-creatures.

The knight having bespoke dinner at a tavern in the Borough,[2] was, together with captain Crowe, conducted to the prison of the King's-bench, which is situated in St. George's-fields,[3] about a mile from the end of Westminster-bridge, and appears like a neat little regular town, consisting of one street, surrounded by a very high wall, including an open piece of ground which may be termed a garden, where the prisoners take the air, and amuse themselves with a variety of diversions. Except the entrance, where the turnkeys keep watch and ward, there is nothing in the place that looks like a jail, or bears the least colour of restraint. The street is crowded with passengers. Tradesmen of all kinds here exercise their different professions. Hawkers of all sorts are admitted to call and vend their wares as in any open street of London. Here are butchers-stands, chandlers-shops, a surgery, a tap-house well frequented, and a public kitchen in which provisions are dressed for all the prisoners gratis, at the expence of the publican. Here the voice of misery never complains, and, indeed, little else is to be heard but the sounds of mirth and jollity. At the farther end of the street, on the right hand, is a little paved court leading to a separate building, consisting of twelve large apartments, called state-rooms, well furnished, and fitted up for the reception of the better sort of crown-prisoners; and on the other side of the street, facing a separate division of ground, called the common side, is a range of rooms occupied by prisoners of the lowest order, who share the profits of a begging-box, and are maintained by this practice, and some established funds of charity. We ought also to observe, that the jail is provided with a neat chapel, in which a clergyman, in consideration of a certain salary, performs divine service every Sunday.

Our adventurer having searched the books, and perused the description of all the female prisoners who had been for some weeks admitted into the jail, obtained not the least intelligence of his concealed charmer, but resolved to alleviate his disappointment by the gratification of his curiosity. Under the auspices of Mr. Norton, he made a tour of the prison, and in particular visited the kitchen, where he saw a number of spits loaded with a variety of provision, consisting of butcher's meat, poultry, and game: he could not help expressing his astonishment with up-lifted hands, and congratulating himself in secret, upon his being a member of that community which had provided such a comfortable asylum for the unfortunate. His ejaculation was interrupted by a tumultuous noise in the street; and Mr. Norton declaring he was sent for to the lodge, consigned our hero to the cure of one Mr. Felton, a prisoner of a very decent appearance, who paid his compliments with a good grace, and invited the company to repose themselves in his apartment, which was large, commodious, and well furnished. When Sir Launcelot asked the cause of that uproar, he told him that it was the prelude to a boxing-match between two of the prisoners, to be decided in the ground, or garden of the place.

Capt. Crowe expressing an eager curiosity to see the battle, Mr. Felton assured him there would be no sport, as the combatants were both reckoned dunghills: 'But, in half an hour (said he) there will be a battle of some consequence between two of the demagogues of the place, Dr. Crabclaw and Mr. Tapley, the first a physician, and the other a brewer. You must know, Gentlemen, that this microcosm or republic in miniature, is like the great world, split into factions.¹ Crabclaw is the leader of one party; and the other is headed by Tapley: both are men of warm and impetuous tempers; and their intrigues have embroiled the whole place, insomuch that it was dangerous to walk the street, on account of the continual skirmishes of their partizans. At length, some of the more sedate inhabitants having met and deliberated upon some remedy for these growing disorders, proposed that the dispute should be at once decided by single combat between the two chiefs, who readily agreed to the proposal. The match was accordingly made for five guineas, and this very day and hour appointed for the trial, on which considerable sums of money are depending. As for Mr. Norton, it is not proper that he should be present, or seem to countenance such violent proceedings, which, however, it is necessary to connive at, as convenient vents for the evaporation of those humours, which being confined, might accumulate and break out with greater fury, in conspiracy and rebellion.'

The knight owned he could not conceive by what means such a number of licentious people, amounting, with their dependants, to above five hundred, were restrained within the bounds of any tolerable discipline, or prevented from making their escape; which they might at any time accomplish, either by stealth or open violence, as it could not be supposed that one or two turnkeys, continually employed in opening and shutting the door, could resist the efforts of a whole multitude. 'Your wonder, good Sir, (said Mr. Felton) will vanish, when you consider it is hardly possible that the multitude should co-operate in the execution of such a scheme; and that the keeper perfectly well understands the maxim *divide et impera*.[1] Many prisoners are restrained by the dictates of gratitude towards the deputy-marshal, whose friendship and good offices they have experienced: some, no doubt, are actuated by motives of discretion. One party is an effectual check upon the other; and I am firmly persuaded that there are not ten prisoners within the place that would make their escape, if the doors were laid open. This is a step which no man would take, unless his fortune was altogether desperate; because it would oblige him to leave his country for life, and expose him to the most imminent risque of being retaken and treated with the utmost severity. The majority of the prisoners live in the most lively hope of being released by the assistance of their friends, the compassion of their creditors, or the favour of the legislature. Some who are cut off from all these proposals, are become naturalized to the place, knowing they cannot subsist in any other situation. I, myself, am one of these. After having resigned all my effects for the benefit of my creditors, I have been detained these nine years in prison, because one person refuses to sign my certificate. I have long outlived all my friends from whom I could expect the least countenance or favour: I am grown old in confinement; and lay my account with ending my days in jail, as the mercy of the legislature in favour of insolvent debtors, is never extended to uncertified bankrupts taken in execution.[2] By dint of industry, and the most rigid oeconomy, I make shift to live independant in this retreat. To this scene my faculty of subsisting, as well as my body, is peculiarly confined. Had I an opportunity to escape, where should I go? All my views of fortune have been long blasted. I have no friends nor connexions in the world. I must, therefore, starve in some sequestred corner, or be recaptivated and confined for ever to close prison, deprived of the indulgences which I now enjoy.'

Here the conversation was broke off by another uproar, which was the signal to battle between the doctor and his antagonist. The company immediately adjourned to the field, where the combatants were already undressed and the stakes deposited. The doctor seemed of the middle age and middle stature, active and alert, with an atrabiliarious aspect, and a mixture of rage and disdain expressed in his countenance. The brewer was large, raw-boned, and round as a but of beer, but very fat, unwieldy, short-winded and phlegmatic. Our adventurer was not a little surprised when he beheld in the character of seconds, a male and a female, stripped naked from the waist upwards, the latter ranging on the side of the physician: but the commencement of the battle prevented his demanding of his guide an explanation of this phœnomenon. The doctor, retiring some paces backwards, threw himself into the attitude of a battering ram, and rushed upon his antagonist with great impetuosity, foreseeing that should he have the good fortune to over-turn him in the first assault, it would not be an easy task to raise him up again and put him in a capacity of offence. But the momentum of Crabclaw's head, and the con-comitant efforts of his knuckles, had no effect upon the ribs of Tapley, who stood firm as the Acroceraunian promontory:[1] and stepping forward with his projected fist, something smaller and softer than a sledge-hammer, struck the physician to the ground. In a trice, however, by the assistance of his female second, he was on his legs again, and grappling with his antagonist, endeavoured to tip him a fall; but, instead of accomplishing his purpose, he received a cross-buttock, and the brewer throwing himself upon him as he fell, had well-nigh smothered him on the spot. The amazon flew to his assistance, and Tapley shewing no inclination to get up, she smote him on the temple 'till he roared. The male second hastening to the relief of his principal, made application to the eyes of the female, which were immediately surrounded with black circles; and she returned the salute with a blow which brought a double stream of blood from his nostrils, greeting him at the same time with the opprobrious appellation of a lousy son of a b—h. A combat more furious than the first would now have ensued, had not Felton interposed with an air of authority, and insisted on the man's leaving the field; an injunction which he forthwith obeyed, saying, 'Well, damme, Felton, you're my friend and commander: I'll obey your order—but the b—h will be foul of me before we sleep—.' Then Felton, advancing to his opponent, 'Madam (said he) I'm very sorry to see a lady of your rank and qualifications expose yourself in this manner.—For God's sake, behave with a little more decorum; if not for the sake of your own family, at least for the credit of your sex in general.' 'Hark ye, Felton, (said she) decorum is founded upon a delicacy of sentiment and deportment, which cannot consist with the disgraces of a jail, and the miseries of indigence.—But I see the dispute is now terminated, and the money is to be drank: if you'll dine with us you shall be welcome; if not, you may die in your sobriety, and be damned.'

By this time the doctor had given out, and allowed the brewer to be the better man; yet he would not honour the festival with his presence, but retired to his chamber, exceedingly mortified at his defeat. Our hero was reconducted to Mr. Felton's apartment, where he sat some time without opening his mouth, so astonished he was at what he had seen and heard. 'I perceive, Sir, (said the prisoner) you are surprised at the manner in which I accosted that unhappy woman; and perhaps you will be more surprised when you hear, that within these eighteen months, she was actually a person of fashion, and her opponent (who by the bye) is her husband, universally respected as a man of honour, and a brave officer.' 'I am, indeed, (cried our hero) overwhelmed with amazement and concern as well as stimulated by an eager curiosity to know the fatal causes which have produced such a deplorable reverse of character and fortune. But, I will rein my curiosity till the afternoon, if you will favour me with your company at a tavern in the neighbourhood, where I have bespoke dinner; a favour which I hope Mr. Norton will have no objection to your granting, as he himself is to be of the party.—' The prisoner thanked him for his kind invitation, and they adjourned immediately to the place, taking up the deputy-marshal in their passage through the lodge or entrance of the prison.

CHAPTER XXI

Containing further Anecdotes relating to the Children of Wretchedness

DINNER being chearfully discussed, and our adventurer expressing an eager desire to know the history of the male and female who
had acted as 'squires or seconds to the champions of the King's-
bench, Felton gratified his curiosity to this effect:

'All that I know of Captain Clewlin,[1] previous to his committ-
ment, is, that he was commander of a sloop of war, and bore the
reputation of a gallant officer; that he married the daughter of a
rich merchant in the city of London against the inclination, and
without the knowledge of her father, who renounced her for this
act of disobedience: that the captain consoled himself for the rigour
of the parent, with the possession of the lady, who was not only
remarkably beautiful in person, but highly accomplished in her
mind, and amiable in her disposition. Such, a few months ago,
were those two persons whom you saw acting in such a vulgar
capacity. When they first entered the prison they were undoubtedly
the handsomest couple mine eyes ever beheld, and their appearance
won universal respect even from the most brutal inhabitants of the
jail. The captain having unwarily involved himself as security for a
man to whom he had lain under obligations, became liable for a
considerable sum; and his own father-in-law being the sole creditor
of the bankrupt, took this opportunity of wreaking vengeance upon
him for having espoused his daughter. He watched an opportunity
until the captain had actually stept into the post-chaise with his
lady, for Portsmouth, where his ship lay, and caused him to be
arrested in the most public and shameful manner. Mrs. Clewlin
had like to have sunk under the first transports of her grief and
mortification; but these subsiding, she had recourse to personal
sollicitation. She went with her only child in her arms (a lovely boy)
to her father's door, and being denied admittance, kneeled down in
the street, imploring his compassion in the most pathetic strain;
but this hard-hearted citizen, instead of recognizing his child, and
taking the poor mourner to his bosom, insulted her from the window with the most bitter reproach, saying, among other shocking
expressions, "Strumpet, take yourself away, with your brat, other-

wise I shall send for the beadle, and have you to Bridewell."

'The unfortunate lady was cut to the heart by this usage, and fainted in the street; from whence she was conveyed to a public house by the charity of some passengers. She afterwards attempted to soften the barbarity of her father, by repeated letters, and by interesting some of his friends to intercede with him in her behalf; but all her endeavours proving ineffectual, she accompanied her husband to the prison of the King's-bench, where she must have felt, in the severest manner, the fatal reverse of circumstance to which she was exposed. The captain being disabled from going to sea, was superseded, and he saw all his hopes blasted in the midst of an active war,[1] at a time when he had the fairest prospects of fame and fortune. He saw himself reduced to extreme poverty, cooped up with the tender partner of his heart in a wretched hovel, amidst the refuse of mankind, and on the brink of wanting the common necessaries of life. The mind of man is ever ingenious in finding resources. He comforted his lady with vain hopes of having friends who would effect his deliverance, and repeated assurances of this kind so long, that he at length began to think they were not altogether void of foundation.

'Mrs. Clewlin, from a principle of duty, recollected all her fortitude, that she might not only bear her fate with patience, but even contributed to alleviate the woes of her husband, whom her affection had ruined. She affected to believe the suggestions of his pretended hope; she interchanged with him assurances of better fortune; her appearance exhibited a calm, while her heart was torn with anguish. She assisted him in writing letters to former friends, the last consolation of the wretched prisoner; she delivered these letters with her own hand, and underwent a thousand mortifying repulses, the most shocking circumstances of which she concealed from her husband. She performed all the menial offices in her own little family, which was maintained by pawning her apparel; and both the husband and wife, in some measure sweetened their cares, by prattling and toying with their charming little boy, on whom they doated with an enthusiasm of fondness.—Yet, even this pleasure was mingled with the most tender and melancholy regret. I have seen the mother hang over him, with the most affecting expression of this kind in her aspect, the tears contending with the smiles upon her countenance, while she exclaimed: "Alas! my poor prisoner, little did your mother once think she should be obliged to nurse you in a jail." The captain's paternal love was dashed with impatience—He would snatch up the boy in a transport of grief, press him to his breast, devour him as it were with kisses, throw up his eyes to heaven in the most emphatic silence; then convey the child hastily to his mother's arms, pull his hat over his eyes, stalk out into the common walk, and finding himself alone, break out into tears and lamentation.

'Ah! little did this unhappy couple know what further griefs awaited them! The small-pox broke out in the prison, and poor Tommy Clewlin was infected. As the eruption appeared unfavourable, you may conceive the consternation with which they were overwhelmed. Their distress was rendered inconceivable by indigence; for, by this time, they were so destitute that they could neither pay for common attendance, nor procure proper advice. I did, on that occasion, what I thought my duty towards my fellow-creatures.—I wrote to a physician of my acquaintance, who was humane enough to visit the poor little patient: I engaged a careful woman prisoner as a nurse, and Mr. Norton supplied them with money and necessaries. These helps were barely sufficient to preserve them from the horrors of despair, when they saw their little darling panting under the rage of a loathsome pestilential malady, during the excessive heat of the dog-days, and struggling for breath in the noxious atmosphere of a confined cabin, where they scarce had room to turn, on the most necessary occasions. The eager curiosity with which the mother eyed the doctor's looks as often as he visited the boy; the terror and trepidation of the father, while he desired to know his opinion; in a word, the whole tenour of their distress, baffled all description.

At length the physician, for the sake of his own character, was obliged to be explicit; and returning with the captain, to the common walk, told him in my hearing, that the child could not possibly recover.—This sentence seemed to have petrified the unfortunate parent, who stood motionless, and seemingly bereft of sense. I led him to my apartment, where he sat a full hour in that state of stupefaction; then he began to groan hideously; a shower of tears burst from his eyes; he threw himself on the floor, and uttered the most piteous lamentation that ever was heard. Mean while, Mrs. Norton being made acquainted with the doctor's prognostic, visited Mrs. Clewlin, and invited her to the lodge. Her prophetic fears immediately took the alarm. "What! (cried she, starting up

with a frantic wildness in her looks) then our case is desperate—I
shall lose my dear Tommy!—the poor prisoner will be released by
the hand of heaven!—Death will convey him to the cold grave!"—
The dying innocent hearing this exclamation, pronounced these
words: "Tommy won't leave you, my dear mamma—if death
comes to take Tommy, pappa shall drive him away with his sword."
This address deprived the wretched mother of all resignation to the
will of Providence. She tore her hair, dashed herself on the pavement, shrieked aloud, and was carried off in a deplorable state of
distraction.

'That same evening the lovely babe expired, and the father grew
frantic. He made an attempt on his own life, and being with difficulty restrained, his agitation sunk into a kind of sudden insensi-
bility, which seemed to absorb all sentiment, and gradually vul-
garized his faculty of thinking. In order to dissipate the violence
of his sorrow, he continually shifted the scene from one company
to another, contracted abundance of low connexions, and drowned
his cares in repeated intoxication. The unhappy lady underwent a
long series of hysterical fits and other complaints, which seemed
to have a fatal effect on her brain as well as constitution. Cordials
were administred to keep up her spirits; and she found it necessary
to protract the use of them to blunt the edge of grief, by over-
whelming reflexion, and remove the sense of uneasiness arising
from a disorder in her stomach. In a word, she became an habitual
dram-drinker; and this practice exposed her to such communication as debauched her reason, and perverted her sense of decorum
and propriety. She and her husband gave a loose to vulgar excess,
in which they were enabled to indulge by the charity and interest of
some friends, who obtained half-pay for the captain. They are now
metamorphosed into the shocking creatures you have seen; he into
a riotous plebeian, and she into a ragged trull. They are both drunk
every day, quarrel and fight one with another, and often insult their
fellow-prisoners. Yet, they are not wholly abandoned by virtue and
humanity. The captain is scrupulously honest in all his dealings,
and pays off his debts punctually every quarter, as soon as he receives his half-pay. Every prisoner in distress is welcome to share
his money while it lasts; and his wife never fails, while it is in her
power, to relieve the wretched; so that their generosity, even in this
miserable disguise, is universally respected by their neighbours.
Sometimes the recollection of their former rank comes over them

like a qualm, which they dispel with brandy, and then humorously rally one another on their mutual degeneracy. She often stops me in the walk, and pointing to the captain, says, "My husband, tho' he's become a black-guard jail-bird, must be allowed to be an handsome fellow still."—On the other hand, he will frequently desire me to take notice of his rib, as she chances to pass.—"Mind that draggle-tail'd drunken drab—(he will say) what an antidote it is—yet, for all that, Felton, she was a fine woman when I married her—Poor Bess, I have been the ruin of her, that is certain, and deserve to be damned for bringing her to this pass."

'Thus they accommodate themselves to each other's infirmities, and pass their time not without some taste of plebeian enjoyment—but, name their child, they never fail to burst into tears, and still feel a return of the most poignant sorrow.'

Sir Launcelot Greaves did not hear this story unmoved. Tom Clark's cheeks were bedewed with the drops of sympathy, while with much sobbing, he declared his opinion, that an action would lie against the lady's father.—Captain Crowe having listened to the story, with uncommon attention, expressed his concern that an honest seaman should be so taken in stays: but he imputed all his calamities to the wife: 'for why? (said he) a sea-faring man may have a sweet-heart in every port; but he should steer clear of a wife, as he would avoid a quick-sand—you see, brother, how this here Clewlin lags astern in the wake of a sniveling b——; otherwise he'd never make a weft[1] in his ensign for the loss of a child—odds heart! he could have done no more if he had sprung a top-mast, or started a timber.—'

The knight declaring that he would take another view of the prison in the afternoon, Mr. Felton insisted upon his doing him the honour to drink a dish of tea in his apartment, and Sir Launcelot accepted his invitation. Thither they accordingly repaired, after having made another circuit of the jail, and the tea-things were produced by Mrs. Felton, when she was summoned to the door, and in a few minutes returning, communicated something in a whisper to her husband. He changed colour, and repaired to the stair-case, where he was heard to talk aloud in an angry tone. When he came back he told the company he had been teazed by a very importunate beggar. Addressing himself to our adventurer, 'You took notice (says he) of a fine lady flaunting about our walk in all the frippery of the fashion—she was lately a gay young widow that made a great figure at the court end of the town; she distinguished herself by her splendid equipage, her rich liveries, her brilliant assemblies, her numerous routs, and her elegant taste in dress and furniture. She is nearly related to some of the best families in England, and it must be owned, mistress of many fine accomplishments. But, being deficient in true delicacy, she endeavoured to hide that defect by affectation. She pretended to a thousand antipathies which did not belong to her nature. A breast of veal threw her into mortal agonies. If she saw a spider she screamed; and at sight of a mouse she fainted away. She could not without horror behold an entire joint of meat; and nothing but fricassees and other made-dishes were seen upon her table. She caused all her floors to be lined with green bays, that she might trip along them with more ease and pleasure. Her footmen wore clogs, which were deposited in the hall, and both they and her chairmen were laid under the strongest injunctions to avoid porter and tobacco. Her jointure amounted to eight hundred pounds per annum, and she made shift to spend four times that sum: at length it was mortgaged for nearly the entire value; but, far from retrenching, she seemed to increase in extravagance until her effects were taken in execution, and her person here deposited in safe custody. When one considers the abrupt transition she underwent from her spacious apartments to an hovel scarce eight feet square; from sumptuous furniture to bare benches; from magnificence to meanness; from affluence to extreme poverty; one would imagine she must have been totally overwhelmed by such a sudden gush of misery. But this was not the case: she has, in fact, no delicate feelings. She forthwith accommodated herself to the exigency of her fortune; yet, she still affects to keep state amidst the miseries of a gaol; and this affectation is truly ridiculous.—She lies abed till two o'clock in the afternoon: she maintains a female attendant for the sole purpose of dressing her person. Her cabin is the least cleanly in the whole prison; she has learned to eat bread and cheese, and drink porter; but she always appears once a day dressed in the pink of the fashion. She has found means to run in debt at the chandler's shop, the baker's, and the tap-house, tho' there is nothing got in this place but with ready money: she has even borrowed small sums from divers prisoners, who were themselves on the brink of starving. She takes pleasure in being surrounded with duns, observing that by such people a person of fashion is to be distinguished. She writes circular letters to her former friends and acquaintance, and by this method has raised pretty considerable contributions; for she writes in a most elegant and irresistible stile. About a fortnight ago she received a supply of twenty guineas; when, instead of paying her little gaol-debts, or withdrawing any part of her apparel from pawn, she laid out the whole sum in a fashionable suit and laces; and next day borrowed of me a shilling to purchase a neck of mutton for her dinner—She seems to think her rank in life intitles her to this kind of assistance. She talks very pompously of her family and connexions, by whom, however, she has been long renounced. She has no sympathy nor compassion for the distresses of her fellow-creatures; but she is perfectly well bred; she bears a repulse the best of any woman I ever knew; and her temper has never been once ruffled since her arrival at the King's-bench—She now intreated me to lend her half a guinea, for which she said she had the most pressing occasion, and promised upon her honour it should be repaid to-morrow; but I lent a deaf ear to her request, and told her in plain terms that her honour was already bankrupt.—'

Sir Launcelot thrusting his hand mechanically into his pocket, pulled out a couple of guineas, and desired Felton to accommodate her with that trifle in his own name; but he declined the proposal, and refused to touch the money. 'God forbid, (said he) that I should attempt to thwart your charitable intention: but, this, my good sir, is no object—she has many resources. Neither should we number the clamorous beggar among those who really feel distress. He is generally gorg'd with bounty misapplied. The liberal hand of charity should be extended to modest want that pines in silence, encountering cold, and nakedness, and hunger, and every species of distress. Here you may find the wretch of keen sensations, blasted by accident in the blossom of his fortune, shivering in the solitary recess of indigence, disdaining to beg, and even ashamed to let his misery be known. Here you may see the parent who has known happier times, surrounded by his tender offspring, naked and forlorn, demanding food, which his circumstances cannot afford.—That man of decent appearance and melancholy aspect, who lifted his hat as you passed him in the yard, is a person of unblemished character. He was a reputable tradesman in the city, and failed through inevitable losses. A commission of bankruptcy was taken out against him by his sole creditor, a quaker, who refused to sign his certificate. He has lived these three years in prison, with a wife and five small children. In a little time after his commitment, he had friends who offered to pay ten shillings in the pound of what he owed, and to give security for paying the remainder in three years, by installments. The honest quaker did not charge the bankrupt with any dishonest practices; but he rejected the proposal with the most mortifying indifference, declaring that he did not want his money. The mother repaired to his house, and kneeled before him with her five lovely children, imploring mercy with tears and exclamations. He stood this scene unmoved, and even seemed to enjoy the prospect, wearing the looks of complacency while his heart was steeled with rancour. "Woman, (said he) these be hopeful babes, if they were duly nurtured. Go thy ways in peace; I have taken my resolution." Her friends maintained the family for some time; but it is not in human charity to persevere: some of them died; some of them grew unfortunate; some of them fell off; and now the poor man is reduced to the extremity of indigence, from whence he has no prospect of being retrieved. The fourth part of what you would have bestowed upon the lady would make this poor man and his family sing with joy.'

He had scarce pronounced these words when our hero desired the man might be called, and in a few minutes he entered the apartment with a low obeisance. 'Mr. Coleby, (said the knight) I have heard how cruelly you have been used by your creditor, and beg you will accept this trifling present, if it can be of any service to you in your distress.' So saying, he put five guineas into his hand. The poor man was so confounded at such an unlooked-for acquisition, that he stood motionless and silent, unable to thank the donor; and Mr. Felton conveyed him to the door, observing that his heart was too full for utterance. But, in a little time, his wife bursting into the room with her five children, looked around, and going up to Sir Launcelot, without any direction, exclaimed: 'This is the angel sent by Providence to succour me and my poor innocents.' Then falling at his feet, she pressed his hand and bathed it with her tears —He raised her up with that complacency which was natural to his disposition. He kissed all her children, who were remarkably handsome and neatly kept, tho' in homely apparel; and, giving her his direction, assured her she might always apply to him in her distress.

After her departure, he produced a bank-note for twenty pounds, and would have deposited it in the hands of Mr. Felton, to be distributed in charities among the objects of the place; but he desired it might be left with Mr. Norton, who was the proper person for managing his benevolence; and he promised to assist the deputy with his advice in laying it out.

CHAPTER XXII

In which Capt. Crowe is sublimed into the Regions of Astrology

THREE whole days had our adventurer prosecuted his inquiry about the amiable Aurelia, whom he sought in every place of public and of private entertainment, or resort, without obtaining the least satisfactory intelligence, when he received one evening, from the hands of a porter, who instantly vanished, the following billet: 'If you would learn the particulars of Miss Darnel's fate, fail not to be in the fields by the Foundling Hospital,[1] precisely at seven o'clock this evening, when you shall be met by a person who will give you the satisfaction you desire, together with his reason for addressing you in this mysterious manner.—' Had this intimation concerned any other subject, perhaps the knight would have deliberated with himself in what manner he should take a hint so darkly communicated: but his eagerness to retrieve the jewel he had lost, divested him of all his caution; the time of assignation was already at hand; and neither the captain nor his nephew could be found to accompany him, had he been disposed to make use of their attendance. He therefore, after a moment's hesitation, repaired to the place appointed, in the utmost agitation and anxiety, lest the hour should be elapsed before his arrival.

Crowe was one of those defective spirits, who cannot subsist for any length of time on their own bottoms.[2] He wanted a familiar prop, upon which he could disburthen his cares, his doubts, and his humours: an humble friend who would endure his caprices, and with whom he could communicate, free of all reserve and restraint. Though he loved his nephew's person, and admired his parts, he considered him often as a little petulant jackanapes, who presumed upon his superior understanding; and as for Sir Launcelot, there was something in his character that overawed the seaman, and kept him at a disagreeable distance. He had, in this dilemma, cast his eyes upon Timothy Crabshaw, and admitted him to a considerable share of familiarity and fellowship. These companions had been employed in smoaking a social pipe at an alehouse in the neighbourhood, when the knight made his excursion; and returning to the house about supper-time, found Mr. Clarke in waiting. The young lawyer was alarmed when he heard the hour of ten, without seeing our adventurer, who had been used to be extremely regular in his œconomy; and the captain and he supped in profound silence. Finding, upon enquiry among the servants, that the knight went out abruptly, in consequence of having received a billet, Tom began to be visited with the apprehension of a duel, and sat the best part of the night by his uncle, sweating with the expectation of seeing our hero brought home a breathless corse: but no tidings of him arriving, he, about two in the morning, repaired to his own lodging, resolved to publish a description of Sir Launcelot in the newspapers, if he should not appear next day. Crowe did not pass the time without uneasiness. He was extremely concerned at the thought of some mischief having befallen his friend and patron; and he was terrified with the apprehension, that in case Sir Launcelot was murdered, his spirit might come and give him notice of his fate. Now he had an insuperable aversion to all correspondence with the dead; and taking it for granted, that the spirit of his departed friend could not appear to him except when he should be alone, and a-bed in the dark, he determined to pass the remainder of the night without going to bed. For this purpose his first care was to visit the garret in which Timothy Crabshaw lay fast asleep, snoring with his mouth wide open. Him the captain with difficulty roused, by dint of promising to regale him with a bowl of rum punch in the kitchen, where the fire, which had been extinguished, was soon rekindled. The ingredients were fetched from a public-house in the neighbourhood; for the captain was too proud to use his interest in the knight's family, especially at these hours when all the rest of the servants had retired to their repose; and he and Timothy drank together until day-break, the conversation turning upon hobgoblins, and God's revenge against murder. The cookmaid lay in a little apartment contiguous to the kitchen; and whether disturbed by these horrible tales of apparitions, or titillated by the savoury steams that issued from the punch-bowl, she made a virtue of necessity, or appetite, and dressing herself in

the dark, suddenly appeared before them, to the no small perturbation of both. Timothy, in particular, was so startled, that in his
endeavours to make an hasty retreat towards the chimney-corner,
he overturned the table; the liquor was spilt, but the bowl was saved
by falling on a heap of ashes. Mrs. Cook having reprimanded him
for his foolish fear, declared she had got up betimes, in order to
scour her saucepans; and the captain proposed to have the bowl
replenished, if materials could be procured. This difficulty was
overcome by Crabshaw; and they sat down with their new associate
to discuss the second edition. The knight's sudden disappearing
being again brought upon the carpet, their female companion gave
it as her opinion, that nothing would be so likely to bring this affair
to light, as going to a cunning man, whom she had lately consulted
about a silver spoon that was mislaid, and who told her all the things
that she ever did, and ever would happen to her through the whole
course of her life.

Her two companions pricked up their ears at this intelligence;
and Crowe asked if the spoon had been found? She answered in
the affirmative, and said, the cunning man described to a hair the
person that should be her true love, and her wedded husband: that
he was a sea-faring man; that he was pretty well stricken in years;
a little passionate or so; and that he went with his fingers clinched
like, as it were. The captain began to sweat at this description, and
mechanically thrust his hands into his pockets, while Crabshaw,
pointing to him, told her he believed she had got the right sow by
the ear. Crowe grumbled, that may hap for all that he should not be
brought up by such a grappling neither. Then he asked if this cunning man dealt with the devil, declaring, in that case he would keep
clear of him: for why? because he must have sold himself to old
scratch; and being a servant of the devil, how could he be a good
subject to his majesty? Mrs. Cook assured him, the conjurer was a
good christian; and that he gained all his knowledge by conversing
with the stars and planets. Thus satisfied, the two friends resolved
to consult him as soon as it should be light; and being directed to
the place of his habitation, set out for it by seven in the morning.
They found the house forsaken, and had already reached the end of
the lane in their return, when they were accosted by an old woman,
who gave them to understand, that if they had occasion for the
advice of a fortune-teller, as she did suppose they had, from their
stopping at the house where Dr. Grubble lived, she would conduct

them to a person of much more eminence in that profession; at the same time she informed them, that the said Grubble had been lately sent to Bridewell; a circumstance which, with all his art, he had not been able to foresee. The captain, without any scruple, put himself and his companion under convoy of this beldame, who, thro' many windings and turnings, brought them to the door of a ruinous house, standing in a blind alley; which door having opened with a key drawn from her pocket, she introduced them into a parlour, where they saw no other furniture than a naked bench, and some frightful figures on the bare walls, drawn, or rather scrawled with charcoal. Here she left them locked in until she should give the doctor notice of their arrival; and they amused themselves with decyphering these characters and hieroglyphics. The first figure that engaged their attention, was that of a man hanging upon a gibbet, which both considered as an unfavourable omen, and each endeavoured to avert from his own person. Crabshaw observed, that the figure so suspended was cloathed in a sailor's jacket and trowsers; a truth which the captain could not deny; but on the other hand he affirmed, that the said figure exhibited the very nose and chin of Timothy, together with the hump on one shoulder. A warm dispute ensued; and being maintained with much acrimonious altercation, might have dissolved the new-cemented friendship of these two originals, had it not been interrupted by the old sybil, who, coming into the parlour, intimated that the doctor waited for them above. She likewise told them that he never admitted more than one at a time. This hint occasioned a fresh contest: the captain insisted upon Crabshaw's making sail ahead, in order to look out afore; but Timothy persisted in refusing this honour, declaring he did not pretend to lead, but he would follow, as in duty bound. The old gentlewoman abridged the ceremony, by leading out Crabshaw with one hand, and locking up Crowe with the other. The former was dragged up stairs like a bear to the stake,[1] not without reluctance and terror, which did not at all abate at sight of the conjurer, with whom he was immediately shut up by his conductress; after she had told him in a whisper, that he must deposit a shilling in a little black coffin, supported by a human skull and thigh bones crossed, on a stool covered with black bays, that stood in one corner of the apartment. The squire having made this offering with fear and trembling, ventured to survey the objects around him, which were very well calculated to augment his confusion. He saw divers skeletons hung by the head; the stuffed skin of a young alligator, a calf with two heads, and several snakes suspended from the cieling, with the jaws of a shark, and a starved weasle. On another funereal table he beheld two spheres, between which lay a book open, exhibiting outlandish characters, and mathematical diagrams. On one side stood an ink-standish with paper, and behind this desk appeared the conjurer himself in sable vestments, his head so overshadowed with hair, that far from contemplating his features, Timothy could distinguish nothing but a long white beard, which, for ought he knew, might have belonged to a four-legged goat, as well as to a two-legged astrologer.

This apparition, which the squire did not eye without manifest discomposure, extending a white wand, made certain evolutions over the head of Timothy, and having muttered an ejaculation, commanded him, in a hollow tone, to come forward and declare his name. Crabshaw thus adjured advanced to the altar; and whether from design or (which is more probable) from confusion, answered 'Samuel Crowe.' The conjuror taking up the pen, and making a few scratches on the paper, exclaimed in a terrific accent; 'How! miscreant! attempt to impose upon the stars?—you look more like a *crab* than a *crow*, and was born under the sign of Cancer.' The squire, almost annihilated by this exclamation, fell upon his knees, crying, 'I pray yaw, my lord conjuror's worship, pardon my ignorance, and down't go to baind me oover to the Red Sea like[1]— I'se a poor Yorkshire tyke,[2] and would no more cheat the stars than I'd cheat my own vather, as the saying is—a must be a good hand at *trapping*, that catches the starns[3] a *napping*—but as your honour's worship observed, my name is Tim Crabshaw, of the East Riding, groom and squair to Sir Launcelot Greaves, baron knaight, and arrant knaight, who ran mad for a wench, as your worship's conjuration well knoweth:—the person below is captain Crowe; and we coom by Margery Cook's recommendation, to seek after my master, who is gone away, or made away, the Lord he knows how and where.'

Here he was interrupted by the conjurer, who exhorted him to sit down and compose himself until he should cast a figure:[4] then he scrawled the paper, and waving his wand, repeated abundance of gibberish concerning the number, the names, the houses, and revolutions of the planets, with their conjunctions, oppositions, signs, circles, cycles, trines, and trigons. When he perceived that this artifice had its proper effect in disturbing the brain of Crab-shaw, he proceeded to tell him from the stars, that his name was Crabshaw, or Crabsclaw; that he was born in the East-riding of Yorkshire, of poor, yet honest parents, and had some skill in horses; that he served a gentleman, whose name began with the letter G——, which gentleman had run mad for love, and left his family; but whether he would return alive or dead the stars had not yet determined. Poor Timothy was thunderstruck to find the conjurer acquainted with all these circumstances, and begged to know if he mought be bauld as to ax a question or two about his own fortune. The astrologer pointing to the little coffin, our squire understood the hint, and deposited another shilling. The sage had recourse to his book, erected another scheme, performed once more his airy evolutions with the wand, and having recited another mystical preamble, expounded the book of fate in these words: 'You shall neither die by war nor water, by hunger or by thirst, nor be brought to the grave by old age or distemper; but, let me see—ay, the stars will have it so,—you shall be—exalted—hah!—ay, that is—hanged for horse-stealing.'—'O, good my lord conjurer! (roared the squire) I'd as lief give forty shillings as be hanged.'—'Peace, sirrah! (cried the other) would you contradict or reverse the immutable decrees of fate. Hanging is your destiny; and hanged you shall be—and comfort yourself with the reflection, that as you are not the first, so neither will you be the last to swing on Tyburn tree.'[1] This com-fortable assurance composed the mind of Timothy, and in a great measure reconciled him to the prediction. He now proceeded in a whining tone, to ask whether he should suffer for the first fact?[2] whether it would be for a horse or a mare? and of what colour? that he might know when his hour was come.—The conjurer gravely answered, that he would steal a dappled gelding on a Wednesday; be cast at the Old Baily[3] on a Thursday, and suffer on a Friday; and he strenuously recommended it to him, to appear in the cart with a nosegay in one hand, and the Whole Duty of Man[4] in the other. 'But if in case it should be in the winter (said the squire) when a nosegay can't be had'—'Why then (replied the conjurer) an orange will do as well.' These material points being adjusted to the entire satisfaction of Timothy, he declared he would bestow another shilling to know the fortune of an old companion, who truly did not deserve so much at his hands; but he could not help loving him better than e'er a friend he had in the world. So saying, he dropped a third offering in the coffin, and desired to know the fate of his horse Gilbert. The astrologer having again consulted his art, pronounced, that Gilbert would die of the staggers, and his carcase be given to the hounds; a sentence, which made a much deeper impression upon Crabshaw's mind, than did the prediction of his own untimely and disgraceful fate. He shed a plenteous shower of tears, and his grief broke forth in some passionate expressions of tenderness:—at length he told the astrologer he would go and send up the captain, who wanted to consult him about Margery Cook, because as how she had informed him that Dr. Grubble had described just such another man as the captain for her true love; and he had no great stomach to the match, if so be as the stars were not bent upon their coming together. Accordingly the squire being dismissed by the conjurer, descended to the parlour with a rueful length of face; which being perceived by the captain, he demanded 'What cheer, ho?' with some signs of apprehension. Crabshaw making no return to this salute, he asked if the conjurer had taken an observation, and told him any thing? Then the other replied, he had told him more than he desired to know. 'Why, an that be the case (said the seaman) I have no occasion to go aloft this trip, brother.' This evasion would not serve his turn: old Tisiphone[1] was at hand, and led him up growling into the hall of audience, which he did not examine without trepidation. Having been directed to the coffin, where he presented half a crown, in hope of rendering the fates propitious, the usual ceremony was performed; and the doctor addressed him in these words: 'Approach, Raven.' The captain advancing, 'You an't much mistaken, brother, (said he) heave your eye into the binnacle, and box your compass; you'll find I'm a Crowe, not a Raven, tho'f indeed they be both fowls of a feather, as the saying is.'—'I know it; (cried the conjurer) thou art a northern crow,—a sea crow; not a crow of prey, but a crow to be preyed upon:—a crow to be plucked,—to be flayed,—to be basted, —to be broiled by Margery upon the gridiron of matrimony—.' The novice changing colour at this denunciation, 'I do understand your signals, brother, (said he,) and if it be set down in the log-book of fate, that we must grapple, why then, 'ware timbers. But as I know how the land lies, d'ye see, and the current of my inclination sets me off, I shall haul up close to the wind, and mayhap we shall clear Cape Margery. But, howsomever, we shall leave that reef in the foretopsail:—I was bound upon another voyage, d'ye see—to look and to see, and to know, if so be as how I could pick up any intelligence along shore, concerning my friend Sir Launcelot, who slipped his cable last night, and has lost company,[1] d'ye see.' 'What! (exclaimed the cunning man) art thou a crow, and can'st not smell carrion? If thou would'st grieve for Greaves, behold his naked carcase lies unburied to feed the kites, the crows, the gulls, the rooks, and ravens.'—'What, broach'd to?' 'Dead! as a boiled lobster.' 'Odd's heart! friend, these are the heaviest tidings I have heard these seven long years—there must have been deadly odds when he lowered his topsails—Smite my eyes! I had rather the Mufti had foundered at sea, with myself and all my generation on board—well fare thy soul, flower of the world! had honest Sam Crowe been within hail—but what signifies palavering.' Here the tears of unaffected sorrow flowed plentifully down the furrows of the seaman's cheeks:—then his grief giving way to his indignation, 'Hark ye, brother conjurer, (said he) you that can spy foul weather before it comes, damn your eyes! why didn't you give us warning of this here squall? Blast my limbs! I'll make you give an account of this here damned, horrid, confounded murder, d'ye see—mayhap you yourself was concerned, d'ye see.—For my own part, brother, I put my trust in God, and steer by the compass; and I value not your paw-wawing, and your conjuration, of a rope's end, d'ye see.'—The conjurer was by no means pleased, either with the matter, or the manner of this address. He therefore began to soothe the captain's choler, by representing that he did not pretend to omniscience, which was the attribute of God alone; that human art was fallible and imperfect; and all that it could perform, was to discover certain partial circumstances of any particular object to which its inquiries were directed: that being questioned by the other man, concerning the cause of his master's disappearing, he had exercised his skill upon the subject, and found reason to believe that Sir Launcelot was assassinated; that he should think himself happy in being the instrument of bringing the murderers to justice, though he foresaw they would, of themselves, save him that trouble; for they would quarrel about dividing the spoil, and one would give information against the other.

The prospect of this satisfaction appeased the resentment, and, in some measure, mitigated the grief of captain Crowe, who took his leave without much ceremony; and being joined by Crabshaw, proceeded with a heavy heart to the house of Sir Launcelot, where they found the domestics at breakfast, without exhibiting the least symptom of concern for their absent master. Crowe had been wise enough to conceal from Crabshaw what he had learned of the knight's fate. This fatal intelligence he reserved for the ear of his nephew, Mr. Clarke, who did not fail to attend him in the forenoon.

As for the squire, he did nothing but ruminate in rueful silence upon the dappled gelding, the nosegay, and the predicted fate of Gilbert. Him he forthwith visited in the stable, and saluted with the kiss of peace. Then he bemoaned his fortune with tears, and by the sound of his own lamentation, was lulled asleep among the litter.

CHAPTER XXIII

In which the Clouds that cover the Catastrophe begin to disperse

WE must now leave Capt. Crowe and his nephew Mr. Clarke, arguing with great vehemence about the fatal intelligence obtained from the conjurer, and penetrate at once the veil that concealed our hero. Know then, reader, that Sir Launcelot Greaves, repairing to the place described in the billet which he had received, was accosted by a person muffled in a cloak, who began to amuse him with a feigned story of Aurelia; to which while he listened with great attention, he found himself suddenly surrounded by armed men, who seized and pinioned down his arms, took away his sword, and conveyed him by force into a hackney-coach provided for the purpose. In vain he expostulated on this violence with three persons, who accompanied him in the vehicle. He could not extort one word by way of reply; and, from their gloomy aspects, he began to be apprehensive of assassination. Had the carriage passed through any frequented place, he would have endeavoured to alarm the inhabitants; but it was already clear of the town, and his conductors took care to avoid all villages and inhabited houses.

After having travelled about two miles, the coach stopped at a large iron-gate, which being opened, our adventurer was led in silence thro' a spacious house into a tolerably decent apartment, which he understood was intended for his bed-chamber. In a few minutes after his arrival, he was visited by a man of no very pre-

possessing appearance, who endeavoured to smoothe his countenance, which was naturally stern, welcomed our adventurer to
his house; exhorted him to be of good chear; assured him he should
want for nothing; and desired to know what he would choose for
supper.

Sir Launcelot, in answer to this civil address, begged he would
explain the nature of his confinement, and the reasons for which his
arms were tied like those of the worst malefactor. The other post-
poned till to-morrow the explanation he demanded; but, in the
mean time, unbound his fetters, and as he declined eating, left him
alone to his repose. He took care, however in retiring, to double-
lock the door of the room, whose windows were grated on the
outside with iron.

The knight, being thus abandoned to his own meditations, began
to ruminate on the present adventure with equal surprize and concern; but the more he revolved circumstances, the more was he
perplexed in his conjectures. According to the state of the mind, a
very subtle philosopher is often puzzled by a very plain proposition;
and this was the case of our adventurer—What made the strongest
impression upon his mind, was a notion that he was apprehended
on suspicion of treasonable practices, by a warrant from the
secretary of state, in consequence of some false malicious information; and that his prison was no other than the house of a messenger,[1] set apart for the accommodation of suspected persons. In
this opinion, he comforted himself by recollecting his own con-
scious innocence, and reflecting that he should be intitled to the
privilege of *habeas corpus*, as the act including that inestimable
jewel, was happily not suspended at this time.[2]

Consoled by this self-assurance, he quietly resigned himself to
slumber; but, before he fell asleep, he was very disagreeably un-
deceived in his conjecture. His ears were all at once saluted with a
noise from the next room, conveyed in distinct bounces against
the wainscot; then an hoarse voice exclaimed: 'Bring up the
artillery—let Brutandorf's brigade advance—detach my black
hussars[3] to ravage the country—let them be new-booted—take
particular care of the spur-leathers—make a desert of Lusatia[4]—
bombard the suburbs of Pera[5]—go, tell my brother Henry to pass
the Elbe at Meissen with forty battalions and fifty squadrons—so
ho, you major-general Donder, why don't you finish your second
parallel?[6]—send hither the engineer Schittenbach—I'll lay all the

shoes in my shop, the breach will be practicable in four and twenty hours—don't tell me of your works[1]—you and your works may be damn'd—'

'Assuredly, (cried another voice from a different quarter) he that thinks to be saved by works[2] is in a state of utter reprobation—I myself was a prophane weaver, and trusted to the rottenness of works—I kept my journeymen and 'prentices at constant work; and my heart was set upon the riches of this world, which was a wicked work—but now I have got a glimpse of the new-light—I feel the operations of grace—I am of the new birth[3]—I abhor good works—I detest all working but the working of the spirit—Avaunt, Satan—O! how I thirst for communication[4] with our sister Jolly[5]—'

'The communication is already open with the Marche,[6] (said the first) but as for thee, thou caitif, who hast presumed to disparage my works, I'll have thee rammed into a mortar with a double charge of powder, and thrown into the enemy's quarters.'

This dialogue operated like a train upon many other inhabitants of the place: one swore he was within three vibrations of finding the longitude,[7] when this noise confounded his calculation: a second, in broken English, complained he vas distorped in the moment of de proshection[8]—a third, in the character of his holiness, denounced interdiction, excommunication, and anathemas; and swore by St. Peter's keys, they should howl ten thousand years in purgatory, without the benefit of a single mass. A fourth began to hollow in all the vociferation of a fox-hunter in the chace; and in an instant the whole house was in an uproar—The clamour, however, was of a short duration. The different chambers being opened successively, every individual was effectually silenced by the sound of one cabalistical word, which was no other than *waistcoat*: a charm which at once cowed the king of P——,[9] dispossessed the fanatic, dumbfounded the mathematician, dismayed the alchemist, deposed the pope, and deprived the 'squire of all utterance.

Our adventurer was no longer in doubt concerning the place to which he had been conveyed; and the more he reflected on his situation, the more he was overwhelmed with the most perplexing chagrin. He could not conceive by whose means he had been immured in a madhouse; but he heartily repented of his knight-errantry, as a frolic which might have very serious consequences,

with respect to his future life and fortune. After mature deliberation, he resolved to demean himself with the utmost circumspec-
tion, well knowing that every violent transport would be interpreted into an undeniable symptom of insanity. He was not without
hope of being able to move his jailor by a due administration of that
which is generally more efficacious than all the flowers of elocution;
but when he rose in the morning, he found his pockets had been
carefully examined, and emptied of all his papers and cash.

The keeper entering, he enquired about these particulars, and
was given to understand that they were all safely deposited for his
use, to be forthcoming at a proper season: but, at present, as he
should want for nothing, he had no occasion for money. The
knight acquiesced in this declaration, and eat his breakfast in quiet.
About eleven, he received a visit from the physician, who con-
templated his looks with great solemnity; and, having examined
his pulse, shook his head, saying, 'Well, sir, how d'ye do?—come,
don't be dejected—every thing is for the best—you are in very
good hands, sir, I assure you; and I dare say will refuse nothing
that may be thought conducive to the recovery of your health.—'

'Doctor, (said our hero) if it is not an improper question to ask,
I should be glad to know your opinion of my disorder—' 'O! sir,
as to that—(replied the physician) your disorder is a—kind of a—
sir, 'tis very common in this country—a sort of a—' 'Do you think
my distemper is madness, doctor?'—'O Lord! sir,—not absolute
madness—no—not madness—you have heard, no doubt, of what
is called a weakness of the nerves, sir,—tho' that is a very inaccurate expression; for this phrase, denoting a morbid excess of
sensation, seems to imply that sensation itself is owing to the loose
cohesion of those material particles which constitute the nervous
substance, inasmuch as the quantity of every effect must be pro-
portionable to its cause; now you'll please to take notice, sir, if the
case were really what these words seem to import, all bodies, whose
particles do not cohere with too great a degree of proximity, would
be nervous; that is, endued with sensation[1]—Sir, I shall order
some cooling things to keep you in due temperature; and you'll do
very well—sir, your humble servant.'

So saying, he returned, and our adventurer could not but think
it was very hard that one man should not dare to ask the most
ordinary question without being reputed mad, while another
should talk nonsense by the hour, and yet be esteemed as an oracle

—The master of the house finding Sir Launcelot so tame and so tractable, indulged him after dinner with a walk in a little private garden, under the eye of a servant who followed him at a distance. Here he was saluted by a brother prisoner, a man seemingly turned of thirty, tall and thin, with staring eyes, a hook-nose, and a face covered with pimples.

The usual compliments having passed, the stranger, without further ceremony, asked if he would oblige him with a chew of tobacco, or could spare him a mouthful of any sort of cordial, declaring he had not tasted brandy since he came to the house— The knight assured him it was not in his power to comply with his request; and began to ask some questions relating to the character of their landlord, which the stranger represented in very unfavourable colours. He described him as a ruffian, capable of undertaking the darkest schemes of villainy. He said his house was a repository of the most flagrant iniquities: that it contained fathers kidnapped by their children, wives confined by their husbands, gentlemen of fortune sequestered by their relations, and innocent persons immured by the malice of their adversaries. He affirmed this was his own case; and asked if our hero had never heard of Dick Distich, the poet and satirist. 'Ben Bullock and I (said he) were confident against the world in arms—did you never see his ode to me, beginning with "Fair blooming youth." We were sworn brothers, admired and praised, and quoted each other, sir: we denounced war against all the world, actors, authors, and critics; and having drawn the sword, threw away the scabbard—we pushed through thick and thin, hacked and hewed helter skelter, and became as formidable to the writers of the age, as the Bœotian band of Thebes.[1] My friend Bullock, indeed, was once rolled in the kennel;[2] but soon

> He vig'rous rose, and from th' effluvia strong
> Imbib'd new life, and scour'd, and stunk along.[3]

Here is a satire, which I wrote in an alehouse when I was drunk—I can prove it by the evidence of the landlord and his wife: I fancy you'll own I have some right to say with my friend Horace,

> *Qui me commorit, melius non tangere clamo;*
> *Flebit et insignis toto cantabitur urbe. . . .*[4]

The knight, having perused the papers, declared his opinion that the verses were tolerably good; but at the same time observed that the author had reviled as ignorant dunces several persons who had writ with reputation, and were generally allowed to have genius: a circumstance that would detract more from his candour, than could be allowed to his capacity.

'Damn their genius! (cried the satyrist) a pack of impertinent rascals! I tell you, sir, Ben Bullock and I had determined to crush all that were not of our own party—besides, I said before, this piece was written in drink.' 'Was you drunk too when it was printed and published?' 'Yes, the printer shall make affidavit that I was never otherwise than drunk or maudlin, till my enemies, on pretence that my brain was turned, conveyed me to this infernal mansion—'

'They seem to have been your best friends, (said the knight) and have put the most tender interpretation on your conduct; for, waving the plea of insanity, your character must stand as that of a man who hath some small share of genius, without an atom of integrity—Of all those whom Pope lashed in his Dunciad,[1] there was not one who did not richly deserve the imputation of dulness; and every one of them had provoked the satirist by a personal attack.[2] In this respect the English poet was much more honest than his French pattern Boileau,[3] who stigmatized several men of acknowledged genius; such as Quinault, Perrault, and the celebrated Lulli; for which reason every man of a liberal turn must, in spite of all his poetical merit, despise him as a rancorous knave. If this disingenuous conduct cannot be forgiven in a writer of his superior genius, who will pardon it in you whose name is not half emerged from obscurity?'

'Heark ye, friend, (replied the bard) keep your pardon and your counsel for those that ask it; or, if you will force them upon people, take one piece of advice in return: If you don't like your present situation, apply for a committee without delay: they'll find you too much of a fool to have the least tincture of madness; and you'll be released without further scruple: in that case I shall rejoice in your deliverance; you will be freed from confinement, and I shall be happily deprived of your conversation.'

So saying, he flew off at a tangent, and our knight could not help smiling at the peculiar virulence of his disposition. Sir Launcelot then endeavoured to enter into conversation with his attendant, by asking how long Mr. Distich had resided in the house; but he might as well have addressed himself to a Turkish mute: the fellow either pretended ignorance, or refused an answer to every question that was proposed. He would not even disclose the name of his landlord, nor inform him whereabouts the house was situated.

Finding himself agitated with impatience and indignation, he returned to his apartment, and the door being locked upon him, began to review, not without horror, the particulars of his fate. 'How little reason (said he to himself) have we to boast of the blessings enjoyed by the British subject, if he holds them on such a precarious tenure: if a man of rank and property may be thus kidnapped even in the midst of the capital; if he may be seized by ruffians, insulted, robbed, and conveyed to such a prison as this, from which there seems to be no possibility of escape! Should I be indulged with, pen, ink, and paper, and appeal to my relations, or to the magistrates of my country, my letters would be intercepted by those who superintend my confinement. Should I try to alarm the neighbourhood, my cries would be neglected as those of some unhappy lunatic under necessary correction. Should I employ the force which heaven hath lent me, I might imbrue my hands in blood, and after all find it impossible to escape through a number of successive doors, locks, bolts, and centinels. Should I endeavour to tamper with the servant, he might discover my design, and then I should be abridged of the little comfort I enjoy. People may inveigh against the Bastile in France, and the Inquisition in Portugal; but I would ask if either of these be in reality so dangerous or dreadful as a private mad-house in England, under the direction of a ruffian. The Bastile is a state prison, the Inquisition is a spiritual tribunal; but both are under the direction of government. It seldom, if ever, happens that a man intirely innocent is confined in either; or, if he should, he lays his account with a legal trial before established judges. But in England, the most innocent person upon earth is liable to be immured for life under the pretext of lunacy, sequestered from his wife, children, and friends, robbed of his fortune, deprived even of necessaries, and subjected to the most brutal treatment from a low-bred barbarian, who raises an ample fortune on the misery of his fellow-creatures, and may, during his whole life, practise this horrid oppression, without question or controul.'

This uncomfortable reverie was interrupted by a very unexpected sound that seemed to issue from the other side of a thick party-wall. It was a strain of vocal music, more plaintive than the widow'd turtle's moan, more sweet and ravishing than Philomel's[1] love-warbled song. Through his ear it instantly pierced into his heart; for at once he recognized it to be the voice of his adored Aurelia. Heavens! what was the agitation of his soul, when he made this discovery! how did every nerve quiver! how did his heart throb with the most violent emotion! He ran round the room in distraction, foaming like a lion in the toil—then he placed his ear close to the partition, and listened as if his whole soul was exerted in his sense of hearing. When the sound ceased to vibrate on his ear, he threw himself on the bed; he groaned with anguish; he exclaimed in broken accents; and, in all probability, his heart would have burst, had not the violence of his sorrow found vent in a flood of tears.

These first transports were succeeded by a fit of impatience, which had well-nigh deprived him of his senses in good earnest. His surprize at finding his lost Aurelia in such a place; the seeming impossibility of relieving her; and his unspeakable eagerness to contrive some scheme for profitting by the interesting discovery he had made, concurred in brewing up a second extasy, during which he acted a thousand extravagancies, which it was well for him the attendants did not observe. Perhaps it was well for the servant that he did not enter while the paroxism prevailed: had this been the case, he might have met with the fate of Lychas, whom Hercules in his frenzy destroyed.[2]

Before the cloth was laid for supper, he was calm enough to conceal the disorder of his mind: but he complained of the headach, and desired he might be next day visited by the physician, to whom he resolved to explain himself in such a manner, as should make an impression upon him, provided he was not altogether destitute of conscience and humanity.

CHAPTER XXIV

*The Knot that puzzles human Wisdom, the Hand of Fortune
sometimes will untie familiar as her Garter*

WHEN the doctor made his next appearance in Sir Launcelot's
apartment, the knight addressed him in these words: 'Sir, the
practice of medicine is one of the most honourable professions
exercised among the sons of men; a profession which hath been
revered at all periods and in all nations, and even held sacred in the
most polished ages of antiquity. The scope of it is to preserve the
being, and confirm the health of our fellow-creatures; of consequence, to sustain the blessings of society, and crown life with
fruition. The character of a physician, therefore, not only supposes
natural sagacity, and acquired erudition, but it also implies every
delicacy of sentiment, every tenderness of nature, and every virtue
of humanity. That these qualities are centered in you, doctor, I
would willingly believe: but it will be sufficient for my purpose,
that you are possessed of common integrity. To whose concern I am
indebted for your visits, you best know: but if you understand the
art of medicine, you must be sensible by this time, that with respect
to me your prescriptions are altogether unnecessary—come, Sir,
you cannot—you don't believe that my intellects are disordered.
Yet, granting me to be really under the influence of that deplorable
malady, no person has a right to treat me as a lunatic, or to sue out a
commission, but my nearest kindred.—That you may not plead
ignorance of my name and family, you shall understand that I am
Sir Launcelot Greaves, of the county of York, baronet; and that
my nearest relation is Sir Reginald Meadows, of Cheshire, the
eldest son of my mother's sister—that gentleman, I am sure, had
no concern in seducing me by false pretences under the clouds of
night into the fields, where I was surprised, overpowered, and kidnapped by armed ruffians. Had he really believed me insane, he
would have proceeded according to the dictates of honour,
humanity, and the laws of his country. Situated as I am, I have a
right, by making application to the lord chancellor, to be tried by a
jury of honest men.—But of that right, I cannot avail myself, while
I remain at the mercy of a brutal miscreant, in whose house I am
inclosed, unless you contribute your assistance. Your assistance,

therefore, I demand, as you are a gentleman, a christian, and a fellow-subject, who, tho' every other motive should be overlooked, ought to interest himself in my case as a common concern, and concur with all your power towards the punishment of those who dare commit such outrages against the liberty of your country.'

The doctor seemed to be a little disconcerted; but after some recollection, resumed his air of sufficiency and importance, and assured our adventurer he would do him all the service in his power; but, in the mean time, advised him to take the potion he had prescribed.

The knight's eyes lightning with indignation, 'I am now convinced, (cried he) that you are accomplice in the villainy which has been practised upon me; that you are a sordid wretch, without principle or feeling, a disgrace to the faculty, and a reproach to human nature—yes, sirrah, you are the most perfidious of all assassins—you are the hireling minister of the worst of all villains, who from motives even baser than malice, envy, and revenge, rob the innocent of all the comforts of life, brand them with the imputation of madness, the most cruel species of slander, and wantonly protract their misery, by leaving them in the most shocking confinement, a prey to reflections infinitely more bitter than death—but I will be calm—do me justice at your peril. I demand the protection of the legislature—if I am refused,—remember, a day of reckoning will come—you and the rest of the miscreants who have combined against me, must, in order to cloak your treachery, have recourse to murder; an expedient which I believe you very capable of embracing, or a man of my rank and character cannot be much longer concealed—Tremble, caitif, at the thoughts of my release—in the mean time, begone, lest my just resentments impel me to dash out your brains upon that marble—away.—'

The honest doctor was not so firmly persuaded of his patient's lunacy as to reject his advice, which he made what haste he could to follow, when an unexpected accident intervened. That this may be properly introduced, we must return to the knight's brace of trusty friends, captain Crowe and lawyer Clarke, whom we left in sorrowful deliberation upon the fate of their patron. Clarke's genius being rather more fruitful in resources, than that of the seaman, he suggested an advertisement, which was accordingly inserted in the daily papers; importing, that, 'whereas a gentleman of considerable rank and fortune had suddenly disappeared on such a night from his house, near Golden-square, in consequence of a letter delivered to him by a porter; and there is great reason to believe some violence hath been offered to his life: any person capable of giving such information as may tend to clear up this dark transaction, shall, by applying to Mr. Thomas Clarke, attorney, at his lodgings in Upper Brook-street, receive proper security for the reward of one hundred guineas, to be paid to him upon his making the discovery required.'

The porter who delivered the letter appeared accordingly; but could give no other information, except that it was put into his hand with a shilling, by a man muffled up in a great coat, who stopped him for the purpose, in his passing through Queen-street. It was necessary that the advertisement should produce an effect upon another person, who was no other than the hackney coach-man who drove our hero to the place of his imprisonment. This fellow had been enjoined secrecy, and indeed bribed to hold his tongue, by a considerable gratification, which, it was supposed, would have been effectual, as the man was a master-coachman in good circumstances, and well known to the keeper of the mad house, by whom he had been employed on former occasions of the same nature. Perhaps his fidelity to his employer, reinforced by the hope of many future jobbs of that kind, might have been proof against the offer of fifty pounds; but double that sum was a tempta-tion he could not resist. He no sooner read the intimation in the Daily Advertiser,[1] over his morning's pot at an alehouse, than he entered into consultation with his own thoughts, and having no reason to doubt that this was the very fare he had conveyed, he resolved to earn the reward, and abstain from all such adventures in time coming. He had the precaution, however, to take an attorney along with him to Mr. Clarke, who entered into a conditional bond; and, with the assistance of his uncle deposited the money, to be forthcoming when the conditions should be fulfilled. These previous measures being taken, the coachman declared what he knew, and discovered the house in which Sir Launcelot had been immured. He moreover accompanied our two adherents to a judge's chamber, where he made oath to the truth of his information; and a warrant was immediately granted to search the house of Bernard Shackle, and set at liberty Sir Launcelot Greaves, if there found.

Fortified with this authority, they engaged a constable with a formidable posse, and embarking them in coaches, repaired, with all possible expedition, to the house of Mr. Shackle, who did not think proper to dispute their claim, but admitted them, tho' not without betraying evident symptoms of consternation. One of the servants directing them, by his master's order, to Sir Launcelot's apartment, they hurried up stairs in a body, occasioning such a noise as did not fail to alarm the physician, who had just opened the door to retire, when he perceived their irruption. Capt. Crowe conjecturing he was guilty, from the confusion that appeared in his countenance, made no scruple of seizing him by the collar, as he endeavoured to retreat; while the tender-hearted Tom Clarke, running up to the knight with his eyes brimfull of joy and affection, forgot all the forms of distant respect, and throwing his arms around his neck, blubbered in his bosom.

Our hero did not receive this proof of his attachment unmoved. He strained him in his embrace, honoured him with the title of his deliverer, and asked him by what miracle he had discovered the place of his confinement. The lawyer began to unfold the various steps he had taken, with equal minuteness and self-complacency, when Crowe dragging the doctor still by the collar, shook his old friend by the hand, protesting he was never so overjoyed since he got clear of a Sallee Rover on the coast of Barbary;[1] and that two glasses ago he would have started[2] all the money he had in the world in the hold of any man who would have shewn Sir Launcelot safe at his moorings. The knight, having made a proper return to this sincere manifestation of good will, desired him to dismiss that worthless fellow, meaning the doctor, who, finding himself released, withdrew with some precipitation.

Then our adventurer, attended by his friends, walked with a deliberate pace to the outward gate, which he found open, and getting into one of the coaches, was entertained by the way to his own house with a detail of every measure which had been pursued for his release. In his own parlour he found Mrs. Dolly Cowslip, who had been waiting with great fear and impatience for the issue of Mr. Clarke's adventure. She now fell upon her knees, and bathed the knight's hand with tears of joy; while the face of this young woman, recalling the idea of her mistress, roused his heart to strong emotion, and stimulated his mind to the immediate atchievement he had already planned. As for Crabshaw, he was not the last to signify his satisfaction at his master's return. After having kissed the hem of his garment, he repaired to the stable, where he communicated these tidings to his friend Gilbert, whom he saddled and bridled: the same office he performed for Bronzomarte: then putting on his squire-like attire and accoutrements, he mounted one, and led the other to the knight's door, before which he paraded, uttering from time to time repeated shouts, to the no small entertainment of the populace, until he received orders to house his companions. Thus commanded, he led them back to their stalls, resumed his livery, and rejoined his fellow-servants, who were resolved to celebrate the day with banquets and rejoicings.

Their master's heart was not sufficiently at ease to share in their festivity. He held a consultation with his friends in the parlour, whom he acquainted with the reasons he had to believe Miss Darnel was confined in the same house which had been his prison: a circumstance which filled them with equal pleasure and astonishment. Dolly, in particular, weeping plentifully, conjured him to deliver her dear lady without delay; nothing now remained but to concert the plan for her deliverance. As Aurelia had informed Dolly of her connection with Mrs. Kawdle, at whose house she proposed to lodge, before she was overtaken on the road by her uncle, this particular was now imparted to the council, and struck a light which seemed to point out the direct way to Miss Darnel's enlargement.

Our hero, accompanied by Mrs. Cowslip, and Tom Clarke, set out immediately for the house of Dr. Kawdle, who happened to be abroad; but his wife received them with great courtesy. She was a well-bred, sensible, genteel woman, and strongly attached to Aurelia by the ties of affection as well as of consanguinity. She no sooner learned the situation of her cousin than she expressed the most impatient concern for her being set at liberty; and assured Sir Launcelot she would concur in any scheme he should propose for that purpose. There was no room for hesitation or choice; he attended her immediately to the judge, who upon proper application issued another search-warrant for Aurelia Darnel. The constable and his posse were again retained; and Sir Launcelot Greaves once more crossed the threshold of Mr. Bernard Shackle. Nor was the search-warrant the only implement of justice with which he had furnished himself for this visit. In going thither, they agreed upon the method in which they should introduce themselves gradually to Miss Darnel, that her tender nature might not be too much shocked by their sudden appearance.

When they arrived at the house therefore, and produced their credentials, in consequence of which, a female attendant was directed to shew the lady's apartment, Mrs. Dolly first entered the chamber of the accomplished Aurelia, who, lifting up her eyes, screamed aloud, and flew into the arms of her faithful Cowslip. Some minutes elapsed before Dolly could make shift to exclaim,— 'Am coom to live and daai with my beloved leady!' 'Dear Dolly! (cried her mistress) I cannot express the pleasure I have in seeing you again—good heaven! what solitary hours of keen affliction have I passed since we parted!—but, tell me, how did you discover the place of my retreat?—has my uncle relented?—do I owe your coming to his indulgence?'

Dolly answered in the negative; and by degrees gave her to understand that her cousin, Mrs. Kawdle, was in the next room; that lady immediately appeared, and a very tender scene of recognition passed between the two relations. It was she who, in the course of conversation, perceiving that Aurelia was perfectly composed, declared the happy tidings of the approaching deliverance. When the other eagerly insisted upon knowing to whose humanity and address she was indebted for this happy turn of fortune, her cousin declared the obligation was due to a young gentleman of Yorkshire called Sir Launcelot Greaves. At mention of that name, her face was overspread with a crimson glow, and her eyes beamed redoubled splendor,—'Cousin, (said she, with a sigh,) I know not what to say—that gentleman,—Sir Launcelot Greaves was surely born—Lord bless me!—I tell you, cousin, he has been my guardian angel.—'

Mrs. Kawdle, who had maintained a correspondence with her by letters, was no stranger to the former part of the connexion subsisting between those two lovers, and had always favoured the pretensions of our hero, without being acquainted with his person. She now observed with a smile, that as Aurelia esteemed the knight her guardian angel, and he adored her as a demi-deity, nature seemed to have intended them for each other; for such sublime ideas exalted them both above the sphere of ordinary mortals. She then ventured to intimate that he was in the house, impatient to pay his respects in person. At this declaration, the colour vanished from her cheeks; which, however, soon underwent a total suffusion. Her heart panted; her bosom heaved; and her gentle frame was agitated by transports rather violent than unpleasing. She soon, however, recollected herself; and her native serenity returned; when rising from her seat, she declared she would see him in the next apartment, where he stood in the most tumultuous suspence, waiting for permission to approach her person. Here she broke in upon him, arrayed in an elegant white undress,[1] the emblem of her purity, beaming forth the emanations of amazing beauty, warmed and improved with a glow of gratitude and affection. His heart was too big for utterance; he ran towards her with rapture, and, throwing himself at her feet, imprinted a respectful kiss upon her lilly hand. 'This, divine Aurelia, (cried he,) is a foretaste of that ineffable bliss, which you was born to bestow!—Do I then live to see you smile again? to see you restored to liberty; your mind at ease, and your health unimpaired!' 'You have lived, (said she,) to see my obligations to Sir Launcelot Greaves accumulated in such a manner, that a whole life spent in acknowledgment will scarce suffice to demonstrate a due sense of his goodness.' 'You greatly overrate my services, which have been rather the duties of common humanity, than the efforts of a generous passion, too noble to be thus evinced;—but let not my unseasonable transports detain you a moment longer on this detested scene—Give me leave to hand you into the coach, and commit you to the care of this good lady, attended by this honest young gentleman, who is my particular friend.' So saying, he presented Mr. Thomas Clarke, who had the honour to salute the fair hand of the ever amiable Aurelia.

The ladies being safely coached under the escorte of the lawyer, Sir Launcelot assured them he should wait on them in the evening, at the house of Dr. Kawdle, whither they immediately directed their course. Our hero, who remained with the constable and his gang, enquired for Mr. Bernard Shackle, upon whose person he intended to serve a writ of conspiracy, over and above a prosecution for robbery, in consequence of his having disencumbered the knight of his money and other effects, on the first night of his confinement. Mr. Shackle had discretion enough to avoid this encounter, and even to anticipate the indictment for felony, by directing one of his servants to restore the cash and papers, which our adventurer accordingly received, before he quitted the house.

In the prosecution of his search after Shackle, he chanced to enter the chamber of the bard, whom he found in dishabille, writing at a table, with a bandage over one eye, and his head covered with a night-cap of bays. The knight, having made an apology for his intrusion, desired to know if he could be of any service to Mr. Distich, as he was now at liberty to use the little influence he had, for the relief of his fellow sufferers.—The poet having eyed him for some time askance, 'I told you, (said he) your stay in this place would be of short duration,—I have sustained a small disaster on my left eye, from the hands of a rascally cordwainer, who pretends to believe himself the king of Prussia; and I am now in the very act of galling his majesty with keen iambicks.[1]—If you can help me to a roll of tobacco, and a bottle of genever, so;—If you are not so inclined, your humble servant—I shall share in the joy of your deliverance.'

The knight declined gratifying him in these particulars, which he apprehended might be prejudicial to his health; but offered his assistance in redressing his grievances, provided he laboured under any cruel treatment, or inconvenience. 'I comprehend the full extent of your generosity: (replied the satyrist) you are willing to assist me, in every thing, except the only circumstances in which assistance is required.—God b' w' ye—If you see Ben Bullock, tell him I wish he would not dedicate any more of his works to me. —Damn the fellow; he has changed his note, and begins to snivel. —For my part, I stick to my former maxim; defy all the world, and will die hard, even if death should be preceded by damnation.'

The knight finding him incorrigible, left him to the slender chance of being one day comforted by the dram-bottle; but resolved, if possible, to set on foot an accurate inquiry into the oeconomy and transactions of this private inquisition, that ample justice might be done in favour of every injured individual confined within its walls. In the afternoon, he did not fail to visit his Aurelia; and all the protestations of their mutual passion were once more interchanged. He now produced the letter, which had caused such fatal disquiet in his bosom; and Miss Darnel no sooner eyed the paper, than she recollected it was a formal dismission, which she had intended and directed for Mr. Sycamore. This the uncle had intercepted, and cunningly inclosed in another cover, addressed to Sir Launcelot Greaves, who was now astonished beyond measure to see the mystery so easily unfolded. The joy that now diffused itself in the hearts of our lovers, is more easily conceived than described; but, in order to give a stability to this mutual satisfaction, it was necessary that Aurelia should be secured from the tyranny of her uncle, whose power of guardianship would not otherwise for some months expire.

Dr. Kawdle and his lady having entered into their deliberations on this subject, it was agreed that Miss Darnel should have recourse to the protection of the lord-chancellor: but such application was rendered unnecessary by the unexpected arrival of John Clump with the following letter to Mrs. Kawdle from the steward of Anthony Darnel, dated at Aurelia's house in the country. 'Madam, it hath pleased God to afflict Mr. Darnel with a severe stroke of the dead palsy.—He was taken yesterday, and now lies insensible, seemingly at the point of death. Among the papers in his pocket, I found the inclosed, by which it appears that my honoured young lady Miss Darnel is confined in a private mad-house. I am afraid Mr. Darnel's fate is a just judgment of God upon him for his cruelty to that excellent person. I need not exhort you, madam, to take, immediately upon the receipt of this, such measures as will be necessary for the enlargement of my poor young lady. In the mean time, I shall do the needful for the preservation of her property in this place, and send you an account of any further alteration that may happen; being very respectfully, Madam, your most obedient humble servant, Ralph Mattocks.'

Clump had posted up to London with this intimation, on the wings of love, and being covered with clay from the heels to the eyes upwards, he appeared in such an unfavourable light at Dr. Kawdle's door, that the footman refused him admittance. Nevertheless, he pushed him aside, and fought his way up-stairs into the dining-room, where the company was not a little astonished at such an apparition. The fellow himself was no less amazed at seeing Aurelia, and his own sweetheart Mrs. Dolly Cowslip. He forthwith fell upon his knees, and, in silence, held out the letter, which was taken by the doctor, and presented to his wife, according to the direction. She did not fail to communicate the contents, which were far from being unwelcome to the individuals who composed this little society. Mr. Clump was honoured with the approbation of his young lady, who commended him for his zeal and expedition; bestowed upon him an handsome gratuity in the mean time, and desired to see him again when he should be properly refreshed after the fatigue he had undergone.

Mr. Thomas Clarke being consulted on this occasion, gave it as his opinion, that Miss Darnel should without delay, choose another guardian for the few months that remained of her minority. This opinion was confirmed by the advice of some eminent lawyers, to whom immediate recourse was had; and Dr. Kawdle, being the person pitched upon for this office, the necessary forms were executed with all possible dispatch. The first use the doctor made of his guardianship was to sign a power, constituting Mr. Ralph Mattocks his attorney *pro tempore*, for managing the estate of Miss Aurelia Darnel; and this was forwarded to the steward by the hands of Clump, who set out with it for the seat of Darnel-hill, though not without a heavy heart, occasioned by some intimation he had received, concerning the connexion between his dear Dolly, and Mr. Clarke the lawyer.

CHAPTER THE LAST

Which, it is to be hoped, will be, on more accounts than one,
agreeable to the reader

SIR LAUNCELOT having vindicated the liberty, confirmed the safety, and secured the heart of his charming Aurelia, now found leisure to unravel the conspiracy which had been executed against his person; and with that view commenced a law-suit against the owner of the house where he and his mistress had been separately confined. Mr. Shackle was, notwithstanding all the submissions and atonement which he offered to make, either in private or in public, indicted on the statute of kidnapping, tried, convicted, punished by a severe fine, and standing in the pillory. A judicial writ *ad inquirendum*[1] being executed, the prisons of his inquisition were laid open, and several innocent captives enlarged.

In the course of Shackle's trial, it appeared that the knight's confinement was a scheme executed by his rival Mr. Sycamore, according to the device of his counsellor Dawdle, who, by this contrivance, had reconciled himself to his patron, after having deserted him in the day of battle. Our hero was so incensed at the discovery of Sycamore's treachery and ingratitude, that he went in quest of him immediately, to take vengeance on his person, accompanied by Capt. Crowe, who wanted to ballance accounts with Mr. Dawdle. But those gentlemen had wisely avoided the impending storm, by retiring to the continent, on pretence of travelling for improvement.

Sir Launcelot was not now so much of a knight-errant, as to leave Aurelia to the care of Providence, and pursue the traitors to the farthest extremities of the earth. He practised a much more easy, certain, and effectual method of revenge, by instituting a process against them, which, after writs of *capias*, *alias*, *& pluries*,[1] had been repeated, subjected them both to outlawry. Mr. Sycamore and his friend being thus deprived of the benefit of the law, by their own neglect, would likewise have forfeited their goods and chattels to the king, had not they made such submissions as appeased the wrath of Sir Launcelot and Capt. Crowe; then they ventured to return, and by dint of interest obtained a reversal of the outlawry. But this grace they did not enjoy, till long after our adventurer was happily established in life.

While the knight waited impatiently for the expiration of Aurelia's minority, and, in the mean time, consoled himself with the imperfect happiness arising from her conversation, and those indulgences which the most unblemished virtue could bestow; Capt. Crowe projected another plan of vengeance against the conjurer, whose lying oracles had cost him such a world of vexation. The truth is, the captain began to be tired of idleness, and undertook this adventure to keep his hand in use. He imparted his design to Crabshaw, who had likewise suffered in spirit from the predictions of the said offender, and was extremely well disposed to assist in punishing the false prophet. He now took it for granted that he should not be hanged for stealing a horse; and thought it very hard to pay so much money for a deceitful prophecy, which, in all likelihood, would never be fulfilled.

Actuated by these motives, they set out together for the house of consultation; but they found it shut up and abandoned, and, upon inquiry in the neighbourhood, learned that the conjurer had moved his quarters that very day on which the captain had recourse to his art. This was actually the case: he knew the fate of Sir Launcelot would soon come to light, and he did not chuse to wait the consequence. He had other motives for decamping. He had run a score at the public house, which he had no mind to discharge, and wanted to disengage himself from his female associate, who knew too much of his affairs, to be kept at her proper distance. All these purposes he had answered, by retreating softly without beat of·drum, while his Sybil was abroad running down prey for his devouring. He had not, however, taken his measures so cunningly, but that this old hag discovered his new lodgings, and in revenge, gave information to the publican. This creditor took out a writ accordingly; and the bailiff had just secured his person as Capt. Crowe and Timothy Crabshaw chanced to pass by the door in their way homewards, through an obscure street near the Seven Dials.[1]

The conjurer having no subterfuge left, but a great many particular reasons for avoiding an explanation with the justice, like the man between the devil and the deep sea, of two evils chose the least; and beckoning to the captain, called him by his name. Crowe, thus addressed, replied with a 'Hilloah!' and looking towards the place from whence he was hailed, at once recognized the negromancer. Without farther hesitation he sprang across the street, and collaring Albumazar,[2] exclaimed, 'Aha! old boy; is the wind in that corner?—I thought we should grapple one day—now will I bring you up by the head, tho' all the devils in hell were blowing abaft the beam.'

The bailiff seeing his prisoner so roughly handled before, and at the same time assaulted behind by Crabshaw, who cried, 'Shew me a liar, and I'll shew you a thief—who is to be hanged now?'— I say, the bailiff, fearing he should lose the benefit of his job, began to put on his contentious face, and, declaring the doctor was his prisoner, swore he could not surrender him, without a warrant from the lord chief justice. The whole groupe adjourning into the parlour, the conjurer desired to know of Crowe, whether Sir Launcelot was found? being answered, 'Ey, ey, safe enough to see you made fast in the bilboes,[3] brother;' he told the captain he had something of consequence to communicate for his advantage; and proposed that Crowe and Crabshaw should bail the action, which lay only for a debt of three pounds.

Crow stormed, and Crabshaw grinned at this modest proposal: but when they understood that they could only be bound for his appearance, and reflected that they needed not part with him, until his body should be surrendered unto justice, they consented to give bail; and the bond being executed, conveyed him directly to the house of our adventurer. The boisterous Crowe introduced him to Sir Launcelot with such an abrupt, unconnected detail of his offence, as the knight could not understand without Timothy's annotations. These were followed by some questions put to the conjurer, who laying aside his black gown, and plucking off his white beard, exhibited to the astonished spectators, the very individual countenance of the empirical politician Ferret, who had played our hero such a slippery trick after the electioneering adventure.

'I perceive (said he) you are preparing to expostulate, and upbraid me for having given a false information against you to the country justice. I look upon mankind to be in a state of nature, a truth which Hobbes[1] hath stumbled upon by accident. I think every man has a right to avail himself of his talents, even at the expence of his fellow-creatures; just as we see the fish, and other animals of the creation, devouring one another.—I found the justice but one degree removed from ideotism, and knowing that he would commit some blunder in the execution of his office, which would lay him at your mercy, I contrived to make his folly the instrument of my escape—I was dismissed without being obliged to sign the information I had given; and you took ample vengeance for his tyranny and impertinence. I came to London, where my circumstances obliged me to live in disguise. In the character of a conjurer, I was consulted by your follower Crowe, and your 'squire Crabshaw. I did little or nothing but eccho back the intelligence they brought me, except prognosticating that Crabshaw would be hanged; a prediction to which I found myself so irresistibly impelled, that I am persuaded it was the real effect of inspiration—I am now arrested for a paultry sum of money; and, moreover, liable to be sent to Bridewell as an impostor—let those answer for my conduct, whose cruelty and insolence have driven me to the necessity of using such subterfuges—I have been oppressed and persecuted by the government for speaking truth—your omnipotent laws have reconciled contradictions. That which is acknowledged to be truth in fact is construed falshood in law; and great reason we have to boast of a constitution founded on the basis of absurdity—But, waving these remarks, I own I am unwilling to be either imprisoned for debt, or punished for imposture—I know how far to depend upon generosity, and what is called benevolence; words to amuse the weak-minded—I build upon a surer bottom—I will bargain for your assistance—it is in my power to put twelve thousand pounds in the pocket of Samuel Crowe, that there sea-ruffian, who by his good-will would hang me to the yard's arm—'

There he was interrupted by the seaman. 'Damn your rat's eyes! none of your—hang thee!—fish[2] my topmasts! if the rope was fairly reeved, and the tackle sound, d'ye see—' Mr. Clarke, who was present, began to stare; while the knight assured Ferret, that if he was really able and willing to serve Capt. Crowe in any thing essential, he should be amply rewarded. In the mean time, he discharged the debt, and assigned him an apartment in his own house. That same day, Crowe, by the advice of Sir Launcelot and his nephew, entered into conditional articles with the Cynic, to allow him the interest of fifteen hundred pounds for life: provided, by his means, the captain should obtain possession of the estate of Hobby-hole in Yorkshire, which had belonged to his grandfather, and of which he was heir of blood.

This bond being executed, Mr. Ferret discovered that he himself was the lawful husband of Bridget Maple, aunt to Samuel Crowe, by a clandestine marriage; which, however, he convinced them he could prove by undeniable evidence. This being the case, she, the said Bridget Maple, alias Ferret, was a *covert femme*,[1] consequently could not transact any deed of alienation without his concurrence; ergo, the docking of the intail of the estate of Hobby-hole was illegal and of none effect.[2] This was a very agreeable declaration to the whole company, who did not fail to congratulate Captain Crowe on the prospect of his being restored to his inheritance. Tom Clarke, in particular, protested, with tears in his eyes, that it gave him unspeakable joy; and his tears trickled the faster, when Crowe, with an arch look, signified that now he was pretty well victualled for life, he had some thoughts of embarking on the voyage of matrimony.

But that point of happiness to which, as the north pole, the course of these adventures hath been invariably directed, was still unattained; we mean, the indissoluble union of the accomplished Sir Launcelot Greaves and the enchanting Miss Darnel. Our hero now discovered in his mistress a thousand charms, which hitherto he had no opportunity to contemplate. He found her beauty excelled by her good sense, and her virtue superior to both. He found her untainted by that giddiness, vanity, and affectation, which distinguish the fashionable females of the present age. He found her uninfected by the rage for diversion and dissipation; for noise, tumult, gewgaws, glitter, and extravagance. He found her not only raised by understanding and taste far above the amusements of little vulgar minds; but even exalted by uncommon genius and refined reflection, so as to relish the more sublime enjoyments of rational pleasure. He found her possessed of that vigour of mind which constitutes true fortitude, and vindicates the empire of reason. He found her heart incapable of disguise or dissimulation; frank, generous, and open; susceptible of the most tender impressions; glowing with a keen sense of honour, and melting with humanity. A youth of his sensibility could not fail of being deeply affected by such attractions. The nearer he approached the centre of happiness, the more did the velocity of his passion increase. Her uncle still remained insensible, as it were, in the arms of death. Time seemed to linger in its lapse, 'till the knight was inflamed to the most eager degree of impatience. He communicated his distress to Aurelia; he pressed her with the most pathetic remonstrances to abridge the torture of his suspence. He interested Mrs. Kawdle in his behalf; and, at length, his importunity succeeded. The banns of marriage were regularly published; and the ceremony was performed in the parish church, in presence of Dr. Kawdle and his lady, Capt. Crowe, lawyer Clarke, and Mrs. Dolly Cowslip.—

The bride, instead of being disguised in tawdry stuffs of gold or silver, and sweating under a harness of diamonds, according to the elegant taste of the times, appeared in a negligee of plain blue sattin, without any other jewels than her eyes, which far outshone all that ever was produced by the mines of Golconda.[1] Her hair had no extraneous ornament, than a small sprig of artificial roses; but the dignity of her air, the elegance of her shape, the sweetness and sensibility of her countenance, added to such warmth of colouring, and such exquisite symmetry of features, as could not be excelled by human nature, attracted the eyes and excited the admiration of all the beholders. The effect they produced in the heart of Sir Launcelot, was such a rapture as we cannot pretend to describe. He made his appearance on this occasion, in a white coat and blue sattin vest, both embroidered with silver; and all who saw him could not but own that he alone seemed worthy to possess the lady whom heaven had destined for his consort. Capt. Crowe had taken off a blue suit of cloaths strongly guarded with bars of broad gold lace, in order to honour the nuptials of his friend: he wore upon his head a bag-wig *a-la pigeon*,[2] made by an old acquaintance in Wapping; and to his side he had girded a huge plate-hilted sword, which he had bought of a recruiting serjeant. Mr. Clarke was dressed in pompadour, with gold buttons, and his lovely Dolly, in a smart checked lutestring,[3] a present from her mistress.

The whole company dined, by invitation, at the house of Dr. Kawdle; and here it was that the two most deserving lovers on the face of the earth attained to the consummation of all earthly felicity. The captain and his nephew had a hint to retire in due time. Mrs. Kawdle conducted the amiable Aurelia, trembling, to the marriage-bed: our hero glowing with a bridegroom's ardour, claimed the husband's privilege: Hymen lighted up his brightest torch at Virtue's lamp, and every star shed its happiest influence on their heaven-directed union. Instructions had been already dispatched to prepare Greavesbury-hall for the reception of its new mistress; and for that place the new-married couple set out next morning, according to the plan which had been previously concerted. Sir Launcelot and lady Greaves, accompanied by Mrs. Kawdle and attended by Dolly, travelled in their own coach drawn by six dappled horses. Dr. Kawdle, with Capt. Crowe, occupied the doctor's post-chariot, provided with four bays: Mr. Clarke had the honour to bestride the loins of Bronzomarte: Mr. Ferret was mounted upon an old hunter: Crabshaw stuck close to his friend Gilbert; and two other horsemen completed the retinue. There was not an aching heart in the whole cavalcade, except that of the young lawyer, which was by turns invaded with hot desires and chilling scruples. Tho' he was fond of Dolly to distraction, his regard to worldly reputation, and his attention to worldly interest, were continually raising up bars to a legal gratification of his love. His pride was startled at the thought of marrying the daughter of a poor country publican; and he moreover dreaded the resentment of his uncle Crowe, should he take any step of this nature without his concurrence. Many a wishful look did he cast at Dolly, the tears standing in his eyes; and many a woeful sigh did he utter.

Lady Greaves immediately perceived the situation of his heart, and, by questioning Mrs. Cowslip, discovered a mutual passion between these lovers. She consulted her dear knight on the subject; and he catechised the lawyer, who pleaded guilty. The captain being sounded, as to his opinion, declared he would be steered in that as well as every other course of life, by Sir Launcelot and his lady, whom he verily revered as beings of an order superior to the ordinary race of mankind. This favourable response being obtained from the sailor, our hero took an opportunity on the road, one day after dinner, in presence of the whole company, to accost the lawyer in these words: 'My good friend Clarke, I have your happiness very much at heart—your father was an honest man, to whom my family had manifold obligations. I have had these many years a personal regard for yourself, derived from your own integrity of heart and goodness of disposition—I see you are affected, and shall be brief— Besides this regard, I am indebted to your friendship for the liberty —what shall I say?—for the inestimable happiness I now enjoy, in possessing the most excellent—But I understand that significant glance of my Aurelia—I will not offend her delicacy—The truth is, my obligation is very great, and it is time I should evince my gratitude—if the stewardship of my estate is worth your acceptance, you shall have it immediately, together with the house and farm of Cockerton in my neighbourhood. I know you have a passion for Mrs. Dolly; and believe she looks upon you with the eyes of tender prepossession—don't blush Dolly—besides, your agreeable person, which all the world must approve, you can boast of virtue, fidelity, and friendship. Your attachment to lady Greaves, neither she or I shall ever forget—if you are willing to unite your fate with Mr. Clarke, your mistress gives me leave to assure you she will stock the farm at her own expence; and we will celebrate the wedding at Greavesbury-hall—'

By this time the hearts of these grateful lovers had overflowed. Dolly was sitting on her knees bathing her lady's hand with her tears; and Mr. Clarke appeared in the same attitude by Sir Launcelot. The uncle, almost as much affected as the nephew, by the generosity of our adventurer, cried aloud, 'I pray God that you and your glorious consort may have smooth seas and gentle gales whithersoever you are bound—as for my kinsman Tom, I'll give him a thousand pounds to set him fairly afloat; and if he do not prove a faithful tender to you his benefactor, I hope he will founder in this world, and be damned in that which is to come.' Nothing now was wanting to the completion of their happiness, but the consent of Dolly's mother, at the Black Lyon, who they did not suppose could have any objection to such an advantageous match for her daughter: but, in this particular, they were mistaken.

In the mean time, they arrived at the village where the knight had exercised the duties of chivalry; and there he received the gratulation of Mr. Fillet, and the attorney who had offered to bail him before justice Gobble. Mutual civilities having passed, they gave him to understand, that Gobble and his wife were turned methodists.[1] All the rest of the prisoners whom he had delivered came to testify their gratitude, and were hospitably entertained. Next day, they halted at the Black Lyon, where the good woman was overjoyed to see Dolly so happily preferred: but, when Sir Launcelot unfolded the proposed marriage, she interrupted him with a scream. 'Christ Jesus forbid—marry and amen! match with her own brother!'[1]

At this exclamation Dolly fainted: her lover stood with his hairs erect, and his mouth wide open; Crowe stared; while the knight and his lady expressed equal surprise and concern. When Sir Launcelot intreated Mrs. Cowslip to explain this mystery, she told him that about sixteen years ago, Mr. Clarke senior had brought Dolly, then an infant, to her house, when she and her late husband lived in another part of the country; and as she had then been lately delivered of a child which did not live, he hired her as nurse to the little foundling. He owned she was a love-begotten babe, and from time to time paid handsomely for the board of Dolly, who he desired might pass for her own daughter. In his last illness, he assured her he had taken care to provide for the child; but since his death she had received no account of any such provision. She, moreover, informed his honour, that Mr. Clarke had deposited in her hands a diamond ring and a sealed paper, never to be opened without his order, until Dolly should be demanded in marriage by the man she should like; and not then, except in presence of the clergyman of the parish. 'Send for the clergyman this instant (cried our hero, reddening, and fixing his eyes on Dolly) I hope all will yet be well.'

The vicar arriving, and being made acquainted with the nature of the case, the landlady produced the paper; which being opened, appeared to be an authentic certificate, that the person, commonly known by the name of Dorothy Cowslip, was in fact Dorothea Greaves, daughter of Jonathan Greaves, esq; by a young gentle-woman who had been some years deceased.—

'The remaining part of the mystery I myself can unfold—(exclaimed the knight, while he ran and embraced the astonished Dolly, as his kinswoman.) Jonathan Greaves was my uncle, and died before he came of age; so that he could make no settlement on his child, the fruit of a private amour founded on a promise of marriage, of which this ring was a token. Mr. Clarke, being his confident, disposed of the child, and at length finding his constitution decay, revealed the secret to my father, who, in his will, bequeathed one hundred pounds a year to this agreeable foundling:

but, as they both died while I was abroad, and some of the memorandums touching this transaction probably were mislaid, I never 'till now could discover where or how my pretty cousin was situated. I shall recompence the good woman for her care and fidelity, and take pleasure in bringing this affair to a happy issue.'

The lovers were now overwhelmed with transports of joy and gratitude, and every countenance was lighted up with satisfaction. From this place to the habitation of Sir Launcelot, the bells were rung in every parish, and the corporation in their formalities congratulated him in every town through which he passed. About five miles from Greavesbury-hall he was met by above five thousand persons of both sexes and every age, dressed out in their gayest apparel, headed by Mr. Ralph Mattocks from Darnel-hill, and the rector from the knight's own parish. They were preceded by music of different kinds, ranged under a great variety of flags and ensigns; and the women, as well as the men, bedizened with fancy-knots and marriage-favours.[1] At the end of the avenue, a select bevy of comely virgins arrayed in white, and a separate band of choice youths, distinguished by garlands of laurel and holly interweaved, fell into the procession, and sung in chorus a rustic epithalamium composed by the curate. At the gate they were received by the venerable house-keeper Mrs. Oakley, whose features were so brightened by the occasion, that with the first glance she made a conquest of the heart of captain Crowe; and this connexion was improved afterwards into a legal conjunction.

Mean while the houses of Greavesbury-hall and Darnel-hill were set open for the entertainment of all comers, and both ecchoed with the sounds of festivity. After the ceremony of giving and receiving visits had been performed by Sir Launcelot Greaves and his lady, Mr. Clarke was honoured with the hand of the agreeable Miss Dolly Greaves; and the captain was put in possession of his paternal estate. The perfect and uninterrupted felicity of the knight and his endearing consort, diffused itself through the whole adjacent country, as far as their example and influence could extend. They were admired, esteemed, and applauded by every person of taste, sentiment, and benevolence; at the same time beloved, revered, and almost adored by the common people, among whom they suffered not the merciless hand of indigence or misery to seize one single sacrifice.

Ferret, at first, seemed to enjoy his easy circumstances; but the novelty of this situation soon wore off, and all his misanthropy returned. He could not bear to see his fellow-creatures happy around him; and signified his disgust to Sir Launcelot, declaring his intention of returning to the metropolis, where he knew there would be always food sufficient for the ravenous appetite of his spleen. Before he departed, the knight made him partake of his bounty, though he could not make him taste of his happiness, which soon received a considerable addition in the birth of a son, destined to be the heir and representative of two worthy families, whose mutual animosity, the union of his parents had so happily extinguished.

EXPLANATORY NOTES

ABBREVIATIONS

Don Quixote   *The History and Adventures of the Renowned Don Quixote*, translated from the Spanish of Miguel De Cervantes . . . by T. Smollett, M.D., 4 vols., second edition, corrected, 1761 (cited by Part, Book, and chapter numbers).

History   Tobias Smollett, *The History of England, from the Revolution to the Death of George the Second*, 5 vols., new edition, 1818.

Kahrl   George M. Kahrl, *Tobias Smollett: Traveler-Novelist*, 1945.

Page 1. (1) *black lion*: 'not a fictitious inn but the famous Black Lion at Weston near Sutton-on-the-Trent and Scarthing Moor, in Nottinghamshire' (Kahrl, p. 57).

(2) *sea-coal*: ordinary fossil coal, brought by sea from Newcastle to London and elsewhere.

(3) *rumbo*: rum punch.

(4) *two-penny*: quality of ale originally sold at twopence per quart.

Page 2. (1) *exercise of his profession . . . corrupt*: For the essence of Smollett's views on the legal profession, see *The Letters of Tobias Smollett*, ed. Knapp (1970), pp. 21–6.

(2) *in forma pauperis*: in the character of a pauper. Under statutes passed in 1495 and 1532, persons who could swear they had not property worth five pounds, except their wearing apparel and the subject-matter of the intended action, could bring court action without court costs or fees to the lawyer appointed them.

(3) *horn of a dark lanthorn*: side (made of animal horn) of a lantern with an arrangement by which the light can be concealed.

Page 3. (1) *Ferret*: a caricature of John Shebbeare. See Introduction.

(2) *all weathers . . . case-hardened . . . Spitzbergen*: Cf. *Humphry Clinker*, ed. Knapp (1966), Bramble's Letter of 26 October. Spitzbergen is a group of islands in the Arctic Ocean, covered with snowfields and glaciers.

(3) *aloft and alow*: above and below decks.

(4) *bottom-planks . . . sheathing*: hull planks, sheathing being the protective covering for underwater surfaces of ships.

(5) *new-pay*: smear with pitch, tar, or the like, as a defence against wet.

Page 4. (1) *Royal Exchange*: building serving as the centre of London's banking and commercial life.

(2) *Belay*: stop; literally, make fast a rope.

(3) *Clap a stopper . . . cable*: literally, put a holding rope on your anchor line to keep it from playing out.

(4) *bring thyself up*: literally, come to anchor.

(5) *knees of a bilander*: A bilander was a small coasting vessel of the North Sea; knees are wood or metal forms connecting and supporting two structural members of a ship.

(6) *finger-braces*: ropes or tackles by which a spar across a mast is adjusted.

(7) *eye-blocks*: blocks or pulleys suspended from loops of rope or the holes (eyes) in sails.

Page 5. (1) *Fill about*: trim a sail so that wind acts on it to change tack.

(2) *docked the intail . . . alien*: cut off or broke the prescribed line of succession to the estate and left it to one not a legal heir.

(3) *Statute Westm. 2, 13 Ed. I.*: Statute Westminster. 2, 13 Edward I., A.D. 1285. This statute created the 'estate tail', so-called because it was an estate the descent of which was cut down (*talliatum*) to the heirs of the body of the donee, or recipient, of the estate. The donee (or possessor) of land in tail could alienate the property (that is, give it to someone other than the heirs of his body), but the estate which he thus created could not last for a longer period than his own life; at his death, the estate became the property of the heirs of his body. The whole series of issue (legal offspring) of the first donee in tail were equally restrained from alienating the estate for a longer period than their own lives.

(4) *contingent remainder*: A remainder is the expectant portion of interest which, on the creation of an estate, is at the same time limited over to another, who is to enjoy it after the determination of the estate. A 'contingent' remainder is limited so as to depend on an event or condition which may never happen or be performed, or which may not happen until after the estate is determined.

(5) *feoffees*: those 'enfeoffed' or put in possession, a 'feoffment' being the transfer of freehold land.

(6) *writ of Intrusion*: writ against a stranger who enters on land on the determination of an estate, before the heir or person entitled in remainder could enter.

(7) *tenant for life*: person entitled to land for the term of his own life or another's life.

(8) *ex gravi querela*: a writ which lay for one to whom lands in fee had been devised (legally given) within any city, town, or borough in which lands were devisable by custom, if the heir of the deviser (giver) entered upon the land.

(9) *conveyancing-way*: a conveyancer was a barrister or solicitor who

chiefly devoted himself to conveyancing, or the transferring of property from one person to another; it was possible to be a conveyancer without being called to the bar.

(10) *serjeant*: serjeant-at-law was the highest degree in the common law.

(11) *tail after . . . issue extinct*: If land is entailed upon a man and his issue from a particular wife and she dies without issue, the interest of the husband becomes reduced to a tenancy in tail after possibility of issue extinct. Only a holder of land in *tail special* can become such a tenant, for if the entail is *general* such a tenancy can never arise; for while he lives he may have issue, the law not admitting the impossibility of having children at any age.

(12) *fee-simple*: freehold estate of inheritance, absolute and unqualified.

(13) *seized in tail*: 'Seisin' means feudal possession, or the relation in which a person stands to land when he has in it an estate of freehold in possession; such a person is said to be 'seised' of the land.

Page 6. (1) *bear up a-head*: put helm to windward, thus turning to leeward.

(2) *militia*: Local British regiments were formed after the passage of William Pitt's Militia Bill in 1757.

(3) *change of hands*: from a Whig to a Tory government.

(4) *party-writer*: one who writes in praise or defence of a political party and attacks its opponents.

Page 7. (1) *cap-a-pie*: from head to foot.

Page 9. (1) *farce of Hamlet's ghost: Hamlet*, I. iv.

(2) *a-has not*: he has not.

Page 10. (1) *buff jerkin*: leather jacket.

(2) *buskins*: boots reaching to the calf or knee.

(3) *back-sword*: sword with only one cutting edge.

(4) *Bodikins*: (God's) dear body, an oath.

Page 11. (1) *Go and teach your grannum to crack filberds*: your grand-mother to crack nuts (filberts); expression applied to one who says what is obvious or advises those more knowledgeable than himself.

(2) *sheet-anchor*: heaviest anchor, used in bad weather.

(3) *balsam*: balm.

(4) *siserari*: corruption of *certiorari* (to be more fully informed of), a writ for making lower courts accountable to higher for their actions.

(5) *cups and balls*: toy consisting of a cup at the end of a stem to which a ball is attached by a string, the object being to toss the ball and catch it in the cup.

Page 12. (1) *Don Quixote*: on Greaves's relation to Don Quixote, see Introduction.

(2) *near two hundred years ago*: *Don Quixote* appeared in 1605 with the second part in 1615.

Page 13. (1) *Brutus*: Lucius Junius Brutus, who feigned idiocy to escape the fate of his brother, murdered by their uncle, Tarquinius Superbus, King of Rome.

(2) *windmill for a giant*: *Don Quixote*, I. I. viii.

(3) *public house . . . castle*: '. . . All the inns he lodged at seemed castles to him' (*Don Quixote*, I. III. ii).

(4) *gentleman . . . the constable*: *Don Quixote*, I. I. iii.

(5) *Elizabat*: Don Quixote has an argument about Elizabat with a 'lunatic' (*Don Quixote*, I. III. x–xi).

(6) *Amadis de Gaul*: Don Quixote's favourite book, a Spanish or Portuguese romance first printed in the early 16th century.

(7) *Alquife*: a magician who appears in the various 'continuations' of the *Amadis de Gaul*; mentioned in *Don Quixote*, II. III. ii.

(8) *Bridewell*: a prison, place of forced labour.

Page 14. (1) *bearward*: one who leads about a bear for public exhibition of its tricks.

(2) *armed and in disguise*: 'A committee having been appointed [in 1759] to enquire what laws were expired, or near expiring . . . the following bills were brought in, and enacted into laws; namely . . . an act for continuing the law relating to the punishment of persons going armed or disguised . . . [etc]' (*History*, iv. 442).

Page 15. (1) *standing army*: feared by many as a threat to civil liberties.

(2) *eat up their fellow subjects*: Innkeepers were 'compelled to lodge, feed, and supply with small beer each foot-soldier billeted on them for 4*d*. a day' (Basil Williams, *The Whig Supremacy*, 1962, p. 215).

(3) *mercenaries abroad*: Hanoverian and Hessian troops hired to fight, in Germany, on behalf of Hanover and England.

(4) *militia*: See *supra*, note 2 to p. 5.

(5) *m——ry*: ministry

(6) *what is your* . . . . . : parliament.

(7) *debt of an hundred millions*: Smollett gives the national debt as around 108 million pounds in 1759 (*History*, v. 174).

(8) *two German electorates*: Hanover and Prussia, with whom England had costly treaty obligations by this time.

(9) *m——y*: ministry, though possibly 'monarchy'; Shebbeare had attacked George II specifically. See Introduction.

(10) *just and necessary war*: Seven Years War.

(11) *British principles*: as opposed to the interests of Hanover.

Page 17. (1) *snatch-block*: kind of pulley on ship's rigging.

(2) *Odd's firkin*: 'Odd's' is a minced form of 'God's', used to avoid overt profanation. A firkin is a small cask.

(3) *old shoes*: A shoe is a board or block in which the heel of a derrick is housed, the step of a mast.

(4) *taffril*: upper edge of ship's stern.

(5) *Morattos*: A Mahratta is one of a warlike Hindu race of India. Smollett's use of the term ante-dates by a year or two the earliest examples in the *OED*.

(6) *Seapoys*: natives of India employed as soldiers under European, especially British, discipline.

(7) *Sir Everhard Greaves*: There was a Gravesburgh or Greasburg Hall in the West Riding of Yorkshire (Kahrl, pp. 57–9). It is likelier, however, that Smollett's 'Greaves' is meant to parallel Cervantes' 'Quixote'. 'Greaves' are the parts of armour that protect the shins (the word appears in chap. xvi), and 'quixote', literally, means the piece of armour that protects the thigh. However, in his translation of *Don Quixote*, Smollett glosses the hero's name thus: '*Quixadas* signifies jaws, of which our knight had an extraordinary provision' (*Don Quixote*, I. I. i, n.). Ferdinand Fathom reappears in *Humphry Clinker* with his name changed to Grieve; see *Humphry Clinker*, ed. Knapp (1966), Bramble's Letter of 26 June.

Page 18. (1) *repetatur of the julep*: repetition (repeated dose) of the medicated drink.

(2) *secundum artem*: according to the art or science of his profession.

(3) *gemmen*: gentlemen.

(4) *exceptio in non exceptis, firmat regulam*: the exception, amongst cases which are not excepted, proves the rule.

(5) *sedente curia*: seated in court.

(6) *Anan*: anon.

(7) *in fault*: in hunting, to be off the scent or track.

Page 19. (1) *Dutch yanky*: *OED* lists this word as of doubtful status, origin, and meaning. Perhaps originally applied to a particular ship and identical with Yankee.

(2) *de mortuis nil nisi bonum*: of the dead (say) nothing but good.

(3) *weepers*: strips of white linen or muslin worn on the cuffs of men's sleeves as signs of mourning.

Page 21. (1) *trollopees*: loose-fitting dresses.

(2) *rout*: fashionable social gathering.

(3) *hips and haws*: fruit of the wild rose and the hawthorn, respectively.

(4) *housen*: old plural of house.

Page 22. (1) *bullies*: wild plums.

(2) *distraining*: seizing as security.

Page 23. (1) *thof*: though.

(2) *portioned*: provided dowries for.

(3) *pitching the bar*: athletic contest of throwing a heavy bar.

(4) *dight*: dressed, attired.

(5) *top-knots*: bows of ribbon worn on top of the head.

(6) *kissing-strings*: bonnet or cap-strings tied under the chin with the ends hanging loose.

(7) *stomachers*: ornamental coverings for the chest.

(8) *cockades*: ribbon or knot of ribbons worn in the hat.

Page 24. (1) *poor's-rate*: tax or assessment for the relief or support of the poor.

(2) *golden age*: the first and best age of the world, in which, according to the Greek and Roman poets, mankind lived in ideal prosperity and happiness, free from all trouble or crime.

(3) *the Temple*: The Middle and Inner Temples (so-called because anciently the Knights-Templars dwelt there) are among the Inns of Court.

(4) *insensibly*: Johnson's *Dictionary*, 1755, defines 'insensible' as 'imperceptible; not discoverable by the senses'.

(5) *Inns of Court*: private associations, in the nature of collegiate houses, with the exclusive privilege of conferring the degree of barrister.

(6) *Serjeant's Inn*: Inn formed by the Serjeants-at-law.

(7) *Templar*: member of the Inner or Middle Temple.

(8) *Butcher-row*: in the Strand, noted for its inns and eating-houses.

(9) *regulated . . . the theatre*: The archetypal Templar-theatre critic is Will Honeycomb in Addison and Steele's *Spectator* (1709–11).

Page 25. (1) *Ashenton*: 'In Smollett's time there was . . . an Ashenton in the hundred of Stafford, West Riding, Yorkshire' (Kahrl, p. 57).

(2) *pactum familiae*: family contract.

(3) *in propria persona*: in his own proper person.

Page 26. (1) *Garrick*: David Garrick (1719–79) the most famous actor of his time. Smollett had satirized him (as Marmozet) in ch. lxii–lxiii of *Roderick Random* and in ch. cii of *Peregrine Pickle*. The revised (1758) edition of *Peregrine Pickle* omits the satire on Garrick. In 1757, Garrick, as manager of Drury Lane Theatre, produced Smollett's play, *The Reprisal*.

(2) *Pitt*: William Pitt, first earl of Chatham (1708–78), perhaps the most important political figure in 18th-century England and, by the accounts of his contemporaries, the greatest orator England had ever had.

(3) *Egmont*: John Perceval, second Earl of Egmont (1711–70).

(4) *Murray*: William Murray (1705–93), an important member first of the House of Commons then of the House of Lords; said to be a close second to Pitt in oratory.

(5) *harangue*: 'a speech; a popular oration' (Johnson's *Dictionary*, 1755).

Page 27. (1) '*O! she is all*, etc.: 'Is she not more than painting can express,/ Or youthful poets fancy, when they love?' (Nicholas Rowe, *The Fair Penitent*, iii, 244–5).

(2) *Venus de Medicis*: the Medici *Aphrodite*, hellenistic sculpture possibly by one of the sons of Praxiteles.

(3) *Dianas*: Diana is goddess of the moon.

(4) *Galateas*: sea-maidens or Nereids.

(5) *Praxiteles*: Greek sculptor, born at Athens, *c*. 390 B.C.

(6) *Roubillac*: Louis François Roubillac (1695–1762), French-born sculptor who lived and worked in England from 1730 until his death.

(7) *Wilton*: Joseph Wilton (1722–1803), English sculptor, friend of Roubillac.

(8) *parva componere magnis*: to compare great things with small.

Page 29. (1) *my poor father say—*': Clarke's over-circumstantial detail parodies the epic genealogy of the hero's steed.

(2) *Odd's heartlikins*: God's little heart.

(3) *running tackle*: all movable rigging, ropes, and tackles.

(4) '*Noint my block*: anoint (beat or hit) my head.

(5) *a rope's end*: length of cordage used for flogging.

Page 30. (1) *Discord . . . sooty wings*: This personification seems to be original with Smollett. It appears in *Roderick Random*, ch. xxxiii.

(2) *Pallas*: an epithet (of unknown meaning) for Athene, the Greek goddess of wisdom.

(3) *Merry-Andrew or Jack-Pudding*: clown, mountebank's assistant.

(4) *Beef-stake Club*: the Sublime Society of Beef Steaks, founded in 1735 and having as its emblem a small gridiron of gold with the motto 'Beef and Liberty'. There was a tradition, apparently based only on this allusion, that Smollett was once a guest of this London social club. See Robert J. Allen, *The Clubs of Augustan London* (1933), pp. 136–45; and Kahrl, p. 76.

Page 31. (1) *Jemmy B——t . . . Billy H——d . . . Johnny B——d*: Jemmy Bencroft, Billy Howard and Johnny Beard were elected to the club in the 1740s. See reference to Allen, *supra*.

(2) *this digressive simile*: which has parodied the histories of heroes' weapons in epic.

(3) *card*: piece of paper on which the 32 points of the mariner's compass are marked.

(4) *bowlings*: bowlines, ropes for keeping the edge of a sail steady when sailing on a wind.

Page 37. (1) *tartan*: small coasting vessel of the Mediterranean.

Page 40. (1) *vi et armis*: by force of arms.

(2) *settle it with the parish*: arrange for the child to be provided for by parish, or public, means.

(3) *cracked pitcher*: woman who has lost her virginity before marriage.

Page 41. (1) *Communis malefactor . . . litium*: a common evil-doer, petti-fogger, and author of quarrels.

(2) *coif in the court of common pleas*: A coif was a white cap (later merely a patch on the wig) worn by serjeants-at-law as a badge that they were graduates in law. The court of common pleas was a permanent civil court established in Westminster Hall by Magna Carta.

Page 42. (1) *certain utensil*: chamberpot

(2) *Wounds*: God's wounds, an oath or asseveration.

(3) *Newgate*: famous London prison.

(4) *Jack Ketch*: the hangman (after Jack Ketch, a particularly cruel executioner of the 17th century).

Page 43. (1) *clerk of the assize*: principal officer of the session of civil and criminal justice held periodically in each county.

(2) *great tythes*: originally a sort of tax for providing for the clergy, later transferred to lay hands and saleable like ordinary property. Great tythes included payment in corn, hay, or wood; little (small) tythes embraced all others.

(3) *St. George*: patron saint of England and (along with the archangel, St. Michael, mentioned below) of knights-errant.

Page 44. (1) *Hamlet*: *Hamlet*, I. iv.

(2) *Drury-lane*: the Theatre Royal in Drury Lane, London. *Hamlet* and *Romeo and Juliet* were the most popular of Shakespeare's plays between 1701 and 1800; *Hamlet* was performed an average of 4 times a year at Drury Lane from 1701–50. See Charles Hogan, *Shakespeare in the Theatre, 1701–1800* (1952, 1957), ii. 716.

(3) *impleat orbem*: let it fill the world.

Page 45. (1) *Bayardo, Brigliadoro*: Bayardo is the magic horse given by Charlemagne to Renaud in Ariosto's *Orlando Furioso*; Brigliadoro is Orlando's own horse. 'Ev'n Rozinante [Don Quixote's horse] wears the bay;/Let Brilladore and Bayard bray' (*Don Quixote*, I. IV. xxv).

(2) *whipper-in*: huntsman's assistant who uses a whip to keep the dogs in a pack.

(3) *Greenland canoe*: unidentified, but probably a kayak.

Page 48. (1) *old king Stephen . . . horse armoury*: Displays of suits of armour were kept in the Tower of London from the times of the earliest

English kings. 'A most singular quaint helmet, probably as early as the time of Stephen, if not actually the helmet of that monarch, or of his son', was bungled away by the warders of the Tower armoury and is now in the Musée d'Artillerie at Paris (Walter Thornbury, *Old and New London* (n.d.), ii. 82).

(2) *fellow that rides armed . . . lord mayor's shew*: For the pageantry of the swearing in of a new lord mayor of London, the armourers provided a man in complete armour. Thornbury (see preceding note) i, 324.

Page 49. (1) *mittimus*: warrant committing a person to jail or prison.

(2) *information or indictment*: An information is an oral statement of the facts of a case by an informant or prosecutor; an indictment is a written accusation.

Page 50. (1) *Ferry-bridge*: an actual place. Kahrl, p. 58.

Page 51. (1) *tip me the traveller*: Eric Partridge (*A Dictionary of Slang and Unconventional English* (1949)) says this phrase means 'to exaggerate, to romance, as a traveller is apt to do'; but Smollett's usage obviously differs from this.

Page 52. (1) *box my compass*: recite the points, or quarter points, of the compass in correct order.

(2) *tipped Clarke the wink*: winked as a private signal.

(3) *Don Quixote was dubbed by his landlord*: *Don Quixote*, I. I. iii.

(4) *eve of St. Martin*: St. Martin served in the Roman army before entering religious life. His feast day is 11 November, which contradicts Smollett's assertion in the novel's first paragraph that it is early October.

Page 55. (1) *black joke*: the 'Coal Black Joke', a popular air. Various songs were set to it, some of them indecent.

(2) *black-ey'd Susan*: The words of this song are by John Gay (*c.* 1720), author of *The Beggar's Opera*. There have been a number of different tunes to it, the one now known being by Richard Leveridge. Neither the 'black joke' nor 'black-ey'd Susan' is sorrowful; Crowe appeals to the 'black' of the titles.

(3) *sea-mew*: sea gull.

(4) *go large . . . haul upon a wind*: To 'go large' is to sail with wind towards the stern; to 'haul upon a wind' is to come closer to the wind.

Page 56. (1) *by the lead*: lead and line used to ascertain depth of water.

(2) *hawse-holes*: holes in ship's bow, through which anchor cable passes.

(3) *disrated*: reduced to a lower rating or rank.

(4) *clap hard aweather*: turn toward the wind as quickly as possible.

Page 57. (1) *peddling*: 'piddling', petty or insignificant.

Page 58. (1) *Bartlemey-tide*: St. Bartholomew's day, 24 August.

(2) *reins*: kidneys.

(3) *harslet*: entrails of a hog or vital organs of other animals.

(4) *Papishes*: Papists, Roman Catholics.

Page 59. (1) *cast a figure*: make a horoscope, interpret astrologically.

Page 60. (1) *furtum*: theft.

(2) *in alta via regia . . . magnum terrorem, &c.*: captured violently and nefariously on the King's Highway and carried off in fear and trembling.

(3) *ousted of his clergy*: deprived of 'benefit of clergy', originally the privilege of exemption from trial by a secular court allowed to clergymen arraigned for felony; in later times the privilege of exemption from the sentence, which, in the case of certain offences, might be pleaded on his first conviction by every one who could read.

Page 61. (1) *A knight-errant ought to under-stand the sciences*, etc: 'Knights errant, replied [Don Quixote] ever had, and ought to have, some knowledge of every thing . . .' (*Don Quixote*, I. III. iv).

Page 62. (1) *plain sailing*: Plane sailing is the method of solving certain navigational problems on the assumption that the earth's surface is a plane.

(2) *mercator*: sailing method by which problems of sailing on the spherical surface of the earth are solved by plane trigonometry.

(3) *viol block*: block having a cut-away part in its shell so that a rope can be put over the sheave.

(4) *geer capstan*: gear capstan.

(5) *St. Catherine's*: in Wapping, on the River Thames just below the Tower of London, an area chiefly inhabited by seafaring men and tradesmen supplying necessities for ships and sailors.

Page 63. (1) *I'se wage a teaster*: I'll wager a tester (slang term for a sixpence).

(2) *dispossess*: drive out the devil who possesses the body.

(3) *murrain*: plague.

Page 64. (1) *horse that was foaled of an acorn*: a wooden horse, the gallows.

Page 68. (1) *the following salutation*: Crabshaw's effusion is very similar to Sancho Panza's when he recovers his stolen 'Dapple'. Crabshaw's horse and Sancho's ass are equally indifferent to their masters' affection. (*Don Quixote*, I. IV. iii).

(2) *an unsocial animal*: in contrast to Don Quixote's horse, Rozinante, and Sancho's ass, who have a great friendship. (*Don Quixote*, II. I. xii.)

Page 71. (1) *NO FOREIGN CONNECTIONS,—OLD-ENGLAND FOR EVER*: This and the preceding slogan assert the Tory opinions of many of the large landholders of England: that land (not commerce) should be the basis of political power in England and that the Hanoverian connections of George I and George II had seriously weakened the country. 'Old' England was pre-Glorious Revolution England, before 'foreign' kings began to rule.

(2) *NO SLAVERY,—NO POPISH PRETENDER*: slavery to the Catholic church if the Catholic Charles Edward were to come over from France and take the throne from the Protestant George II. Threats of a French invasion during the Seven Years War (1756–63) made these fears (or desires, if you were a Jacobite Tory) stronger than they had been since Charles's invasion of England in 1745.

(3) *orange ribbons*: symbolic of Protestantism, from its defender, William of Orange.

Page 72. (1) *the schoolman's ass*: example used by scholastic philosophers or theologians (schoolmen) in discussions of free will.

(2) *the peacock and the ladies*: unidentified. Perhaps a vow to Juno, goddess of women, with whom the peacock is associated. The expression appears in one of the notes to Smollett's translation of *Don Quixote* (*Don Quixote*, I. II. ii). 'By the peacock' is an obsolete oath.

Page 73. (1) *Valentine Quickset*: Like virtually all Smollett's names, this one is suggestive, a quickset being a hedge, one of the fox-hunter's obsessions.

(2) *Isaac Vanderpelft*: another 'loaded' name. A special act for naturalization of Jews was passed in 1753 and, because of public protest, repealed in the same year. A Sir George Vandeput was a candidate in the City of Westminster's election of a member to Parliament in 1750; Smollett recounts his fate in the election in *History*, iii. 289–90, 312–13.

(3) *high-flying*: making or upholding lofty claims for authority in church or state.

(4) *stock-jobber*: dealer in stocks.

(5) *copy-holders*: holders of land under claim of having their names enrolled in the 'copy' or manorial court-roll. In 1758 a bill was passed voiding the votes of those holding estates by 'copy of court role'. (*History*, iv. 248–9.)

(6) *dissenters*: Although there were laws depriving dissenters from the Anglican Church of their full rights, dissenters were such firm supporters of Protestantism that the Whig government of George II's reign did various things to appeal to them at election time or when particularly threatened by Catholic France. See Basil Williams, *The Whig Supremacy* (1962), pp. 70–2.

Page 74. (1) *Haman*: In the Book of Esther (vii. 9–10), Haman and his sons die on gallows Haman had prepared for Mordecai.

(2) *H——r*: Hanover.

(3) *vour shillings in the pound*: The land tax (at four shillings in the pound in 1759) was the main source of the country's revenue (*History*, v. 173).

Page 77. (1) *hoicksed*: 'Hoicks' is a call used to incite hunting hounds.

Page 78. (1) *to set up for himself*: In Fielding's play, Don Quixote is asked to stand for a county election, to ensure opposition and promote bribery (*Don Quixote in England* (1734), II. iii).

(2) *he who plays . . . rubbers*: A 'rubber' is a decisive game in a series when bowling. This expression occurs in *Humphry Clinker*, ed. Knapp (1966), Jery's Letter of 3 October.

Page 79. (1) *tye-periwig*: wig having the hair gathered together behind and tied with a knot of ribbon.

(2) *ad captandum vulgus*: to catch the vulgar.

(3) *high German doctor*: quack who claims special knowledge acquired in Germany; below, of course, the phrase refers to the Hanoverian Kings of England and their ministers.

(4) *people of Nineveh*: 'Nineveh, that great city, in which there are more than a hundred and twenty thousand persons who do not know their right hand from their left' (Jonah, iv. 11).

(5) *Westphalian*: Westphalia was a Prussian province bordering on Hanover.

(6) *H——n*: Hanoverian.

(7) *Aristotle's four principles*, etc.: In Aristotle's writings, the male and female principles of generation in the microcosm are related to, respectively, the sun and moon as principles of generation in the macrocosm. 'Unformed matter' ('privation' being Aristotle's term for the state of matter lacking form) Aristotle held to be one of the three principles necessary for any change to occur. He posited four 'causes' involved in any change: the efficient cause is whatever initiates the process of change (the sculptor in the case of a sculpture); the final cause is the end or purpose toward which change is directed (the pleasure of the viewer, in the case of the sculpture). (The other two causes are the formal and the material.)

(8) *Dioscorides, with his faculties*, etc.: Pendanius Dioscorides (*flor. c.* A.D. 50), Greek medical man. His *De Materia Medica* details the properties of about 600 medicinal plants and was the leading text on pharmacology for 16 centuries. 'Faculties of simples' means: medical powers of substances free from foreign elements. I cannot discover the exact expressions for the three 'virtues', but presumably they are expressions for various kinds of healing powers (virtues) which medicinal plants have.

(9) *Galen, with his four elements*, etc.: Greek physician (*c.* A.D. 130–

200). The four elements are earth, air, fire, and water, each element having two of the 'elementary qualities' of heat, dryness, moisture, and coldness. The 'complexions' (humours or mental dispositions) are traditionally only four: sanguine, choleric, melancholic, phlegmatic; perhaps combinations make up the eight. 'Harmonies' and 'discords' could refer to the elements, which Galen held to be compatible or antipathetic; or to the complexions, the proper mixture of which he maintained was necessary to health.

Page 80. (1) *alkahest of . . . Paracelsus*: Paracelsus was the adopted name of Theophrastus Bombastus von Hohenheim (1493–1541), Swiss alchemist, medical man, and scientist. 'Alkahest' was his term for a supposed universal solvent. Salt, mercury, and sulphur were the three alchemical elements in his system or theory.

(2) *archæus or spiritus rector of . . . Van Helmont*: Jean Baptiste van Helmont (1577–1644), Belgian scientist. His 'archaeus' or 'Spiritus rector' was the soul or master spirit dwelling in all things and determining their natures. He thought water to be the elementary matter of all things and invented the term 'gas' for air, or the other primary metaphysical reality. Much of his theory was concerned with digestion and all modes of transmuting substances from one form to another. Ferment, analogous to ferment in brewing, he imagined responsible for all vital phenomena.

(3) *acidum vagum*: vague acid. See G. S. Rousseau, 'Smollett's *Acidum Vagum*', *Isis*, lviii (1967), 244–5.

(4) *Germanized m——r*: the Duke of Newcastle, who long defended George II's policies and accompanied him as minister in attendance on his visits to Hanover. For Smollett's satire on Newcastle in *Humphry Clinker* and attacks on him in the *Briton*, see Byron Gassman, 'The *Briton* and *Humphry Clinker*' (SEL iii (1963), 397–414).

(5) *dry-salter*: dealer in chemical products used in drugs.

(6) *stump-turner*: one who makes and fits wooden limbs for amputees.

(7) *insolvent debtor . . . parliament*: In the 1750s various Insolvent Acts were passed which released certain classes of debtors from prison.

(8) *led-captains*: sycophants.

(9) *chrusion pepuromenon ek puros*: gold tried in the fire.

Page 81. (1) *Revelations*: Rev. iii. 18.

(2) *caput mortuum*: 'dead head', the residuum left after exhaustive distillation.

(3) *menstruum*: any agent that dissolves a solid substance.

(4) *catholicon*: universal remedy.

Page 82. (1) '*The Life and Adventures of Valentine and Orson*': There was an early French romance about Valentine and Orson, but Crowe is probably reading *The History of Valentine and Orson*, a novel which appeared about the mid-18th century. See Andrew Block, *The English Novel: 1740–1850* (1961).

(2) *barricadoes*: barricades.

(3) *stream-anchor*: supplementary anchor, lighter than main anchor.

(4) *boltsprit*: bowsprit, spar projecting over the stem, on which it rests.

(5) *athwart hawse*: position of a ship when she is ahead of, and at right angles to, the fore and aft line of a nearby ship.

(6) *round-top* circular platform near mast head.

(7) *dead lights*: shutters fixed outside port holes in a storm, to prevent water from entering.

(8) *broached upon my broadside—'*: The delightfully elliptical speech of Mr. Jingle in Dickens's *Pickwick Papers* may owe something to Crowe's staccato outbursts.

Page 83. (1) *auditâ querela*: the suit having been heard.

(2) *last legal settlement*: Poor people and lunatics were returned to their legal residence or home parish which was then responsible for providing for them.

Page 84. (1) *vi et armis*: see *supra*, note 1 to p. 40.

Page 85. (1) *to lie upon litter*: Crabshaw's stringing of proverbs together is his nearest similarity to Sancho Panza.

(2) *all long of*: all because of.

(3) *frog in the stocks*: unidentified. The expression may mean simply finding other than what one is looking for.

(4) *cast*: defeated at law.

Page 87. (1) *hackney-writers*: hack writers, hirelings.

(2) *Lammas-market*: harvest festival, 1 August.

Page 88. (1) *certificate*: cancelling financial obligation.

Page 93. (1) *vestry and quarter-sessions*: parochial assembly commonly convened in the vestry; court of criminal and civil jurisdiction, held quarterly by justices of the peace in the counties.

(2) *socius criminis*: partner in crime.

Page 94. (1) *ferk you with a primineery*: 'Ferk' is a form of the obsolete 'firk', to beat, trounce, drub. 'Primineery' is Mrs. Gobble's corruption of *praemunire*, the name of a writ against one charged with introducing a foreign power into the land.

Page 95. (1) *fore-foot*: part of ship's keel.

(2) *Hogarth ... Dutch stile*: William Hogarth (1697–1764). The reference is to 'Paul Before Felix Burlesqued', a satire on the style of

Rembrandt which was a subscription ticket for Hogarth's engraving (pub. 1751) of his serious painting, 'Paul Before Felix' (1748). This same reference occurs in *The History and Adventures of an Atom* (1769), i. 94.

(3) *mainprize*: action of procuring release of a prisoner by becoming surety for his appearance in court at a specified time.

Page 96. (1) *coram non judice*: before a non-judge, one who has no jurisdiction in a case presented to him.

(2) *in Banco Regis*: in the King's Bench (Court).

Page 99. (1) *fish a man's yard-arm . . . snapt in the slings*: put a splint on an arm broken in the mast chains or ropes.

Page 100. (1) *prize-money*: share of wealth seized from enemy ships.

Page 101. (1) *dues*: Prisons were privately run and prisoners had to pay for their room and supplies.

Page 102. (1) *admiral P——'s*: Admiral Sir George Pocock (1706–92), who fought several battles against the French in the East Indies about this time, the most ferocious in September 1758.

Page 105. (1) *crazy bark*: damaged ship.

(2) *spank*: sail quickly and smartly.

(3) *'ware timbers*: beware ship's frames, liable to burst in battle.

(4) *hap*: chance.

(5) *ratline*: small rope stretched between shrouds to make climbing aloft possible.

(6) *tricks upon travellers*: advantages taken of strangers.

(7) *a-pize*: ape, simulate; here an interjection.

(8) *bunt-lines*: lines for hauling up a square sail when furling it.

Page 106. (1) *started a hoop in rolling*: unidentified; perhaps to instigate merriment or love-making.

(2) *tight as a nut-shell*: chaste.

(3) *sail upon a parallel*: sail along a parallel of latitude.

(4) *northward of fifty*: of fifty degrees latitude, England lying just north of fifty degrees latitude.

Page 108. (1) *confine him to his cage*: To get Don Quixote home from his mad wanderings his friends, the curate and the barber, trick him into a cage placed on an ox-wagon (*Don Quixote*, I. IV. xix–xxv).

(2) *Dulcinea*: the mistress in whose name Don Quixote's exploits are undertaken.

(3) *Rowland for their Oliver*: tit for tat, with reference to the evenly matched combat between Roland and Oliver in the Charlemagne cycle of legends.

Page 109. (1) *Don Bethlem*: 'Bethlem' or 'Bedlam' is a shortened form of Bethlehem, the Hospital of St. Mary of Bethlehem, the madhouse in Moorfields, London, where inmates were given straw to lie on.

Page 110. (1) *stockholder at Jonathan's . . . Derby*: Jonathan's Coffee House in London was frequented mostly by dealers in stocks and shares. Derby was associated with the height of English fear and financial panic during the rebellion of 1745, because it was the nearest point to London reached by the forces of Charles Edward, the Young Pretender.

Page 111. (1) *joseph*: long cloak.

Page 114. (1) *tract*: track.
   (2) *sucking giant*: 'Sucking' means childlike or dependent.

Page 120. (1) *Natura il fece . . . stampa*: *Orlando Furioso*, x. 84.

Page 124. (1) *'aive yeaten hool-cheese*: have eaten Hull cheese; that is, got drunk, Hull being famous for strong ale.

Page 126. (1) *winged steed*: For Don Quixote's adventure on a 'winged' horse, see *Don Quixote*, II. III. vii–ix.
   (2) *oilet holes*: eyelet holes.
   (3) *for every zow there's a zirreverence*: *OED* cites Greene (1592): 'As far as a hungry sow can smell a sir reverence (lump of excrement)'.

Page 127. (1) *'Thatch your house with t[ur]d . . . reachers'*: Engage in a troublesome business, and you'll have more advice givers than helpers.
   (2) *Venetian masques*: masks, of Venetian origin, covering the upper part of the face.

Page 130. (1) *as the zaying goes.'*: Cf. the style and spelling of Win Jenkins' Letters in *Humphry Clinker*, ed. Knapp (1966).

Page 132. (1) *pia mater*: innermost of the three meninges which invest the brain and spinal cord.

   (2) *pothecary to be his friend*: Normally, doctor and apothecary worked together, the apothecary seeing the patient and then calling the doctor to prescribe medicines compounded by the apothecary.

Page 133. (1) *acrosaline*: acrid and salty.
   (2) *atrabilious*: affected by black bile.
   (3) *borborygmata*: rumbling in the intestines.
   (4) *venæsection*: opening of a vein to let blood as a medical treatment, phlebotomy.
   (5) *vesicatory . . . inter scapulas*: irritating ointment causing blisters on the skin, applied between the shoulder blades.
   (6) *apozem*: decoction or infusion.

(7) *alexipharmic*: antidote or counter-poison.

(8) *boluses*: pills.

(9) *neutral*: neither acid nor alkaline.

Page 135. (1) *bumboat*: shore boat for taking provisions to ships in harbour.

Page 136. (1) *hop-pole*: long pole used to support a hop-vine.

(2) *basket-hilt broad sword . . . Hudibras*: Hudibras (modelled on Don Quixote) is the pedantic Presbyterian anti-hero of *Hudibras*, a satiric poem by Samuel Butler (1612–80).

> His puissant *Sword* unto his side
> Near his undaunted heart was ty'd,
> With Basket-hilt, that would hold broth,
> And serve for fight and dinner both.
> (*Hudibras*, i. 349–52).

(3) *temporal and spiritual chivalry . . . reconciled*: In the legend of St. George and the dragon, St. George slays a pestilence-causing dragon which preys upon the people of Selena in Libya and, as a consequence, converts the Selenians to Christianity.

Page 139. (1) *journal*: journey.

(2) *bring-to*: bring a ship to stop.

(3) *clew up*: furl and tie up (a sail).

(4) *broad pendant*: broad pennant, the swallow-tailed flag denoting a commodore.

(5) *broached to*: turned toward the wind while running free.

(6) *hand-spike*: short wooden lever.

(7) *mosqueto fleet*: fleet of small, light vessels adapted for rapid manoeuvring.

(8) *pooped with a sea*: swept by following waves coming inboard from astern.

(9) *crowd away*: sail with all sails set.

Page 141. (1) *'size*: assize.

Page 142. (1) *small tythes*: See *supra*, note 2 to p. 43.

Page 143. (1) *scot and lot*: customary contribution laid upon all subjects according to their ability to pay.

Page 145. (1) *sack-whey*: medicinal drink made with sack (a white wine) and the watery part of milk.

Page 147. (1) *Sampson Carrasco . . . injunctions of the victor*: Twice Sampson Carrasco challenges Don Quixote, with the stipulation that the vanquished will obey the commands of the victor, as a scheme for getting Don Quixote to return home. (*Don Quixote*, II. I. xiv and II. IV. xiii.)

(2) *Z*[ound]*s*: oath formed by running together 'his (God's) wounds'.

Page 150. (1) *lie board and board . . . glasses*: side by side; intervals of time at sea were measured in 'glasses' (sand glasses taking half an hour to empty) until the end of the 18th century.

(2) *'Angels and ministers . . . goblin damn'd'*: 'Angels and ministers of grace defend us!/Be thou a spirit of health or goblin damn'd. . . . (*Hamlet*, I. iv. 39–40).

(3) *'What man dare . . . never tremble . . .'*: *Macbeth*, III. iv. 98–102.

Page 151. (1) *raw head and bloody bones*: ghastly spectre, a phrase used to frighten children.

(2) *bear and ragged staff*: crest of the Earls of Warwick used as a public house sign; it shows a bear chained to a ragged staff.

Page 154. (1) *charge to battle.*: These arrangements and the following battle amplify the masters and squires 'combat' in *Don Quixote*, II. I. xiv–xv.

Page 156. (1) *blown bladder . . . smooth pebbles*: The same trick is played on Don Quixote and Sancho Panza (*Don Quixote*, II. I. xi).

(2) *spolia optima*: noble spoils, arms taken on the field of battle.

(3) *calves*: The second meaning of 'calf' here is 'stupid fellow', 'dolt'.

Page 157. (1) *crow-trodden*: beaten with a crow-bar.

Page 158. (1) *Crown-office*: department belonging to the court of King's Bench.

(2) *sea room*: enough room for a ship to manoeuver.

Page 159. (1) *in Banco Regis*: See *supra*, note 2 to p. 96.

(2) *Bilkum Regis*: 'Bilkum Regis' is Crowe's mockery of Clarke's Latin. As a Latinizing of English 'bilk', it would mean 'the king's fraud'.

(3) *stink-pots*: earthenware containers filled with a foul-smelling composition, used as projectiles in naval warfare.

(4) *Bugden*: an actual village (Kahrl, p. 58).

(5) *May-fair*: near Piccadilly in London. Smollett lived there in 1747–8. See Knapp, *Tobias Smollett: Doctor of Men and Manners* (1949), p. 73.

Page 161. (1) *Caffre*: member of a South African race.

(2) *Hatfield*: another actual place (Kahrl, p. 58).

(3) *Bull and Gate inn in Holborn*: one of the most famous of the inns in the Holborn area where the stages for London ended up. In *Tom Jones* (xiii, 2) Tom and Partridge retire to the Bull and Gate inn, Holborn. There are other parallels between *Launcelot Greaves* and *Tom Jones*: both Tom and Greaves recover money lost by the heroine; each narrowly misses seeing the heroine while stopping at an inn; each pursues the heroine, who is supposed to be in London with relatives. Sycamore's

interest in Aurelia for her fortune more than her person is comparable to Blifil's attitude toward Sophia in *Tom Jones*.

(4) *Golden-square*: just north of Piccadilly. Later (in 1765) Smollett lived in a street bordering this square. (Knapp, *Tobias Smollett: Doctor of Men and Manners* (1949), p. 259.) Bramble and his group stay in Golden Square. See *Humphry Clinker*, ed. Knapp (1966), Jery's Letter of 24 May.

(5) *Wapping*: See *supra*, note 5 to p. 62.

Page 162. (1) *alderman Parsons' great brewhouse*: Humphrey Parsons (1676–1741), a highly successful brewer; elected alderman of Portsohen in 1720–1 and later twice lord mayor of London.

(2) *Rotherhithe*: parish on the right bank of the Thames; like Wapping, much inhabited by seafaring people.

(3) *spunging-house*: 'sponging-house', house kept by a bailiff or sheriff's officer, formerly in regular use as a place of preliminary confinement for debtors.

Page 163. (1) *King's-bench*: For Smollett's imprisonment in the King's Bench, see Introduction.

(2) *Borough*: short name for the Borough of Southwark.

(3) *St. George's-fields*: The King's Bench Prison was moved to this new site in 1758. An open space of great extent, it took its name from the adjoining church of St. George the Martyr in Southwark.

Page 164. (1) *split into factions*: Cf. the factions in the Newgate Prison scenes of Fielding's *Jonathan Wild* (1743).

Page 165. (1) *divide et impera*: divide and conquer.

(2) *mercy of the legislature . . . in execution*: See *supra*, note 7 to p. 80. Smollett wrote at length and compassionately about the unfairness of the laws for the relief of insolvent debtors, which exempted people with debts over 100 pounds. (*History*, iv, 442–5, 455–60.)

Page 166. (1) *Acroceraunian promontory*: in ancient geography, projecting from what is now S.W. Albania into the Ionian Sea.

Page 168. (1) *Captain Clewlin*: There are parallels between Clewlin's story and that of a real Captain George Walker who was in prison with Smollett and whose case was specially presented to a parliamentary committee on bankruptcy laws. See *History*, iv, 456; and Alice Parker, 'Tobias Smollett and the Law' (*SP*, xxxix (1942), 554).

Page 169. (1) *active war*: Seven Years War.

Page 172. (1) *weft*: waft, signal.

Page 176. (1) *Foundling Hospital*: founded in 1739 by Captain Thomas Coram as a hospital for exposed and deserted children; still thriving.

(2) *on their own bottoms*: on their own resources.

Page 179. (1) *bear to the stake*: Bear-baiting, a popular 18th-century sport, involved setting dogs to attack a bear chained to a stake.

Page 180. (1) *baind me oover to the Red Sea like*: Perhaps the astrologer's long white beard reminds Crabshaw of Moses and his connection with the supernatural terrors of the Red Sea, the crossing of which is one of the types of Baptism and of the victory of the elect over death. I have found no clear account of Crabshaw's folk version of the idea of the departed soul's crossing the Red Sea, but, in Matthew Lewis's novel *The Monk* (1795), ch. ix, Ambrosio, for his presumed holiness as a monk, is asked to lay a tormented soul to rest in the Red Sea. See Jean Danielou, S.J., *The Bible and the Liturgy* (1956), pp. 86–98.

(2) *tyke*: common Yorkshire term for dog.

(3) *starns*: dial. for 'stars'.

(4) *cast a figure*: compose a horoscope.

Page 181. (1) *Tyburn tree*: the gallows, Tyburn being the place of public execution in London until the late 18th century.

(2) *fact*: crime

(3) *cast at the Old Baily*: defeated at law at London's central criminal court (Old Bailey).

(4) *Whole Duty of Man*: popular devotional tract published in 1658 and probably written by Richard Allestree. Crabshaw is advised to carry this to make a good impression on the spectators as he rides in the cart that took condemned men from prison to the gallows. Cf. 'The Idle 'Prentice Executed at Tyburn', plate 11 of Hogarth's *Industry and Idleness* (1747), where Tom Idle carries *The Whole Duty of Man* in the cart.

Page 182. (1) *Tisiphone*: one of the Furies or avenging deities in Greek mythology.

Page 183. (1) *lost company*: separated from the rest of the fleet.

Page 185. (1) *messenger*: government official employed to carry dispatches, and, formerly, to apprehend state prisoners.

(2) *habeas corpus . . . not suspended at this time*: Earlier in the century, in times of national crisis, *habeas corpus* had been suspended, but Pitt, as Secretary of State, opposed its suspension during the Seven Years War. See Basil Williams, *The Whig Supremacy* (1962), p. 357.

(3) *black hussars*: light horsemen, originally Hungarian, who wore black uniforms.

(4) *Lusatia*: region now part of E. Germany and S.W. Poland.

(5) *Pera*: northern quarter of Istanbul.

(6) *parallel*: trench used in siege warfare.

Page 186. (1) *works*: fortifications.

(2) *saved by works*: Christian charity, active goodness as opposed to faith.

(3) *new-light . . . new birth*: Methodist terms for a sense of being directly infused with the divine spirit. In reviewing the reign of George II, Smollett wrote that 'imposture and fanaticism still hung upon the skirts of religion. Weak minds were seduced by the delusion of a superstition styled Methodism, raised upon the affectation of superior sanctity, and maintained by pretensions to divine illumination . . . they denied the merit of good works . . .' (*History*, v. 376). Smollett's satire on Methodism is much more elaborate in *Humphry Clinker*.

(4) *communication*: sexual union as well as religious communion.

(5) *sister Jolly*: 'Sister' was a slang term for prostitute, and 'jolly' could mean 'amatory'. The identification of spiritual with sexual inspiration was a commonplace of 18th-century satire on Methodism and all forms of 'enthusiasm'; cf. Swift's *Tale of a Tub*.

(6) *Marche*: the Mark of Brandenburg, Prussia.

(7) *finding the longitude*: In 1759 'several persons invented methods for discovering the longitude at sea, that great *desideratum* in navigation, for the ascertainment of which so many nations have offered a public recompense [England offered up to 20,000 pounds], and in the investigation of which so many mathematical heads have been disordered' (*History*, iv. 483).

(8) *proshection*: 'projection', in alchemy, was use of the 'powder of projection' (philosopher's stone) to transmute base metal into gold.

(9) *P——*: Prussia.

Page 187. (1) *weakness of the nerves . . . with sensation*: This passage is reproduced, almost verbatim, from William Battie's *Treatise on Madness* (1758). See Richard A. Hunter and Ida Macalpine, 'Smollett's Reading in Psychiatry' (*MLR*, li (1956), 409–11).

Page 188. (1) *Bœotian band of Thebes*: the comparison is self-satiric; the Bœotians were thought to be rude and illiterate, preferring bodily strength to mental.

(2) *kennel*: gutter or open sewer.

(3) *He vig'rous rose . . . stunk along*: In the original the lines read: 'Vig'rous he rises; from th'effluvia strong/Imbibes new life, and scours and stinks along'. (Alexander Pope, *The Dunciad* ii. 97–8.)

(4) *Qui me commorit . . . cantabitur urbe*: But if one stir me up ('Better not touch me!' I shout), he shall smart for it and have his name sung up and down the town. (Horace, *Satires* II. i. 45–6 (Loeb).)

Page 189. (1) *Pope . . . Dunciad*: Smollett greatly admired Pope; his early verse satires, *Advice* and *Reproof*, are largely modelled on Pope's satiric epistles.

(2) *deserve the imputation of dulness . . . personal attack*: Neither statement is literally true.

(3) *Boileau*: Nicholas Boileau-Despreaux (1636–1711), French poet, satirist, and critic, much admired by Pope. Among those of his contemporaries Boileau satirized individually were the writers Quinault and Parrault and the opera composer Lilli.

Page 191. (1) *Philomel*: the nightingale.

(2) *Lychas . . . destroyed*: The poisoned tunic sent to Hercules by his wife Deianira is delivered by Lychas, Hercules' servant. When he realizes he is dying from the effect of the gift, Hercules hurls Lychas into the sea. Ovid, *Metamorphoses*, viii–ix.

Page 194. (1) *Daily Advertiser*: first published 3 February 1730.

Page 195. (1) *Sallee Rover . . . Barbary*: Moorish pirate ship on the coast of Barbary, North Africa.

(2) *started*: loaded.

Page 198. (1) *undress*: dress not ordinarily worn in public.

Page 199. (1) *iambicks*: the traditional metre of satiric verse.

Page 201. (1) *ad inquirendum*: writ inquiring into the facts of a case in the superior courts.

Page 202. (1) *writs of capias, alias, & pluries*: *Capias* is the generic name of several writs directing the sheriff to arrest a particular person; an *alias* writ is issued after an initial writ has been unsuccessful, and a *pluries* when the alias is ineffective.

Page 203. (1) *Seven Dials*: area in the parish of St. Giles-in-the-Fields from which seven streets radiated, with a central column bearing seven sun-dials, a dial facing each of the streets. Henry B. Wheatley, *London Past and Present* (1891), 3 vols., *sub verbo*.

(2) *Albumazar*: Arabian astronomer (A.D. 805–85), the subject of a comedy by Thomas Tomkis (*flor.* 1604–15) which was revived in 1747–8.

(3) *bilboes*: bars to which men in ankle shackles are attached.

Page 204. (1) *Hobbes*: Thomas Hobbes (1588–1679), English philosopher famous for a political theory based on the assumption that man is essentially a selfish creature who lives in a 'state of nature' or state of war, with the strongest prevailing, until a powerful external force imposes peace.

(2) *fish*: splice.

Page 205. (1) *covert femme*: legal term for a married woman, in this case one who has no legal rights apart from her husband.

(2) *deed of alienation . . . none effect*: For the legalities here, see *supra*, notes 2 and 3 to p. 5.

Page 206. (1) *mines of Golconda*: ancient kingdom and city in India, proverbially famous for its diamonds.

(2) *bag-wig a-la pigeon*: wig the back-hair of which was enclosed in an ornamental bag, worn in the style of a pigeon.

(3) *lutestring*: dress of glossy silk.

Page 208. (1) *turned methodists*: See *supra*, note 3, p. 186.

Page 209. (1) *her own brother*: Cf. the threat of incest in *Joseph Andrews* and *Tom Jones*.

Page 210. (1) *marriage-favours*: knots of white ribbons or bunches of white flowers worn at weddings.